JOHN SPLENDID

THE TALE OF A POOR GENTLEMAN, AND THE LITTLE WARS OF LORN

BY

NEIL MUNRO

WILLIAM BLACKWOOD & SONS LTD.

EDINBURGH AND LONDON

First published in August 1898
By Wm. Blackwood & Sons
45 George Street, Edinburgh

Second Impression, September 1898
Third Impression, September 1898
Fourth Impression, November 1898
Fifth Impression, November 1898
Sixth Impression, March 1899

CHEAP EDITION, April 1903

3/6 EDITION
    January 1905
    August 1910
    July 1915

UNIFORM EDITION (3/6)
    March 1923
    October 1923
    October 1924
    March 1929
    March 1931
    October 1933

POPULAR EDITION
    February 1920
    January 1931
    December 1936

INVERARAY EDITION
    February 1935
    August 1935
    March 1943
    January 1945
    August 1948
    February 1955

Printed in Scotland
By Wm. Blackwood & Sons Ltd.

JOHN SPLENDID

THE WORKS OF NEIL MUNRO.

INVERARAY EDITION.

DEDICATION.

To read this tale, dear Hugh, without any association of its incidents with the old respectable chronicles of the Historians is what I should wish you could always do. That is the happy manner with Romance; that is the enviable aptness of the child. But when (by the favour of God) you grow older and more reflective, seeking perhaps for more in these pages than they meant to give, you may wonder that the streets, the lanes, the tenements herein set forth so much resemble those we know to-day, though less than two hundred years ago the bracken waved upon their promontory. You may wonder, too, that the Silver Mines of Coillebhraid, discovered in the time of your great-grandfather, should have so strangely been anticipated in the age of Gillesbeg Gruamach. Let not those chronological divergencies perturb you; they were in the manuscript (which you will be good enough to assume) of Elrigmore, and I would not alter them. Nor do I diminish by a single hour Elrigmore's estimate that two days were taken on the Miraculous Journey to Inverlochy, though numerous histories have made it less. In that, as in a few other details, Elrigmore's account is borne out by one you know to whom The Little Wars of Lorn and Lochaber are yet, as it were, an impulse of yesterday, and the name of Athole is utterly detestable.

I give you this book, dear Hugh, not for History, though a true tale—a sad old tale—is behind it, but for a picture of times and manners, of a country that is dear to us in every rock and valley, of a people we know whose blood is ours. And that you may grow in wisdom as in years, and gain the riches of affection, and escape the giants of life as Connal did the giants of Erin O, in our winter tale, is my fervent prayer.

N. M.

September 1898.

CONTENTS

JOHN SPLENDID.

CHAPTER I.

FROM THE FOREIGN FIELD.

MANY a time, in college or in camp, I had planned the
style of my home-coming. Master Webster, in the
Humanities, droning away like a Boreraig bagpipe, would
be sending my mind back to Shira Glen, its braes and
corries and singing waters, and Ben Bhuidhe over all, and
with my chin on a hand I would ponder on how I should
go home again when this weary scholarship was over. I
had always a ready fancy and some of the natural vanity
of youth, so I could see myself landing off the lugger at
the quay of Inneraora town, three inches more of a man
than when I left with a firkin of herring and a few bolls of
meal for my winter's provand; thicker too at the chest,
and with a jacket of London green cloth with brass
buttons. Would the fishermen about the quay-head not
lean over the gun'les of their skiffs and say, "There goes
young Elrigmore from Colleging, well-knit in troth, and
a pretty lad"? I could hear (all in my day-dream in
yon place of dinghy benches) the old women about the
well at the town Cross say, "Oh *laochain!* thou art come
back from the Galldach, and Glascow College; what a
thousand curious things thou must know, and what
wisdom thou must have, but never a change on thine
affability to the old and to the poor!" But it was not
till I had run away from Glascow College, and shut the
boards for good and all, as I thought, on my humane

letters and history, and gone with cousin Gavin to the German wars in Mackay's Corps of true Highlanders, that I added a manlier thought to my thinking of the day when I should come home to my native place. I've seen me in the camp at night, dog-wearied after stoury marching on their cursed foreign roads, keeping my eyes open and the sleep at an arm's-length, that I might think of Shira Glen. Whatever they may say of me or mine, they can never deny but I had the right fond heart for my own country-side, and I have fought men for speaking of its pride and poverty—their ignorance, their folly!—for what did they ken of the Highland spirit? I would be lying in the lap of the night, and my Ferrara sword rolled in my plaid as a pillow for my head, fancying myself—all those long wars over, march, siege, and sack—riding on a good horse down the pass of Aora and through the arches into the old town. Then, it was not the fishermen or the old women I thought of, but the girls, and the winking stars above me were their eyes, glinting merrily and kindly on a stout young gentleman soldier with jack and morion, sword at haunch, spur at heel, and a name for bravado never a home-biding laird in our parish had, burgh or landward. I would sit on my horse so, the chest well out, the back curved, the knees straight, one gauntlet off to let my white hand wave a salute when needed, and none of all the pretty ones would be able to say Elrigmore thought another one the sweetest. Oh! I tell you we learnt many arts in the Lowland wars, more than they teach Master of Art in the old biggin' in the Hie Street of Glasgow.

One day, at a place called Nordlingen near the Mid Franken, binding a wound Gavin got in the sword-arm, I said, "What's your wish at this moment, cousin?"

He looked at me with a melting eye, and the flush hove to his face.

"'Fore God, Colin," said he, "I would give my twelve months' wage to stand below the lintel of my mother's door and hear her say 'Darling scamp!'"

"If you had your wish, Gavin, when and how would you go into Inneraora town after those weary years away?"

2

" Man, I've made that up long syne," said he, and the tear was at his cheek. " Let me go into it cannily at night-fall from the Cromalt end, when the boys and girls were dancing on the green to the pipes at the end of a harvest-day. Them in a reel, with none of the abulzie-ments of war about me, but a plain civil lad like the rest, I would join in the strathspey and kiss two or three of the girls ere ever they jaloused a stranger was among them."

Poor Gavin, good Gavin! he came home no way at all to his mother and his mountains ; but here was I, with some of his wish for my fortune, riding cannily into Inneraora town in the dark.

It is wonderful how travel, even in a marching company of cavaliers of fortune, gives scope to the mind. When I set foot, twelve years before this night I speak of, on the gabert that carried me down to Dunbarton on my way to the Humanities classes, I could have sworn I was leaving a burgh most large and wonderful. The town houses of old Stonefield, Craignish, Craignure, Asknish, and the other cadets of Clan Campbell, had such a strong and genteel look ; the windows, all but a very few, had glass in every lozen, every shutter had a hole to let in the morning light, and each door had its little ford of stones running across the gutter that sped down the street, smelling fishily a bit, on its way to the shore. For me, in those days, each close that pierced the tall lands was as wide and high as a mountain *eas*, the street itself seemed broad and substantial, crowded with people worth kenning for their graces and the many things they knew.

I came home now on this night of nights with Munchen and Augsburg, and the fine cities of all the France, in my mind, and I tell you I could think shame of this mean rickle of stones I had thought a town, were it not for the good hearts and kind I knew were under every roof. The broad street crowded with people, did I say ? A little lane rather ; and Elrigmore, with schooling and the wisdom of travel, felt he could see into the heart's core of the cunningest merchant in the place.

But anyway, here I was, riding into town from the Cromalt end on a night in autumn. It was after ten by my Paris watch when I got the length of the Creags, and

I knew that there was nothing but a sleeping town before me, for our folks were always early bedders when the fishing season was on. The night hung thick with stars, but there was no moon ; a stiff wind from the east prinked at my right ear and cooled my horse's skin, as he slowed down after a canter of a mile or two on this side of Pennymore. Out on the loch I could see the lights of a few herring-boats lift and fall at the end of their trail of nets.

" Too few of you there for the town to be busy and cheerful," said I to myself ; " no doubt the bulk of the boats are down at Otter, damming the fish in the narrow gut, and keeping them from searching up to our own good townsmen."

I pressed my brute to a trot, and turned round into the nether part of the town. It was what I expected—the place was dark, black out. The people were sleeping ; the salt air of Loch Finne went sighing through the place in a way that made me dowie for old days. We went over the causeway-stones with a clatter that might have wakened the dead, but no one put a head out, and I thought of the notion of a cheery home-coming poor Gavin had—my dear cousin, stroked out and cold under foreign clods at Velshiem, two leagues below the field of Worms of Hessen, on the banks of the Rhine, in Low Germanie.

It is a curious business this riding into a town in the dark waste of night ; curious even in a strange town when all are the same for you that sleep behind those shutters and those doors, but doubly curious when you know that behind the dark fronts are folk lying that you know well, that have been thinking, and drinking, and thriving when you were far away. As I went clattering slowly by, I would say at one house front, " Yonder's my old comrade, Tearlach, who taught me my one tune on the pipe-chanter ; is his beard grown yet, I wonder ? " At another, " There is the garret window of the schoolmaster's daughter—does she sing so sweetly nowadays in the old kirk ? "

In the dead middle of the street I pulled my horse up, just to study the full quietness of the hour. Leaning over, I put a hand on his nostrils and whispered in his ear for a silence, as we do abroad in ambuscade. Town Inneraora slept sound, sure enough! All to hear was the spilling of the river at the cascade under the bridge and the plopping of the waves against the wall we call the ramparts, that keeps the sea from thrashing on the Tolbooth. And then over all I could hear a most strange moaning sound, such as we boys used to make with a piece of lath nicked at the edges and swung hurriedly round the head by a string. It was made by the wind, I knew, for it came loudest in the gusty bits of the night and from the east, and when there was a lull I could hear it soften away and end for a second or two with a dunt, as if some heavy, soft thing struck against wood.

Whatever it was, the burghers of Inneraora paid no heed, but slept, stark and sound, behind their steeked shutters.

The solemnity of the place that I knew so much better in a natural lively mood annoyed me, and I played there and then a prank more becoming a boy in his first kilt than a gentleman of education and travel and some repute for sobriety. I noticed I was opposite the house of a poor old woman they called Black Kate, whose door was ever the target in my young days for every lad that could brag of a boot-toe, and I saw that the shutter, hanging ajee on one hinge, was thrown open against the harled wall of the house. In my doublet-pocket there were some carabeen bullets, and taking one out, I let bang at the old woman's little lozens. There was a splinter of glass, and I waited to see if any one should come out to find who had done the damage. My trick was in vain; no one came. Old Kate, as I found next day, was dead since Martinmas, and her house was empty.

Still the moaning sound came from the town-head, and I went slowly riding in its direction. It grew clearer and yet uncannier as I sped on, and mixed with the sough of it I could hear at last the clink of chains.

"What in God's name have I here?" said I to myself, turning round Islay Campbell's corner, and yonder was my answer!

The town gibbets were throng indeed! Two corpses swung in the wind, like net bows on a drying-pole, going from side to side, making the woeful sough and clink of chains, and the dunt I had heard when the wind dropped.

I grued more at the sound of the soughing than at the sight of the hanged fellows, for I've seen the Fell Sergeant in too many ugly fashions to be much put about at a hanging match. But it was such a poor home-coming! It told me as plain as could be, what I had heard rumours of in the low country, riding round from the port of Leith, that the land was uneasy, and that pit and gallows were bye-ordinar busy at the gates of our castle. When I left for my last session at Glascow College, the countryside was quiet as a village green, never a raider nor a reiver in the land, and so poor the Doomster's trade (Black George) that he took to the shoeing of horses.

" There must be something wicked in the times, and cheatery rampant indeed," I thought, " when the common gibbet of Inneraora has a drunkard's convoy on either hand to prop it up."

But it was no time for meditation. Through the rags of plaiding on the chains went the wind again so eerily that I bound to be off, and I put my horse to it, bye the town-head and up the two miles to Glen Shira. I was sore and galled sitting on the saddle ; my weariness hung at the back of my legs and shoulders like an ague, and there was never a man in this world came home to his native place so eager for taking supper and sleep as young Elrigmore.

What I expected at my father's door I am not going to set down here. I went from it a fool, with not one grace about me but the love of my good mother, and the punishment I had for my hot and foolish cantrip was many a wae night on foreign fields, vexed to the core for the sore heart I had left at home.

My mind, for all my weariness, was full of many things, and shame above all, as I made for my father's house. The horse had never seen Glen Shira, but it smelt the comfort of the stable and whinnied cheerfully as I pulled up at the gate. There was but one window to the gable-end of Elrigmore, and it was something of a surprise to me to find a light in it, for our people were not overly rich in these days, and candle or cruisie was wont to be doused at bedtime. More was my surprise when, leading my horse round to the front, feeling my way in the dark by memory, I found the oak door open and my father, dressed, standing in the light of it.

A young *sgalag* came running to the reins, and handing them to him, I stepped into the light of the door, my bonnet in my hand.

" Step in, sir, caird or gentleman," said my father— looking more bent at the shoulder than twelve years before.

I went under the door-lintel, and stood a little abashed before him.

" Colin ! Colin ! " he cried in the Gaelic. " Did I not ken it was you? " and he put his two hands on my shoulders.

" It is Colin sure enough, father dear," I said, slipping readily enough into the mother tongue they did their best to get out of me at Glascow College. " Is he welcome in this door ? " and the weariness weighed me down at the hip and bowed me my very legs.

He gripped me tight at the elbows, and looked me hungrily in the face.

" If you had a murdered man's head in your oxter, Colin," said he, " you were still my son. Colin, Colin ! come ben and put off your boots ! "

" Mother——" I said, but he broke in on my question.

" Come in, lad, and sit down. You are back from the brave wars you never went to with my will, and you'll find stirring times here at your own parish. It's the way of the Sennachies' stories."

" How is that, sir ? "

" They tell, you know, that people wander far on the going foot for adventure, and adventure is in the first turning of their native lane."

I was putting my boots off before a fire of hissing logs that filled the big room with a fir-wood smell right homely and comforting to my heart, and my father was doing what I should have known was my mother's office if weariness had not left me in a sort of stupor—he was laying on the board a stout and soldierly supper and a tankard of the red Bordeaux wine the French traffickers bring to Loch Finne to trade for cured herring. He would come up now and then where I sat fumbling sleepily at my belt, and put a hand on my head, a curious unmanly sort of thing I never knew my father do before, and I felt put-about at this petting, which would have been more like my sister if ever I had had the luck to have one.

"You are tired, Colin, my boy?" he said.

"A bit, father, a bit," I answered; "rough roads you know. I was landed at break of day at Skipness and—Is mother——?"

"Sit in, *laochain!* Did you meet many folks on the road?"

"No, sir; as pestilent barren a journey as ever I trotted on, and the people seemingly on the hill, for their crops are unco late in the field."

"Ay, ay, lad, so they are," said my father, pulling back his shoulders a bit—a fairly straight wiry old man, with a name for good swordsmanship in his younger days.

I was busy at a cold partridge, and hard at it, when I thought again how curious it was that my father should be a-foot in the house at such time of night and no one else about, he so early a bedder for ordinary and never the last to sneck the outer door.

"Did you expect any one, father," I asked, "that you should be waiting up with the collation, and the outer door unsnecked?"

"There was never an outer door snecked since you left, Colin," said he, turning awkwardly away and looking hard into the loof of his hand like a wife spaeing fortunes—for sheer want, I could see, of some engagement for his eyes. "I could never get away with the notion that some way like this at night would ye come back to Elrigmore."

"Mother would miss me?"

"She did, Colin, she did; I'm not denying."

"She'll be bedded long syne, no doubt, father?"

My father looked at me and gulped at the throat.

"Bedded indeed, poor Colin," said he, "this very day in the clods of Kilmalieu!"

And that was my melancholy home-coming to my father's house of Elrigmore, in the parish of Glenaora, in the shire of Argile.

CHAPTER II.

GILLESBEG GRUAMACH.

EVERY land, every glen or town, I make no doubt, has its own peculiar air or atmosphere that one familiar with the same may never puzzle about in his mind, but finds come over him with a waft at odd moments like the scent of bog-myrtle and tansy in an old clothes-press. Our own air in Glen Shira had ever been very genial and encouraging to me. Even when a young lad, coming back from the low country or the scaling of school, the cool fresh breezes of the morning and the riper airs of the late afternoon went to my head like a mild white wine ; very heartsome too, rousing the laggard spirit that perhaps made me, before, over-apt to sit and dream of the doing of grand things instead of putting out a hand to do them. In Glascow the one thing that I had to grumble most about next to the dreary hours of schooling was the clammy air of street and close ; in Germanie it was worse, a moist weakening windiness full of foreign smells, and I've seen me that I could gaily march a handful of leagues to get a sniff of the salt sea. Not that I was one who craved for wrack and bilge at my nose all the time. What I think best is a stance inland from the salt water, where the mountain air, brushing over gall and heather, takes the sting from the sea air, and the two blended give a notion of the fine variousness of life. We had a herdsman once in Elrigmore, who could tell five miles up the glen when the tide was out on Loch Finne. I was never so keen-scented as that, but when I awakened next day in a camceiled room in Elrigmore, and put my head out at the window to look around, I smelt the heather for a second like an escapade in a dream.

Down to Ealan Eagal I went for a plunge in the linn in the old style, and the airs of Shira Glen hung about me like friends and lovers, so well acquaint and jovial.

Shira Glen, Shira Glen! if I was bard I'd have songs to sing to it, and all I know is one sculduddry verse on a widow that dwelt in Maam! There, at the foot of my father's house, were the winding river, and north and south the brown hills, split asunder by God's goodness, to give a sample of His bounty. Maam, Elrigmore and Elrigbeg, Kilblaan and Ben Bhuidhe—their steep sides hung with cattle, and below crowded the reeking homes of tacksman and cottar; the burns poured hurriedly to the flat beneath their borders of hazel and ash; to the south, the fresh water we call Dubh Loch, flapping with ducks and fringed with shelisters or water-flags and bul-rush, and farther off the Cowal hills; to the north, the wood of Drimlee and the wild pass the red Macgregors sometimes took for a back-road to our cattle-folds in cloud of night and darkness. Down on it all shone the polished and hearty sun, birds chirmed on every tree, though it was late in the year; blackcock whirred across the alders, and sturdy heifers bellowed tunefully, knee-deep at the ford.

"Far have I wandered," thought I to myself, "warring other folk's wars for the humour of it and small wages, but here's the one place I've seen yet that was worth hacking good steel for in earnest!"

But still my heart was sore for mother, and sore, too, for the tale of changed times in Campbell country my father told me over a breakfast of braddan, fresh caught in a creel from the Gearron river, oaten bannock, and cream.

After breakfast I got me into my kilt for town. There are many costumes going about the world, but, with allowance for every one, I make bold to think our own tartan duds the gallantest of them all. The kilt was my wear when first I went to Glasgow College, and many a St Mungo keelie, no better than myself at classes or at

English language, made fun of my brown knees, sometimes not to the advantage of his headpiece when it came
to argument and neifs on the Fleshers' Haugh. Pulling
on my old *breacan* this morning in Elrigmore was like
donning a fairy garb, and getting back ten years of youth.
We have a way of belting on the kilt in real Argile I have
seen nowhere else. Ordinarily, our lads take the whole
web of tartan cloth, of twenty ells or more, and coil it
once round their middle, there belting it, and bring the
free end up on the shoulder to pin with a brooch—not
a bad fashion for display and long marches and for
sleeping out on the hill with, but somewhat discom-
modious for warm weather. It was our plan sometimes
to make what we called a philabeg, or little kilt, maybe
eight yards long, gathered in at the haunch and hung
in many pleats behind, the plain brat part in front decked
off with a leather sporran, tagged with thong points
tied in knots, and with no plaid on the shoulder. I've
never seen a more jaunty and suitable garb for campaigning, better by far for short sharp tulzies with an
enemy than the philamore or the big kilt our people
sometimes throw off them in a skirmish, and fight (the
coarsest of them) in their gartered hose and scrugged
bonnets.

With my kilt and the memory of old times about me,
I went walking down to Inneraora in the middle of the
day. I was prepared for change from the complaints
of my father, but never for half the change I found in the
burgh town of MacCailein Mor. In my twelve foreign
years the place was swamped by incomers, black unwelcome Covenanters from the shires of Air and Lanrick—
Brices, Yuilles, Rodgers, and Richies—all brought up
here by Gillesbeg Gruamach, Marquis of Argile, to teach
his clans the arts of peace and merchandise. Half the
folk I met between the arches and the Big Barns were
strangers that seemingly never had tartan on their hur-
dies, but settled down with a firm foot in the place, I could
see by the bold look of them as I passed on the plainstanes of the street. A queer town this on the edge of
Loch Finne, and far in the Highlands! There were shops
with Lowland stuffs in them, and over the doors sign-

boards telling of the most curious trades for a Campbell burgh—horologers, cordiners, baxters, and such like mechanicks that I felt sure poor Donald had small call for. They might be incomers, but they were thirled to Gillesbeg all the same, as I found later on.

It was the court day, and his lordship was sitting in judgment on two Strathlachlan fellows, who had been brawling at the Cross the week before and came to knives, more in a frolic than in hot blood, with some of the town lads. With two or three old friends I went into the Tolbooth to see the play—for play it was, I must confess, in town Inneraora, when justice was due to a man whose name by ill-luck was not Campbell, or whose bonnet-badge was not the myrtle stem.

The Tolbooth hall was, and is to this day, a spacious high-ceiled room, well lighted from the bay-side. It was crowded soon after we got in, with Cowalside fishermen and townpeople all the one way or the other—for or against the poor lads in bilboes, who sat, simple-looking enough, between the town officers, a pair of old *bodachs* in long scarlet coats and carrying *tuaghs*, Lochaber axes, or halberds that never smelt blood since they came from the smith.

It was the first time ever I saw Gillesbeg Gruamach sitting on the bench, and I was startled at the look of the man. I've seen some sour dogs in my day—few worse than Ruthven's rittmasters whom we met in Swabia—but I never saw a man who, at the first vizzy, had the dour sour countenance of Archibald, Marquis of Argile and Lord of Lochow. Gruamach, or grim-faced, our good Gaels called him in a bye-name, and well he owned it, for over necklace or gorget I've seldom seen a sterner jowl or a more sinister eye. And yet, to be fair and honest, this was but the notion one got at a first glint; in a while I thought little was amiss with his looks as he leaned on the table and cracked in a humoursome laughing way with the pannelled jury.

He might have been a plain cottar on Glen Aora side rather than King of the Highlands for all the airs he assumed, and when he saw me, better put-on in costume than my neighbours in court, he seemingly asked my name in a whisper from the clerk beside him, and finding who I was, cried out in St Andrew's English—

"What! Young Elrigmore back to the Glens! I give you welcome, sir, to Bailie Inneraora!"

I but bowed, and in a fashion saluted, saying nothing in answer, for the whole company glowered at me, all except the home-bred ones who had better manners.

The two MacLachlans denied in the Gaelic the charge the sheriff clerk read to them in a long farrago of English with more foreign words to it than ever I learned the sense of in College.

His lordship paid small heed to the witnesses who came forward to swear to the unruliness of the Strathlachlan men, and the jury talked heedlessly with one another in a fashion scandalous to see. The man who had been stabbed—it was but a jag at the shoulder, where the dirk had gone through from front to back with only some loss of blood—was averse from being hard on the panels. He was a jocular fellow with the right heart for a duello, and in his nipped burgh Gaelic he made light of the disturbance and his injury.

"Nothing but a bit play, my jurymen—MacCailein—my lordship—a bit play. If the poor lad didn't happen to have his dirk out and I to run on it, nobody was a bodle the worse."

"But the law"—started the clerk to say.

"No case for law at all," said the man. "It's an honest brawl among friends, and I could settle the account with them at the next market-day, when my shoulder's mended."

"Better if you would settle my account for your last pair of brogues, Alasdair M'Iver," said a black-avised juryman.

"What's your trade?" asked the Marquis of the witness.

"I'm at the Coillebhraid silver-mines," said he. "We had a little too much drink, or these MacLachlan gentlemen and I had never come to variance."

The Marquis gloomed at the speaker and brought down his fist with a bang on the table before him.

"Damn those silver-mines!" said he; "they breed more trouble in this town of mine than I'm willing to thole. If they put a penny in my purse it might not be so irksome, but they plague me sleeping and waking, and I'm not a plack the richer. If it were not to give my poor cousin, John Splendid, a chance of a living and occupation for his wits, I would drown them out with the water of Cromalt Burn."

The witness gave a little laugh, and ducking his head oddly like one taking liberties with a master, said, "We're a drouthy set, my lord, at the mines, and I wouldn't be saying but what we might drink them dry again of a morning, if we had been into town the night before."

His lordship cut short his sour smile at the man's fancy, and bade the officers on with the case.

"You have heard the proof," he said to the jury when it came to his turn to charge them. "Are they guilty, or not? If the question was put to me I should say the Laird of MacLachlan, arrant Papist! should keep his men at home to Mass on the other side of the loch instead of loosing them on honest, or middling honest, Campbells, for the strict virtue of these Coillebhraid miners is what I am not going to guarantee."

Of course the fellows were found guilty—one of stabbing, the other of art and part—for MacLachlan was no friend of MacCailein Mor, and as little friend to the merchant burghers of Inneraora, for he had the poor taste to buy his shop provand from the Lamont towns of Low Cowal.

"A more unfriendly man to the Laird of MacLachlan might be for hanging you on the gibbet at the town-head," said his lordship to the prisoners, spraying ink-sand idly on the clean page of a statute-book as he spoke; "but our three trees upbye are leased just now to other tenants, —Badenoch hawks a trifle worse than yourselves, and more deserving."

The men looked stupidly about them, knowing not one word of his lordship's English, and he was always a man who disdained to converse much in Erse. He looked a little cruelly at them and went on.

"Perhaps clipping your lugs might be the bonniest way of showing you what we think of such on-goings in honest Inneraora; or getting the Doomster to bastinado you up and down the street. But we'll try what a fortnight in the Tolbooth may do to amend your visiting manners. Take them away, officers."

"*Abair moran taing*—say 'many thanks' to his lordship," whispered one of the red-coat halberdiers in the ear of the bigger of the two prisoners. I could hear the command distinctly where I sat, well back in the court, and so no doubt could Gillesbeg Gruamach, but he was used to such obsequious foolishness and he made no dissent or comment.

"*Taing! taing!*" said one spokesman of the two MacLachlans in his hurried Cowal Gaelic, and his neighbour, echoing him word for word in the comic fashion they have in these parts; "*Taing! taing!* I never louted to the horseman that rode over me yet, and I would be ill-advised to start with the Gruamach one!"

The man's face flushed up as he spoke. It's a thing I've noticed about our own poor Gaelic men : speaking before them in English or Scots, their hollow look and aloofness would give one the notion that they lacked sense and sparkle ; take the muddiest-looking among them and challenge him in his own tongue, and you'll find his face fill with wit and understanding.

I was preparing to leave the court-room, having many people to call on in Inneraora, and had turned with my two friends to the door, when a fellow brushed in past us—a Highlander, I could see, but in trews—and he made to go forward into the body of the court, as if to speak to his lordship, now leaning forward in a cheerful conversation with the Provost of the burgh, a sonsy gentleman in a peruke and figured waistcoat.

"Who is he, this bold fellow?" I asked one of my friends, pausing with a foot on the door-step, a little surprised at the want of reverence to MacCailein in the man's bearing.

"Iain Aluinn—John Splendid," said my friend. We were talking in the Gaelic, and he made a jocular remark there is no English for. Then he added, "A poor cousin of the Marquis, a M'Iver Campbell (*on the wrong side*), with little schooling, but some wit and gentlemanly parts. He has gone through two fortunes in black cattle, fought

15

some fighting here and there, and now he manages the
silver-mines so adroitly that Gillesbeg Gruamach is ever
on the brink of getting a big fortune, but never done
launching out a little one instead to keep the place going.
A decent soul the Splendid! throughither a bit, and
better at promise than performance, but at the core as
good as gold, and a fellow you would never weary of
though you tramped with him in a thousand glens. We
call him Splendid, not for his looks but for his style."

The object of my friend's description was speaking into
the ear of MacCailein Mor by this time, and the Marquis's face showed his tale was interesting, to say the least
of it.

We waited no more, but went out into the street. I
was barely two closes off from the Tolbooth when a messenger came running after me, sent by the Marquis, who
asked if I would oblige greatly by waiting till he made up
on me. I went back, and met his lordship with his kinsman and mine-manager coming out of the court-room
together into the lobby that divided the place from the
street.

"Oh, Elrigmore!" said the Marquis, in an offhand
jovial and equal way; "I thought you would like to meet
my cousin here—M'Iver of the Barbreck; something of a
soldier like yourself, who has seen service in Lowland
wars."

"In the Scots Brigade, sir?" I asked M'Iver, eyeing
him with greater interest than ever. He was my senior
by about a dozen years seemingly, a neat, well-built fellow,
clean-shaven, a little over the middle height, carrying a
rattan in his hand, though he had a small sword tucked
under the skirt of his coat.

"With Lumsden's regiment," he said. "His lordship
here has been telling me you have just come home from
the field."

"But last night. I took the liberty while Inneraora
was snoring. You were before my day in foreign service,
and yet I thought I knew by repute every Campbell that
ever fought for the hard-won dollars of Gustavus even
before my day. There were not so many of them from
the West Country."

16

"I trailed a pike privately," laughed M'Iver, "and for the honour of Clan Diarmaid I took the name Munro. My cousin here cares to have none of his immediate relatives make a living by steel at any rank less than a cornal's, or a major's at the very lowest. Frankfort, and Landsberg, and the stark field of Leipzig were the last I saw of foreign battles, and the God's truth is they were my bellyful. I like a bit splore, but give it to me in our old style, with the tartan instead of buff, and the target for breastplate and taslets. I came home sick of wars."

"Our friend does himself injustice, my dear Elrigmore," said Argile, smiling; "he came home against his will, I have no doubt, and I know he brought back with him a musketoon bullet in the hip, that couped him by the heels down in Glassary for six months."

"The result," M'Iver hurried to exclaim, but putting out his breast with a touch of vanity, "of a private *ren contre*, an affair of my own with a Reay gentleman, and not to be laid to my credit as part of the war's scaith at all."

"You conducted your duello in odd style under Lumsden, surely," said I, "if you fought with powder and ball instead of steel, which is more of a Highlander's weapon to my way of thinking. All our affairs in the Reay battalion were with claymore—sometimes with targe, sometimes wanting."

"This was a particular business of our own," laughed John Splendid (as I may go on to call M'Iver, for it was the name he got oftenest behind and before in Argile). "It was less a trial of valour than a wager about which had the better skill with the musket. If I got the bullet in my groin, I at least showed the Mackay gentleman in question that an Argile man could handle arquebus as well as *arme blanche* as we said in the France. I felled my man at one hundred and thirty paces, with six to count from a ritt-master's signal. Blow, present, God sain Mackay's soul! But I'm not given to braggadocio."

"Not a bit, cousin," said the Marquis, looking quizzingly at me.

"I could not make such good play with the gun against a fort gable at so many feet," said I.

"You could, sir, you could," said John Splendid in an easy, offhand, flattering way, that gave me at the start of our acquaintance the whole key to his character. "I've little doubt you could allow me half-a-dozen paces and come closer on the centre of the target."

By this time we were walking down the street, the Marquis betwixt the pair of us commoners, and I to the left side. Lowlanders and Highlanders quickly got out of the way before us and gave us the crown of the causeway. The main part of them the Marquis never let his eye light on; he kept his nose cocked in the air in the way I've since found peculiar to his family. It was odd to me that had in wanderings got to look on all honest men as equal (except Camp-Master Generals and Pike Colonels), to see some of his lordship's poor clansmen cringing before him. Here indeed was the leaven of your low-country scum, for in all the broad Highlands wandering before and since I never saw the like! "Blood of my blood, brother of my name!" says our good Gaelic old-word: it made no insolents in camp or castle, yet it kept the poorest clansmen's head up before the highest chief. But there was, even in Baile Inneraora, sinking in the servile ways of the incomer, something too of honest worship in the deportment of the people. It was sure enough in the manner of an old woman with a face peat-tanned to crinkled leather who ran out of the Vennel or lane, and, bending to the Marquis his lace wrist-bands, kissed them as I've seen Papists do the holy duds in Notre Dame and Bruges Kirk.

This display before me, something of a stranger, a little displeased Gillesbeg Gruamach. "Tut, tut!" he cried in Gaelic to the *cailleach*, "thou are a foolish old woman!"

"God keep thee, MacCailein!" said she; "thy daddy put his hand on my head like a son when he came back from his banishment in Spain, and I keened over thy mother dear when she died. The hair of Peggy Bheg's head is thy door-mat, and her son's blood is thy will for a foot-bath."

"Savage old harridan!" cried the Marquis, jerking away; but I could see he was not now unpleased altogether that a man new from the wide world and its ways should behold how much he was thought of by his people.

He put his hands in a friendly way on the shoulders of us on either hand of him, and brought us up a bit round turn, facing him at a stand-still opposite the door of the English kirk. To this day I mind well the rumour of the sea that came round the corner.

"I have a very particular business with both you gentlemen," he said. "My friend here, M'Iver, has come hot-foot to tell me of a rumour that a body of Irish banditty under Alasdair MacDonald, the MacColkitto as we call him, has landed somewhere about Kinlochaline or Knoydart. This portends damnably, if I, an elder ordained of this kirk, may say so. We have enough to do with the Athole gentry and others nearer home. It means that I must on with plate and falchion again, and out on the weary road for war I have little stomach for, to tell the truth."

"You're able for the best of them, MacCailein," cried John Splendid, in a hot admiration. "For a scholar you have as good judgment on the field and as gallant a seat on the saddle as any man ever I saw in haberschone and morion. With your schooling I could go round the world conquering."

"Ah! flatterer, flatterer! Ye have all the guile of the tongue our enemies give Clan Campbell credit for, and that I wish I had a little more of. Still and on, it's no time for fair words. Look! Elrigmore. You'll have heard of our kittle state in this shire for the past ten years, and not only in this shire but all over the West Highlands. I give you my word I'm no sooner with the belt off me and my chair pulled in to my desk and papers than its some one beating a point of war or a piper blowing the warning under my window. To look at my history for the past few years any one might think I was Dol' Gorm himself, fight and plot, plot and fight! How can I help it—thrust into this hornet's nest from the age of sixteen, when my father (*beannachd leis!*) took me out warring against the islesmen, and I only in the humour for playing at shinty or fishing like the boys on the moorlochs behind the town. I would sooner be a cottar in

Auchnagoul down there, with porridge for my every meal, than constable, chastiser, what not, or whatever I am, of all these vexed Highlands. Give me my book in my closet, or at worst let me do my country's work in a courtier's way with brains, and I would ask no more."

"Except Badenoch and Nether Lochaber—fat land, fine land, MacCailein!" said John Splendid, laughing cunningly.

The Marquis's face flamed up.

"You're an ass, John," he said; "picking up the countryside's gossip. I have no love for the Athole and Great Glen folks as ye ken; but I could long syne have got letters of fire and sword that made Badenoch and Nether Lochaber mine if I had the notion. Don't interrupt me with your nonsense, cousin; I'm telling Elrigmore here, for he's young and has skill of civilised war, that there may, in very few weeks, be need of every arm in the parish or shire to baulk Colkitto. The MacDonald and other malignants have been robbing high and low from Lochow to Loch Finne this while back; I have hanged them a score a month at the town-head there, but that's dealing with small affairs, and I'm sore mistaken if we have not cruel times to come."

"Well, sir," I said, "what can I do?"

The Marquis bit his moustachio and ran a spur on the ground for a little without answering, as one in a quandary, and then he said, "You're no vassal of mine, Baron" (as if he were half sorry for it), "but all you Glen Shira folk are well disposed to me and mine, and have good cause, though that Macnachtan fellow's a Papisher. What I had in my mind was that I might count on you taking a company of our fencible men, as John here is going to do, and going over-bye to Lorn with me to cut off those Irish blackguards of Alasdair MacDonald's from joining Montrose."

For some minutes I stood turning the thing over in my mind, being by nature slow to take on any scheme of high emprise without some scrupulous balancing of chances. Half-way up the closes, in the dusk, and in their rooms, well back from the windows, or far up the street, all aloof from his Majesty MacCailein Mor, the good curious people of Inneraora watched us. They could little guess the pregnancy of our affairs. For me, I thought how wearily I had looked for some rest from wars, at home in Glen Shira after my years of foreign service. Now that I was here, and my mother no more, my old father needed me on hill and field, and Argile's quarrel was not my quarrel until Argile's enemies were at the foot of Ben Bhuidhe or coming all boden in fier of war up the pass of Shira Glen. I liked adventure, and a captaincy was a captaincy, but——

"Is it boot and saddle at once, my lord?" I asked.

"It must be that or nothing. When a viper's head is coming out of a hole, crunch it incontinent, or the tail may be more than you can manage."

"Then, my lord," said I, "I must cry off. On this jaunt at least. It would be my greatest pleasure to go with you and my friend M'Iver, not to mention all the good fellows I'm bound to know in rank in your regiment, but for my duty to my father and one or two other considerations that need not be named. But—if this be any use—I give my word that should MacDonald or any other force come this side the passes at Accurach Hill, or anywhere east Lochow, my time and steel are yours."

MacCailein Mor looked a bit annoyed, and led us at a fast pace up to the gate of the castle that stood, high towered and embrasured for heavy pieces, stark and steeve above town Inneraora. A most curious, dour, and moody man, with a mind roving from key to key. Every now and then he would stop and think a little without a word, then on, and run his fingers through his hair or fumble nervously at his leathern buttons, paying small heed to the Splendid and I, who convoyed him, so we got into a crack about the foreign field of war.

"Quite right, Elrigmore, quite right!" at last cried the Marquis, pulling up short, and looked me plump in the eyes. "Bide at hame while bide ye may. I would never go on this affair myself if by God's grace I was not Marquis of Argile and son of a house with many bitter foes. But, hark ye! a black day looms for these our home-lands if ever Montrose and those Irish dogs get through our passes. For twenty thousand pounds Saxon I would not have the bars off the two roads of Accurach! And I thank you, Elrigmore, that at the worst I can count on your service at home. We may need good men here on Loch Finneside as well as farther afield, overrun as we are by the blackguardism of the North and the Papist clans around us. Come in, friends, and have your meridian. I have a flagon of French brown brandy you never tasted the equal of in any town you sacked in all Low Germanie."

CHAPTER III.

THE LADY ON THE STAIR.

JOHN SPLENDID looked at me from the corner of an eye as we came out again and daundered slowly down the town.

"A queer one yon!" said he, as it were feeling his way with a rapier-point at my mind about his Marquis.

"Do you tell me?" I muttered, giving him parry of low quarte like a good swordsman, and he came to the recover with a laugh.

"Foil, Elrigmore!" he cried. "But we're soldiers and lads of the world, and you need hardly be so canny. You see MacCailein's points as well as I do. His one weakness is the old one—books, books,—the curse of the Highlands and every man of spirit, say I. He has the stuff in him by nature, for none can deny Clan Diarmaid courage and knightliness; but for four generations court, closet, and college have been taking the heart out of our chiefs. Had our lordship in-bye been sent a fostering in the old style, brought up to the chase and the sword and manly comportment, he would not have that wan cheek this day, and that swithering about what he must be at next!"

"You forget that I have had the same ill-training," I said (in no bad humour, for I followed his mind). "I had a touch of Glasgow College myself."

"Yes, yes," he answered quickly; "you had that, but by all accounts it did you no harm. You learned little of what they teach there."

This annoyed me, I confess, and John Splendid was gleg enough to see it.

"I mean," he added, "you caught no fever for paper and ink, though you may have learned many a quirk I was the better of myself. I could never even write my name; and I've kept compt of wages at the mines with a pickle chuckie-stones."

"That's a pity," says I, drily.

"Oh, never a bit," says he, gaily, or at any rate with a way as if to carry it off vauntingly. "I can do many things as well as most, and a few others colleges never learned me. I know many winter tales, from 'Minochag and Morag' to 'The Shifty Lad'; I can make passable poetry by word of mouth; I can speak the English and the French, and I have seen enough of courtiers to know that half their canons are to please and witch the eye of women in a way that I could undertake to do by my looks alone and some good-humour. Show me a beast on hill or in glen I have not the history of; and if dancing, singing, the sword, the gun, the pipes—ah, not the pipes, —it's my one envy in the world to play the bagpipes with some show of art and delicacy, and I cannot. Queer is that, indeed, and I so keen on them! I would tramp right gaily a night and a day on end to hear a scholar fingering 'The Glen is Mine.'"

There was a witless vanity about my friend that sat on him almost like a virtue. He made parade of his crafts less, I could see, because he thought much of them, than because he wanted to keep himself on an equality with me. In the same way, as I hinted before, he never, in all the time of our wanderings after, did a thing well before me but he bode to keep up my self-respect by maintaining that I could do better, or at least as good.

"Books, I say," he went on, as we clinked heels on the causeway-stones, and between my little bit cracks with old friends in the by-going,—"books, I say, have spoiled MacCailein's stomach. Ken ye what he told me once? That a man might readily show more valour in a conclusion come to in the privacy of his bed-closet than in a victory won on the field. That's what they teach by way of manly doctrine down there in the new English church, under the pastorage of Maister Alexander Gordon, chaplain to his lordship and minister to his lordship's people!

It must be the old Cavalier in me, but somehow (in your lug) I have no broo of those Covenanting cattle from the low country—though Gordon's a good soul, there's no denying."

"Are you Catholic ? " I said, in a surprise.

"What are you yourself ? " he asked, and then he flushed, for he saw a little smile in my face at the transparency of his endeavour to be always on the pleasing side.

"To tell the truth," he said, " I'm depending on salvation by reason of a fairly good heart, and an eagerness to wrong no man, gentle or semple. I love my fellows, one and all, not offhand as the Catechism enjoins, but heartily, and I never saw the fellow, carl or king, who, if ordinary honest and cheerful, I could not lie heads and thraws with at a camp-fire. In matters of strict ritual, now,—ha—um ! "

"Out with it, man ! " I cried, laughing.

"I'm like Parson Kilmalieu upbye. You've heard of him—easy-going soul, and God sain him ! When it came to the bit, he turned the holy-water font of Kilcatrine blue-stone upside-down, scooped a hole in the bottom, and used the new hollow for Protestant baptism. ' There's such a throng about heaven's gate,' said he, ' that it's only a mercy to open two ; ' and he was a good and humoursome Protestant-Papist till the day he went under the flagstones of his chapel upbye."

Now here was not a philosophy to my mind. I fought in the German wars less for the kreutzers than for a belief (never much studied out, but fervent) that Protestantism was the one good faith, and that her ladyship of Babylon, that's ever on the ran-don, cannot have her downfall one day too soon. You dare not be playing corners-change-corners with religion as you can with the sword of what the ill-bred have called a mercenary (when you come to ponder on't, the swords of patriot or paid man are both for selfish ends unsheathed) ; and if I set down here word for word what John Splendid said, it must not be thought to be in homologation on my part of such latitudinarianism.

I let him run on in this key till we came to the change-house of a widow—one Fraser—and as she curtsied at the door, and asked if the braw gentlemen would favour her poor parlour, we went in and tossed a quaich or two of aqua, to which end she set before us a little brown bottle and two most cunningly contrived and carven cups made of the Coillebhraid silver.

The houses in Inneraora were, and are, built all very much alike, on a plan I thought somewhat cosy and genteel, ere ever I went abroad and learned better. I do not even now deny the cosiness of them, but of the genteelity it were well to say little. They were tall lands or tenements, three storeys high, with through-going closes, or what the English might nominate passages, running from front to back, and leading at their midst to stairs, whereby the occupants got to their domiciles in the flats above. Curved stairs they were, of the same blue-stone the castle is built of, and on their landings at each storey they branched right and left to give access to the single apartments or rooms and kitchens of the residenters. Throng tenements they are these, even yet, giving, as I write, clever children to the world. His Grace nowadays might be granting the poor people a little more room to grow in, some soil for their kail, and a better prospect from their windows than the white-washed wall of the opposite land; but in the matter of air there was and is no complaint. The sea in stormy days came bellowing to the very doors, salt and stinging, tremendous blue and cold. Staying in town of a night, I used to lie awake in my relative's, listening to the spit of the waves on the window-panes and the grumble of the tide, that rocked the land I lay in till I could well fancy it was a ship. Through the closes the wind ever stalked like something fierce and blooded, rattling the iron snecks with an angry finger, breathing beastily at the hinge, and running back a bit once in a while to leap all the harder against groaning lintel and post.

The change-house of the widow was on the ground-flat, a but and ben, the ceilings arched with stone—a strange device in masonry you'll seldom find elsewhere, Highland or Lowland. But she had a garret-room up two stairs where properly she abode, the close flat being reserved for trade of vending *uisgebeatha* and ale. I describe all this old place so fully because it bears on a little affair that happened therein on that day John Splendid and I went in to clink glasses.

The widow had seen that neither of us was very keen on her aqua, which, as it happened, was raw new stuff brewed over at Kames, Lochow, and she asked would we prefer some of her brandy.

" After his lordship's it might be something of a down-come," said John Splendid, half to me and half to the woman.

She caught his meaning, though he spoke in the English ; and in our own tongue, laughing toothlessly, she said—

" The same stilling, Barbreck, the same stilling I make no doubt. MacCailein gets his brown brandy by my brother's cart from French Foreland ; it's a rough road, and sometimes a bottle or two spills on the way. I've a flagon up in a cupboard in my little garret, and I'll go fetch it."

She was over-old a woman to climb three steep stairs for the sake of two young men's drought, and I (having always some regard for the frail) took the key from her hand and went, as was common enough with her younger customers, seeking my own liquor up the stair.

In those windy flights in the fishing season there is often the close smell of herring-scale, of bow tar and the bark-tan of the fishing nets ; but this stair I climbed for the wherewithal was unusually sweet-odoured and clean, because on the first floor was the house of Provost Brown —a Campbell and a Gael, but burdened by accident with a Lowland-sounding cognomen. He had the whole flat to himself—half-a-dozen snug apartments with windows facing the street or the sea as he wanted. I was just at the head of the first flight when out of a door came a girl, and I clean forgot all about the widow's flask of French brandy.

Little more than twelve years syne the Provost's daughter had been a child at the grammar-school, whose one annoyance in life was that the dominie called her Betsy instead of Betty, her real own name : here she was, in the flat of her father's house in Inneraora town, a full-grown woman, who gave me check in my stride and set

27   c

my face flaming. I took in her whole appearance at one glance—a way we have in foreign armies. Between my toe on the last step of the stair and the landing I read the picture : a well-bred woman, from her carriage, the neatness of her apparel, the composure of her pause to let me bye in the narrow passage to the next stair ; not very tall (I have ever had a preference for such as come no higher than neck and oxter) ; very dark brown hair, eyes sparkling, a face rather pale than ruddy, soft skinned, full of a keen nervousness.

In this matter of a woman's eyes—if I may quit the thread of my history—I am a trifle fastidious, and I make bold to say that the finest eyes in the world are those of the Highland girls of Argile—burgh or landward—the best bred and gentlest of them, I mean. There is in them a full and melting friendliness, a mixture to my sometimes notion of poetry and of calm—a memory, as I've thought before, of the deep misty glens and their sights and secrets. I have seen more of the warm heart and merriment in a simple Loch Finne girl's eyes than in all the faces of all the grand dames ever I looked on, Lowland or foreign.

What pleased me first and foremost about this girl Betty, daughter of Provost Brown, were her eyes, then, that showed, even in yon dusky passage, a humoursome interest in young Elrigmore in a kilt coming up-stairs swinging on a finger the key of Lucky Fraser's garret. She hung back doubtfully, though she knew me (I could see) for her old school-fellow and sometime boy-lover, but I saw something of a welcome in the blush at her face, and I gave her no time to chill to me.

" Betty lass, 'tis you," said I, putting out a hand and shaking her soft fingers. " What think you of my cere-mony in calling at the earliest chance to pay my devoirs to the Provost of this burgh and his daughter ? "

I put the key behind my back to give colour a little to my words ; but my lady saw it and jumped at my real errand on the stair, with that quickness ever accompany-ing eyes of the kind I have mentioned.

" Ceremony here, devoir there ! " said she, smiling, " there was surely no need for a key to our door, Elrig-more——"

"Colin, Mistress Brown, plain Colin, if you please."

"Colin, if you will, though it seems daftlike to be so free with a soldier of twelve years' fortune. You were for the widow's garret. Does some one wait on you below?"

"John Splendid."

"My mother's in-bye. She will be pleased to see you back again if you and your friend call. After you've paid the lawing," she added, smiling like a rogue.

"That will we," said I; but I hung on the stair-head, and she leaned on the inner sill of the stair window.

We got into a discourse upon old days, that brought a glow to my heart the brandy I forgot had never brought to my head. We talked of school, and the gay days in wood and field, of our childish wanderings on the shore, making sand-keps and stone houses, herding the crabs of God—so little that bairns dare not be killing them, of venturings to sea many ells out in the fishermen's coracles, of journeys into the brave deep woods that lie far and wide round Inneraora, seeking the branch for the Beltane fire; of nutting in the hazels of the glens, and feasts upon the berry on the brae. Later, the harvest-home and the dance in green or barn when I was at almost my man's height, with the pluck to put a bare lip to its apprenticeship on a woman's cheek; the songs at *ceilidh* fires, the telling of *sgeulachdan* and fairy tales up on the mountain sheiling——

"Let me see," said I; "when I went abroad, were not you and one of the Glenaora Campbells chief?"

I said it as if the recollection had but sprung to me, while the truth is I had thought on it often in camp and field, with a regret that the girl should throw herself off on so poor a partner.

She laughed merrily with her whole soul in the business, and her face without art or pretence—a fashion most wholesome to behold.

"He married some one nearer him in years long syne," said she. "You forget I was but a bairn when we romped in the hay-dash." And we buckled to the crack again, I more keen on it than ever. She was a most marvellous fine girl, and I thought her (well I mind me now) like the blue harebell that nods upon our heather hills.

29

We might, for all I dreamt of the widow's brandy, have been conversing on the stair-head yet, and my story had a different conclusion, had not a step sounded on the stair, and up banged John Splendid, his sword-scabbard clinking against the wall of the stair with the haste of him.

"Set a cavalier at the side of an anker of brandy," he cried, "and——"

Then he saw he was in company. He took off his bonnet with a sweep I'll warrant he never learned anywhere out of France, and plunged into the thick of our discourse with a query.

"At your service, Mistress Brown," said he. "Half my errand to town to-day was to find if young Mac-Lachlan, your relative, is to be at the market here to-morrow. If so——"

"He is," said Betty.

"Will he be intending to put up here all night, then ? "

"He comes to supper at least," said she, "and his biding overnight is yet to be settled."

John Splendid toyed with the switch in his hand in seeming abstraction, and yet as who was pondering on how to put an unwelcome message in plausible language.

"Do you know," said he at last to the girl, in a low voice, for fear his words should reach the ears of her mother in-bye. "I would as well see MacLachlan out of town the morn's night. There's a waft of cold airs about this place not particularly wholesome for any of his clan or name. So much I would hardly care to say to himself ; but he might take it from you, madam, that the other side of the loch is the safest place for sound sleep for some time to come."

"Is it the MacNicolls you're thinking of ? " asked the girl.

"That same, my dear."

"You ken," he went on, turning fuller round to me, to tell a story he guessed a new-comer was unlikely to know the ins and outs of—"you ken that one of the MacLachlans, a cousin-german of old Lachie the chief, came over in a boat to Braleckan a few weeks syne on an old feud, and put a bullet into a MacNicoll, a peaceable lad who was at work in a field. Gay times, gay times, aren't they? From behind a dyke wall too—a far from gentlemanly escapade even in a MacLa—— Pardon, mistress; I forgot your relationship, but this was surely a very low dog of his kind. Now from that day to this the murtherer is to find; there are some to say old Lachie could put his hand on him at an hour's notice if he had the notion. But his lordship, Justiciar-General, upbye, has sent his provost-marshal with letters of arrest to the place in vain. Now here's my story. The MacNicolls of Elrig have joined cause with their cousins and name-sakes of Braleckan; there's a wheen of both to be in the town at the market to-morrow, and if young Mac-Lachlan bides in this house of yours overnight, Mistress Betty Brown, you'll maybe have broken delf and worse ere the day daw."

Mistress Brown took it very coolly; and as for me, I was thinking of a tiny brown mole-spot she used to have low on the white of her neck when I put daisy-links on her on the summers we played on the green, and wondering if it was still to the fore and hid below her collar. In by the window came the saucy breeze and kissed her on a curl that danced above her ear.

"I hope there will be no lawlessness here," said she : "whether he goes or bides, surely the burghers of Inner-aora will not quietly see their Provost's domicile invaded by brawlers."

"Exactly so," said John Splendid, drily. "Nothing may come of it, but you might mention the affair to MacLachlan if you have the chance. For me to tell him would be to put him in the humour for staying—dour fool that he is—out of pure bravado and defiance. To tell the truth, I would bide myself in such a case. 'Thole feud' is my motto. My granddad writ it on his sword-blade in clear round print letters I've often marvelled at the skill of. If it's your will, Elrigmore, we may be doing without the brandy, and give the house-dame a call now."

We went in and paid our duties to the goodwife—a silver-haired dame with a look of Betty in every smile.

CHAPTER IV.

A NIGHT ALARM.

WRITING all this old ancient history down, I find it hard to riddle out in my mind the things that have really direct and pregnant bearing on the matter in hand. I am tempted to say a word or two anent my Lord Marquis's visit to my father, and his vain trial to get me enlisted into his corps for Lorn. Something seems due, also, to be said about the kindness I found from all the old folks of Inneraora, ever proud to see a lad of their own of some repute come back among them ; and of my father's grieving about his wae widowerhood : but these things must stand by while I narrate how there arose a wild night in town Inneraora, with the Highlandmen from the glens into it with dirk and sword and steel Doune pistols, the flambeaux flaring against the tall lands, and the Lowland burghers of the place standing up for peace and tranquil sleep.

The market-day came on the morning after the day John Splendid and I foregathered with my Lord Archibald. It was a smaller market than usual, by reason of the troublous times ; but a few black and red cattle came from the landward part of the parish and Knapdale side, while Lochow and Bredalbane sent hoof nor horn. There was never a blacker sign of the time's unrest. But men came from many parts of the shire, with their chieftains or lairds, and there they went clamping about this Lowland-looking town like foreigners. I counted ten tartans in as many minutes between the Cross and the kirk, most of them friendly with MacCailein Mor, but a few, like that of MacLachlan of that ilk, at variance, and

the wearers with ugly whingers or claymores at their belts.
Than those MacLachlans one never saw a more barbarous-
looking set. There were a dozen of them in the tail or
retinue of old Lachie's son—a henchman, piper, piper's
valet, *gille-mor*, *gille* wet-sole, or running footman, and
such others as the more vain of our Highland gentry at
the time ever insisted on travelling about with, all stout
junky men of middle size, bearded to the brows, wearing
flat blue bonnets with a pervenke plant for badge on the
sides of them, on their feet deerskin brogues with the hair
out, the rest of their costume all belted tartan, and with
arms clattering about them. With that proud pretence
which is common in our people when in strange unfamiliar
occasions—and I would be the last to dispraise it—they
went about by no means braggardly but with the aspect of
men who had better streets and more shops to show at
home ; surprised at nothing in their alert moments, but
now and again forgetting their dignity and looking into
little shop-windows with the wonder of bairns and great
gabbling together, till MacLachlan fluted on his whistle,
and they came, like good hounds, to heel.

All day the town hummed with Gaelic and the round
bellowing of cattle. It was clear warm weather, never a
breath of wind to stir the gilding trees behind the burgh.
At ebb-tide the sea-beach whitened and smoked in the
sun, and the hot air quivered over the stones and the
crisping wrack. In such a season the bustling town in
the heart of the stern Highlands seemed a fever spot.
Children came boldly up to us for fairings or gifts, and
they strayed—the scamps !—behind the droves and
thumped manfully on the buttocks of the cattle. A
constant stream of men passed in and out at the change-
house closes and about the Fisherland tenements, where
seafarers and drovers together sang the maddest love-
ditties in the voices of roaring bulls ; beating the while
with their feet on the floor in our foolish Gaelic fashion,
or, as one could see through open windows, rugging and
riving at the corners of a plaid spread between them,—
a trick, I daresay, picked up from women, who at the
waulking or washing of woollen cloth new spun, pull out
the fabric to tunes suited to such occasions.

I spent most of the day with John Splendid and one Tearlach Fraser, an old comrade, and as luck, good or ill, would have it, the small hours of morning were on me before I thought of going home. By dusk the bulk of the strangers left the town by the highroads, among them the MacNicolls, who had only by the cunning of several friends (Splendid as busy as any) been kept from coming to blows with the MacLachlan tail. Earlier in the day, by a galley or wherry, the MacLachlans also had left, but not the young laird, who put up for the night at the house of Provost Brown.

The three of us I have mentioned sat at last playing cartes in the ferry-house, where a good glass could be had and more tidiness than most of the hostelries in the place could boast of. By the stroke of midnight we were the only customers left in the house, and when, an hour after, I made the move to set out for Glen Shira, John Splendid yoked on me as if my sobriety were a crime.

"Wait, man, wait, and I'll give you a convoy up the way," he would say, never thinking of the road he had himself to go down to Coillebhraid.

And aye it grew late and the night more still. There would be a foot going by at first at short intervals, sometimes a staggering one and a voice growling to itself in Gaelic; and anon the wayfarers were no more, the world outside in a black and solemn silence. The man who kept the ferry-house was often enough in the custom of staying up all night to meet belated boats from Kilcatrine; we were gentrice and good customers, so he composed himself in a lug chair and dovered in a little room opening off ours, while we sat fingering the book. Our voices as we called the cartes seemed now and then to me like a discourtesy to the peace and order of the night.

"I must go," said I a second time.

"Another one game," cried John Splendid. He had been winning every bout, but with a reluctance that shone honestly on his face, and I knew it was to give Tearlach and me a chance to better our reputation that he would have us hang on.

"You have hard luck indeed," he would say. "Or, "You played that trick as few could do it." Or, "Am

34

not I in the key to-night? there's less craft than luck here." And he played even slovenly once or twice, flushing, we could read, lest we should see the stratagem. At these times, by the curious way of chance, he won more surely than ever.

"I must be going," I said again. And this time I put the cartes bye, firmly determined that my usual easy and pliant mood in fair company would be my own enemy no more.

"Another chappin of ale," said he. "Tearlach, get Elrigmore to bide another bit. Tuts, the night's but young, the chap of two and a fine clear clean air with a wind behind you for Shira Glen."

"Wheest!" said Tearlach of a sudden, and he put up a hand.

There was a skliffing of feet on the road outside—many feet and wary, with men's voices in a whisper caught at the teeth—a sound at that hour full of menace. Only a moment and then all was by.

"There's something strange here!" said John Splendid, "let's out and see." He put round his rapier more on the groin, and gave a jerk at the narrow belt creasing his fair-day crimson vest. For me I had only the dirk to speak of, for the *sgian dubh* at my leg was a silver toy, and Tearlach, being a burgh man, had no arm at all. He lay hold on an oaken shinty stick that hung on the wall, property of the ferry-house landlord's son.

Out we went in the direction of the footsteps, round Gillemor's corner and the jail, past the Fencibles' armroom and into the main street of the town, that held no light in door or window. There would have been moon, but a black wrack of clouds filled the heavens. From the kirk corner we could hear a hushed tumult down at the Provost's close-mouth.

"Pikes and pistols!" cried Splendid. "Is it not as I said? yonder's your MacNicolls for you."

In a flash I thought of Mistress Betty with her hair down, roused by the marauding crew, and I ran hurriedly down the street shouting the burgh's slogan, "Slochd!"

"Damn the man's hurry!" said John Splendid, trotting at my heels, and with Tearlach too he gave lungs to the shout.

" Slochd ! " I cried, and " Slochd ! " they cried, and the whole town clanged like a bell. Windows opened here and there, and out popped heads, and then—

" Murder and thieves ! " we cried stoutly again.

" Is't the Athole dogs ? " asked some one in bad English from a window, but we did not bide to tell him.

" Slochd ! slochd ! club and steel ! " more nimble burghers cried, jumping out at closes in our rear, and following with neither hose nor brogue, but the kilt thrown at one toss on the haunch and some weapon in hand. And the whole wide street was stark awake.

The MacNicolls must have numbered fully threescore. They had only made a pretence (we learned again) of leaving the town, and had hung on the riverside till they fancied their attempt at seizing MacLachlan was secure from the interference of the townfolk. They were packed in a mass in the close and on the stair, and the foremost were solemnly battering at the night door at the top of the first flight of stairs, crying, " *Fuil airson fuil !* —blood for blood, out with young Lachie ! "

We fell to on the rearmost with a will, first of all with the bare fist, for half of this midnight army were my own neighbours in Glen Shira, peaceable men in ordinary affairs, kirk-goers, law-abiders, though maybe a little common in the quality, and between them and the mustering burghers there was no feud. For a while we fought it dourly in the darkness with the fingers at the throat or the fist in the face, or wrestled warmly on the plain-stones, or laid out, such as had staves, with good vigour on the bonneted heads. Into the close we could not—soon I saw it—push our way, for the enemy filled it—a dense mass of tartan—stinking with peat and oozing with the day's debauchery.

" We'll have him out, if it's in bits," they said, and aye upon the stair-head banged the door.

" No remedy in this way for the folks besieged," thought I, and stepping aside I began to wonder how best to aid our friends by strategy rather than force of arms. All at once I had mind that at the back of the land facing the shore an outhouse with a thatched roof ran at a high pitch well up against the kitchen window, and I stepped through a close farther up and set, at this outhouse, to the climbing, leaving my friends fighting out in the darkness in a town tumultuous. To get up over the eaves of the outhouse was no easy task, and I would have failed without a doubt had not the stratagem of John Splendid come to his aid a little later than my own and sent him after me. He helped me first on the roof, and I had him soon beside me. The window lay unguarded (all the inmates of the house being at the front), and we stepped in and found ourselves soon in a household vastly calm considering the rabble dunting on its doors.

"A pot of scalding water and a servant wench at that back-window we came in by would be a good sneck against all that think of coming after us," said John Splendid, stepping into the passage where we had met Mistress Betty the day before—now with the stair-head door stoutly barred and barricaded up with heavy chests and napery-aumries.

"God! I'm glad to see you, sir!" cried the Provost, "and you, Elrigmore!" He came forward in a trepidation which was shared by few of the people about him.

Young MacLachlan stood up against the wall facing the barricaded door, a lad little over twenty, with a steel-grey quarrelsome eye, and there was more bravado than music in a pipe-tune he was humming in a low key to himself. A little beyond, at the door of the best room, half in and half out, stood the goodwife Brown and her daughter. A long-legged lad, of about thirteen, with a brog or awl was teasing out the end of a flambeau in preparation to light it for some purpose not to be guessed at, and a servant lass, pock-marked, with one eye on the pot and the other up the lum, as we say of a glee or cast, made a storm of lamentation, crying in Gaelic—

"My grief! my grief! what's to come of poor Peggy?" (Peggy being herself.) "Nothing for it but the wood and cave and the ravishing of the Ben Bhuidhe wolves."

Mistress Betty laughed at her notion, a sign of humour and courage in her (considering the plight) that fairly took me.

"I daresay, Peggy, they'll let us be," she said, coming

forward to shake Splendid and me by the hand. "To keep me in braws and you in ashets to break would be more than the poor creatures would face, I'm thinking. You are late in the town, Elrigmore."

"Colin," I corrected her, and she bit the inside of her nether lip in a style that means temper.

"It's no time for dalliance, I think. I thought you had been up the glen long syne, but we are glad to have your service in this trouble, Master—Colin " (with a little laugh and a flush at the cheek), "also Barbreck. Do you think they mean seriously ill by MacLachlan ? "

"Ill enough, I have little doubt," briskly replied Splendid. "A corps of MacNicolls, arrant knaves from all airts, worse than the Macaulays or the Gregarach themselves, do not come banging at the burgh door of Inneraora at this uncanny hour for a child's play. Sir " (he went on, to MacLachlan), "I mind you said last market-day at Kilmichael, with no truth to back it, that you could run, shoot, or sing any Campbell ever put on hose ; let a Campbell show you the way out of a bees'-bike. Take the back-window for it, and out the way we came in. I'll warrant there's not a wise enough (let alone a sober enough) man among all the idiots battering there who'll think of watching for your retreat."

MacLachlan, a most extraordinarily vain and pompous little fellow, put his bonnet suddenly on his head, scrugged it down vauntingly on one side over the right eye, and stared at John Splendid with a good deal of choler or hurt vanity.

"Sir," said he, " this was our affair till you put a finger into it. You might know me well enough to understand that none of our breed ever took a back-door if a front offered."

"Whilk it does not in this case," said John Splendid, seemingly in a mood to humour the man. "But I'll allow there's the right spirit in the objection—to begin with in a young lad. When I was your age I had the same good Highland notion that the hardest way to face the foe was the handsomest. ' Pallas Armata ' [1] (is't that

---

[1] It could hardly be ' Pallas Armata.' The narrator anticipates Sir James Turner's ingenious treatise by several years.—N. M.

you call the book of arms, Elrigmore?) tells different; but 'Pallas Armata' (or whatever it is) is for old men with cold blood."

Of a sudden MacLachlan made dart at the chests and pulled them back from the door with a most surprising vigour of arm before any one could prevent him. The Provost vainly tried to make him desist; John Splendid said in English, "Wha will to Cupar maun to Cupar," and in a jiffy the last of the barricade was down, but the door was still on two wooden bars slipping into stout staples. Betty in a low whisper asked me to save the poor fellow from his own hot temper.

At the minute I grudged him the lady's consideration —too warm, I thought, even in a far-out relative, but a look at her face showed she was only in the alarm of a woman at the thought of any one's danger.

I caught MacLachlan by the sleeve of his shirt—he had on but that and a kilt and vest—and jerked him back from his fool's employment; but I was a shave late. He ran back both wooden bars before I let him.

With a roar and a display of teeth and steel the Mac-Nicolls came into the lobby from the crowded stair, and we were driven to the far parlour end. In the forefront of them was Nicol Beg MacNicoll, the nearest kinsman of the murdered Braleckan lad. He had a targe on his left arm—a round buckler of *darach* or oakwood covered with dun cow-hide, hair out, and studded in a pleasing pattern with iron bosses—a prong several inches long in the middle of it. Like every other scamp in the pack, he had dirk out. *Beg* or little he was in the countryside's bye-name, but in truth he was a fellow of six feet, as hairy as a brock and in the same straight bristly fashion. He put out his arms at full reach to keep back his clansmen, who were stretching necks at poor MacLachlan like weasels, him with his nostrils swelling and his teeth biting his bad temper.

"Wait a bit, lads," said Nicol Beg; "perhaps we may get our friend here to come peaceably with us. I'm sorry " (he went on, addressing the Provost) "to put an honest house to rabble at any time, and the Provost of Inneraora specially, for I'm sure there's kin's blood by my mother's side between us; but there was no other way to get MacLachlan once his tail was gone."

"You'll rue this, MacNicoll," fumed the Provost—as red as a bubblyjock at the face—mopping with a napkin at his neck in a sweat of annoyance; "you'll rue it, rue it, rue it!" and he went into a coil of lawyer's threats against the invaders, talking of brander-irons and gallows, hame-sucken and housebreaking.

We were a daft-like lot in that long lobby in a wan candle-light. Over me came that wonderment that falls on one upon stormy occasions (I mind it at the sally of Lecheim), when the whirl of life seems to come to a sudden stop, all's but wooden dummies and a scene empty of atmosphere, and between your hand on the basket-hilt and the drawing of the sword is a lifetime. We could hear at the close-mouth and far up and down the street the shouting of the burghers, and knew that at the stair-foot they were trying to pull out the bottom-most of the marauders like tods from a hole. For a second or two nobody said a word to Nicol MacNicoll's remark, for he put the issue so cool (like an invitation to saunter along the road) that all at once it seemed a matter between him and MacLachlan alone. I stood between the house-breakers and the women-folk beside me—John Splendid looking wonderfully ugly for a man fairly clean fashioned at the face by nature. We left the issue to MacLachlan, and I must say he came up to the demands of the moment with gentlemanliness, minding he was in another's house than his own.

"What is it ye want?" he asked MacNicoll, burring out his Gaelic r's with punctilio.

"We want you in room of a murderer your father owes us," said MacNicoll.

"You would slaughter me, then?" said MacLachlan, amazingly undisturbed, but bringing again to the front, by a motion of the haunch accidental to look at, the sword he leaned on.

"*Fuil airson fuil!*" cried the rabble on the stairs, and it seemed ghastly like an answer to the young laird's question; but Nicol Beg demanded peace, and assured MacLachlan he was only sought for a hostage.

"We but want your red-handed friend Dark Neil," said he; "your father kens his lair, and the hour he puts him in our hands for justice, you'll have freedom."

"Do you warrant me free of scaith?" asked the young laird.

"I'll warrant not a hair of your head's touched," answered Nicol Beg—no very sound warranty, I thought, from a man who, as he gave it, had to put his weight back on the eager crew that pushed at his shoulders, ready to spring like weasels at the throat of the gentleman in the red tartan.

He was young, MacLachlan, as I said; for him this was a delicate situation, and we about him were in no less a quandary than himself. If he defied the Glen Shira men, he brought bloodshed on a peaceable house, and ran the same risk of bodily harm that lay in the alternative of his going with them that wanted him.

Round he turned and looked for guidance—broken just a little at the pride, you could see by the lower lip. The Provost was the first to meet him eye for eye.

"I have no opinion, Lachie," said the old man, snuffing rappee with the butt of an egg-spoon and spilling the brown dust in sheer nervousness over the night-shirt bulging above the band of his breeks. "I'm wae to see your father's son in such a corner, and all my comfort is that every tenant in Elrig and Braleckan pays at the Tolbooth or gallows of Inneraora town for this night's frolic."

"A great consolation to think of!" said John Splendid.

The goodwife, a nervous body at her best, sobbed away with her pock-marked hussy in the parlour, but Betty was to the fore in a passion of vexation. To her the lad made next his appeal.

"Should I go?" he asked, and I thought he said it more like one who almost craved to stay. I never saw a woman in such a coil. She looked at the dark MacNicolls, and syne she looked at the fair-haired young fellow, and her eyes were swimming, her bosom heaving under her screen of Campbell tartan, her fingers twisting at the pleated hair that fell in sheeny cables to her waist.

"If I were a man I would stay, and yet—if you stay

—— Oh, poor Lachlan! I'm no judge," she cried; "my cousin, my dear cousin!" and over brimmed her tears.

All this took less time to happen than it takes to tell with pen and ink, and though there may seem in reading it to be too much palaver on this stair-head, it was but a minute or two, after the bar was off the door, that John Splendid took me by the coat-lapel and back a bit to whisper in my ear—

"If he goes quietly or goes gaffed like a grilse, it's all one on the street. Out-bye the place is hotching with the towns-people. Do you think the MacNicolls could take a prisoner bye the Cross?"

"It'll be cracked crowns on the causeway," said I.

"Cracked crowns any way you take it," said he, "and better on the causeway than on Madame Brown's parlour floor. It's a gentleman's policy, I would think, to have the squabble in the open air, and save the women the likely sight of bloody gashes."

"What do you think, Elrigmore?" Betty cried to me the next moment, and I said it were better the gentleman should go. The reason seemed to flash on her there and then, and she backed my counsel; but the lad was not the shrewdest I've seen, even for a Cowal man, and he seemed vexed that she should seek to get rid of him, glancing at me with a scornful eye as if I were to blame.

"Just so," he said, a little bitterly; "the advice is well meant," and on went his jacket that had hung on a peg behind him, and his bonnet played scrug on his forehead. A wiry young scamp, spirited too! He was putting his sword into its scabbard, but MacNicoll stopped him, and he went without it.

Now it was not the first time "Slochd a Chubair!" was cried as slogan in Baile Inneraora in the memory of the youngest lad out that early morning with a cudgel. The burgh settled to its Lowlandishness with something of a grudge. For long the landward clans looked upon the incomers to it as foreign and unfriendly. More than once in fierce or drunken escapades they came into the place in their *mogans* at night, quiet as ghosts, mischievous as the winds, and set fire to wooden booths, or shot in wantonness at any mischancy unkilted citizen late returning from the change-house. The tartan was at those times the only passport to their good favour; to them the black cloth knee-breeches were red rags to a bull, and ill luck to the lad who wore the same anywhere outside the Crooked Dyke that marks the town and policies of his lordship! If he fared no worse, he came home with his coat-skirts scantily filling an office unusual. Many a time " Slochd ! " rang through the night on the Athole winter when I dosed far off on the fields of Low Germanie, or sweated in sallies from leaguered towns. And experience made the burghers mighty tactical on such occasions. Old Leslie or ' Pallas Armata ' itself conferred no better notion of strategic sally than the simple one they used when the MacNicolls came down the stair with their prisoner; for they had dispersed themselves in little companies up the closes on either side the street, and past the close the invaders bound to go.

They might have known, the MacNicolls, that mischief was forward in that black silence, but they were, like all Glen men, unacquaint with the quirks of urban war. For them the fight in earnest was only fair that was fought on the heather and the brae ; and that was always my shame of my countrymen, that a half company of hag-butiers, with wall cover to depend on, could worst the most chivalrous clan that ever carried triumph at a rush.

For the middle of the street the invaders made at once, half ready for attack from before or behind, but ill pre-pared to meet it from all airts as attack came. They were not ten yards on their way when Splendid and I, emerging behind them, found them pricked in the rear by one company, brought up short by another in front at Stonefield's land, and harassed on the flanks by the lads from the closes. They were caught in a ring.

Lowland and Highland, they roared lustily as they came to blows, and the street boiled like a pot of herring : in the heart of the commotion young MacLachlan tossed hither and yond—a stick in a linn. A half-score more of MacNicolls might have made all the difference in the end of the story, for they struck desperately, better men by

D

far as weight and agility went than the burgh half-breds,
but (to their credit) so unwilling to shed blood, that they
used the flat of the claymore instead of the edge and fired
their pistols in the air.

The long-legged lad flung up a window and lit the street
with the flare of the flambeau he had been teasing out so
earnestly, and dunt, dunt went the oaken rungs on the
bonnets of Glen Shira, till Glen Shira smelt defeat and
fell slowly back.

In all this horoyally I took but an onlooker's part.
MacLachlan's quarrel was not mine, the burgh was none
of my blood, and the Glen Shira men were my father's
friends and neighbours. Splendid, too, candidly kept out
of the turmoil when he saw that young MacLachlan was
safely free of his warders, and that what had been a cause
militant was now only a Highland diversion.

"Let them play away at it," he said; "I'm not keen
to have wounds in a burgher's brawl in my own town
when there's promise of braver sport over the hills among
other tartans."

Up the town drifted the little battle, no dead left as
luck had it, but many a gout of blood. The white gables
clanged back the cries, in claps like summer thunder, the
crows in the beech-trees complained in a rasping roupy
chorus, and the house-doors banged at the back of men,
who, weary or wounded, sought home to bed. And
Splendid and I were on the point of parting, secure that
the young laird of MacLachlan was at liberty, when that
gentleman himself came scouring along, hard pressed by
a couple of MacNicolls ready with brands out to cut him
down. He was without steel or stick, stumbling on the
causeway-stones in a stupor of weariness, his mouth
gasping and his coat torn wellnigh off the back of him.
He was never in his twenty years of life nearer death than
then, and he knew it; but when he found John Splendid
and me before him he stopped and turned to face the
pair that followed him—a fool's vanity to show fright had
not put the heels to his hurry! We ran out beside him,
and the MacNicolls refused the *rencontre*, left their quarry,
and fled again to the town-head, where their friends were
in a dusk the long-legged lad's flambeau failed to mitigate.

" I'll never deny after this that you can outrun me ! "
said John Splendid, putting up his small sword.

" I would have given them their kail through the reek
in a double dose if I had only a simple knife," said the
lad angrily, looking up the street, where the fighting was
now over. Then he whipped into Brown's close and up
the stair, leaving us at the gable of Craignure's house.

John Splendid, ganting sleepily, pointed at the fellow's
disappearing skirts. " Do you see yon ? " said he, and
he broke into a line of a Gaelic air that told his meaning.

" Lovers ? " I asked.

" What do you think yourself ? " said he.

" She is mighty put about at his hazard," I confessed,
reflecting on her tears.

" Cousins, ye ken, cousins ! " said Splendid, and he put
a finger in my side, laughing meaningly.

I got home when the day stirred among the mists over
Strone.

CHAPTER V.

KIRK LAW.

OF course Clan MacNicoll was brought to book for this frolic on Inneraora fair-day, banned by Kirk, and soundly beaten by the Doomster in name of law. To read some books I've read, one would think our Gaels in the time I speak of, and even now, were pagan and savage. We are not, I admit it, fashioned on the prim style of London dandies and Italian fops; we are—the poorest of us—coarse a little at the hide, too quick, perhaps, to slash out with knife or hatchet, and over-ready to carry the most innocent argument the dire length of a thrust with the sword. That's the blood; it's the common understanding among ourselves. But we were never such thieves and marauders, caterans bloody and unashamed, as the Galloway kerns and the Northmen, and in all my time we had plenty to do to fend our straths against reivers and cattle-drovers from the bad clans round about us. We lift no cattle in all Campbell country. When I was a lad some of the old-fashioned tenants in Glenaora once or twice went over to Glen Nant and Rannoch and borrowed a few beasts; but the Earl (as he was then) gave them warning for it that any vassal of his found guilty of such practice again should hang at the town-head as readily as he would hang a Cowal man for theftuously awaytaking a board of kipper salmon. My father (peace with him!) never could see the logic of it. "It's no theft," he would urge, "but war on the parish scale: it needs coolness of the head, some valour, and great genius to take fifty or maybe a hundred head of bestial hot-hoof over hill and moor. I

46

would never blame a man for lifting a mart of black cattle
any more than for killing a deer : are not both the natural
animals of these mountains, prey lawful to the first lad who
can tether or paunch them ? "

" Not in the fold, father ! " I mind of remonstrating
once.

" In the fold too," he said. " Who respects Bredalbane's fenced deer ? Not the most Christian elders in
Glenurchy : they say grace over venison that crossed
a high dyke in the dead of night tail first, or game birds
that tumbled out of their dream on the bough into the
reek of a brimstone fire. A man might as well claim the
fish of the sea and the switch of the wood, and refuse
the rest of the world a herring or a block of wood, as put
black cattle in a fank and complain because he had to
keep watch on them ! "

It was odd law, but I must admit my father made the
practice run with the precept, for more than once he
refused to take back cattle lifted by the Macgregors from
us, because they had got over his march-stone.

But so far from permitting this latitude in the parish of
Inneraora, Kirk and State frowned it down, and sins far
less heinous. The session was bitterly keen on Sabbath-
breakers, and to start on a Saturday night a kiln-drying
of oats that would claim a peat or two on Sabbath, was
accounted immorality of the most gross kind.

Much of this strict form, it is to be owned, was im-
ported by the Lowland burghers, and set up by the
Lowland session of the English kirk, of which his lordship was an elder, and the Highlanders took to it badly
for many a day. They were aye, for a time, driving their
cattle through the town on the Lord's day or stravaiging
about the roads and woods, or drinking and listening to
pipers piping in the change-houses at time of sermon,
fond, as all our people are by nature, of the hearty open
air, and the smell of woods, and lusty sounds like the
swing of the seas and pipers playing old tunes. Out
would come elders and deacons to scour the streets and
change-houses for them, driving them, as if with scourges,
into worship. Gaelic sermon (or Irish sermon, as the
Scots called it) was but every second Sabbath, and on the

blank days the landward Highlanders found in town
bound to go to English sermon whether they knew the
language or not, a form which it would be difficult nowadays to defend. And it was, in a way, laughable to see
the big Gaels driven to chapel like boys by the smug light
burghers they could have crushed with a hand. But time
told ; there was sown in the landward mind by the blessing
of God (and some fear of the Marquis, no doubt) a respect
for Christian ordinance, and by the time I write of there
were no more devout churchgoers and respecters of the
law ecclesiastic than the umquhile pagan small-clans of
Loch Finne and the Glens.

It is true that Nicol Beg threatened the church-officer
with his dirk when he came to cite him before the session
a few days after the splore in Inneraora, but he stood his
trial like a good Christian all the same, he and half a score
of his clan, as many as the church court could get the
names of. I was a witness against them, much against
my will, with John Splendid, the Provost, and other towns-
folk.

Some other defaulters were dealt with before the Mac-
Nicolls, a few throughither women and lads from the
back-lanes of the burghs, on the old tale, a shoreside
man for houghing a quey, and a girl MacVicar, who had
been for a season on a visit to some Catholic relatives in
the Isles, and was charged with malignancy and profanity.

Poor lass ! I was wae for her. She stood bravely
beside her father, whose face was as begrutten as hers
was serene, and those who put her through her catechism
found to my mind but a good heart and tolerance where
they sought treachery and rank heresy. They convicted
her notwithstanding.

"You have stood your trials badly, Jean MacVicar,"
said Master Gordon. "A backslider and malignant
proven ! You may fancy your open profession of piety,
your honesty and charity, make dykes to the narrow
way. A fond delusion, woman ! There are, sorrow on
it ! many lax people of your kind in Scotland this day,
hangers-on at the petticoat tails of the whore of Babylon,
sitting like you, as honest worshippers at the tables of the
Lord, eating Christian elements that but for His mercy

choked them at the thrapple. You are a wicked woman ! "

" She's a good daughter," broke in the father through his tears ; but his Gaelic never stopped the minister.

" An ignorant besom."

" She's leech-wife to half Kenmore," protested the old man.

" And this court censures you, ordains you to make public confession at both English and Gaelic kirks before the congregations, thereafter to be excommunicate and banished furth and from this parish of Inneraora and Glenaora."

The girl never winced.

Her father cried again. " She can't leave me," said he, and he looked to the Marquis, who all the time sat on the hard deal forms, like a plain man. " Your lordship kens she is motherless and my only kin ; that's she true and honest."

The Marquis said yea nor nay, but had a minute's talk with the clergyman, as I thought at the time, to make him modify his ruling. But Master Gordon enforced the finding of the session.

" Go she must," said he ; " we cannot have our young people poisoned at the mind."

" Then she'll bide with me," said the father, angrily.

" You dare not, as a Christian professor, keep an excommunicate in your house," said Gordon ; " but taking to consideration that excommunication precludes not any company of natural relations, we ordain you never to keep her in your house in this parish any more ; but if you have a mind to do so with her, to follow her wherever she goes."

And that sorry small family went out at the door, in tears.

Some curious trials followed, and the making of quaint bylaws ; for now that his lordship, ever a restraining influence on his clans, was bound for new wars elsewhere, a firmer hand was wanted on the people he left behind, and Master Gordon pressed for stricter canons. Notification was made discharging the people of the burgh from holding lyke-wakes in the smaller houses, from unnecessary travel on the Sabbath, from public flyting and abusing, and from harbouring ne'er-do-weels from other parishes ; and seeing it had become a practice of the women attending kirk to keep their plaids upon their heads and faces in time of sermon as occasion of sleeping, as also that they who slept could not be distinguished from those who slept not, that they might be wakened, it was ordained that such be not allowed hereafter, under pain of taking the plaids from them.

With these enactments too came evidence of the Kirk's paternity. It settled the salary (200 pounds Scots) of a new master for the grammar-school, agreed to pay the fees of divers poor scholars, instructed the administering of the funds in the poor's-box, fixed a levy on the town for the following week to help the poorer wives who would be left by their fencible husbands, and paid ten marks to an elderly widow woman who desired, like a good Gael, to have her burial clothes ready, but had not the wherewithal for linen.

"We are," said Master Gordon, sharpening a pen in a pause ere the MacNicolls came forward, " the fathers and guardians of this parish people high and low. Too long has Loch Finne side been ruled childishly. I have no complaint about its civil rule—his lordship here might well be trusted to that ; but its religion was a thing of rags. They tell me old Campbell in the Gaelic end of the church (peace with him !) used to come to the pulpit with a broadsword belted below his Geneva gown. Savagery, savagery, rank and stinking ! I'll say it to his face in another world, and a poor evangel and ensample truly for the quarrelsome landward folk of this parish, that even now, in the more unctuous times of God's grace, doff steel weapons so reluctantly. I found a man with a dirk at his hip sitting before the Lord's table last Lammas !"

"Please God," said the Marquis, " the world shall come to its sight some day. My people are of an unruly race, I ken, good at the heart, hospitable, valorous, even with some Latin chivalry ; but, my sorrow ! they are sorely unamenable to policies of order and peace."

"Deil the hair vexed am I," said John Splendid in my ear ; " I have a wonderful love for nature that's raw and human, and this session-made morality is but a gloss. They'll be taking the tartan off us next maybe! Some day the old dog at the heart of the Highlands will bark for all his sleek coat. Man! I hate the very look of those Lowland cattle sitting here making kirk laws for their emperors, and their bad-bred Scots speech jars on my ear like an ill-tuned bagpipe."

Master Gordon possibly guessed what was the topic of Splendid's confidence,—in truth, few but knew my hero's mind on these matters ; and I have little doubt it was for John's edification he went on to sermonise, still at the shaping of his pen.

"Your lordship will have the civil chastisement of these MacNicolls after this session is bye with them. We can but deal with their spiritual error. Nicol Beg and his relatives are on our kirk rolls as members or adherents, and all we can do is to fence the communion-table against them for a period, and bring them to the stool of repentance. Some here may think a night of squabbling and broken heads in a Highland burgh too trifling an affair for the interference of the kirk or the court of law : I am under no such delusion. There is a valour better than the valour of the beast unreasoning. Your lordship has seen it at its proper place in your younger wars ; young Elrigmore, I am sure, has seen it on the Continent, where men live quiet burgh lives while left alone, and yet comport themselves chivalrously and gallantly on the stricken fields when their country or a cause calls for them so to do. In the heart of man is hell smouldering, always ready to leap out in flames of sharpened steel ; it's a poor philosophy that puffs folly in at the ear to stir the ember, saying, ' Hiss, catch him, dog ! ' I'm for keeping hell (even in a wild Highlandman's heart) for its own business of punishing the wicked."

"Amen to yon ! " cried MacCailein, beating his hand on a book-board, and Master Gordon took a snuff like a man whose doctrine is laid out plain for the world and who dare dispute it. In came the beadle with the MacNicolls, very much cowed, different men truly from the brave gentlemen who cried blood for blood on Provost Brown's stair.

They had little to deny, and our evidence was but a word ere the session passed sentence of suspension from the kirk tables, as Gordon had said, and a sheriff's officer came to hale them to the Tolbooth for their trial on behalf of the civil law.

With their appearance there my tale has nothing to do ; the Doomster, as I have said, had the handling of them with birch. What I have described of this kirk-session's cognisance of those rough fellows' ill behaviour is designed ingeniously to convey a notion of its strict ceremony and its wide dominion,—to show that even in the heart of Arraghael we were not beasts in that year when the red flash of the sword came on us and the persecution of the torch. The MacNicoll's Night in the Hie Street of MacCailein Mor's town was an adventure uncommon enough to be spoken of for years after, and otherwise (except for the little feuds between the Glensmen and the burghers without tartan), our country-side was as safe as the heart of France—safer even. You might leave your purse on the open road anywhere within the Crooked Dyke with uncounted gold in it and be no penny the poorer at the week's end ; there was never lock or bar on any door in any of the two glens—locks, indeed, were a contrivance the Lowlanders brought for the first time to the town ; and the gardens lay open to all who had appetite for kail or berry. There was no man who sat down to dinner (aye in the landward part I speak of ; it differed in the town) without first going to the door to look along the high road to see if wayfarers were there to share the meal with him and his family. " There he goes," was the saying about any one who passed the door at any time without coming in to take a spoon— " there he goes ; I'll warrant he's a miser at home to be so much of a churl abroad." The very gipsy claimed the cleanest bed in a Glenman's house whenever he came that way, and his gossip paid handsomely for his shelter.

It was a fine fat land this of ours, mile upon mile thick with herds, rolling in the grassy season like the seas, growing such lush crops as the remoter Highlands never dreamt of. Not a foot of good soil but had its ploughing, or at least gave food to some useful animal, and yet so rocky the hills between us and lower Lochow, so tremendous steep and inaccessible the peaks and corries north of Ben Bhuidhe, that they were relegated to the chase. There had the stag his lodging and the huntsman a home almost perpetual. It was cosy, indeed, to see at evening the peat-smoke from well-governed and comfortable hearths lingering on the quiet air, to go where you would and find bairns toddling on the braes or singing women bent to the peat-creel and the reaping-hook.

In that autumn I think nature gave us her biggest cup brimmingly, and my father, as he watched his servants binding corn head high, said he had never seen the like before. In the hazel-woods the nuts bent the branches, so thick were they, so succulent ; the hip and the haw, the blaeberry and the rowan, swelled grossly in a constant sun ; the orchards of the richer folks were in a revelry of fruit. Somehow the winter grudged, as it were, to come. For ordinary, October sees the trees that beard Dunchuach and hang for miles on the side of Creag Dubh searing and falling below the frost ; this season the cold stayed aloof long, and friendly winds roved from the west and south. The forests gleamed in a golden fire that only cooled to darkness when the firs, my proud tall friends, held up their tasselled heads in unquenching green. Birds swarmed in the heather, and the sides of the bare hills moved constantly with deer. Never a stream in all real Argile but boiled with fish ; you came down to Eas-a-chleidh on the Aora with a creel and dipped it into the linn to bring out salmon rolling with fat.

All this I dwell on for a sensible purpose, though it may seem to be but an old fellow's boasting and a childish vanity about my own calf-country. 'Tis the picture I would paint—a land laughing and content, well governed by Gillesbeg, though Gruamach he might be by name and by nature. Fourpence a-day was a labourer's wage, but what need had one of even fourpence, with his hut free and the food piling richly at his very door ?

CHAPTER VI.

MY LADY OF MOODS.

ON the 27th of July in this same year 1644 we saw his lordship and his clan march from Inneraora to the dreary north. By all accounts (brought in to the Marquis by foot-runners from the frontier of Lorn), the Irishry of Colkitto numbered no more than 1200, badly armed with old matchlocks and hampered by two or three dozen camp-women bearing the bairns of this dirty regiment at their breasts. Add to this as many Highlanders under Montrose and his cousin Para Dubh of Inchbrackie, and there was but a force of 3500 men for the good government of Argile to face. But what were they ? If the Irish were poorly set up in weapons the Gaels were worse. On the spring before, Gillesbeg had harried Athole, and was cunning enough to leave its armouries as bare as the fields he burned, so now its clans had but home-made claymores, bows, and arrows, Lochaber *tuaghs* and cudgels, with no heavy pieces. The cavalry of this unholy gang was but three garrons, string and bone. Worse than their ill-arming, as any soldier of experience will allow, were the jealousies between the two bodies of the scratched-up army. Did ever one see a Gael that nestled to an Irishman ? Here's one who will swear it impossible, though it is said the blood is the same in both races, and we nowadays read the same Gaelic Bible. Colkitto MacDonald was Gael by birth and young breeding, but Erinach by career, and repugnant to the most malignant of the west clans before they got to learn, as they did later, his quality as a leader. He bore down on Athole, he and his towsy rabble, hoping to get the clans there to join him greedily for the sake of

54

the old feud against MacCailein Mor, but the Stewarts would have nothing to say to him, and blows were not far off when Montrose and his cousin Black Pate came on the scene with his king's licence.

To meet this array now playing havoc on the edge of Campbell country, rumour said two armies were moving from the north and east : if Argile knew of them he kept his own counsel on the point, but he gave colour to the tale by moving from Inneraora with no more than 2000 foot and a troop of horse. These regimentals had mustered three days previously, camping on the usual camping-ground at the Maltland, where I spent the last day and night with them. They were, for the main part, the Campbells of the shire : of them alone the chief could muster 5000 half-merkland men at a first levy, all capable swordsmen, well drilled and disciplined *soldadoes*, who had, in addition to the usual schooling in arms of every Gael, been taught many of the niceties of new-fashioned war, countermarch, wheeling, and pike-drill. To hear the orders, " Pouldron to pouldron ; keep your files ; and middlemen come forth ! " was like an echo from my old days in Germanie. These manœuvres they were instructed in by hired veterans of the Munro and Mackay battalions who fought with Adolphus. Four or five companies of Lowland soldiers from Dunbarton and Stirling eked out the strength ; much was expected from the latter, for they were, unlike our clansmen, never off the parade-ground, and were in receipt of pay for their militant service ; but as events proved, they were MacCailein's poor reed.

I spent, as I have said, a day and a night in the camp between Aora river and the deep wood of Tarradubh. The plain hummed with our little army, where now are but the nettle and the ivied tower, and the yellow bee booming through the solitude ; morning and night the shrill of the *piob-mhor* rang cheerily to the ear of Dunchuach ; the sharp call of the chieftains and sergeants, the tramp of the brogued feet in their simple evolutions, the clatter of arms, the contention and the laughing, the song, the reprimand, the challenge, the jest,—all these were pleasant to me.

One morning I got up from a bed of gall or bog-myrtle
I shared with John Splendid after a late game of chess,
and fared out on a little eminence looking over the scene.
Not a soldier stirred in his plaid ; the army was drugged
by the heavy fir-winds from the forest behind. The light
of the morning flowed up wider and whiter from the
Cowal hills, the birds woke to a rain of twittering prayer
among the bushes ere ever a man stirred more than from
side to side to change his dream. It was the most melancholy hour I ever experienced, and I have seen fields in
the wan morning before many a throng and bloody day.
I felt " fey," as we say at home—a premonition that
here was no conquering force, a sorrow for the glens raped
of their manhood, and hearths to be desolate. By-and-by
the camp moved into life, Dunbarton's drums beat the
reveille, the pipers arose, doffed their bonnets to the sun,
and played a rouse ; my gloom passed like a mist from
the mountains.

They went north by the Aora passes into the country of
Bredalbane, and my story need not follow them beyond.

Inneraora burghers went back to their commercial
affairs, and I went to Glen Shira to spend calm days on
the river and the hill. My father seemed to age per-
ceptibly, reflecting on his companion gone, and he clung
to me like the *crotal* to the stone. Then it was (I think)
that some of the sobriety of life first came to me, a more
often cogitation and balancing of affairs. I began to see
some of the tanglement of nature, and appreciate the
solemn mystery of our travel across this vexed and care-
warped world. Before, I was full of the wine of youth,
giving doubt of nothing a lodgment in my mind, acting
ever on the impulse, sucking the lemon, seeds and all,
and finding it unco sappy and piquant to the palate. To
be face to face day after day with this old man's grief,
burdened with his most apparent double love, conscious
that I was his singular bond to the world he would otherwise be keen to be leaving, set me to chasten my dalliance
with fate. Still and on, our affection and its working on
my prentice mind is nothing to dwell on publicly. I've
seen bearded men kiss each other in the France, a most
scandalous exhibition surely, one at any rate that I never

gazed on without some natural Highland shame, and I would as soon kiss my father at high noon on the open street as dwell with paper and ink upon my feeling to him.

We settled down to a few quiet weeks after the troops had gone. Rumours came of skirmishes at Tippermuir and elsewhere. I am aware that the fabulous Wishart makes out that our lads were defeated by Montrose at every turning, claiming even Dundee, Crief, Strathbogie, Methven Wood, Philiphaugh, Inverness, and Dunbeath. Let any one coldly calculate the old rogue's narrative, and it will honestly appear that the winner was more often Argile, though his lordship never followed up his advantage with slaughter and massacre as did his foes at Aberdeen. All these doings we heard of but vaguely, for few came back except an odd lad wounded and cut off in the wilds of Athole from the main body.

Constant sentinels watched the land from the fort of Dunchuach, that dominates every pass into our country, and outer guards took day and night about on the remoter alleys of Aora and Shira Glens. South, east, and west, we had friendly frontiers; only to the north were menace and danger, and from the north came our scaith—the savage north and jealous.

These considerations seemed, on the surface, little to affect Inneraora and its adjacent parts. We slept soundly at night, knowing the warders were alert; the women with absent husbands tempered their anxiety with the philosophy that comes to a race ever bound to defend its own doors.

The common folks had *ceilidhs* at night—gossip parties in each other's houses, and in our own hall the herds and shepherds often convocat to change stories, the tales of the Fingalians, Ossian and the Finne. The burgh was a great place for suppers too, and never *ceilidh* nor supper went I to but the daughter of Provost Brown was there before me. She took a dislike to me, I guessed at last, perhaps thinking I appeared too often; and I was never fully convinced of this till I met her once with some companions walking in the garden of the castle, that always stood open for the world.

I was passing up the Dame's Pad, as it was called, a

little turfed road, overhung by walnut trees brought by the old Earl from England. I had on a Lowland costume with a velvet coat and buckled shoes, and one or two vanities a young fellow would naturally be set up about, and the consciousness of my trim clothing put me in a very complacent mood as I stopped and spoke with the damsels.

They were pretty girls all, and I remember particularly that Betty had a spray of bog-myrtle and heather fastened at a brooch at her neck.

She was the only one who received me coldly, seemed indeed impatient to be off, leaving the conversation to her friends while she toyed with a few late flowers on the bushes beside her.

"You should never put heather and gall together," I said to her, rallyingly.

"Indeed!" she said, flushing. "Here's one who wears what she chooses, regardless of custom or freit."

"But you know," I said, "the badge of the Campbell goes badly with that of so bitter a foe as the MacDonald. You might as well add the oak-stalk of Montrose, and make the emblem tell the story of those troubles."

It was meant in good-humour, but for some reason it seemed to sting her to the quick. I could see it in the flash of her eyes and the renewed flush at her temples.

There was a little mischievous girl in the company, who giggled and said, "Betty's in a bad key to-day; her sweetheart has vexed her surely."

It was a trivial remark, but I went off with it in my mind.

A strange interest in the moods of this old school-friend had begun to stir me. Meeting her on my daily walks to town by the back way through the new avenue, I found her seemingly anxious to avoid me, and difficult to warm to any interest but in the most remote and abstract affairs. Herself she would never speak of, her plans, cares, ambitions, preferences, or aversions; she seemed dour set on aloofness. And though she appeared to listen to my modestly phrased exploits with attention and respect, and some trepidation at the dangerous portions, she had notably more interest in my talk of others.

Ours was the only big house in the glen she never came calling to, though her father was an attentive visitor and supped his curds-and-cream of a Saturday with friendly gusto, apologising for her finding something to amuse and detain her at Roderick's over the way, or the widow's at Gearran Bridge.

I would go out on these occasions and walk in the open air with a heart uneasy.

And now it was I came to conclude, after all, that much as a man may learn of many women studied indifferently, there is something magical about his personal regard for one, that sets up a barrier of mystery between them. So long as I in former years went on the gay assumption that every girl's character was on the surface, and I made no effort to probe deeper, I was the confidant, the friend, of many a fine woman. They all smiled at my douce sobriety, but in the end they preferred it to the gaudy recklessness of more handsome men.

But here was the conclusion of my complacent belief in my knowledge of the sex. The oftener I met her the worse my friendship progressed. She became a problem behind a pretty mask, and I would sit down, as it were, dumb before it and guess at the real woman within. Her step on the road as we would come to an unexpected meeting, her handling of a flower I might give her in a courtesy, her most indifferent word as we met or parted, became a precious clue I must ponder on for hours. And the more I weighed these things, the more confused thereafter I became in her presence. " If I were in love with the girl," I had to say to myself at last, " I could not be more engrossed on her mind."

The hill itself, with days of eager hunting after the red-deer, brought not enough distraction, and to stand by the mountain tarns and fish the dark trout was to hold a lonely carnival with discontent.

It happened sometimes that on the street of Inneraora I would meet Betty convoying her cousin young MacLachlan to his wherry (he now took care to leave for home betimes), or with his sister going about the shops. It would be but a bow in the bye-going, she passing on with equanimity and I with a maddening sense of awkwardness, that was not much bettered by the tattle of the plainstanes, where merchant lads and others made audible comment on the cousinly ardour of young Lachie.

On Sundays, perhaps worst of all, I found my mind's torment. Our kirk to-day is a building of substantiality and even grace ; then it was a somewhat squalid place of worship, in whose rafters the pigeon trespassed and the swallow built her home. We sat in torturous high-backed benches so narrow that our knees rasped the boards before us, and sleep in Master Gordon's most dreary discourse was impossible. Each good family in the neighbourhood had its own pew, and Elrigmore's, as it is to this day, lay well in the rear among the shadows of the loft, while the Provost's was a little to the left and at right angles, so that its occupants and ours were in a manner face to face.

Gordon would be into many deeps of doctrine no doubt while I was in the deeper depths of speculation upon my lady's mind. I think I found no great edification from the worship of those days—shame to tell it !—for the psalms we chanted had inevitably some relevance to an earthly affection, and my eyes were for ever roaming from the book or from the preacher's sombre face.

They might rove far and long, but the end of each journey round that dull interior was ever in the Provost's pew, and, as if by some hint of the spirit, though Betty might be gazing steadfastly where she ought, I knew that she knew I was looking on her. It needed but my glance to bring a flush to her averted face. Was it the flush of annoyance or of the conscious heart? I asked myself, and remembering her coldness elsewhere, I was fain to think my interest was considered an impertinence. And there I would be in a cold perspiration of sorry apprehension.

CHAPTER VII.

CHILDREN OF THE MIST.

THE Highlanders of Lochaber, as the old saying goes,
" pay their daughters' tochers by the light of the Michaelmas moon." Then it was that they were wont to come
over our seven hills and seven waters to help themselves
to our cattle when the same were at their fattest and best.
It would be a skurry of bare knees down pass and brae,
a ring of the robbers round the herd sheltering on the
bieldy side of the hill or in the hollows among the ripe
grass, a brisk change of shot and blow if alarm rose, and
then hie ! over the moor by Macfarlane's lantern.

This Michaelmas my father put up a *buaile-mhart*, a
square fold of wattle and whinstone, into which the herds-
men drove the lowing beasts at the mouth of every evening, and took turn about in watching them throughout
the clear season. It was perhaps hardly needed, for
indeed the men of Lochaber and Glenfalloch and the
other dishonest regions around us were too busy dipping
their hands in the dirty work of Montrose and his Irish
major-general to have any time for their usual autumn's
recreation. But a *buaile-mhart* when shifted from time
to time in a field is a profitable device in agriculture, and
custom had made the existence of it almost a necessity to
the sound slumber of our glens. There was a pleasant
habit, too, of neighbours gathering at night about a fire
within one of the spaces of the fold and telling tales and
singing songs. Our whole West Country is full of the
most wonderful stories one might seek in vain for among
the world of books and scholars—of giants and dwarfs,

61

fairies, wizards, water-horse, and sea-maiden. The most unlikely-looking peasant that ever put his foot to a *caschrom*, the most uncouth hunter that ever paunched a deer, would tell of such histories in the most scrupulous language and with cunning regard for figure of speech. I know that nowadays, among people of esteemed cultivation in the low country and elsewhere, such a diversion might be thought a waste of time, such narratives a sign of superstition. Of that I am not so certain. The practice, if it did no more, gave wings to our most sombre hours, and put a point on the imagination. As for the superstition of the tales of *ceilidh* and *buaile-mhart* I have little to say. Perhaps the dullest among us scarce credited the giant and dwarf; but the Little Folks are yet on our topmost hills.

A doctor laughed at me once for an experience of my own at the Piper's Knowe, on which any man, with a couchant ear close to the grass, may hear fairy tunes piped in the under-world.

" A trick of the senses," said he.

"But I can bring you scores who have heard it ! " said I.

" So they said of every miracle since time began," said he ; " it but proves the widespread folly and credulity of human nature."

I protested I could bring him to the very spot or whistle him the very tunes ; but he was busy, and wondered so sedate a man as myself could cherish so strange a delusion.

Our fold on Elrigmore was in the centre of a flat meadowland that lies above Dhu Loch, where the river winds among rush and willow-tree, a constant whisperer of love and the distant hills and the salt inevitable sea. There we would be lying under moon and star, and beside us the cattle deeply breathing all night long. To the simple tale of old, to the humble song, these circumstances gave a weight and dignity they may have wanted elsewhere. Never a teller of tale, or a singer of song so artless in that hour and mood of nature, but he hung us breathless on his every accent : we were lone inhabitants of a little space in a magic glen, and the great

world outside the flicker of our fire hummed untenanted
and empty through the jealous night.

It happened on a night of nights—as the saying goes
—that thus we were gathered in the rushy flat of Elrigmore and our hearts easy as to reivers—for was not Mac-
Cailein scourging them over the north ?—when a hint
came to us of a strange end to these Lorn wars, and of
the last days of the Lord of Argile. A night with a sky
almost pallid, freckled with sparkling stars ; a great moon
with an aureole round it, rolling in the east, and the
scent of fern and heather thick upon the air.

We had heard many stories, we had joined in a song
or two, we had set proverb and guess and witty saying
round and round, and it was the young morning when
through the long grass to the fold came a band of
strangers. We were their equal in numbers, whatever
their mission might be, and we waited calmly where we
were, to watch.

The bulk of them stood back from the pin-fold wall,
and three of them came forward and put arms upon the
topmost divots, so that they could look in and see the
watchers gathered round the fire.

"Co tha'n sud's an uchd air a bhuaile ? " (" Who is
there leaning on the fold ? ") asked one of our men, with
a long bow at stretch in his hands.

He got no answer from any of the three strangers, who
looked ghastly eerie in their silence on the wall.

" Mar freagar sibh mise bithidh m'inthaidh aig an
fhear as gile broilleach agaibh " (" My arrow's for the
whitest breast, if ye make no answer "), said my man, and
there was no answer.

The string twanged, the arrow sped, and the stranger
with the white breast fell—shot through her kerchief.
For she was a woman of the clan they name Macaulay,
children of the mist, a luckless dame that, when we
rushed out to face her company, they left dying on the
field.

They were the robber widows of the clan, a gang then
unknown to us, but namely now through the west for
their depredations when the absence of their men in
battles threw them upon their own resource.

And she was the oldest of her company, a half-witted creature we grieved at slaying, but reptile in her malice, for as she lay passing, with the blood oozing to her breast, she reviled us with curses that overran each other in their hurry from her foul lips.

"Dogs! dogs!—heaven's worst ill on ye, dogs!" she cried, a waeful spectacle, and she spat on us as we carried her beside the fire to try and staunch her wound. She had a fierce knife at her waist and would have used it had she the chance, but we removed it from her reach, and she poured a fresher, fuller stream of malediction.

Her voice at last broke and failed to a thin piping whisper, and it was then—with the sweat on her brow—she gave the hint I speak of, the hint of the war's end and the end of MacCailein Mor.

"Wry-mouths, wry-mouths!" said she; "I see the heather above the myrtle on Lhinne-side, and MacCailein's head on a post."

That was all.

It is a story you will find in no books, and yet a story that has been told sometime or other by every fireside of the shire—not before the prophecy was fulfilled but after, when we were loosed from our bonded word. For there and then we took oath on steel to tell no one of the woman's saying till the fulness of time should justify or disgrace the same.

Though I took oath on this melancholy business like the rest, there was one occasion, but a day or two after, that I almost broke my pledged word, and that to the lady who disturbed my Sunday worship and gave me so much reflection on the hunting-road. Her father, as I have said, came up often on a Saturday and supped his curds-and-cream and grew cheery over a Dutch bottle with my father, and one day, as luck had it, Betty honoured our poor doorstep. She came so far, perhaps, because our men and women were at work on the field I mention, whose second crop of grass they were airing for the winter byres—a custom brought to the glen from foreign parts, and with much to recommend it.

I had such a trepidation at her presence that I had

almost fled on some poor excuse to the hill; but the Provost, who perhaps had made sundry calls in the bye-going at houses farther down the glen, and was in a mellow humour, jerked a finger over his shoulder towards the girl as she stood hesitating in the hall after a few words with my father and me, and said, "I've brought you a good harvester here, Colin, and she'll give you a day's darg for a kiss."

I stammered a stupid comment that the wage would be well earned on so warm a day, and could have choked, the next moment, at my rusticity.

Mistress Betty coloured and bit her lip.

"Look at the hussy!" said her father again, laughing with heaving shoulders. "'Where shall we go to-day on our rounds?' said I; 'Where but to Elrigmore,' said she; 'I have not seen Colin for an age!' Yet I'll warrant you thought the cunning jade shy of a gentleman soldier! Ah, those kirtles, those kirtles! I'll give you a word of wisdom, sir, you never learned in Glascow Hie Street nor in the army."

I looked helplessly after the girl, who had fled, incontinent, to the women at work in the field.

"Well, sir," I said, "I shall be pleased to hear it. If it has any pertinence to the harvesting of a second crop it would be welcome."

My father sighed. He never entered very heartily into diversion nowadays—small wonder!—so the Provost laughed on with his counsel.

"You know very well it has nothing to do with harvesting nor harrowing," he cried; "I said kirtles, didn't I! And you needn't be so coy about the matter; surely to God you never learned modesty at your trade of sacking towns. Many a wench——"

"About this counsel," I put in; "I have no trick or tale of wenchcraft beyond the most innocent. And beside, sir, I think we were just talking of a lady who is your daughter."

Even in his glass he was the gentleman, for he saw the suggestion at once.

"Of course, of course, Colin," he said hurriedly, coughing in a confusion. "Never mind an old fool's havering."

Then said he again, " There's a boy at many an old man's heart. I saw you standing there and my daughter was yonder, and it just came over me like the verse of a song that I was like you when I courted her mother. My sorrow! it looks but yesterday, and yet here's an old done man! Folks have been born and married (some of them) and died since syne, and I've been going through life with my eyes shut to my own antiquity. It came on me like a flash three minutes ago, that this gross oidster, sitting of a Saturday sipping the good *aqua* of Elrigmore, with a pendulous waistcoat and a wrinkled hand, is not the lad whose youth and courtship you put me in mind of."

" Stretch your hand, Provost, and fill your glass," said my father. He was not merry in his later years, but he had a hospitable heart.

The two of them sat dumb a space, heedless of the bottle or me, and at last, to mar their manifest sad reflections, I brought the Provost back to the topic of his counsel.

" You had a word of advice," I said, very softly. There was a small tinge of pleasure in my guess that what he had to say might have reference to his daughter.

" Man! I forget now," he said, rousing himself. " What were we on ? "

" Harvesting," said father.

" No, sir ; kirtles," said I.

" Kirtles—so it was," said the Provost. " My wife at Betty's age, when I first sought her company, was my daughter's very model, in face and figure."

" She was a handsome woman, Provost," said my father.

" I can well believe it," said I.

" She is that to-day," cried the Provost, pursing his lips and lifting up his chin in a challenge. " And I learned one thing at the courting of her which is the gist of my word of wisdom to you, Colin. Keep it in mind till you need it. It's this : There's one thing a woman will put up with blandly in every man but the one man she has a notion of, and that's the absence of conceit about himself or her."

In the field by the river, the harvesters sat at a mid-day

meal, contentedly eating their bannock and cheese. They were young folks all, at the age when toil and plain living but give a zest to the errant pleasures of life, so they filled their hour of leisure with gallivanting among the mown and gathered grass.

And oh! *mo chridhe*, but that was long ago! Let no one, remembering the charm of an autumn field in his youth, test its cheerfulness when he has got up in years. For he will find it lying under a sun less genial than then; he will fret at some influence lost; the hedges tall and beautiful will have turned to stunted boundaries upon his fancy; he will ache at the heart at the memory of those old careless crops and reapers when he sits, a poor man or wealthy, among the stubble of grass and youth.

As I lay on the shady side of an alder bank watching our folk at their gambols, I found a serenity that again set me at my ease with the Provost's daughter. I gathered even the calmness to invite her to sit beside me, and she made no demur.

"You are short of reapers, I think, by the look of them," she said; "I miss some of the men who were here last year."

They were gone with MacCailein, I explained, as paid volunteers.

"Oh! those wars!" she cried sadly. "I wish they were ended. Here are the fields, good crops, food and happiness for all, why must men be fighting?"

"Ask your Highland heart," said I. "We are children of strife."

"In my heart," she replied, "there's but love for all. I toss sleepless, at night, thinking of the people we know —the good, kind, gallant, merry lads we know—waging savage battle for something I never had the wit to discover the meaning of."

"The Almighty's order—we have been at it from the birth of time."

"So old a world might have learned," she said, "to break that order when they break so many others. Is his lordship likely to be back soon?"

"I wish he might be," said I, with a dubious accent,

thinking of the heather above the myrtle and MacCailein's head on a post. " Did you hear of the Macaulay beldame shot by Roderick ? "

" Yes," she said ; " an ugly business ! What has that to do with MacCailein's home-coming ? "

" Very little indeed," I answered, recalling our bond ; " but she cursed his lordship and his army with a zeal that was alarming, even to an old soldier of Sweden."

" God ward all evil ! " cried Betty in a passion of earnestness. " You'll be glad to see your friend M'Iver back, I make no doubt."

" Oh ! he's an old hand at war, madam ; he'll come safe out of this by his luck and skill, if he left the army behind him."

" I'm glad to hear it," said she, smiling.

" What ! " I cried in raillery ; " would you be grateful for so poor a balance left of a noble army ? "

And she reddened and smiled again, and a servant cried us in to the dinner-table.

In spite of the Macaulay prophecy, MacCailein and his men came home in the fulness of time. They came with the first snowstorm of winter, the clan in companies down Glenaora and his lordship roundabout by the Lowlands, where he had a mission to the Estates. The war, for the time, was over, a truce of a kind was patched up, and there was a cheerful prospect—too briefly ours—that the country would settle anon to peace.

CHAPTER VIII.

THE BALE-FIRES ON THE BENS.

HARD on the heels of the snow came a frost that put shackles on the very wind. It fell black and sudden on the country, turning the mud floors of the poorer dwellings into iron that rang below the heel, though the peat-fires burned by day and night, and Loch Finne, lying flat as a girdle from shore to shore, crisped and curdled into ice on the surface in the space of an afternoon. A sun almost genial to look at, but with no warmth at the heart of him, rode among the white hills that looked doubly massive with their gullies and corries, for ordinary black or green, lost in the general hue, and at mid-day bands of little white birds would move over the country from the north, flapping weakly to a warmer clime. They might stay a little, some of them, deceived by the hanging peat-smoke into the notion that somewhere here were warmth and comfort ; but the cold searched them to the core, and such as did not die on the roadside took up their dismal voyaging anew.

The very deer came down from the glens—*cabarfeidh* stags, hinds, and prancing roes. At night we could hear them bellowing and snorting as they went up and down the street in herds from Ben Bhrec or the barren sides of the Black Mount and Dalness in the land of Bredalbane, seeking the shore and the traveller's illusion—the content that's always to come. In those hours, too, the owls seemed to surrender the fir-woods and come to the junipers about the back-doors, for they keened in the darkness, even on, woeful warders of the night, telling the constant hours.

'Twas in these bitter nights, shivering under blanket and plaid, I thought ruefully of foreign parts, of the frequented towns I had seen elsewhere, the cleanly paven streets, swept of snow, the sea-coal fires, and the lanterns swinging over the crowded causeways, signs of friendly interest and companionship. Here were we, poor peasants, in a waste of frost and hills, cut off from the merry folks sitting by fire and flame at ease! Even our gossiping, our *ceilidh* in each other's houses, was stopped; except in the castle itself no more the song and story, the pipe and trump.

In the morning when one ventured abroad he found the deer-slot dimpling all the snow on the street, and down at the shore, unafeared of man, would be solitary hinds, widows and rovers from their clans, sniffing eagerly over to the Cowal hills. Poor beasts! poor beasts! I've seen them in their madness take to the ice for it when it was little thicker than a groat, thinking to reach the oak-woods of Ardchyline. For a time the bay at the river mouth was full of long-tailed ducks, that at a whistle almost came to your hand, and there too came flocks of wild-swan, flying in wedges, trumpeting as they flew. Fierce otters quarrelled over their eels at the mouth of the Black Burn that flows underneath the town and out below the Tolbooth to the shore, or made the gloaming melancholy with their doleful whistle. A roebuck in his winter jacket of mouse-brown fur died one night at my relative's door, and a sea-eagle gorged himself so upon the carcass that at morning he could not flap a wing, and fell a ready victim to a knock from my staff.

The passes to the town were head-high with drifted snow, our warders at the heads of Aora and Shira could not themselves make out the road, and the notion of added surety this gave us against Antrim's Irishmen was the only compensation for the ferocity of nature.

In three days the salt loch, in that still and ardent air, froze like a fishpond, whereupon the oddest spectacle ever my country-side saw was his that cared to rise at morning to see it. Stags and hinds in tremendous herds, black cattle, too, from the hills, trotted boldly over the ice to the other side of the loch, that in the clarity of the air seemed but a mile off. Behind them went skulking foxes,

pole-cats, badgers, cowering hares, and bead-eyed weasels.
They seemed to have a premonition that Famine was stalk-
ing behind them, and they fled our luckless woods and
fields like rats from a sinking ship.

To Master Gordon I said one morning as we watched
a company of dun heifers mid-way on the loch, "This is
an ill omen or I'm sore mistaken."

He was not a man given to superstitions, but he could
not gainsay me. "There's neither hip nor haw left in our
woods," he said ; "birds I've never known absent here in
the most eager winters are gone, and wild-eyed strangers,
their like never seen here before, tamely pick crumbs at
my very door. Signs! signs! It beats me sometimes
to know how the brute scents the circumstance to come,
but—what's the Word ?—' Not a sparrow shall fall.'"

We fed well on the wild meat driven to our fireside,
and to it there never seemed any end, for new flocks took
up the tale of the old ones, and a constant procession of
fur and feather moved across our white prospect. Even
the wolf—from Benderloch no doubt—came baying at
night at the empty gibbets at the town-head, that spoke
of the law's suspense.

Only in Castle Inneraora was there anything to be called
gaiety. MacCailein fumed at first at the storm that kept
his letters from him and spoiled the laburnums and elms
he was coaxing to spring about his garden ; but soon he
settled down to his books and papers, ever his solace in
such homely hours as the policy and travel of his life permitted. And if the burgh was dull and dark, night after
night there was merriment over the drawbrig of the castle.
It would be on the 10th or the 15th of the month that I
first sampled it. I went up with a party from the town
and neighbourhood, with their wives and daughters, finding an atmosphere wondrous different from that of the
cooped and anxious tenements down below. Big logs
roared behind the fire-dogs, long candles and plenty lit
the hall, and pipe and harp went merrily. Her ladyship
had much of the French manner—a dainty dame with
long thin face and bottle shoulders, attired always in Saxon
fashion, and indulgent in what I then thought a wholesome levity, that made up for the Gruamach husband.

And she thought him, honestly, the handsomest and noblest in the world, though she rallied him for his over-much sobriety of deportment. To me she was very gracious, for she had liked my mother, and I think she planned to put me in the way of the Provost's daughter as often as she could.

When his lordship was in his study, our daffing was in Gaelic, for her ladyship, though a Morton, and only learning the language, loved to have it spoken about her. Her pleasure was to play the harp—a clarsach of great beauty, with Iona carving on it—to the singing of her daughter Jean, who knew all the songs of the mountains and sang them like the bird. The town girls, too, sang, Betty a little shyly, but as daintily as her neighbours, and we danced a reel or two to the playing of Paruig Dall, the blind piper. Venison and wine were on the board, and whiter bread than the town baxters afforded. It all comes back on me now—that lofty hall, the skins of seal and otter and of stag upon the floor, the flaring candles and the glint of glass and silver, the banners swinging upon the walls over devices of pike, gun, and claymore—the same to be used so soon !

The castle, unlike its successor, sat adjacent to the river-side, its front to the hill of Dunchuach on the north, and its back a stone-cast from the mercat cross and the throng street of the town. Between it and the river was the small garden consecrate to her ladyship's flowers, a patch of level soil, cut in dice by paths whose tiny pebbles and broken shells crunched beneath the foot at any other season than now when the snow covered all.

John Splendid, who was of our party, in a lull of the entertainment was looking out at the prospect from a window at the gable end of the hall, for the moon sailed high above Strone, and the outside world was beautiful in a cold and eerie fashion. Of a sudden he faced round and beckoned to me with a hardly noticeable toss of the head.

I went over and stood beside him. He was bending a little to get the top of Dunchuach in the field of his vision, and there was a puzzled look on his face.

"Do you see any light up yonder ? " he asked, and I

followed his query with a keen scrutiny of the summit, where the fort should be lying in darkness and peace.

There was a twinkle of light that would have shown fuller if the moonlight were less.

" I see a spark," I said, wondering a little at his interest in so small an affair.

" That's a pity," said he, in a rueful key. " I was hoping it might be a private vision of my own, and yet I might have known my dream last night of a white rat meant something. If that's flame there's more to follow. There should be no lowe on this side of the fort after nightfall, unless the warders on the other side have news from the hills behind Dunchuach. In this matter of fire at night Dunchuach echoes Ben Bhuidhe or Ben Bhrec, and these two in their turn carry on the light of our friends farther ben in Bredalbane and Cruachan. It's not a state secret to tell you we were half feared some of our Antrim gentry might give us a call ; but the Worst Curse on the pigs who come guesting in such weather ! "

He was glowering almost feverishly at the hill-top, and I turned round to see that the busy room had no share in our apprehension. The only eyes I found looking in our direction were those of Betty, who finding herself observed, came over, blushing a little, and looked out into the night.

" You were hiding the moonlight from me," she said with a smile, a remark which struck me as curious, for she could not, from where she sat, see out at the window.

" I never saw one who needed it less," said Splendid, and still he looked intently at the mount. " You carry your own with you."

Having no need to bend, she saw the top of Dunchuach whenever she got close to the window, and by this time the light on it looked like a planet, wan in the moonlight, but unusually large and angry.

" I never saw star so bright," said the girl, in a natural enough error.

" A challenge to your eyes, madam," retorted Splendid again, in a raillery wonderful considering his anxiety, and he whispered in my ear—" or to us to war."

As he spoke, the report of a big gun boomed through

the frosty air from Dunchuach to the plain, and the beacon flashed up, tall, flaunting, and unmistakable.

John Splendid turned into the hall and raised his voice a little, to say with no evidence of disturbance—

" There's something amiss up the glens, your ladyship."

The harp her ladyship strummed idly on at the moment had stopped on a ludicrous and unfinished note, the hum of conversation ended abruptly. Up to the window the company crowded, and they could see the bale-fire blazing hotly against the cool light of the moon and the widely sprinkled stars. Behind them in a little came Argile, one arm only thrust hurriedly in a velvet jacket, his hair in a disorder, the pallor of study on his cheek. He very gently pressed to the front, and looked out with a lowering brow at the signal.

" Ay, ay ! " he said in the English, after a pause that kept the room more intent on his face than on the bale-fire. " My old luck bides with me. I thought the weather guaranteed me a season's rest, but here's the claymore again ! Alasdair, Craignish, Sir Donald, I wish you gentlemen would set the summons about with as little delay as need be. We have no time for any display of militant science, but as these beacons carry their tale fast we may easily be at the head of Glen Aora before the enemy is down Glenurchy."

Sir Donald, who was the eldest of the officers his lordship addressed, promised a muster of five hundred men in three hours' time. " I can have a *crois-tara*," he said, " at the very head of Glen Shira in an hour."

" You may save yourself the trouble," said John Splendid ; " Glen Shira's awake by this time, for the watchers have been in the hut on Ben Bhuidhe since ever we came back from Lorn, and they are in league with other watchers at the Gearron town, who will have the alarm miles up the Glen by now if I make no mistake about the breed."

By this time a servant came in to say Sithean Sluaidhe hill on Cowal was ablaze, and likewise the hill of Ardno above the Ardkinglas lands.

" The alarm will be over Argile in two hours," said his lordship. " We're grand at the beginnings of things," and as he spoke he was pouring, with a steady hand, a glass of wine for a woman in the tremors. "I wish to God we were better at the endings," he added, bitterly. "If these Athole and Antrim caterans have the secret of our passes, we may be rats in a trap before the morn's morning."

The hall emptied quickly, a commotion of folks depart-ing rose in the courtyard, and candle and torch moved about. Horses put over the bridge at a gallop, striking sparks from the cobble-stones, swords jingled on stirrups. In the town, a piper's tune hurriedly lifted, and numerous lights danced to the windows of the burghers. John Splendid, the Marquis, and I were the only ones left in the hall, and the Marquis turned to me with a smile—

"You see your pledge calls for redemption sooner than you expected, Elrigmore. The enemy's not far from Ben Bhuidhe now, and your sword is mine by the contract."

"Your lordship can count on me to the last ditch," I cried ; and indeed I might well be ready, for was not the menace of war as muckle against my own hearth as against his ?

"Our plan," he went on, "as agreed upon at a council after my return from the north, was to hold all above Inneraora in simple defence while lowland troops took the invader behind. Montrose or the MacDonalds can't get through our passes."

"I'm not cock-sure of that, MacCailein," said Splendid. "We're here in the bottom of an ashet ; there's more than one deserter from your tartan on the outside of it, and once they get on the rim they have, by all rules strategic, the upper hand of us in some degree. I never had much faith (if I dare make so free) in the surety of our retreat here. It's an old notion of our grandads that we could bar the passes."

"So we can, sir, so we can ! " said the Marquis, nerv-ously picking at his buttons with his long white fingers, the nails vexatiously polished and shaped.

"Against horse and artillery, I allow, surely not against Gaelic foot. This is not a wee foray of broken men, but an attack by an army of numbers. The science of war —what little I learned of it in the Low Countries with gentlemen esteemed my betters—convinces me that if a big enough horde fall on from the rim of our ashet, as I call it, they might sweep us into the loch like rattons."

I doubt MacCailein Mor heard little of this uncheery criticism, for he was looking in a seeming blank abstraction out of the end window at the town lights increasing in number as the minutes passed. His own piper in the close behind the buttery had tuned up and into the gathering—

" Bha mi air banais 'am bail' Inneraora.
  Banais bu mhiosa bha riamh air an t-saoghal ! "

I felt the tune stir me to the core, and M'Iver, I could see by the twitch of his face, kindled to the old call.

"Curse them!" cried MacCailein; "Curse them!" he cried in the Gaelic, and he shook a white fist foolishly at the north; "I'm wanting but peace and my books. I keep my ambition in leash, and still and on they must be snapping like curs at Argile. God's name! and I'll crush them like ants on the ant-heap."

From the door at the end of the room, as he stormed, a little bairn toddled in, wearing a night-shirt, a curly gold-haired boy with his cheeks like the apple for hue, the sleep he had risen from still heavy on his eyes. Seemingly the commotion had brought him from his bed, and up he now ran, and his little arms went round his father's knees. On my word I've seldom seen a man more vastly moved than was Archibald, Marquis of Argile. He swallowed his spittle as if it were wool, and took the child to his arms awkwardly, like one who has none of the handling of his own till they are grown up, and I could see the tear at the cheek he laid against the youth's ruddy hair.

"Wild men coming!" said the child, not much put about after all.

"They shan't touch my little Illeasbuig," whispered his lordship, kissing him on the mouth. Then he lifted his head and looked hard at John Splendid. "I think," he said, "if I went post-haste to Edinburgh, I could be of some service in advising the nature and route of the harassing on the rear of Montrose. Or do you think—do you think——? "

He ended in a hesitancy, flushing a little at the brow, his lips weakening at the corner.

John Splendid, at my side, gave me with his knee the least nudge on the leg next him.

" Did your lordship think of going to Edinburgh at once ? " he asked, with an odd tone in his voice, and keeping his eyes very fixedly on a window.

" If it was judicious, the sooner the better," said the Marquis, nuzzling his face in the soft warmth of the child's neck.

Splendid looked helpless for a bit, and then took up the policy that I learned later to expect from him in every similar case. He seemed to read (in truth it was easy enough !) what was in his master's mind, and he said, almost with gaiety—

" The best thing you could do, my lord. Beyond your personal encouragement (and a Chief's aye a consoling influence on the field, I'll never deny), there's little you could do here that cannot, with your pardon, be fairly well done by Sir Donald and myself, and Elrigmore here, who have made what you might call a trade of tulzie and brulzie."

MacCailein Mor looked uneasy for all this open assurance. He set the child down with an awkward kiss, to be taken away by a servant lass who had come after him.

" Would it not look a little odd ! " he said, eyeing us keenly.

" Your lordship might be sending a trusty message to Edinburgh," I said ; and John Splendid with a " Pshaw ! " walked to the window, saying what he had to say with his back to the candle-light.

" There's not a man out there but would botch the whole business if you sent him," he said ; " it must be his lordship or nobody. And what's to hinder her lady-ship and the children going too ? Snugger they'd be by far in Stirling Lodge, than here, I'll warrant. If I were not an old runt of a bachelor, it would be my first thought to give my women and bairns safety."

MacCailein flew at the notion. " Just so, just so," he cried, and of a sudden he skipped out of the room.

John Splendid turned, pushed the door to after the

nobleman, and in a soft voice broke into the most terrible torrent of bad language ever I heard (and I've known cavaliers of fortune free that way). He called his Marquis everything but a man.

"Then why in the name of God do you urge him on to a course that a fool could read the poltroonery of? I never gave MacCailein Mor credit for being a coward before," said I.

"Coward!" cried Splendid. "It's no cowardice but selfishness—the disease, more or less, of us all. Do you think yon gentleman a coward? Then you do not know the man. I saw him once, empty-handed, in the forest, face the white stag and beat it off a hunter it was goring to death, and they say he never blenched when the bonnet was shot off his head at Drimtyne, but jested with a 'Close on't: a nail-breadth more, and Colin was heir to an earlhood!'"

"I'm sorry to think the worst of an Argile and a Campbell, but surely his place is here now."

"It is, I admit; and I egged him to follow his inclination because I'm a fool in one thing, as you'll discover anon, because it's easier and pleasanter to convince a man to do what he wants to do than to convince him the way he would avoid is the only right one."

"It's not an altogether nice quirk of the character," I said, drily. It gave me something of a stroke to find so weak a bit in a man of so many notable parts.

He spunked up like tinder.

"Do you call me a liar?" he said, with a face as white as a clout, his nostrils stretching in his rage.

"Liar!" said I, "not I. It would be an ill time to do it with our common enemy at the door. A lie (as I take it in my own Highland fashion) is the untruth told for cowardice or to get a mean advantage of another: your way with MacCailein was but a foolish way (also Highland, I've noticed) of saving yourself the trouble of spurring up your manhood to put him in the right."

"You do me less than half justice," said Splendid, the blood coming back to his face, and him smiling again; "I allow I'm no preacher. If a man must to hell, he must, his own gait. The only way I can get into argu-

ment with him about the business is to fly in a fury. If
I let my temper up I would call MacCailein coward to
his teeth, though I know it's not his character. But I've
been in a temper with my cousin before now, and I ken
the stuff he's made of: he gets as cold as steel the hotter
I get, and with the poorest of causes he could then put
me in a black confusion——"

" But you——"

" Stop, stop! let me finish my tale. Do you know, I
put a fair face on the black business to save the man
his own self-respect. He'll know himself his going looks
bad without my telling him, and I would at least leave
him the notion that we were blind to his weakness. After
all it's not much of a weakness—the wish to save a wife
and children from danger. Another bookish disease,
I admit: their over-much study has deadened the man
to a sense of the becoming, and in an affair demanding
courage he acts like a woman, thinking of his household
when he should be thinking of his clan. My only consolation is that after all (except for the look of the thing)
his leaving us matters little."

I thought different on that point, and I proved right.
If it takes short time to send a fiery cross about, it takes
shorter yet to send a naughty rumour, and the story that
MacCailein Mor and his folks were off in a hurry to the
Lowlands was round the greater part of Argile before the
clansmen mustered at Inneraora. They never mustered
at all, indeed, for the chieftains of the small companies
that came from Glen Finne and down the country no
sooner heard that the Marquis was off than they took the
road back, and so Montrose and Colkitto MacDonald
found a poltroon and deserted countryside waiting them.

CHAPTER IX.

INVASION.

EIGHT hours after the beacon kindled on Dunchuach, the enemy was feeling at the heart of Argile.

It came out years after, that one Angus Macalain, a Glencoe man, a branded robber off a respectable Water-of-Douglas family, had guided the main body of the invaders through the mountains of the Urchy and into our territory. They came on in three bands, Alasdair Mac-Donald and the Captain of Clanranald (as they called John MacDonald, the beast—a scurvy knave!), separating at Accurach at the forking of the two glens, and entering both, Montrose himself coming on the rear as a support. As if to favour the people of the Glens, a thaw came that day with rain and mist that cloaked them largely from view as they ran for the hills to shelter in the sheiling bothies. The ice, as I rode up the water-side, home to Glen Shira to gather some men and dispose my father safely, was breaking on the surface of the loch and roaring up on the shore in the incoming tide. It came piling in layers in the bays—a most wonderful spectacle! I could not hear my horse's hooves for the cracking and crushing and cannonade of it as it flowed in on a south wind to the front of the Gearran, giving the long curve of the land an appearance new and terrible, filled as it was far over high-water mark with monstrous blocks, answering with groans and cries to every push of the tide.

I found the glen wrapped in mist, the Gearran hamlet empty of people, Maam, Kilblaan, Stuchgoy, and Ben Bhuidhe presenting every aspect of desolation. A weeping rain was making sodden all about my father's house when I galloped to the door, to find him and the *sgalag* the only ones left.

The old man was bitter on the business.

" Little I thought," said he, " to see the day when Glen Shira would turn tail on an enemy."

" Where are they ? " I asked, speaking of our absent followers ; but indeed I might have saved the question, for I knew before he told me they were up in the corries between the mounts, and in the caves of Glen Finne.

He was sitting at a fire that was down to its grey ash, a mournful figure my heart was vexed to see. Now and then he would look about him, at the memorials of my mother, her chair and her Irish Bible (the first in the parish), and a posy of withered flowers that lay on a bowl on a shelf where she had placed them, new cut and fresh, the day she took to her deathbed. Her wheel, too, stood in the corner, with the thread snapped short in the heck —a hint, I many times thought, at the sundered interests of life.

" I suppose we must be going with the rest," I ventured ; " there's small sense in biding here to be butchered."

He fell in a rain of tears, fearing nor death nor hardship, I knew, but wae at the abandonment of his home. I had difficulty in getting him to consent to come with me, but at last I gave the prospect of safety in the town and the company of friends there so attractive a hue that he consented. So we hid a few things under a *bruach* or overhanging brae beside the burn behind the house, and having shut all the doors—a comical precaution against an army, it struck me at the time—we rode down to Inneraora, to the town house of our relative Craignure.

It was a most piteous community, crowded in every lane and pend with men, women, and children dreadful of the worst. All day the people had been trooping in from the landward parts, flying before the rumour of the Athole advance down Cladich. For a time there was the hope that the invaders would but follow the old Athole custom and plunder as they went, sparing unarmed men and women, but this hope we surrendered when a lad came from Carnus with a tale of two old men, who were weavers there, and a woman, nailed into their huts and burned to death.

Had Inneraora been a walled town, impregnable, say, as a simple Swabian village with a few sconces and redoubts, and a few pieces of cannon, we old soldiers would have counselled the holding of it against all comers ; but it was innocently open to the world, its back windows looking into the fields, its through-going wynds and closes leading frankly to the highway.

A high and sounding wind had risen from the south, the sea got in a tumult, the ice-blocks ran like sheep before it to the Gearran bay and the loch-head. I thought afterwards it must be God's providence that opened up for us so suddenly a way of flight from this lamentable trap, by the open water now free from shore to shore in front of the town. Generalling the community as if he was a marshal of brigade, John Splendid showed me the first of his manly quality in his preparation for the removal of the women and children. He bade the men run out the fishing smacks, the wherries and skiffs, at the Cadger's Quay, and moving about that frantic people, he disposed them in their several places on the crafts that were to carry them over the three-mile ferry to Cowal. A man born to enterprise and guidance, certes ! I never saw his equal. He had the happy word for all, the magic hint of hope, a sober merriment when needed, sometimes a little raillery and laughing, sometimes (with the old) a farewell in the ear. Even the better gentry, Sir Donald and the rest, took a second place in the management, beholding in this poor gentleman the human heart that at a pinch is better than authority in a gold-braided coat.

By noon we had every bairn and woman (but for one woman I'll mention) on their way from the shore, poor dears ! tossing on the turbulent sea, the women weeping bitterly for the husbands and sons they left, for of men there went with them but the oldsters, able to guide a boat, but poorly equipped for battling with Irish banditty. And my father was among them, in the kind hands of his *sgalag* and kinswomen, but in a vague indifference of grief.

A curious accident, that in the grace of God made the

greatest difference on my after-life, left among them that
found no place in the boats the daughter of Provost
Brown. She had made every preparation to go with her
father and mother, and had her foot on the beam of the
boat, when an old woman set up a cry for an oe that had
been forgot in the confusion, and was now, likely, crying
in the solitude of the back lands. It was the love-bairn
of a dead mother, brought up in the kindly Highland
fashion, free of every girnel and kail-pot. Away skirted
Betty up the causeway of the Cadger's Quay, and in
among the lanes for the little one, and (I learned again)
she found it playing well content among puddled snow,
chattering to itself in the loneliness of yon war-menaced
town. And she had but snatched it up to seek safety
with her in the boats when the full tide of Colkitto's
robbers came pelting in under the Arches. They cut
her off from all access to the boats by that way, so she
turned and made for the other end of the town, hoping
to hail in her father's skiff when he had put far enough
off shore to see round the point and into the second
bay.

We had but time to shout her apparent project to her
father, when we found ourselves fighting hand-to-hand
against the Irish gentry in trews. This was no market-
day brawl, but a stark assault-at-arms. All in the sound
of a high wind, broken now and then with a rain blattering
even-down, and soaking through tartan and *clo-dubh*,
we at it for dear life. Of us Clan Campbell people,
gentrice and commoners, and so many of the Lowland
mechanics of the place as were left behind, there would
be something less than two hundred, for the men who
had come up the loch-side to the summon of the beacons
returned the way they came when they found MacCailein
gone, and hurried to the saving of wife and bairn. We
were all well armed with fusil and sword, and in that we
had some advantage of the caterans bearing down on us;
for they had, for the main part, but rusty matchlocks,
pikes, billhooks—even bows and arrows, antique enough
contrivance for a time of civilised war! But they had
hunger and hate for their backers, good guidance in their
own savage fashion from MacDonald, and we were fighting

on a half heart, a body never trained together, and stupid to the word of command.

From the first, John took the head of our poor defence. He was *duine-uasail* enough, and he had, notoriously, the skill that earned him the honour, even over myself (in some degree), and certainly over Sir Donald.

The town-head fronted the upper bay, and between it and the grinding ice on the shore lay a broad tract of what might be called esplanade, presenting ample space for our encounter.

"Gentlemen," cried John, picking off a man with the first shot from a silver-butted *dag* he pulled out of his waist-belt at the onset, "and with your leave, Sir Donald (trusting you to put pluck in these Low Country shopkeepers), it's Inneraora or Ifrinn for us this time. Give them cold steel, and never an inch of arm-room for their bills!"

Forgotten were the boats, behind lay all our loves and fortunes—was ever Highland heart but swelled on such a time? Sturdy black and hairy scamps the Irish—never German boor so inelegant—but venomous in their courage! Score upon score of them ran in on us through the Arches. Our lads had but one shot from the muskets, then into them with the dirk and sword.

"Montrose! Montrose!" cried the enemy, even when the blood glucked at the thrapple, and they twisted to the pain of the knife.

"A papist dog!" cried Splendid, hard at it on my right, for once a zealous Protestant, and he was whisking around him his broadsword like a hazel wand, facing half-a-dozen Lochaber-axes. "Cruachan, Cruachan!" he sang. And we cried the old slogan but once, for time pressed and wind was dear.

Sitting cosy in taverns with friends long after, listening to men singing in the cheery way of taverns the ditty that the Leckan bard made upon this little spulzie, I could weep and laugh in turns at minding of yon winter's day. In the hot stress of it I felt but the ardour that's in all who wear tartan—less a hatred of the men I thrust and slashed at with Sir Claymore than a zest in the busy traffic, and something of a pride (God help me!) in the pretty way my blade dirled on the harn-pans of the rascals.

There was one trick of the sword I had learned off an old sergeant of pikes in Mackay's Scots, in a leisure afternoon in camp, that I knew was alien to every man who used the targe in home battles, and it served me like a Mull wife's charm. They might be sturdy, the dogs, valorous too, for there's no denying the truth, and they were gleg, gleg with the target in fending, but, man, I found them mighty simple to the feint and lunge of Alasdair Mor !

Listening, as I say, to a song in a tavern, I'm sad for the stout fellows of our tartan who fell that day, and still I could laugh gaily at the amaze of the ragged corps who found gentlemen before them. They pricked at us, for all their natural ferocity, with something like apology for marring our fine clothes ; and when the end came, and we were driven back, they left the gentlemen of our band to retreat by the pends to the beech-wood, and gave their attention to the main body of our common townsmen.

We had edged, Splendid and Sir Donald and I, into a bit of green behind the church, and we held a council of war on our next move.

Three weary men, the rain smirring on our sweating faces, there we were ! I noticed that a trickle of blood was running down my wrist, and I felt at the same time a beat at the shoulder that gave the explanation, and had mind that a fellow in the Athole corps had fired a pistolet point-blank at me, missing me, as I had thought, by the thickness of my doublet-sleeve.

" You've got a cut," said Sir Donald. " You have a face like the clay."

" A bit of the skin off," said I, unwilling to vex good company.

" We must take to Eas-a-chosain for it," said Splendid, his eyes flashing wild upon the scene, the gristle of his red neck throbbing.

Smoke was among the haze of the rain ; from the thatch of the town-head houses the wind brought on us the smell of burning heather and brake and fir-joist.

" Here's the lamentable end of town Inneraora ! " said John, in a doleful key.

And we ran, the three of us, up the Fisherland burn-side to the wood of Creag Dubh.

CHAPTER X.

THE FLIGHT TO THE FOREST.

WE made good speed up the burn-side, through the
fields, and into the finest forest that was (or is to this
day, perhaps) in all the wide Highlands. I speak of
Creag Dubh, great land of majestic trees, home of the
red-deer, rich with glades carpeted with the juiciest grass,
and endowed with a cave or two where we knew we were
safe of a sanctuary if it came to the worst, and the Athole
men ran at our heels. It welcomed us from the rumour
of battle with a most salving peace. Under the high fir
and oak we walked in a still and scented air, aisles lay
about and deep recesses, the wind sang in the tops and
in the vistas of the trees, so that it minded one of Catholic
kirks frequented otherwhere. We sped up by the quarries
and through Eas-a-chosain (that little glen so full of fondest
memorials for all that have loved and wandered), and
found our first resting-place in a cunning little hold on
an eminence looking down on the road that ran from the
town to Coillebhraid mines. Below us the hillside dipped
three or four hundred feet in a sharp slant bushed over
with young *darach* wood ; behind us hung a tremendous
rock that few standing upon would think had a hollow
heart. Here was our refuge, and the dry and stoury
alleys of the fir-wood we had traversed gave no clue of
our track to them that might hunt us.

We made a fire whose smoke curled out at the back of
the cave into a linn at the bottom of a fall the Cromalt
burn has here, and had there been any to see the reek
they would have thought it but the finer spray of the

thawed water rising among the melting ice-lances. We made, too, couches of fir-branches—the springiest and most wholesome of beds in lieu of heather or gall, and laid down our weariness as a soldier would relinquish his knapsack, after John Splendid had bandaged my wounded shoulder.

In the cave of Eas-a-chosain we lay for more days than I kept count of, I immovable, fevered with my wound, Sir Donald my nurse, and John Splendid my provider. They kept keen scrutiny on the road below, where sometimes they could see the invaders passing in bands in their search for scattered townships or crofts.

On the second night John ventured into the edge of the town to see how fared Inneraora and to seek provand. He found the place like a fiery cross,—burned to char at the ends, and only the mid of it—the solid Tolbooth and the gentle houses—left to hint its ancient pregnancy. A corps of Irish had it in charge while their comrades scoured the rest of the country, and in the dusk John had an easy task to find brandy in the cellars of Craignure (the invaders never thought of seeking a cellar for anything more warming than peats), a boll of meal in handfuls here and there among the meal-girnels of the commoner houses that lay open to the night, smelling of stale hearth-fires, and harried.

To get fresh meat was a matter even easier, though our guns we dare not be using, for there were blue hares to snare, and they who have not taken fingers to a roasted haunch of badger harried out of his hiding with a club have fine feeding yet to try. The good Gaelic soldier will eat, sweetly, crowdy made in his brogue—how much better off were we with the stout and well-fired oaten cakes that this Highland gentleman made on the flagstone in front of our cave-fire !

Never had a wounded warrior a more rapid healing than I. "*Ruigidh an ro-ghiullach air an ro-ghalar*"—good nursing will overcome the worst disease, as our antique proverb says, and I had the best of nursing and but a baggage-master's wound after all. By the second week I was hale and hearty. We were not uncomfortable in our forest sanctuary ; we were well warmed by the perfumed roots of the candle-fir ; John Splendid's foraging was richer than we had on many a campaign, and a pack of cartes lent some solace to the heaviest of our hours. To our imprisonment we brought even a touch of scholarship. Sir Donald was a student of Edinburgh College— a Master of Arts—learned in the moral philosophies, and he and I discoursed most gravely of many things that had small harmony with our situation in that savage foe-haunted countryside.

To these, our learned discourses, John Splendid would listen with an impatient tolerance, finding in the most shrewd saying of the old scholars we dealt with but a paraphrase of some Gaelic proverb or the roundabout expression of his own views on life and mankind. " Tuts ! tuts ! " he would cry, " I think the dissensions of you two are but one more proof of the folly of book-learning. Your minds are not your own, but the patches of other people's bookish duds. A keen eye, a custom of puzzling everything to its cause, a trick of balancing the different motives of the human heart, get John M'Iver as close on the bone when it comes to the bit. Every one of the scholars you are talking of had but my own chance (maybe less, for who sees more than a Cavalier of fortune ?) of witnessing the real true facts of life. Did they live to-day poor and hardy, biting short at an oaten bannock to make it go the farther, to-morrow gorging on fat venison and red rich wine ? Did they parley with cunning lawyers, cajole the boor, act the valorous on a misgiving heart, guess at the thought of man or woman oftener than we do ? Did ever you find two of them agree on the finer points of their science ? Never the bit ! "

We forgave him his heresies for the sake of their wit, that I but poorly chronicle, and he sang us wonderful Gaelic songs that had all of that same wisdom he bragged of—no worse, I'll allow, than the wisdom of print ; not all love-songs, laments, or such naughty ballads as you will hear to-day, but the poetry of the more cunning bards. Our cavern, in its inner recesses, filled with the low rich chiming of his voice ; his face, and hands, and whole body took part in the music. In those hours his character borrowed just that touch of sincerity it was in want of at ordinary times, for he was one of those who need trial and trouble to bring out their better parts.

We might have been happy, we might have been content, living thus in our cave the old hunter's life ; walking out at early mornings in the adjacent parts of the wood for the wherewithal to breakfast ; rounding in the day with longer journeys in the moonlight, when the shadows were crowded with the sounds of night bird and beast ; —we might have been happy, I say, but for thinking of our country's tribulation. Where were our friends and neighbours ? Who were yet among the living ? How fared our kin abroad in Cowal or fled farther south to the Rock of Dunbarton ? These restless thoughts came oftener to me than to my companions, and many an hour I spent in woeful pondering in the alleys of the wood.

At last it seemed the Irish who held the town were in a sure way to discover our hiding if we remained any longer there. Their provender was running low, though they had driven hundreds of head of cattle before them down the Glens ; the weather hardened to frost again, and they were pushing deeper into the wood to seek for bestial. It was full of animals we dare not shoot, but which they found easy to the bullet ; red-deer with horns —even at three years old—stunted to knobs by a constant life in the shade and sequestration of the trees they threaded their lives through, or dun-bellied fallow-deer unable to face the blasts of the exposed hills, light-coloured yeld hinds and hornless " heaviers " (or winterers) the size of oxen. A flock or two of wild goat, even, lingered on the upper slopes towards Ben Bhrec, and they were down now browsing in the ditches beside the Marriage Tree.

We could see little companies of the enemy come closer and closer on our retreat each day—attracted up the side of the hill from the road by birds and beast that found cover under the young oaks.

" We'll have to be moving before long," said Sir Donald, ruefully looking at them one day—so close at hand that we unwittingly had our fingers round the dirk-hilts.

He had said the true word.

It was the very next day that an Irishman, bending under a bush to lift a hedgehog that lay sleeping its winter sleep tightly rolled up in grass and bracken, caught sight of the narrow entrance to our cave. Our eyes were on him at the time, and when he came closer we fell back into the rear of our dark retreat, thinking he might not push his inquiry further.

For once John Splendid's cunning forsook him in the most ludicrous way. " I could have stabbed him where he stood," he said afterwards, " for I was in the shadow at his elbow ; " but he forgot that the fire whose embers glowed red within the cave would betray its occupation quite as well as the sight of its occupants, and that we were discovered only struck him when the man, after but one glance in, went bounding down the hill to seek for aid in harrying this nest of ours.

It was " Bundle and Go " on the bagpipes. We hurried to the top of the hill and along the ridge just inside the edge of the pines in the direction of the Aora, apprehensive that at every step we should fall upon bands of the enemy, and if we did not come upon themselves, we came upon numerous enough signs of their employment. Little farms lay in the heart of the forest of Creag Dubh, —or rather more on the upper edge of it,—their fields scalloped into the wood, their hills a part of the mountains that divide Loch Finne from Lochow. To-day their roof-trees lay humbled on the hearth, the gable-walls stood black and eerie, with the wind piping between the stones, the cabars or joists held charred arms to heaven, like poor martyrs seeking mercy. Nothing in or about these once happy homesteads, and the pertinents and pendicles near them, had been spared by the robbers.

But we had no time for weeping over such things as we sped on our way along the hillside for Dunchuach, the fort we knew impregnable and sure to have safety for us if we could get through the cordon that was bound to be round it.

It was a dull damp afternoon, an interlude in the frost, chilly and raw in the air, the forest filled with the odours of decaying leaves and moss. The greater part of our way lay below beechwood neither thick nor massive, giving no protection from the rain to the soil below it, so that we walked noisily and uncomfortably in a mash of rotten vegetation. We were the length of the Cherry Park, moving warily, before our first check came. Here, if possible, it were better we should leave the wood and cut across the mouth of the Glen to Dunchuach on the other side. But there was no cover to speak of in that case. The river Aora, plopping and crying on its hurried way down, had to be crossed, if at all, by a wooden bridge, cut at the parapets in the most humorous and useless way in embrasures, every embrasure flanked by port-holes for musketry—a laughable pretence about an edifice in itself no stronger against powder than a child's toy.

On the very lowest edges of the wood, in the shade of a thick plump of beech, strewed generously about the foot by old bushes of whin and bramble, we lay at last studying the open country before us, and wondering how we should win across it to the friendly shelter of Dunchuach. Smoke was rising from every chimney in the castle, which, with its moat and guns, and its secret underground passage to the seashore, was safe against surprises or attacks through all this disastrous Antrim occupation. But an entrance to the castle was beyond us ; there was nothing for it but Dunchuach, and it cheered us wonderfully too, that from the fort there floated a little stream of domestic reek, white-blue against the leaden grey of the unsettled sky.

"Here we are, dears, and yonder would we be," said John, digging herb-roots with his knife and chewing them in an abstraction of hunger, for we had been disturbed at a meal just begun to.

I could see a man here and there between us and the lime-kiln we must pass on our way up Dunchuach. I confessed myself in as black a quandary as ever man experienced. As for Sir Donald—good old soul !—he was now, as always, unable to come to any conclusion except such as John Splendid helped him to.

We lay, as I say, in the plump, each of us under his bush, and the whole of us overhung a foot or two by a brow of land bound together by the spreading beech-roots.

To any one standing on the *bruach* we were invisible, but a step or two would bring him round to the foot of our retreat and disclose the three of us.

The hours passed, with us ensconced there—every hour the length of a day to our impatience and hunger ; but still the way before was barred, for the coming and going of people in the valley was unceasing. We had talked at first eagerly in whispers, but at last grew tired of such un-natural discourse, and began to sleep in snatches for sheer lack of anything else to do. It seemed we were prisoned there till nightfall at least, if the Athole man who found our cave did not track us to our hiding.

I lay on the right of my two friends, a little more awake, perhaps, than they, and so I was the first to perceive a little shaking of the soil, and knew that some one was coming down upon our hiding. We lay tense, our breathing caught at the chest, imposing on ourselves a stillness that swelled the noises of nature round about us—the wind, the river, the distant call of the crows—to a most clamorous and appalling degree.

We could hear our visitor breathing as he moved about cautiously on the stunted grass above us, and so certain seemed discovery that we had our little black knives lying naked along our wrists.

The suspense parched me at the throat till I thought the rasping of my tongue on the roof of my palate seemed like the scraping of a heath-brush in a wooden churn. Unseen we were, we knew, but it was patent that the man above us would be round in front of us at any moment, and there we were to his plain eyesight ! He was within three yards of a steel death, even had he been Fin MacCoul ; but the bank he was standing on—or lying on, as we learned again—crumbled at the edge and threw him among us in a different fashion from that we had looked for.

My fingers were on his throat before I saw that we had for our visitor none other than young MacLachlan.

He had his *sgian dubh* almost at my stomach before our mutual recognition saved the situation.

" You're a great stranger," said John Splendid, with a fine pretence at more coolness than he felt, " and yet I thought Cowal side would be more to your fancy than real Argile in this vexatious time."

"I wish to God I was on Cowal side now!" said the lad, ruefully. "At this minute I wouldn't give a finger-length of the Loch Eck road for the whole of this rich strath."

"I don't suppose you were forced over here," I commented.

"As well here in one way as another," he said. "I suppose you are unaware that Montrose and MacDonald have overrun the whole country. They have sacked and burned the greater part of Cowal; they have gone down as far as Knapdale. I could have been in safety with my own people (and the bulk of your Inneraora people too) by going to Bute or Dunbarton, but I could hardly do that with my kinsfolk still hereabouts in difficulties."

"Where, where?" I cried; "and who do you mean?"

He coughed, in a sort of confusion, I could see, and said he spoke of the Provost and his family.

"But the Provost's gone, man!" said I, "and his family too."

"My cousin Betty is not gone among them," said he; "she's either in the castle yonder—and I hope to God she is—or a prisoner to the MacDonalds, or——"

"The Worst Curse on their tribe!" cried John Splendid, in a fervour.

Betty, it seemed, from a narrative that gave me a stound of anguish, had never managed to join her father in the boats going over to Cowal the day the MacDonalds attacked the town. Terror had seemingly sent her, carrying the child, away behind the town; for though her father and others had put ashore again at the south bay, they could not see her, and she was still unfound when the triumph of the invader made flight needful again.

"Her father would have bided too," said MacLachlan, "but that he had reason to believe she found the safety of the castle. Lying off the quay when the fight was on, some of the people in the other boats saw a woman with a burden run up the riverside to the back of the castle garden, and there was still time to get over the draw-brig then."

MacLachlan himself had come round by the head of the loch, and by going through the Barrabhreac wood and over the shoulder of Duntorval, had taken Inneraora on the rear flank. He had lived several days in a bothy above the Beannan on High Balantyre, and, like ourselves, depended on his foraging upon the night and the luck of the woods.

We lay among the whins and bramble undisturbed till the dusk came on. The rain had stopped, a few stars sedately decked the sky. Bursts of laughing, the cries of comrades, bits of song, came on the air from the town where the Irish caroused. At last between us and Dunchuach there seemed to be nothing to prevent us venturing on if the bridge was clear.

"If not," said Sir Donald, "here's a doomed old man, for I know no swimming."

"There's Edinburgh for you, and a gentleman's education!" said John Splendid, with a dry laugh; and he added, "But I daresay I could do the swimming for the both of us, Sir Donald. I have carried my accoutrements dry over a German river ere now, and I think I could convey you safely over yon bit burn even if it were not so shallow above the bridge as I expect it is after these long frosts."

"I would sooner force the bridge if ten men held it," said MacLachlan. "I have a Highland hatred of the running stream, and small notion to sleep a night in wet tartan."

John looked at the young fellow with a struggle for tolerance. "Well, well," he said; "we have all a touch of the fop in our youth."

"True enough, you're not so young as you were once," put in MacLachlan, with a sly laugh.

"I'm twenty at the heart," cried John,—"at the heart, man,—and do my looks make me more than twice that age? I can sing you, or run you, or dance you. What I thought was that at your age I was dandified too about my clothing. I'll give you the benefit of believing that it's not the small discomfort of a journey in wet tartan you vex yourself over. Have we not—we old campaigners of Lumsden's—soaked our plaids in the running rivers of Low Germanie, and rolled them round us at night to make our hides the warmer, our sleep the snugger? Oh, the old days! Oh, the stout days! God's name, but I ken one man who wearies of these tame and comfortable times!"

"Whether or not," said Sir Donald, anxious to be on, "I wish the top of Dunchuach was under our brogues."

"*Allons, mes amis,* then," said John, and out we set.

Out we went, and we sped swiftly down to the bridge, feeling a sense of safety in the dark and the sound of the water that mourned in a hollow way under the wooden cabars. There was no sentinel, and we crossed dry and safely. On the other side, the fields, broken here and there by dry-stone dykes, a ditch or two, and one long thicket of shrubs, rose in a gentle ascent to the lime-kiln. We knew every foot of the way as 'twere in our own pockets, and had small difficulty in pushing on in the dark. The night, beyond the kiln and its foreign trees, was loud with the call of white-horned owls, sounding so human sometimes that it sent the heart vaulting and brought us to pause in a flurried cluster on the path that we followed closely as it twisted up the hill.

However, we were in luck's way for once. Never a creature challenged our progress until we landed at the north wall of the fort, and crouching in the rotten brake, cried, "Gate, oh!" to the occupants.

A stir got up within; a torch flared on the wall, and a voice asked our tartan and business.

"Is that you, Para Mor?" cried John Splendid. "It's a time for short ceremony. Here are three or four of your closest friends terribly keen to see the inside of a wall."

"Barbreck, is't?" cried Para Mor, holding the flambeau over his head that he might look down on us.

"Who's that with the red tartan?" he asked, speaking of MacLachlan, whose garments shone garish in the light beside our dull Campbell country war-cloth.

"Condemn your parley, Para Mor," cried Sir Donald; "it's young MacLachlan,—open your doors!"

And the gate in a little swung on its hinges to pass us in.

CHAPTER XI.

ON BENS OF WAR.

THIS mount of Dunchuach, on which we now found ourselves ensconced, rises in a cone shape to a height of about eight hundred feet, its bottom being but a matter of a quarter-mile from the castle door. It is wooded to the very nose, almost, except for the precipitous *sgornach* or scaur, that, seen from a distance, looks like a red wound on the face of it. The fort, a square tower of extraordinarily stout masonry, with an eminent roof, had a sconce with escarpment round it, placed on the very edge of the summit. Immediately behind Dunchuach is Duntorvil, its twin peak, that, at less distance than a shout will carry, lifts a hundred feet higher on the north. The two hills make, indeed, but one, in a manner of talking, except for this hundred feet of a hollow worn by a burn lost midway in long sour grasses. It had always been a surprise to me that Argile's grandfather, when he set the fort on the hill, chose the lower of the two eminences, contrary to all good guidance of war. But if he had not full domination on Dunchuach, he had, at any rate, a fine prospect. I think, in all my time, I have never witnessed a more pleasing scene than ever presents itself in clear weather from the brow of this peak. Loch Finne—less, as the whim of the fancy might have it, a loch than a noble river—runs south in a placid band ; the Cowal hills rise high on the left, bare but of heather and gall ; in front is the heart of Argile, green with the forest of Creag Dubh, where the stag bays in the gloaming. For miles behind the town and castle lies a plain, flat and rich, growing the most lush crops. The town itself, that one could almost throw a stone down on, looks like a child's toy. And away to the north and west are the abundant hills, rising higher and higher, sprinkled here and there with spots of moor loch.

The fort this night was held by a hundred men of the body called the Marquis his Halberdiers, a corps of antique heroes whose weapon for ordinary was a long axe, a pretty instrument on a parade of state, but small use, even at close quarters, with an enemy. They had skill of artillery, however, and few of them but had a Highlander's training in the use of the broadsword. Besides two culverins mounted on the less precipitous side of the hill—which was the way we came—they had smaller firearms in galore on the sconce, and many kegs of powder disposed in a recess or magazine at the base of the tower. To the east of the tower itself, and within the wall of the fort (where now is but an old haw-tree), was a governor's house perched on the sheer lip of the hill, so that, looking out at its window, one could spit farther than a musket-ball would carry on the level.

We were no sooner in than MacLachlan was scenting round and into this little house. He came out crestfallen, and went over to the group of halberdiers, who were noisily telling their story to myself and Splendid.

"Are no people here but men?" he asked Para Mor, who was sergeant of the company, and to all appearance in charge of the place.

He caught me looking at him in some wonder, and felt bound, seemingly, to explain himself.

"I had half the hope," said he, "that my cousin had come here; but she'll be in the castle after all, as her father thought."

John Splendid gave me the pucker of an eye and a line of irony about the edge of his lips, that set my blood boiling. I was a foolish and ungoverned creature in those days of no-grace. I cried in my English, "One would think you had a goodman's interest in this bit girl."

MacLachlan leered at me with a most devilish light in his black eyes, and said, "Well, well, I might have even more. Marriage, they say, makes the sweetest woman wersh. But I hope you'll not grudge me, my dear Elrigmore, some anxiety about my own relatives."

The fellow was right enough (that was the worst of it), for a cousin's a cousin in the friendly North; but I found myself for the second time since I came home grudging him the kinship to the Provost of Inneraora's daughter.

That little tirravee passed, and we were soon heartily employed on a supper that had to do duty for two meals. We took it at a rough table in the tower, lighted by a flambeau that sent sparks flying like pigeons into the sombre height of the building which tapered high overhead as a lime-kiln upside down. From this retreat we could see the proof of knavery in the villages below. Far down on Knapdale, and back in the recesses of Lochow, were burning homes, to judge from the blotched sky.

Dunchuach had never yet been attacked, but that was an experience expected at any hour, and its holders were ready for it. They had disposed their guns round the wall in such a way as to command the whole gut between the hills, and consequently the path up from the glens. The town side of the fort wall, and the east side, being on the sheer face (almost) of the rock, called for no artillery.

It was on the morning of the second day there that our defence was put to the test by a regiment of combined Irish and Athole men. The day was misty, with the frost in a hesitancy, a raw gowsty air sweeping over the hills. Para Mor, standing on the little north bastion or ravelin, as his post of sergeant always demanded, had been crooning a ditty and carving a scroll with his hunting-knife on a crook he would maybe use when he got back to the tack where his home was in ashes and his cattle were far to seek, when he heard a crackle of bushes at the edge of the wood that almost reached the hill-top, but falls short for lack of shelter from the sinister wind. In a second a couple of scouts in dirty red and green tartans, with fealdags or pleatless kilts on them instead of the better class philabeg, crept cannily out into the open, unsuspicious that their position could be seen from the fort.

Para Mor stopped his song, projected his firelock over

the wall as he ducked his body behind it—all but an eye and shoulder—and, with a hairy cheek against the stock, took aim at the foremost. The crack of the musket sounded odd and moist in the mist, failing away in a dismal slam that carried but a short distance, yet it was enough to rouse Dunchuach.

We took the wall as we stood,—myself, I remember me, in my kilt, with no jacket, and my shirt-sleeves rolled up to the shoulder ; for I had been putting the stone, a pleasant Highland pastime, with John Splendid, who was similarly disaccoutred.

" All the better for business," said he, though the raw wind, as we lined the wall, cut like sharp steel.

Para Mor's unfortunate gentleman was the only living person to see when we looked into the gut, and he was too little that way to say much about. Para had fired for the head, but struck lower, so that the scout writhed to his end with a red-hot coal among his last morning's viands.

Long after, it would come back to me, the oddity of that spectacle in the hollow—a man in a red fealdag, with his hide-covered buckler grotesquely flailing the grass, he, in the Gaelic custom, making a great moan about his end, and a pair of bickering rooks cawing away heartily as if it was no more than a sheep in the throes of braxy.

After a little the moan of the MacDonald stopped, the crows slanted down to the loch-side, stillness came over the place. We talked in whispers, sped about the walls on the tiptoes of our brogues, and peered wonderingly down to the edge of the wood. Long we waited and wearily, and by-and-by who came out high on the shoulder of Duntorvil but a band of the enemy, marching in good order for the summit of that paramount peak ?

" I hope to God they have no large pieces with them yonder," said John ; " for they'll have a coign there to give us trouble if once they get mother of muskets in train."

But, fortunately for us, no artillery ever came to Duntorvil.

Fully two hundred of the enemy massed on the hill, commanded by a squat officer in breeks and wearing a peruke *Anglicè*, that went oddly with his tartan plaid. He was the master of Clanranald, we learned anon, a cunning person, whose aim was to avail himself of the impetuousness of the kilts he had in his corps. Gaels on the attack, as he knew, are omnipotent as God's thunderbolts : give them a running start at a foe, with no waiting, and they might carry the gates of hell against the Worst One and all his clan ; on a standing defence where coolness and discipline are wanted they have less splendid virtues. Clanranald was well aware that to take his regiment all into the hollow where his scout was stiffening was not only to expose them to the fire of the fort without giving them any chance of quick reply, but to begin the siege off anything but the bounding shoe-sole the Highlander has the natural genius for. What he devised was to try musketry at long range (and to shorten my tale, that failed), then charge from his summit, over the rushy gut, and up the side of Dunchuach, disconcerting our aim and bringing his men in on their courageous heat.

We ran back our pieces through the gorge of the bastions, wheeled them in on the terre-plein back from the wall, and cocked them higher on their trunnions to get them in train for the opposite peak.

" Boom ! " went the first gun, and a bit of brown earth spat up to the left of the enemy, low by a dozen paces.

A silly patter of poor musketry made answer, but their bullets might as well have been aimed at snipe for all the difference it made to us : they came short or spattered against our wall. We could hear the shouts of the foe, and saw their confusion as our third gun sent its message into the very heart of them.

Then they charged Dunchuach.

Our artillery lost its value, and we met them with fusil and caliver.

They came on in a sort of echelon of four companies, close ordered, and not as a more skilly commander would make them, and the leading company took the right. The rushy grass met them with a swish as they bounded over it like roebucks, so fast that our few score of muskets made no impression on them until they were climbing up the steep brae that led to our walls.

Over a man in a minority, waiting, no matter how well ensconced, the onslaught of numbers carried on the wings of hate, there comes a strange feeling—I'll never deny it —a sort of qualm at the pit of the stomach, a notion to cry parley or turn a tail disgraceful. I felt it but for a second, and then I took to my old practice of making a personal foe of one particular man in front of me. This time I chose a lieutenant or sergeant of the MacDonalds (by his tartan), a tall lean rascal, clean shaved, in trews and a tight-fitting *cota gearr* or short coat, with an otter-skin cap on his head, the otter-tail still attached and dangling behind like a Lowlander's queue. He was striding along zealfully, brandishing his sword, and disdaining even to take off his back the bull-hide targe, though all his neighbours kept theirs in front of them on the left arm.

" You have wrecked honest homes ! " I argued with him in my mind. " You put the torch to the widow's thatch, you have driven the cattle from Elrigmore, and what of a girl with dark eyes like the sloe ? Fancy man, man of my fancy ! Oh ! here's the end of your journey ! "

Our assailants, after their usual custom, dropped their pieces, such as had them, when they had fired the first shot, and risked all on the push of the target and the slash of the broad brand, confident even that our six or seven feet of escarpment would never stay their onset any time to speak of. An abattis or a fosse would have made this step futile ; but as things were, it was not altogether impossible that they might surmount our low wall. Our advantage was that the terre-plein on which we stood was three or four feet higher than they were at the outer side of the wall, apart from the fact that they were poised precariously on a step brae. We leaned calmly over the wall and spat at them with pistols now and then as they ran up the hill, with Clanranald and some captains crying them on at the flank or middle. In the plain they left a piper who had naturally not enough wind to keep his instrument going and face the hill at the same time. He strode up and down in the deadliest part of the valley where a well-sent musket ball would never lose him, and played a tune they call "The Galley of the Waves," a Stewart rant with a hint of the zest of the sea in it. Nobody thought of firing at him, though his work was an encouragement to our foes, and anon the hill-tops rang with a duel of pibrochs between him and a lad of our garrison, who got round on the top of the wall near the governor's house and strutted high-shouldered up and down, blasting at the good braggart air of "Baile Inneraora."

Those snorting, wailing, warring pipes mingled oddly with the shout of the fighting men, who had ways of battle new to me in practice though they were in a sense my own countrymen. Gaelic slogans and maledictions they shouted, and when one of them fell in the mob, his immediate comrades never failed to stop short in their charge and coolly rob him of a silver button from his coat, or a weapon if it seemed worth while.

In a little they were soon clamouring against our wall. We laughed and prodded them off with the long-handed axes to get free play with the fusils, and one after another of them fell off, wounded or dead.

"This is the greatest folly ever I saw," said Sir Donald, wiping his brow with a bloody hand.

"I wish I was sure there was no trick in it," said John. He was looking around him and taking a tug at his belt, that braced him by a couple of holes. Then he spat, for luck, on a ball he dropped into his fusil, said a Glassary charm on it as he rammed home the charge and brought the butt to his cheek, aiming at a white-faced Irisher with a leathern waistcoat, who fell backward into a dub of mud and stirred no more.

"Four!" said John; "I could scarcely do better with my own French fusil Mairi Og."

The enemy drew off at a command of their captain, and into the edge of the wood that came up on the left near our summit. We lost our interest in them for a time, watching a man running up the little valley from the right, above Kilmalieu. He came on waving his arms wildly and pointing ahead; but though he was plain to our view, he was out of sight of the enemy on the left.

A long black coat hampered his movements, and he looked gawky enough, stumbling through the rushes.

"If I didn't think the inside of Castle Inneraora was too snug to quit for a deadly hillside," said John, "I could believe yon was our friend the English minister."

"The English minister sure enough!" said half-a-dozen beside us.

"Here's ill-luck for us then!" cried John, with irony. "He'll preach us to death: the fellow's deadlier than the Clanranald banditty."

Some one ran to the post beside the governor's house, and let the gentleman in when he reached it. He was panting like a winded hound, the sweat standing in beads on his shaven jowl, and for a minute or two he could say nothing, only pointing at the back of our fort in the direction of the town.

"A parish visit, is it, sir?" asked John, still in his irony.

The minister sat him down on a log of wood and clutched his side, still pointing eagerly to the south of our fort. No one could understand him, but at last he found a choked and roupy voice.

"A band behind there," he said; "your—front—attack is—but—a—feint."

As he spoke, half-a-dozen men in a north-country tartan got on the top of our low rear wall that we thought impregnable on the lip of the hill, and came on us with a most ferocious uproar. "Badenoch!" they cried in a fashion to rend the hills, and the signal (for such it was more than slogan) brought on our other side the Clanranald gentry.

What followed in that hearthstone fight so hot and brisk took so short a space of time, and happened in so confused and terrible a moment, that all but my personal feeling escapes me. My every sense stirred with something horrible—the numb sound of a musket-butt on a head, the squeal of men wounded at the vitals, and the deeper roar of hate; a smell of blood as I felt it when a boy holding the candle at night to our shepherds slaughtering sheep in the barn at home; before the eyes a red blur cleared at intervals when I rubbed the stinging sweat from my face.

Half a hundred of those back-gait assailants were over our low wall with their axe-hooks and ladders before we could charge and prime, engaging us hand to hand in the cobbled square of our fort, at the tower foot. The harassment on this new side gave the first band of the enemy the chance to surmount our front wall, and they were not slow to take it.

Luckily our halberdiers stood firm in a mass that faced both ways, and as luckily, we had in Master John M'Iver a general of strategy and experience.

"Stand fast, Campbell Halberdiers!" he cried. "It's bloody death, whether we take it like cravens or Gaelic gentlemen!" He laid about him with a good purpose, and whether they tried us in front or rear, the scamps found the levelled pikes and the ready swords. Some dropped beside, but more dropped before us, for the tod in a hole will face twenty times what he will flee from in the open wood, but never a man of all our striving company fought sturdier than our minister, with a weapon snatched from an Athole man he had levelled at a first blow from an oaken rung.

"The sword of the Lord and of Gideon!" he would cry; "for all the kings of the Amorites that dwell in the mountains are gathered together against us." A slim elder man he was, ordinarily with a wan sharp face; now it was flushed and hoved in anger, and he hissed his texts through his teeth as he faced the dogs. Some of youth's schooling was there, a Lowland youth's training with the broadsword, for he handled it like no novice, and even M'Iver gave him "Bravo, *suas e!*"

That we held our ground was no great virtue—we could scarcely do less; but we did more, for soon we had our enemy driven back on the walls. They fought with a frenzy that made them ill to beat, but when a couple of scores of our lads lined the upper wall again and kept back the leak from that airt by the command of John Splendid, it left us the chance of sweeping our unwelcome tenants back again on the lower wall. They stayed stubbornly, but we had weight against them and the advantage of the little brae, and by-and-by we pinned them, like foumarts, against the stones. Most of them put back against the wall, and fought, even with the pike at their vitals, slashing empty air with sword or dirk ; some got on the wall again and threw themselves over the other side, risking the chance of an uglier death on the rocks below.

In less than an hour after the shot of Para Mor (himself a stricken corpse now) rang over Dunchuach, our piper, with a gash on his face, was playing some vaunting air on the walls again, and the fort was free of the enemy, of whom the bulk had fallen back into the wood, and seemingly set out for Inneraora.

Then we gathered and stroked our dead—twenty-and-three ; we put our wounded in the governor's house, and gave them the rough leech-craft of the fighting field ; the dead of the assailants we threw over the rock, and among them was a clean-shaven man in trews and a tight-fitting *cota gearr*, who left two halves of an otter-skin cap behind him.

CHAPTER XII.

A CUP OF WATER.

"I WISH to God!" cried John Splendid, "that I had a drink of Altan-aluinn at this minute, or the well of Beai-loch-an-uarain."

It was my own first thought, or something very like it, when the fighting was over, for a most cruel thirst crisped my palate, and, as ill luck had it, there was not a cup of water in the fort.

"I could be doing with a drop myself," said the English minister. "I'll take a stoup and go down to the well yonder and fetch it."

He spoke of the spout in the gut, a clean little well of hill-water that, winter or summer, kept full to the lip and accessible.

We had gathered into the tower itself (all but a few sentinels), glad for a time to escape the sight of yon shambles of friend and foe that the battle had left us. The air had softened of a sudden from its piercing cold to a mildness balmy by comparison ; the sky had leadened over with a menacing vapour, and over the water—in the great glen between Ben Ime and Ardno—a mist hurried to us like driving smoke. A few flakes of snow fell, lingering in the air as feathers from a nest in spring.

"Here's a friend of Argile back again," said an old halberdier, staunching a savage cut on his knee, and mumbling his words because he was chewing as he spoke an herb that's the poultice for every wound.

"Frost and snow might have been Argile's friend when that proverb was made," said John Splendid, "but here are changed times; our last snow did not keep Colkitto on the safe side of Cladich. Still, if this be snow in earnest," he added with a cheerier tone, "it may rid us of these vermin, who'll find provand iller to get every extra day they bide. Where are you going, Master Gordon?"

"To the well," said the minister, simply, stopping at the port, with a wooden stoup in his hand. "Some of our friends must be burning for a mouthful, poor dears; the wounded flesh is drouthy."

John turned himself round on a keg he sat on, and gave a French shrug he had picked up among foreign cavaliers.

"Put it down, sir," he said; "there's a wheen less precious lives in this hold than a curate's, and for the turn you did us in coming up to alarm us of the rear attack, if for nothing else, I would be sorry to see you come to any skaith. Do you not know that between us and the well there might be death half-a-dozen times? The wood, I'll warrant, is hotching still with those disappointed warriors of Clanranald, who would have no more reverence for your life than for your Geneva bands."

"There's no surer cure for the disease of death in a hind than for the same murrain in a minister of the Gospel—or a landed gentleman," said Gordon, touched in his tone a little by the austerity of his speeches as we heard them at the kirk-session.

John showed some confusion in his face, and the minister had his feet on the steps before he could answer him.

"Stop, stop!" he cried. "Might I have the honour of serving the Kirk for once? I'll get the water from the well, minister, if you'll go in again and see how these poor devils of ours are thriving. I was but joking when I hinted at the risk; our Athole gentry are, like enough, far off by this time."

"I liked you better when you were selfish and told the truth, than now that you're valiant (in a small degree) and excuse it with a lie," quo' the minister, and off he set.

He was beyond the wall, and stepping down the brae before we could be out at the door to look after him.

" Damn his nipped tongue ! " fumed John. " But man ! there's a lovable quirk in his character too. I'll give twenty pounds (Scots) to his kirk-plate at the first chance if he wins out of this fool's escapade of his without injury."

There was no doubt the minister's task had many hazards in it, for he carried stave nor steel as he jogged on with the stoup, over the frank open brae-side, down to the well. Looking at him going down into the left of the gut as unafeared as he had come up on the right of it, I put myself in his place, and felt the skin of my back pimpling at the instinct of lurking enemies.

But Gordon got safely to the well, through the snow, now falling in a heavy shower, dipped out a stoupful, and turned about to come home. A few yards off his path back, to the right and closer to the wood, lay the only man of all the bodies lying in the valley who seemed to have any life left in him. This fellow lay on his side, and was waving his hands feverishly when the minister went up to him, and—as we saw in a dim way through the snow—gave him a drink of the water from the lip of the stoup.

" Sassenach fool ! " said young MacLachlan, parched with thirst, gathering in with a scooped hand the snow as it fell on the wall, and gluttonously sucking it.

" There are many kinds of folly, man," said I ; " and I would think twice before I would grudge a cleric's right to give a mouthful of water to a dying man, even if he was a MacDonald on his way to the Pit."

" Tuts, tuts ! Elrigmore," cried John, " let the young cock crow ; he means no more than that it's hard to be hungry and see your brother feed a foeman. Indeed I could be wishing myself that his reverence was the Good Samaritan on a more fitting occasion."

We were bandying words now, and not so closely watching our friend in the hollow, and it was Sir Donald, standing to a side a little, who called our attention anew, with a cry of alarm.

" Look, lads, look ! " he cried, " God help Gordon ! "

We looked through the snow—a grey veil—and saw two or three men fall on the minister.

John Splendid but stopped a second to say, " It may

be a feint to draw us off the fort ; bide where ye are," and then he leaped over the wall, armed with a claymore picked from the haunch of a halberdier beside him. I was over at his heels, and the pair of us scoured down the brae.

There was some hazard in the enterprise ; I'm ashamed to this day to tell I thought that, at every foot of the way as we ran on. Never before nor since have I felt a wood so sinister, so ghastly, so inspired by dreadful airs, and when it was full on our flank, I kept my head half turned to give an eye to where I was going and an eye to what might come out on my rear. People tell you fear takes wings at a stern climax, that a hot passion fills the brain with blood and the danger blurs to the eye. It's a theory that works but poorly on a forlorn-hope, with a certainty that the enemy are outnumbering you on the rear. With man and ghost, I have always felt the same : give me my back to the wall, and I could pluck up valour enough for the occasion, but there's a spot between the shoulders that would be coward flesh in Hector himself. That, I'm thinking, is what keeps some armies from turning tail to heavy odds.

Perhaps the terror behind (John swore anon he never thought on't till he learned I had, and then he said he felt it worse than I) gave our approach all the more impetuousness, for we were down in the gut before the MacDonald loiterers (as they proved) were aware of our coming. We must have looked unco numerous and stalwart in the driving snow, for the scamps dashed off into the wood as might children caught in a mischief. We let them go, and bent over our friend, lying with a very gashly look by the body of the MacDonald, a man well up in years, now in the last throes, a bullet-wound in his neck and the blood frothing at his mouth.

" Ar't hurt, sir ? " asked John, bending on a knee, but the minister gave no answer.

We turned him round and found no wound but a bruise on the head, that showed he had been attacked with a cudgel by some camp-followers of the enemy, who had neither swords, nor reverence for a priest who was giving a brotherly sup to one of their own tartan. In that driving snow we rubbed him into life again, cruelly pallid, but with no broken bit about him.

"Where's my stoup?" were his first words; "my poor lads upbye must be wearying for water." He looked pleased to see the same beside him where he had set it down, with its water untouched, and then he cast a wae glance on the dead man beside him.

"Poor wretch, poor wretch!" said he.

We took the stoup and our minister up to the summit, and had got him but safely set there when he let out what gave me the route again from Dunchuach, and led to divers circumstances that had otherwise never come into this story if story there was, which I doubt there had never been. Often I've thought me since how pregnant was that Christian act of Gordon in giving water to a foe. Had I gone, or had John gone, for the stoup of water, none of us, in all likelihood, had stirred a foot to relieve yon enemy's drouth; but he found a godly man, though an austere one too on occasion, and paid for the cup of water with a hint in broken English that was worth all the gold in the world to me. Gordon told us the man's dying confidence whenever he had come to himself a little more in the warmth of the fort fire.

"There's a woman and child," said he, "in the wood of Strongara."

CHAPTER XIII.

WHERE TREADS THE DEER.

WHEN the English minister, in his odd lalland Scots, had told us this tale of the dying MacDonald, I found for the first time my feeling to the daughter of the Provost of Inneraora. Before this the thought of her was but a pleasant engagement for the mind at leisure moments; now it flashed on my heart with a stound that yon black eyes were to me the dearest jewels in the world, that lacking her presence these glens and mountains were very cold and empty. I think I gave a gasp that let John Splendid into my secret there and then; but at least I left him no doubt about what I would be at.

"What's the nearer way to Strongara?" I asked; "alongside the river, or through Tombreck?"

He but peered at me oddly a second under his brows —a trifle wistfully, though I might naturally think his mood would be quizzical, then he sobered in a moment. That's what I loved about the man; a fool would have laughed at the bravado of my notion, a man of thinner sentiment would have marred the moment by pointing out difficulties.

"So that's the airt the wind's in!" he said, and then he added, "I think I could show you, not the shortest, but the safest road."

"I need no guidance," I cried in a hurry, "only——"

"Only a friend who knows every wood in the country-side, and has your interest at heart, Colin," he said softly, putting a hand on my elbow and gripping it in a homely way. It was the first time he gave me my Christian name since I made his acquaintance.

His company was not to be denied.

We made up some bear-meal bannocks, and a collop of boiled venison in a knapsack that I carried on my back, borrowed plaids from some of the common soldiery, and set out for Strongara at the mouth of the night, with the snow still driving over the land.

MacLachlan was for with us, but John turned on him with a great deal of determination, and dared him to give extra risk to our enterprise by adding another man to the chance of the enemy seeing us.

The lad met the objection ungraciously, and John took to his flattery.

"The fact is, MacLachlan," said he, taking him aside with a hand on his lapel, and a show of great confidence —"the fact is, we can't be leaving this place in charge of a lot of old *bodachs*—Sir Donald the least able of them all,—and if there's another attack the guidance of the defence will depend on you. You may relish that or you may not ; perhaps after all you would be safer with us——"

MacLachlan put up his chest an inch or two, unconscious that he did it, and whistled a stave of music to give evidence of his indifference. Then he knitted his brows to cogitate, as it were, and—

"Very well ! " said he. "If you come on my coz, you'll bring her back here, or to the castle, I suppose ? "

"I had no thought of running away with the lass, I'll take my oath," cried John, sticking his tongue in the cheek nearest me.

"I wish I could fathom yon fellow's mind," I said to my comrade, as we stepped out through the snow and into the wooded brae-side, keeping a wary eye about for spies of the enemy, whose footprints we came on here and there, but so faint in the fresh snowfall that it was certain they were now in the valley.

"Do you find it difficult ? " asked John. "I thought a man of schooling, with Latin at his tongue's-end, would see to the deepest heart of MacLachlan."

"He's crafty."

"So's the polecat till the fox meets him. Tuts, man, you have a singular jealousy of the creature."

"Since the first day I saw him."

John laughed.

"That was in the Provost's," quo' he, and he hummed a song I caught the meaning of but slightly.

"Wrong, wrong!" said I, striding under the trees as we slanted to the right for Tombreck. "His manner is provoking."

"I've seen him polish it pretty well for the ladies."

"His temper's always on the boil."

"Spirit, man; spirit! I like a fellow of warmth now and then."

"He took it most ungraciously when we put him out of the Provost's house on the night of the squabble in the town."

"It was an awkward position he was in. I'd have been a bit black-browed about it myself," said John. "Man! it's easy to pick holes in the character of an unfriend, and you and MacLachlan are not friendly, for one thing that's not his fault any more than yours."

"You're talking of the girl," I said, sharply, and not much caring to show him how hot my face burned at having to mention her.

"That same," said he; "I'll warrant that if it wasn't for the girl (the old tale! the old tale!), you had thought the young sprig not a bad gentleman after all."

"Oh, damn his soul!" I blurted out. "What is he that he should pester his betters with his attentions?"

"A cousin, I think, a simple cousin-german they tell me," said John, drily; "and in a matter of betters, now —eh?"

My friend coughed on the edge of his plaid, and I could swear he was laughing at me. I said nothing for a while, and with my skin burning, led the way at a hunter's pace. But John was not done with the subject.

"I'm a bit beyond the age of it myself," he said; "but that's no reason why I shouldn't have eyes in my head. I know how much put about you are to have this young fellow gallivanting round the lady."

"Jealous, you mean," I cried.

"I didn't think of putting it that way."

"No; it's too straightforward a way for you,—ever the roundabout way for you. I wish to God you would sometimes let your Campbell tongue come out of the kink, and say what you mean."

With a most astonishing steady voice for a man as livid as the snow on the hair of his brogues, and with his hand on the hilt of his dirk, John cried—

"Stop a bit."

I faced him in a most unrighteous humour, ready to quarrel with my shadow.

"For a man I'm doing a favour to, Elrigmore," he said, "you seem to have a poor notion of politeness. I'm willing to make some allowance for a lover's tirravee about a woman who never made tryst with him; but I'll allow no man to call down the credit of my clan and name."

A pair of gowks, were we not, in that darkening wood, quarrelling on an issue as flimsy as a spider's web, but who will say it was not human nature? I daresay we might have come to hotter words and bloody blows there and then, but for one of the trifles that ever come in the way to change—not fate, for that's changeless, but the semblance of it.

"My mother herself was a Campbell of an older family than yours," I started to say, to show I had some know-ledge of the breed, and at the same time a notion of fairness to the clan.

This was fresh heather on the fire.

"Older!" he cried; "she was a MacVicar as far as ever I heard; it was the name she took to kirk with her when she married your father."

"So," said I; "but——"

"And though I allow her grandfather Dol-a-mhonadh [Donald-of-the-Hills] was a Campbell, it was in a round-about way; he was but the son of one of the Craignish gentry."

"You yourself——"

"Sir!" said he in a new tone, as cold as steel and as sharp, misjudging my intention.

"You yourself are no more than a M'Iver."

"And what of that?" he cried, cooling down a bit. "The M'Ivers of Asknish are in the direct line from Duncan, Lord of Lochow. We had Pennymore, Stronshira, and Glenaora as cadets of Clan Campbell when your Craignish cross-breeds were under the salt."

"Only by the third cousin," said I; "my father has told me over and over again that Duncan's son had no heir."

And so we went into all this perplexity of Highland pedigree like old wives at a waulking, forgetting utterly that what we began to quarrel about was the more serious charge of lying. M'Iver was most frantic about the business, and I think I was cool, for I was never a person that cared a bodle about my history bye the second genera- tion. They might be lairds or they might be lackeys for all the differ it made to me. Not that there were any lackeys among them. My grandfather was the grandson of Tormaid Mor, who held the whole east side of Lochow from Ford to Sonachan, and we have at home the four- posted bed that Tormaid slept on when the heads of the house of Argile were lying on white-hay or chaff.

At last John broke into a laugh.

"Aren't you the *amadan* to be biting the tongue between your teeth?" he said.

"What is it?" I asked, constrained to laugh too.

"You talk about the crook in our Campbell tongue in one breath," said he, "and in the next you would make yourself a Campbell more sib to the chief than I am my- self. Don't you think we might put off our little affairs of family history till we find a lady and a child in Stron- gara?"

"No more of it, then," said I. "Our difference began on my fool's notion that because I had something of what you would call a liking for this girl, no one else should let an eye light on her."

By now we were in a wide glade in the Tombreck wood. On our left we could see lying among the grey snow the house of Tombreck, with no light nor lowe (as the saying goes); and though we knew better than to expect there might be living people in it, we sped down to see the place.

"There's one chance in a million she might have ven- tured here," I said.

A most melancholy dwelling! Dwelling indeed no

more but for the hoodie-crow, and for the fawn of the hill that years after I saw treading over the grass-grown lintel of its door. To-night the place was full of empty airs and ghosts of sounds inexplicable, wailing among the cabars that jutted black and scarred mid-way from wall to wall. The byre was in a huddle of damp thatch, and strewn (as God's my judge) by the bones of the cattle the enemy had refused to drive before them in the sauciness of their glut. A desolate garden slept about the place, with bush and tree—once tended by a family of girls, left orphan and desolate for evermore.

We went about on tiptoes as it might be in a house of the dead, and peeped in at the windows at where had been chambers lit by the cheerful cruisie or dancing with peat-fire flame—only the dark was there, horrible with the odours of char, or the black joist against the dun sky. And then we went to the front door (for Tombreck was a gentle-house), and found it still on the hinges, but hanging half back to give view to the gloomy interior. It was a spectacle to chill the heart, a house burned in hatred, the hearth of many songs and the chambers of love, merry-making, death, and the children's feet, robbed of every interest but its ghosts and the memories of them they came to.

"It were useless to look here ; she is not here," I said in a whisper to my comrade.

He stood with his bonnet in his hand, dumb for a space, then speaking with a choked utterance.

"Our homes, our homes, Colin ! " he cried. "Have I not had the happy nights in those same walls, those harmless hospitable halls, those dead halls ? "

And he looked broadcast over the country-side.

"The curse of Conan and the black stones on the hands that wrought this work ! " he said. "Poison to their wells ; may the brutes die far afield ! "

The man was in a tumult of grief and passion, the tears, I knew by his voice, welling to his eyes. And indeed I was not happy myself, had not been happy indeed, by this black home, even if the girl I loved was waiting me at the turn of the road.

"Let us be going," I said at last.

" She might be here ; she might be in the little plantation ! " he said (and still in the melancholy and quiet of
the place we talked in whispers).

" Could you not give a call, a signal ? " he asked ; and
I had mind of the call I had once taught her, the doleful
pipe of the curlew.

I gave it with hesitancy to the listening night. It
came back an echo from the hills, but brought no other
answer.

A wild bird roosting somewhere in the ruined house
flapped out by the door and over us. I am not a believer
in the ghostly—at least to the extent of some of our
people ; yet I was alarmed, till my reason came to me
and the badinage of the professors at college, who had
twitted me on my fears of the mischancy. But M'Iver
clutched me by the shoulder in a frenzy of terror. I
could hear his teeth chittering as if he had come out of
the sea.

" Name of God ! " he cried, " what was yon ? "

" But a night-hag," said I.

He was ashamed of his weakness ; but the night, as he
said, had too many holes in it for his fancy.

And so we went on again across the hill-face in the
sombre gloaming. It was odd that the last time I had
walked on this hillside had been for a glimpse of that same
girl we sought to-night. Years ago, when I was a lad, she
had on a summer been sewing with a kinswoman in Carlunnan, the mill croft beside a linn of the river, where the
salmon plout in a most wonderful profusion, and I had
gone at morning to the hill to watch her pass up and down
in the garden of the mill, or feed the pigeons at the round
doo-cot, content (or wellnigh content) to see her and
fancy the wind in her tresses, the song at her lip. In these
mornings the animals of the hill and the wood and I
were friendly ; they guessed somehow, perhaps, no harm
was in my heart : the young roes came up unafraid, almost
to my presence, and the birds fluttered like comrades
about me, and the little animals that flourish in the wild
dallied boldly in my path. It was a soft and tranquil
atmosphere, it was a world (I think now) very happy and
unperplexed. And at evening, after a hurried meal, I

was off over the hills to this brae anew, to watch her who gave me an unrest of the spirit, unappeasable but precious. I think, though the mornings were sweet, 'twas the eve that was sweeter still. All the valley would be lying soundless and sedate, the hills of Salachary and the forest of Creag Dubh purpling in the setting sun, a rich gold tipping Dunchuach like a thimble. Then the eastern woods filled with dark caverns of shade, wherein the tall trunks of the statelier firs stood grey as ghosts. What was it, in that precious time, gave me, in the very heart of my happiness, a foretaste of the melancholy of coming years? My heart would swell, the tune upon my lip would cease, my eyes would blur foolishly, looking on that prospect most magic and fine. Rarely, in that happy age, did I venture to come down and meet the girl, but—so contrary is the nature of man!—the day was happier when I worshipped afar, though I went home fuming at my own lack of spirit.

To-day, my grief! how different the tale! That by-gone time loomed upon me like a wave borne down on a mariner on a frail raft, the passion of the past ground me inwardly in a numb pain.

We stumbled through the snow, and my comrade—good heart!—said never a word to mar my meditation. On our right the hill of Meall Ruadh rose up like a storm-cloud ere the blackest of the night fell; we walked on the edges of the plantations, surmising our way by the aid of the grey snow around us.

It was not till we were in the very heart of Strongara wood that I came to my reason and thought what folly was this to seek the wanderer in such a place in dead of night. To walk that ancient wood, on the coarse and broken ground, among fallen timber, bog, bush, water-pass, and hillock, would have tried a sturdy forester by broad day; it was, to us weary travellers, after a day of sturt, a madness to seek through it at night for a woman and child whose particular concealment we had no means of guessing.

M'Iver, natheless, let me flounder through that perplexity for a time, fearful, I suppose, to hurt my feelings by showing me how little I knew of it, and finally he hinted at three cairns he was acquaint with, each elevated somewhat over the general run of the country, and if not the harbourage a refugee would make for, at least the most suitable coign to overlook the Strongara wood.

" Lead me anywhere, for God's sake ! " said I ; " I'm as helpless as a mowdie on the sea-beach."

He knew the wood as 'twere his own garden, for he had hunted it many times with his cousin, and so he led me briskly, by a kind of natural path, to the first cairn. Neither there nor at the second did I get answer to my whistle.

" We'll go up on the third," said John, " and bide there till morning ; scouring a wood in this fashion is like hunting otters in the deep sea."

We reached the third cairn when the hour was long past midnight. I piped again in vain, and having ate part of our collop, we set us down to wait the dawn. The air, for mid-winter, was almost congenial ; the snow fell no longer ; the north part of the sky was wondrous clear and even jubilant with star.

CHAPTER XIV.

MY LADY AND THE CHILD.

I WOKE with a shiver at the hour before dawn, that strange hour when the bird turns on the bough to change his dream, when the wild-cat puts out his tongue to taste the air and curls more warmly into his own fur, when the leaf of the willows gives a tremor in the most airless morning. M'Iver breathed heavily beside me, rolled in his plaid to the very nose, but the dumb cry of the day in travail called him, too, out of the chamber of sleep, and he turned on his back with a snatch of a soldier's drill on his lips, but without opening his eyes.

We were on the edge of a glade of the wood, at the watershed of a small burn that tinkled among its ice along the ridge from Tombreck, dividing close beside us, half of it going to Shira Glen and half to Aora. The tall trees stood over us like sentinels, coated with snow in every bough; a cool crisp air fanned me, with a hint in it, somehow, of a smouldering wood-fire. And I heard close at hand the call of an owl, as like the whimper of a child as ever howlet's vesper mocked. Then to my other side, my plaid closer about me, and to my dreaming anew.

It was the same whimper waked me a second time, too prolonged to be an owl's complaint, and I sat upright to listen. It was now the break of day. A faint grey light brooded among the tree-tops.

" John ! John ! " I said in my companion's ear, shaking his shoulder.

He stood to his feet in a blink, wide awake, fumbling

at his sword-belt as a man at hurried wakings on foreign shores.

"What is it ? " he asked, in a whisper.

I had no need to answer him, for anew the child's cry rose in the wood—sharp, petulant, hungry. It came from a thick clump of undergrowth to the left of our night's lodging, not sixty yards away, and in the half-light of the morning had something of the eerie about it.

John Splendid crossed himself ere he had mind of his present creed, and " God sain us ! " he whispered ; " have we here banshee or warlock ! "

" I'll warrant we have no more than what we seek," said I, with a joyous heart, putting my tartan about me more orderly, and running a hand through my hair.

" I've heard of unco uncanny things assume a wean's cry in a wood," said he, very dubious in his aspect.

I laughed at him, and " Come away, 'ille," I said ; " here's the Provost's daughter." And I was hurrying in the direction of the cry.

M'Iver put a hand on my shoulder.

" Canny, man, canny ; would ye enter a lady's chamber (even the glade of the wood) without tirling at the pin ? "

We stopped, and I softly sounded my curlew-call— once, twice, thrice.

The echo of the third time had not ceased on the hill when out stepped Betty. She looked miraculous tall and thin in the haze of the dawn, with the aspiring firs behind her, pallid at the face, wearied in her carriage, and torn at her kirtle by whin or thorn. The child clung at her coats, a ruddy brat, with astonishment stilling its whimper.

For a little the girl half misdoubted us, for the wood behind us and the still sombre west left us in a shadow, and there was a tremor in her voice as she challenged in English—

" Is that you, Elrigmore ? "

I went forward at a bound, in a stupid rapture that made her shrink in alarm ; but M'Iver lingered in the rear, with more discretion than my relations to the girl gave occasion for.

" Friends ! oh, am not I glad to see you ? " she said simply, her wan face lighting up. Then she sat down on a hillock and wept in her hands. I gave her awkward comfort, my wits for once failing me, my mind in a confusion, my hands, to my own sense, seeming large, coarse, and in the way. Yet to have a finger on her shoulder was a thrill to the heart, to venture a hand on her hair was a passionate indulgence.

The bairn joined in her tears till M'Iver took it in his arms. He had a way with little ones that had much of magic in it, and soon this one was nestling to his breast with its sobs sinking, an arm round his neck.

More at the pair of them than at me did Betty look with interest when her tears were concluded.

"Amn't I like myself this morning?" asked John, jocularly, dandling the bairn in his arms.

Betty turned away without a reply, and when the child was put down and ran to her, she scarcely glanced on it, but took it by the hand and made to go before us, through the underwood she had come from.

"Here's my home, gentlemen," she said, "like the castle of Colin Dubh, with the highest ceiling in the world and the stars for candles."

We might have passed it a score of times in broad daylight and never guessed its secret. It was the beildy side of the hill. Two fir-trees had fallen at some time in the common fashion of wind-blown pines, with their roots clean out of the earth, and raised up, so that coming together at two edges they made two sides of a triangle. To add to its efficiency as a hiding-place, some young firs grew at the open third side of the triangle.

In this confined little space (secure enough from any hurried search) there was still a *greasach*, as we call it, the ember of a fire that the girl had kindled with a spark from a flint the night before, to warm the child, and she had kept it at the lowest extremity short of letting it die out altogether, lest it should reveal her whereabouts to any searchers in the wood.

We told her our story and she told us hers. She had fled on the morning of the attack, in the direction of the castle, but found her way cut off by a wing of the enemy, a number of whom chased her as she ran with the child up the river-side to the Cairnbaan, where she eluded her pursuers among his lordship's shrubberies, and discovered a road to the wood. For a week she found shelter and food in a cow-herd's abandoned bothy among the alders of Tarra-dubh; then hunger sent her travelling again, and she reached Leacainn Mhor, where she shared the cotter's house with a widow woman who went out to the burn with a kail-pot and returned no more, for the tardy bullet found her. The murderers were ransacking the house when Betty and the child were escaping through the byre. This place of concealment in Strongara she sought by the advice of a Glencoe man well up in years, who came on her suddenly, and, touched by her predicament, told her he and his friends had so well beaten that place, it was likely to escape further search.

"And so I am here with my charge," said the girl, affecting a gaiety it were hard for her to feel. "I could be almost happy and content, if I were assured my father and mother were safe, and the rest of my kinsfolk."

"There's but one of them in all the countryside," I said. "Young MacLachlan, and he's on Dunchuach."

To my critical scanning her cheek gave no flag.

"Oh, my cousin!" she said. "I am pleased that he is safe, though I would sooner hear he was in Cowal than in Campbell country."

"He's honoured in your interest, madam," I could not refrain from saying, my attempt at raillery I fear a rather forlorn one.

She flushed at this, but said never a word, only biting her nether lip and fondling the child.

I think we put together a cautious little fire and cooked some oats from my *dorlach*, though the ecstasy of the meeting with the girl left me no great recollection of all that happened. But in a quiet part of the afternoon we sat snugly in our triangle of fir roots and discoursed of trifles that had no reasonable relation to our precarious state. Betty had almost an easy heart, the child slept on my comrade's plaid, and I was content to be in her company and hear the little turns and accents of her voice, and watch the light come and go in her face, and the smile hover, a little wae, on her lips at some pleasant tale of M'Iver's.

"How came you round about these parts?" she asked —for our brief account of our doings held no explanation of our presence in the wood of Strongara.

I

" Ask himself here," said John, cocking a thumb over his shoulder at me ; " I have the poorest of scents on the track of a woman."

Betty turned to me with less interest in the question than she had shown when she addressed it first to my friend.

I told her what the Glencoe man had told the parson, and she sighed. " Poor man ! " said she, " (blessing with him !) it was he that sent me here to Strongara, and gave me tinder and flint."

" We could better have spared any of his friends, then," said I. " But you would expect some of us to come in search of you ? "

" I did," she said in a hesitancy, and crimsoning in a way that tingled me to the heart with the thought that she meant no other than myself. She gave a caressing touch to the head of the sleeping child, and turned to M'Iver, who lay on his side with his head propped on an elbow, looking out on the hill-face.

" Do you know the bairn ? " she asked.

" No," he said, with a careless look where it lay as peaceful as in a cradle rocked by a mother's foot.

" It's the oe of Peggie Mhor," she said.

" So," said he ; " poor dear ! " and he turned and looked out again at the snow.

We were, in spite of our dead Glencoe man's assurance, in as wicked a piece of country as well might be. No snow had fallen since we left Tombreck, and from that dolorous ruin almost to our present retreat was the patent track of our march.

" I'm here, and I'm making a fair show at an easy mind," said M'Iver ; " but I've been in cheerier circumstances ere now."

" So have I, for that part of it," said Betty with spirit, half humorously, half in an obvious punctilio.

" Mistress," said he, sitting up gravely, " I beg your pardon. Do you wonder if I'm not in a mood for saying dainty things ? Our state's precarious (it's needless to delude ourselves otherwise), and our friend Sandy and his bloody gang may be at a javelin's throw from us as we sit here. I wish——"

He saw the girl's face betray her natural alarm, and

amended his words almost too quickly for the sake of the illusion.

"Tuts, tuts!" he cried. "I forgot the wood was searched before, and here I'm putting a dismal black face on a drab business. We might be a thousand times worse. I might be a clay-cold corp with my last week's wage unspent in my sporran, as it happens to be, and here I'm to the fore with four or five MacDonalds to my credit. If I've lost my mercantile office as mine-manager (curse your trades and callings!) my sword is left me; you have equal fortune, Elrigmore; and you, Mistress Brown, have them you love spared to you."

Again the girl blushed most fiercely. "Thank God! Thank God!" she cried in a stifled ecstasy, "and O! but I'm grateful." And anew she fondled the little bye-blow as it lay with its sunny hair on the soldier's plaid.

John glanced at her from the corners of his eyes with a new expression, and asked her if she was fond of bairns.

"Need you ask that of a woman?" she said. "But for the company of this one on my wanderings, my heart had failed me a hundred times a-day. It was seeing him so helpless that gave me my courage: the dark at night in the bothy and the cot and the moaning wind of this lone spot had sent me crazy if I had not this little one's hand in mine, and his breath in my hair as we lay together."

"To me," said John, "they're like flowers, and that's the long and the short of it."

"You're like most men, I suppose," said Betty, archly; "fond of them in the abstract, and with small patience for the individuals of them. This one now—you would not take half the trouble with him I found a delight in. But the nursing of bairns—even their own—is not a soldier's business."

"No, perhaps not," said M'Iver, surveying her gravely; "and yet I've seen a soldier, a rough hired cavalier, take a wonderful degree of trouble about a duddy little bairn of the enemy in the enemy's country. He was struck —as he told me after—by the look of it sitting in a scene of carnage, orphaned without the sense of it, and he carried it before him on the saddle for a many leagues' march till he found a peaceful wayside cottage, where he gave it in the charge of as honest a woman, to all appearance, as these parts could boast. He might even—for all I know to the contrary—have fairly bought her attention for it by a season's paying of the kreutzers, and I know it cost him a duel with a fool who mocked the sentiment of the deed."

"I hope so brave and good a man was none the worse for his duel in a cause so noble," said the girl, softly.

"Neither greatly brave nor middling good," said John, laughing, "at least to my way of thinking, and I know him well. But he was no poorer but by the kreutzers for his advocacy of an orphan bairn."

"I think I know the man," said I, innocently, "and his name would be John."

"And John or George," said the girl, "I could love him for his story."

M'Iver lifted a tress of the sleeping child's hair and toyed with it between his fingers.

"My dear, my dear!" said he; "it's a foolish thing to judge a man's character by a trifle like yon; he's a poor creature who has not his fine impulse now and then; and the man I speak of, as like as not, was dirling a wanton flagon (or maybe waur) ere nightfall, or slaying with cruelty and zest the bairn's uncles in the next walled town he came to. At another mood he would perhaps balance this lock of hair against a company of burghers but fighting for their own fire-end."

"The hair is not unlike your own," said Betty, comparing with quick eyes the curl he held and the curls that escaped from under the edge of his flat blue bonnet.

"May every hair of his be a candle to light him safely through a mirk and dangerous world," said he, and he began to whittle assiduously at a stick, with a little black oxter-knife he lugged from his coat.

"Amen!" said the girl, bravely; "but he were better with the guidance of a good father, and that there seems small likelihood of his enjoying—poor thing!"

A constraint fell on us; it may have been there before, but only now I felt it myself. I changed the conversation, thinking that perhaps the child's case was too delicate a subject, but unhappily made the plundering of our glens my dolorous text, and gloom fell like a mort-cloth on our little company. If my friend was easily uplifted, made buoyantly cheerful by the least accident of life, he was as prone to a hellish melancholy when fate lay low. For the rest of the afternoon he was ever staving with a gloomy brow about the neighbourhood, keeping an eye, as he said, to the possible chance of the enemy.

Left thus for long spaces in the company of Betty and the child, that daffed and croodled about her, and even became warmly friendly with me for the sake of my Paris watch and my glittering waistcoat buttons, I made many gallant attempts to get on my old easy footing. That was the wonder of it : when my interest in her was at the lukewarm, I could face her repartee with as good as she gave ; now that I loved her (to say the word and be done with it), my words must be picked and chosen and my tongue must stammer in a contemptible awkwardness. Nor was she, apparently, quite at her ease, for when our talk came at any point too close on her own person, she was at great pains adroitly to change it to other directions.

I never, in all my life, saw a child so muckle made use of. It seemed, by the most wonderful of chances, to be ever needing soothing or scolding or kissing or running after in the snow, when I had a word to say upon the human affections, or a compliment to pay upon some grace of its most assiduous nurse.

"I'm afraid," said Betty at last, "you learned some courtiers' flatteries and coquetries in your travels. You should have taken the lesson like your friend and fellow-cavalier M'Iver, and got the trick of keeping a calm heart."

"M'Iver!" I cried. "He's an old hand at the business."

She put her lips to the child's neck and kissed it tumultuously.

"Not—not at the trade of lovier?" she asked after a while, carelessly keeping up the crack.

"Oh no!" I said, laughing. "He's a most religious man."

"I would hardly say so much," she answered, coldly ; "for there have been tales—some idle, some otherwise—about him, but I think his friend should be last to hint at any scandal."

Good heavens ! here was a surprise for one who had no more notion of traducing his friend than of miscalling

the Shorter Catechism. The charge stuck in my gizzard.
I fumed and sweat, speechless at the injustice of it, while
the girl held herself more aloof than ever, busy preparing
for our evening meal.

But I had no time to put myself right in her estimate
of me before M'Iver came back from his airing with an
alarming story.

" It's time we were taking our feet from here," he cried
running up to us. " I've been up on Meall Ruadh there,
and I see the whole countryside's in a confusion. Pipers
are blowing away down the glen and guns are firing ; if
it's not a muster of the enemy preparatory to their quitting
the country, it's a call to a more particular search in the
hills and woods. Anyway we must be bundling."

He hurriedly stamped out the fire, that smoked a faint
blue reek which might have advertised our whereabouts,
and Betty clutched the child to her arms, her face again
taking the hue of hunt and fear she wore when we first
set eyes on her in the morning.

" Where is safety ? " she asked, hopelessly. " Is there
a sheep-fank or a sheiling-bothy in Argile that is not at
the mercy of those blood-hounds ? "

" If it wasn't for the snow on the ground," said M'Iver,
" I could find a score of safe enough hidings between
here and the Beannan." " Heavens ! " he added, " when
I think on it, the Beannan itself is the place for us ; it's
the one safe spot we can reach by going through the
woods without leaving any trace, if we keep under the
trees and in the bed of the burn."

We took the bairn in turns, M'Iver and I, and the four
of us set out for the opposite side of Glenaora for the *eas*
or gully called the Beannan, that lay out of any route
likely to be followed by the enemy, whether their object
was a retreat or a hunting. But we were never to reach
this place of refuge, as it happened ; for M'Iver, leading
down the burn by a yard or two, had put his foot on the
path running through the pass beside the three bridges,
when he pulled back, blanching more in chagrin than
apprehension.

" Here they are," he said. " We're too late ; there's a
band of them on the march up this way."

At our back was the burned ruin of a house that had

belonged to a shepherd who was the first to flee to the
town when the invaders came. Its byre was almost
intact, and we ran to it up the burn as fast as we could,
and concealed ourselves in the dark interior. Birds came
chirping under the eaves of thatch and by the vent-holes,
and made so much bickering to find us in their sanctuary
that we feared the bye-passers, who were within a whisper
of our hiding, would be surely attracted. Band after
band of the enemy passed, laden in the most extraordinary
degree with the spoil of war. They had only a rough sort
of discipline in their retirement : the captains or chieftains
marched together, leaving the companies to straggle as
they might, for was not the country deserted by every
living body but themselves ? In van of them they drove
several hundreds of black and red cattle, and with the
aid of some rough ponies, that pulled such sledges (called
carns) as are used for the hauling home of peat on hilly
land, they were conveying huge quantities of household
plenishing and the merchandise of the burgh town.

Now we had more opportunity of seeing those coarse
savage forces than on any occasion since they came to
Argile, for the whole of them had mustered at Inneraora
after scouring the shire, and were on their march out of
the country to the north, fatter men and better put-on
than when they came. Among them were numerous
tartans, either as kilt, trews, or plaid ; the bonnet was
universal, except that some of the officers wore steel
helms, with a feather tip in them, and a clan badge of
heather or whin or moss, and the dry oak-stalk whimsy
of Montrose. They had come bare-footed and bare-
buttocked (many of the privates of them) to Campbell
country ; now, as I say, they were very snod, the scurviest
of the knaves set up with his hosen and brogues. Sturdy
and black, or lank and white-haired like the old sea-
rovers, were they, with few among them that ever felt
the razor edge, so that the hair coated them to the very
eyeholes, and they looked like wolves. The pipers, of
whom there were three, were blasting lustily at Clanranald's march when they came up the lower part of the
Glen, according to M'Iver, who had heard them from
Meall Ruadh ; but now the music was stopped, and all
were intent upon driving the cattle or watching their

stolen gear, for doubtless among such thieves there was not as much honour as would prevent one from picking his neighbour's sporran.

We lay buried to the head in bracken that filled one side of the byre, and keeked through the plenteous holes in the dry-stone wall at the passing army. Long gaps were between the several clans, and the Irish came last. It seemed—they moved so slowly on account of the cattle—that the end of the cavalcade was never to come ; but at length came the baggage and the staff of Montrose himself. Then I got my first look of the man whose name stinks in the boar's snout to this day. A fellow about thirty-three years of age, of mid height, hair of a very dark red, hanging in a thick fell on the shoulders of the tartan jacket (for he wore no armour), with a keen scrutinising eye, and his beard trimmed in the foreign vein. He sat his horse with considerable ease and grace, and was surrounded by half-a-dozen of the chiefs who had come under his banner. The most notable-looking of these was Alasdair MacDonald, the Major-General, an uncouth dog, but a better general, as I learned later, than ever God or practice made James Grahame of Montrose ; with John of Moidart, the Captain of Clanranald, Donald Glas MacRanald of Keppoch, the laird of Glencoe, Stewart of Appin, and one of the Knoydart house, all of whilk we distinguished by their tartans and badges.

In the mien of these savage chiefs there was great elation that Montrose had little share in, to all appearance. He rode moodily, and when fair opposite our place of concealment he stopped his horse as if to quit the sell, but more likely to get, for a little, out of the immediate company of his lawless troops. None of those home-returning Gaels paid heed to his pause, for they were more Alasdair Macdonald's men than his ; MacDonald brought them to the lair of the boar, MacDonald glutted their Highland thirst for Campbell blood, MacDonald had compelled this raid in spite of the protests of the nobleman who held the King's Commission and seal.

For some minutes his lordship stood alone on the pathway. The house where we lay was but one, and the meanest, among a numerous cluster of such drear memorials of a black business, and it was easy to believe this generalissimo had some gloomy thoughts as he gazed on the work he had lent consent to. He looked at the ruins and he looked up the pass at his barbarians, and shrugged his shoulders with a contempt there was no mistaking.

"I could bring him down like a capercailzie," said M'Iver, coolly, running his eye along his pistol and cocking it through his keek-hole.

"For God's sake don't shoot!" I said, and he laughed quietly.

"Is there anything in my general deportment, Colin, that makes ye think me an assassin or an idiot? I never wantonly shot an unsuspecting enemy, and I'm little likely to shoot Montrose and have a woman and bairn suffer the worst for a stupid moment of glory."

As ill luck would have it, the bairn, that had been playing peacefully in the dusk, at this critical minute let up a cry Montrose plainly heard.

"We're lost, we're lost," said Betty, trembling till the crisp dry bracken rustled about her, and she was for instant flight.

"If we're lost, there's a marquis will go travelling with us," said M'Iver, covering his lordship's heart with his pistol.

Had Montrose given the slightest sign that he intended to call back his men to tread out this last flicker of life in Aora Glen he would never have died on the gibbet at the Grassmarket of Dunedin. Years after, when Grahame met his doom (with much more courtliness and dignity than I could have given him credit for), M'Iver would speak of his narrow escape at the end of the raiding.

"I had his life in the crook of my finger," he would say; "had I acted on my first thought, Clan Campbell would never have lost Inverlochy; but *bha e air an dàn*, —what will be will be,—and Grahame's fate was not in the crook of my finger, though so I might think it. Aren't we the fools to fancy sometimes our human wills decide the course of fate, and the conclusions of circumstances? From the beginning of time, my Lord Marquis of Montrose was meant for the scaffold."

Montrose, when he heard the child's cry, only looked to either hand to see that none of his friends heard it, and finding there was no one near him, took off his Highland bonnet, lightly, to the house where he jaloused there was a woman with the wean, and passed slowly on his way.

"It's so honest an act," said John, pulling in his pistol, "that I would be a knave to advantage myself of the occasion."

A generous act enough. I daresay there were few in the following of James Grahame would have borne such a humane part at the end of a bloody business, and I never heard our people cry down the name of Montrose (bitter foe to me and mine) but I minded to his credit that he had a compassionate ear for a child's cry in the ruined hut of Aora Glen.

Montrose gave no hint to his staff of what he had heard, for when he joined them, he nor they turned round to look behind. Before us now, free and open, lay the way to Inneraora. We got down before the dusk fell, and were the first of its returning inhabitants to behold what a scandal of charred houses and robbed chests the Athole and Antrim caterans had left us.

In the grey light the place lay tenantless and melancholy, the snow of the silent street and lane trodden to a slush, the evening star peeping between the black roof-timbers, the windows lozenless, the doors burned out or hanging off their hinges. Before the better houses were piles of goods and gear turned out on the causeway. They had been turned about by pike-handles and trodden upon with contemptuous heels, and the pick of the plenishing was gone. Though upon the rear of the kirk there were two great mounds, that showed us where friend and foe had been buried, that solemn memorial was not so poignant to the heart as the poor relics of the homes gutted and sacked. The Provost's tenement, of all the lesser houses in the burgh, was the only one that stood in its outer entirety, its arched ceils proof against the malevolent fire. Yet its windows gaped black and empty. The tide was in close on the breast-wall behind, and the sound of it came up and moaned in the close like the sough of a sea-shell held against the ear.

We stood in the close, the three of us (the bairn clinging in wonder to the girl's gown), with never a word for a space, and that sough of the sea was almost a coronach.

CHAPTER XV.

CONFESSIONS OF A MARQUIS.

In a few hours, as it were, the news that the enemy had left the country was put about the shire, and people returned to pick up the loose ends of the threads of family and affairs. Next day my lord the Marquis came round Lochlong and Glencroe in a huge chariot with four wheels, the first we had ever seen in these parts, a manner of travel incumbent upon him because of a raxed shoulder he had met with at Dunbarton. He came back to a poor reception: the vestiges of his country's most bitter extremity were on every hand, and, what was bound to be embarrassing to any nobleman of spirit, there was that in the looks and comportment of his clansmen that must have given MacCailein some unpleasant thought.

Behind his lordship came eleven hundred Lowland levies that had been with Baillie in England, and to command them came his cousin, Sir Duncan Campbell of Auchinbreac, luckily new over from Ireland, and in the spirit for campaigning. A fiery cross was sent round the clan, that in better times should easily have mustered five thousand of the prettiest lads ever trod heather, but it brought only a remnant of a thousand, and the very best that would have been welcome under the galley flag were too far afield for the summons to reach them in time. But every well-affected branch of Clan Campbell sent its gentlemen to officer our brigade.

A parley of war held in the castle determined on immediate pursuit of Montrose to Lochaber, keeping within easy distance, but without attacking till he was checked

in front by troops that had gone up to flank him by way
of Stirling. I was at the council, but had little to do with
its decision, though the word of M'Iver and myself (as
was due to cavaliers of experience) was invited with
respect.

We were to march in two days; and as I had neither
house nor ha' to shelter me, seeing the old place up the
glen was even more of a ruin than in Donald Gorm's
troubles, when the very roof-tree was thrown in Dhuloch,
I shared quarters with M'Iver in the castle, where every
available corner was occupied by his lordship's guests.

When these other guests were bedded, and the house
in all our wing of it was still, my comrade and I sat down
to a tasse of brandy in our chamber, almost blythe, as
you would say, at the prospect of coming to blows with
our country's spoilers. We were in the midst of a most
genial crack when came a faint rap at the door, and in
steps the goodman, as solemn as a thunder-cloud, in spite
of the wan smile he fixed upon his countenance. He bore
his arm out of his sleeve in a sling, and his hair was un-
trim, and for once a most fastidious nobleman was anything but perjink.

"I cry pardon, gentlemen!" he said in Gaelic, "for
breaking in on my guests' privacy; but I'm in no humour
for sleeping, and I thought you might have a spare glass
for a friend."

"It's your welcome, Argile," said I, putting a wand
chair to the front for him. He sat himself down in it
with a sigh of utter weariness, and nervously poking the
logs on the fire with a purring-iron, looked sadly about
the chamber.

It was his wife's tiring-room, or closet, or something of
that nature, fitted up hastily for our accommodation, and
there were signs of a woman's dainty hand and occupation
about it. The floor was carpeted, the wall was hung with
arras; a varnish 'scrutoire, some sweet-wood boxes, two
little statues of marble, two raised silver candlesticks with
snuffers conform, broidery-work unfinished, and my lord's
picture, in a little gilded frame hanging over a dressing-
table, were among its womanly plenishing.

"Well, coz," said his lordship, breaking an awkward

silence, "we have an enormous and dastardly deed here to avenge."

"We have that!" said M'Iver. "It's a consolation that we are in the mood and in the position to set about paying the debt. Before the glad news came of your return, I was half afraid that our quarry would be too far gone ere we set loose the dogs on him. Luckily he can be little farther than Glenurchy now. Elrigmore and I had the honour to see the visitors make their departure. They carried so much stolen gear, and drove so big a prize of cattle, that I would not give them more than a twenty miles' march to the day."

"Will they hang together, do you think?" asked his lordship, fingering a crystal bottle for essence that lay on the 'scrutoire.

"I misdoubt it," said M'Iver. "You know the stuff, MacCailein? He may have his Irish still; but I'll wager the MacDonalds, the Stewarts, and all the rest of that reiving crowd are off to their holds, like the banditty they are, with their booty. A company of pikes on the rear of him, as like as not, would settle his business."

The Marquis, besides his dishevelment, was looking very lean and pale. I am wrong if I had not before me a man who had not slept a sound night's sleep in his naked bed since the point of war beat under his castle window.

"Your arm, my lord"—I said in a pause of his conversation with M'Iver, "is it a fashious injury? You look off your ordinary."

"I do," he said. "I daresay I do, and I wish to God it was only this raxed arm that was the worst of my ailment."

His face burned up red in the candle-light, his nostrils swelled, and he rose in his chair. A small table was between us. He put his uninjured hand on it to steady himself, and leaned over to me to make his words more weighty for my ear.

"Do you know," he added, "I'm Archibald, Marquis of Argile, and under the cope and canopy of heaven this January night there's not a creature of God's making more down in the heart and degraded than I? If the humblest servant in my house pointed a scornful finger at me and cried 'Coward,' I would bow my head. Ay, ay! it's good of you, sir, to shake a dissenting head; but I'm a chief discredited. I know it, man. I see it in the faces about me. I saw it at Rosneath, when my very gardener fumbled, and refused to touch his bonnet when I left. I saw it to-night at my own table, when the company talked of what they should do, and what my men should do, and said never a word of what was to be expected of Mac-Cailein Mor."

" I think, my lord," I cried, " that you're exaggerating a very small affair."

" Small affair ! " he said (and he wetted his lips with his tongue before the words came). " Small affair ! Hell's flame ! is there anything smaller than the self-esteem of a man who by some infernal quirk of his nature turns his back on his most manifest duty—leaves the blood of his blood and the skin of his skin to perish for want of his guidance and encouragement, and wakens at morning to find it no black nightmare but the horrible fact ? Answer me that, Elrigmore ! "

" Tut, tut," said M'Iver, pouring his cousin a glass ; " you're in the vapours, and need a good night's sleep. There's no one in Argile dare question your spirit, whatever they may think of your policy."

Argile relapsed into his chair, and looked with a pitiful eye at his kinsman.

" My good Iain," he said, " do you ken the old Lochow wife's story of the two daws ? ' Thou didst well,' said the one, ' though thy wings *are* cut ; thou didst well to do as I told thee.' I'm not blaming you ; you are a brave man of your own hands, and a middling honest man too, as honesty goes among mercenaries ; but your tongue's plausible, plausible, and you are the devil's counsellor to any other man who slackens his will by so much as a finger-length."

M'Iver took on a set stern jaw, and looked his chief very dourly in the face.

" My Lord of Argile," he said, " you're my cousin-german, and you're in a despondent key, and small blame to you with your lands smoking about you from

Cruachan to Kilmartin ; but if you were King Tearlach himself, I would take no insult from you. Do you charge me with any of your misfortunes ? "

" I charge you with nothing, John," said Argile, wearily. " I'm only saying that at a time of stress, when there's a conflict in a man's mind between ease and exertion, you're not the best of consciences. Are we two going to quarrel about a phrase while our clansmen's blood is crying from the sod ? Sit down, sir ; sit down, if it please you," he said more sternly, the scowl that gave him the *gruamach* reputation coming on his face ; " sit down, if it please you, and instead of ruffling up like the bubbly-jock over words, tell me, if you can, how to save a reputation from the gutter. If it was not that I know I have your love, do you think I should be laying my heart bare here and now ? You have known me some time now, M'Iver—did you ever find me without some reserve in my most intimate speech ? Did you ever hear me say two words that I had not a third in the background to bring forward if the policy of the moment called for it ? "

M'Iver laughed slyly, and hesitated to make any answer.

" It's a simple question," said the Marquis ; " am I to think it needs too straightforward an answer for John Splendid to give it ? "

" I'm as frank as my neighbours," said M'Iver.

" Well, sir, do not check the current of my candour by any picking and choosing of words. I ask if you have ever found me with the babbling and unbridled tongue of a fool in my mouth, giving my bottom-most thought to the wind and the street ? "

" You were no Gael if you did, my lord. That's the sin of the shallow wit. I aye kept a bit thought of my own in the corner of my vest."

MacCailein sighed, and the stem of the beaker he was fingering broke in his nervous fingers. He threw the fragments with an impatient cry into the fireplace.

" It's the only weakness of our religion (God pardon the sin of hinting at any want in that same !) that we have no chance of laying the heart bare to mortal man.

Many a time I could wish for the salving influence of the confessional, even without the absolution to follow."

"I think," said John Splendid, "it would be a strange day when MacCailein Mor, Marquis of Argile, would ask or need shriving from anything or any one. There was never a priest or vicar in the shire you couldn't twist the head off."

The Marquis turned to me with a vexed toss of his shoulder. "It's a hopeless task to look for a pagan's backbone," said he. "Come, I'll confess. I dare not hint at my truant thought to Auchinbreac or before any of these fiery officers of mine, who fear perhaps more than they love me. At the black tale of my weakness they would make no allowance for my courage as the same was shown before."

"Your courage, sir," said I, "has been proved; it is the inheritance of your race. But I dare not strain my conscience, my lord, much as I love and honour your house, to say I could comprehend or concur in the extraordinary retirement you made from these parts when our need for your presence was the sorest."

"I thank you for that, Elrigmore," said his lordship, cordially. "You say no more now than you showed by your face (and perhaps said too) on the night the beacon flamed on Dunchuach. To show that I value your frankness—that my kinsman here seems to fancy a flaw of character—I'll be explicit on the cause of my curious behaviour in this crisis. When I was a boy I was brought up loyally to our savage Highland tradition, that feuds were to carry on, and enemies to confound, and that no logic under heaven should keep the claymore in its sheath while an old grudge was to wipe out in blood or a wrong to right."

"A most sensible and laudable doctrine!" cried M'Iver. "With that and no more of a principle in life—except paying your way among friends—a good man of his hands could make a very snug and reputable progress through the world."

"Some men might," said Argile, calmly; "I do not know whether to envy or pity their kind. But they are not my kind. I think I bore myself not ungracefully in the Cabinet, in the field too, so long as I took my father's logic without question. But I have read, I have pondered——"

"Just so," whispered M'Iver, not a bit abashed that a sneer was in his interjection and his master could behold it.

"—And I have my doubts about the righteousness of much of our warfare, either before my day or now. I have brought the matter to my closet. I have prayed——"

"Pshaw!" exclaimed M'Iver, but at once he asked pardon.

"—I am a man come—or wellnigh come—to the conclusion that his life was never designed by the Creator to be spent in the turmoil of faction and field. There is, I allow, a kind of man whom strife sets off, a middling good man in his way, perhaps, with a call to the sword whose justice he has never questioned. I have studied the philosophies; I have reflected on life—this unfathomable problem—and 'fore God I begin to doubt my very right to wear a breastplate against the poignard of fate. Dubiety plays on me like a flute."

To all this I listened soberly, at the time comprehending that this was a gentleman suffering from the disease of being unable to make up his mind. I would have let him go on in that key while he pleasured it, for it's a vein there's no remedy for at the time being; but M'Iver was not of such tolerant stuff as I. He sat with an amazed face till his passion simmered over into a torrent of words.

"MacCailein!" said he, "I'll never call you coward, but I'll call you mad, book mad, closet mad! Was this strong fabric your house of Argile (John M'Iver the humblest of its members) built up on doubt and whim and shilly-shally hither and yond? Was't that made notable the name of your ancestor Cailein Mor na Sringe, now in the clods of Kilchrenan, or Cailein Iongataich who cooled his iron hide in Linne-na-luraich; or your father himself (peace with him!), who did so gallantly at Glenlivet?"

"—And taught me a little of the trade of slaughter at the Western Isles thirty years ago come Candlemas,"

K

said the Marquis. "How a man ages! Then—then I had a heart like the bird of spring."

"He could have taught you worse! I'm your cousin, and I'll say it to your beard, sir! Your glens and howes are ruined, your cattle are houghed and herried, your clan's name is a bye-word this wae day in all Albainn, and you sit there like a chemist weighing the wind on your stomach."

"You see no farther than your nose, John," said the Marquis, petulantly, the candle-light turning his eyes blood-red.

"Thank God for that same!" said M'Iver, "if it gives me the wit to keep an enemy from striking the same. If the nose was Argile's, it might be twisted off his face while he debated upon his right to guard it."

"You're in some ways a lucky man," said the Marquis, still in the most sad and tolerant humour. "Did you never have a second's doubt about the right of your side in battle?"

"Here's to the doubt, sir!" said M'Iver. "I'm like yourself and every other man in a quandary of that kind, that thinking on it rarely brought me a better answer to the guess than I got from my instinct to start with."

Argile put his fingers through his hair, clearing the temples, and shutting wearied eyes on a perplexing world.

"I have a good deal of sympathy with John's philosophy," I said, modestly. "I hold with my father that the sword is as much God's scheme as the cassock. What are we in this expedition about to start but the instruments of Heaven's vengeance on murtherers and unbelievers?"

"I could scarcely put it more to the point myself," cried M'Iver. "A soldier's singular and essential duty is to do the task set him with such art and accomplishment as he can—in approach, siege, trench, or stronghold."

"Ay, ay! here we are into our dialectics again," said his lordship, laughing, with no particular surrender in his merriment. "You gentlemen make no allowance for the likelihood that James Grahame, too, may be swearing himself Heaven's chosen weapon. 'Who gave Jacob to the spoil and Israel to the robbers—did not I, the Lord?' Oh, it's a confusing world!"

"Even so, MacCailein; I'm a plain man," said M'Iver, "though of a good family, brought up roughly among men, with more regard to my strength and skill of arm than to book-learning; but I think I can say that here and in this crisis I am a man more fit, express, and appropriate than yourself. In the common passions of life, in hate, in love, it is the simple and confident act that quicker achieves its purpose than the cunning ingenuity. A man in a swither is a man half absent, as poor a fighter as he is indifferent a lover; the enemy and the girl will escape him ere he has throttled the doubt at his heart. There's one test to my mind for all the enterprises of man—are they well contrived and carried to a good conclusion? There may be some unco quirks to be performed, and some sore hearts to confer at the doing of them, but Heaven itself, for all its puissance, must shorten the pigeon's wing that the gled of the wood may have food to live on."

"Upon my word, M'Iver," said Argile, "you beat me at my own trade of debate, and—have you ever heard of a fellow Machiavelli?"

"I kent a man of that name in a corps we forgathered with at Mentz—a 'provient schriever,' as they called him. A rogue, with a hand in the sporran of every soldier he helped pay wage to."

"This was a different person; but no matter. Let us back to the beginning of our argument—why did you favour my leaving for Dunbarton when Montrose came down the Glen?"

The blood swept to M'Iver's face, and his eye quailed.

"I favoured no such impolitic act," said he, slowly. "I saw you were bent on going, and I but backed you up, to leave you some rags of illusion to cover your naked sin."

"I thought no less," said Argile, sadly, "and yet, do you know, Iain, you did me a bad turn yonder. You made mention of my family's safety, and it was the last straw that broke the back of my resolution. One word of honest duty from you at that time had kept me in Inneraora though Abijah's array and Jeroboam's horse and foot were coming down the glens."

For a little M'Iver gave no answer, but sat in a chair of torture.

"I am sorry for it," he said at last, in a voice that was scarce his own; "I'm in an agony for it now; and your horse was not round Strone before I could have bit out the tongue that flattered your folly."

MacCailein smiled with a solemn pity that sat oddly on the sinister face that was a mask to a complex and pliable soul.

"I have no doubt," said he, "and that's why I said you were a devil's counsellor. Man, cousin! have we not played together as boys on the shore, and looked at each other on many a night across a candid bowl? I know you like the open book; you and your kind are the weak, strong men of our Highland race. The soft tongue and the dour heart; the good man at most things but at your word!"

CHAPTER XVI.

OUR MARCH FOR LOCHABER.

THE essence of all human melancholy is in the sentiment of farewells. There are people roving about the world, to-day here, to-morrow afar, who cheat fate and avoid the most poignant wrench of this common experience by letting no root of their affection strike into a home or a heart. Self-contained, aloof, unloved, and unloving, they make their campaign through life in movable tents that they strike as gaily as they pitch, and, beholding them thus evade the one touch of sorrow that is most inevitable and bitter to every sensitive soul, I have sometimes felt an envy of their fortune. To me the world was almost mirthful if its good-byes came less frequent. Cold and heat, the contumely of the slanderer, the insult of the tyrant, the agues and fevers of the flesh, the upheavals of personal fortune, were events a robust man might face with calm valiancy if he could be spared the cheering influence of the homely scene or the unchanged presence of his familiars and friends. I have sat in companies and put on an affected mirth, and laughed and sung with the most buoyant of all around, and yet ever and anon I chilled at the intruding notion of life's brevity.

Thus my leaving town Inneraora—its frozen hearths, its smokeless vents, its desecrated doorways, and the few of my friends who were back to it—was a stupendous grief. My father and my kinspeople were safe—we had heard of them by the returners from Lennox; but a girl with dark tresses gave me a closer passion for my native burgh than ever I felt for the same before. If love of his lady had been Argile's reason for retreat (thought I), there was no great mystery in his act.

What enhanced my trouble was that Clan MacLachlan —as Catholics always safe to a degree from the meddling of the invaders—had re-established themselves some weeks before in their own territory down the loch, and that young Lachlan, as his father's proxy, was already manifesting a guardian's interest in his cousin. The fact came to my knowledge in a way rather odd, but characteristic of John Splendid's anxiety to save his friends the faintest breeze of ill-tidings.

We were up early betimes in the morning of our departure for Lorn, though our march was fixed for the afternoon, as we had to await the arrival of some officers from Ceanntyre ; and John and I, preparing our accoutrements, began to talk of the business that lay heaviest at my heart—the leaving of the girl we had found in Strongara wood.

" The oddest thing that ever happened to me," he said, after a while, " is that in the matter of this child she mothers so finely she should be under the delusion that I have the closest of all interests in its paternity. Did you catch her meaning when she spoke of its antecedents as we sat, the four of us, behind the fir-roots ? "

" No, I can't say that I did," said I, wonderingly.

" You're not very gleg at some things, Elrigmore," he said, smiling. " Your Latin gave you no clue, did it, to the fact that she thought John M'Iver a vagabond of the deepest dye ? "

" If she thought that," I cried, " she baffles me ; for a hint I let drop in a mere careless badinage of your gallanting reputation made her perilously near angry."

John with pursed lips stroked his chin, musing on my words. I was afraid for a little he resented my indiscretion, but resentment was apparently not in his mind, for his speech found no fault with me.

" Man, Colin," he said, " you could scarcely have played a more cunning card if you had had myself to advise you. But no matter about that."

" If she thinks so badly of you, then," I said, " why not clear yourself from her suspicions, that I am willing to swear (less because of your general character than because of your conduct since she and you and the child met) are without foundation ? "

" I could scarcely meet her womanly innuendo with a coarse and abrupt denial," said he. " There are some shreds of common decency left in me yet."

" And you prefer to let her think the worst ? "

He looked at me with a heightened colour, and he laughed shortly.

" You'll be no loser by that, perhaps," he said ; and before I could answer he added, " Pardon a foolish speech, Colin ; I learned the trick of fanfaron among foreign gentry who claimed a *conquête d'amour* for every woman who dropped an eye to their bold scrutiny. Do not give me any share of your jealousy for Lachlan MacLachlan of that ilk—I'm not deserving the honour. And that reminds me——"

He checked himself abruptly.

" Come, come," said I, " finish your story ; what about MacLachlan and the lady ? "

" The lady's out of the tale this time," he said, shortly. " I met him stravaiging the vacant street last night ; that was all."

" Then I can guess his mission without another word from you," I cried, after a little dumfounderment. " He would be on the track of his cousin."

" Not at all," said John, with a bland front ; " he told me he was looking for a boatman to ferry him over the loch."

This story was so plainly fabricated to ease my apprehension that down I went, incontinent, and sought the right tale in the burgh.

Indeed it was not difficult to learn the true particulars, for the place rang all the worse for its comparative emptiness with the scandal of M'Iver's encounter with Mac-Lachlan, whom, it appeared, he had found laying a gallant's siege to the upper window of Askaig's house, whose almost unharmed condition had made it a convenient temporary shelter for such as had returned to the town. In the chamber behind the window that Mac-Lachlan threw his peebles at, were his cousin and the child, as M'Iver speedily learned, and he trounced him from the neighbourhood with indignities.

"What set you on the man?" I asked John when I came back after learning this.

"What do you think?" said he.

"You could have done no more if you had an eye on the girl yourself," I said, "and that, you assure me, is out of the question."

"The reason was very simple," he answered. "I have a sort of elder man's mischievous pleasure in spoiling a young buck's ploy, and—and—there might be an extra interest in my entertainment in remembering that you had some jealous regard for the lady."

All I had that was precious to take with me when we left Inneraora to follow the track of Montrose was the friendly wave of Mistress Betty's hand as we marched out below the Arches on our way to the North.

Argile and Auchinbreac rode at our head—his lordship on a black horse called Lepanto, a spirited beast that had been trained to active exercises and field-practice; Auchinbreac on a smaller animal, but of great spirit and beauty. M'Iver and I walked, as did all the officers. We had for every one of our corps twelve shot apiece, and in the rear a sufficiency of centners of powder, with ball and match. But we depended more on the prick of pike and the slash of sword than on our culverins. Our Lowland levies looked fairly well disciplined and smart, but there was apparent among them no great gusto about our expedition, and we had more hope of our vengeance at the hands of our uncouth but eager clansmen who panted to be at the necks of their spoilers and old enemies.

M'Iver confided to me more than once his own doubts about the mettle of the companies from Dunbarton.

"I could do well with them on a foreign strand," he said, "fighting for the bawbees against half-hearted soldiery like themselves, but I have my doubts about their valour or their stomach for this broil with a kind of enemy who's like to surprise them terribly when the time comes. This affair's decision must depend, I'm afraid, for the most part on our own lads, and I wish there were more of them."

We went up the Glen at a good pace, an east wind behind us, and the road made a little easier for us since the snow had been trodden by the folks we were after. To-day you will find Aora Glen smiling—happy with crop and herd on either hand and houses at every turn of the road, with children playing below the mountain-ash that stands before each door. You cannot go a step but human life's in sight. Our march was in a desolate valley—the winds with the cold odour (one might almost think) of ruin and death.

Beyond Lecknamban, where the time by the shadow on Tom-an-Uarader was three hours of the afternoon, a crazy old *cailleach*, spared by some miracle from starvation and doom, ran out before us wringing her hands, and crying a sort of coronach for a family of sons of whom not one had been spared to her. A gaunt, dark woman, with a frenzied eye, her cheeks collapsed, her neck and temples like crinkled parchment, her clothes dropping off her in strips, and her bare feet bleeding in the snow.

Argile scoffed at the superstition, as he called it, and the Lowland levies looked on it as a jocular game, when we took a few drops of her blood from her forehead for luck—a piece of chirurgy that was perhaps favourable to her fever, and one that, knowing the ancient custom, and respecting it, she made no fraca about.

She followed us in the snow to the ruins of Carnus, pouring out her curses upon Athole and the men who had made her home desolate and her widowhood worse than the grave, and calling on us a thousand blessings.

Lochow—a white, vast meadow, still bound in frost—we found was able to bear our army and save us the toilsome bend round Stronmealchan. We put out on its surface fearlessly. The horses pranced between the isles ; our cannon trundled on over the deeps ; our feet made a muffled thunder, and that was the only sound in all the void. For Cruachan had looked down on the devastation of the enemy. And at the falling of the night we camped at the foot of Glen Noe.

It was a night of exceeding clearness, with a moon almost at the full, sailing between us and the south. A certain jollity was shed by it upon our tired brigade, though all but the leaders (who slept in a tent) were resting in the snow on the banks of the river, with not even a saugh-tree to give the illusion of a shelter. There was but one fire in the bivouac, for there was no fuel at hand, and we had to depend upon a small stock of peats that came with us in the stores-sledge.

Deer came to the hill and belled mournfully, while we ate a frugal meal of oat-bannock and wort. The Low-landers—raw lads—became boisterous; our Gaels, stern with remembrance and eagerness for the coming business, thawed to their geniality, and soon the laugh and song went round our camp. Argile himself for a time joined in our diversion. He came out of his tent and lay in his plaid among his more immediate followers, and gave his quota to the story or the guess. In the deportment of his lordship now there was none of the vexatious hesitancy that helped him to a part so poor as he played in his frowning tower at home among the soothing and soften-ing effects of his family's domestic affairs. He was true Diarmaid the bold, with a calm eye and steadfast, a worthy general for us his children, who sat round in the light of the cheerful fire. So sat his forebears and ours on the close of many a weary march, on the eve of many a perilous enterprise. That cold pride that cocked his head so high on the causeway-stones of Inneraora relin-quished to a mien generous, even affectionate, and he brought out, as only affection may, the best that was of accomplishment and grace in his officers around.

"Craignure," he would say, "I remember your story of the young King of Easaidh Ruadh; might we have it anew?"

Or, "Donald, is the Glassary song of the Target in your mind? It haunts me like a charm."

And the stories came free, and in the owercome of the songs the dark of Glen Noe joined most lustily.

Songs will be failing from the memory in the ranging of the years, the passions that rose to them of old burned low in the ash, so that many of the sweetest ditties I heard on that night in Glen Noe have long syne left me for ever—all but one that yet I hum to the children at my knee. It was one of John Splendid's; the words and air

148

were his as well as the performance of them, and though
the English is a poor language wherein to render any fine
Gaelic sentiment, I cannot forbear to give something of
its semblance here. He called it in the Gaelic "The
Sergeant of Pikes," and a few of its verses as I mind
them might be Scotticed so—

When I sat in the service o' foreign commanders,
  Selling a sword for a beggar man's fee,
Learning the trade o' the warrior who wanders,
  To mak' ilka stranger a sworn enemie ;
There was ae thought that nerved me, and brawly it served me.
  With pith to the claymore wherever I won,—
'Twas the auld sodger's story, that, gallows or glory,
  The Hielan's, the Hielan's were crying me on !

I tossed upon swinging seas, splashed to my kilted knees,
  Ocean or ditch, it was ever the same ;
In leaguer or sally, tattoo or revally,
  The message on every pibroch that came,
Was " Cruachan, Cruachan, O son remember us,
  Think o' your fathers and never be slack ! "
Blade and buckler together, though far off the heather,
  The Hielan's, the Hielan's were all at my back !

The ram to the gate-way, the torch to the tower,
  We rifled the kist, and the cattle we maimed ;
Our dirks stabbed at guess through the leaves o' the bower,
  And crimes we committed that needna be named :
Moonlight or dawning grey, Lammas or Lady-day,
  Donald maun dabble his plaid in the gore ;
He maun hough and maun harry, or should he miscarry,
  The Hielan's, the Hielan's will own him no more !

And still, O strange Providence ! mirk is your mystery,
  Whatever the country that chartered our steel
Because o' the valiant repute o' our history,
  The love o' our ain land we maistly did feel ;
Many a misty glen, many a sheiling pen,
  Rose to our vision when slogans rang high ;
And this was the solace bright came to our starkest fight,
  A' for the Hielan's, the Hielan's we die !

A Sergeant o' Pikes, I have pushed and have parried O
  (My heart still at tether in bonny Glenshee) ;
Weary the marches made, sad the towns harried O,
  But in fancy the heather was aye at my knee :
The hill-berry mellowing, stag o' ten bellowing,
  The song o' the fold and the tale by the hearth,
Bairns at the crying and auld folks a-dying,
  The Hielan's sent wi' me to fight round the earth !

O the Hielan's, the Hielan's, praise God for His favour,
  That ane sae unworthy should heir sic estate,
That gi'ed me the zest o' the sword, and the savour
  That lies in the loving as well as the hate.
Auld age may subdue me, a grim death be due me,
  For even a Sergeant o' Pikes maun depart,
But I'll never complain o't, whatever the pain o't,
  The Hielan's, the Hielan's were aye at my heart!

We closed in our night's diversion with the exercise of prayer, wherein two clerics led our devotion, one Master Mungo Law, a Lowlander, and the other his lordship's chaplain—Master Alexander Gordon, who had come on this expedition with some fire of war in his face, and never so much as a stiletto at his waist.

They prayed a trifle long and drearily the pair of them, and both in the English that most of our clansmen but indifferently understood. They prayed as prayed David, that the counsel of Ahithophel might be turned to foolishness; and "Lo," they said, "be strong and courageous; fear not, neither be afraid of the King of Ashur, neither for all the multitude that is with him; for there be more with us than with him," and John Splendid turned to me at this with a dry laugh.

"Colin, my dear," said he, "thus the hawk upon the mountain-side, and the death of the winged eagle to work up a valour for! 'There be more with us than with him.' I never heard it so bluntly put before. But perhaps Heaven will forgive us the sin of our caution, seeing that half our superior number are but Lowland levies."

And all night long deer belled to deer on the braes of Glen Noe.

CHAPTER XVII.

IN THE LAND OF LORN.

WE might well be at our prayers. Appin paid dearly for its merriment in the land of Cailein Mor, and the MacDonalds were mulct most generously for our every hoof and horn. For when we crossed Loch Etive there came behind us from the ruined glens of Lower Lorn hordes of shepherds, hunters, small men of small families, who left their famished dens and holes, hunger sharping them at the nose, the dead bracken of concealment in their hair, to join in the vengeance on the cause of their distress. Without chieftains or authority, they came in savage bands, affronting the sea with their shouts as they swam or ferried ; they made up with the wildest of our troops, and ho, ro ! for the plaids far and wide on the errands of Hell. In that clear, cold, white weather—the weather of the badger's dream, as our proverb calls it— we brought these glens unfriendly, death in the black draught and the red wine of fire. A madness of hate seized on us ; we glutted our appetites to the very gorge. I must give Argile the credit of giving no licence to our on-goings. He rode after us with his Lowlanders, pro- testing, threatening, cajoling in vain. Many a remon- strance, too, made Gordon, many an opening fire he stamped out in cot and barn. But the black smoke of the granary belching against the white hills, or the kyloe, houghed and maimed, roaring in its agony, or the fugitive brought bloody on his knees among the rocks—God's mercy !

Do you know why those unco spectacles were sometimes almost sweet to me, though I was more often a looker-on than a sharer in their horror? It was because I never saw a barn blaze in Appin or Glencoe but I minded on our own black barns in Shira Glen; nor a beast slashed at the sinew with a wanton knife, but I thought of Moira, the dappled one that was the pride of my mother's byre, made into hasty collops for a Stewart meal. Through this remoter Lorn I went, less conscious of cruelty than when I plied fire and sword with legitimate men of war, for ever in my mind was the picture of real Argile, scorched to the vitals with the invading flame, and a burgh town I cherished reft of its people, and a girl with a child at her neck flying and sobbing among the hills.

Montrose and MacColkitto were far before us, marching up the Great Glen. They had with them the pick of the clans, so we lived, as it were, at free quarters, and made up for weeks of short fare by a time of high feeding.

Over Etive and through the Benderloch, and through Appin and even up to Glencoe, by some strange spasm of physique—for she was frail and famished—the bare-footed old *cailleach* of Carnus came after us, a bird of battle, croaking in a horrible merriment over our operations. The Dark Dame we called her. She would dance round the butchery of the fold, chanting her venomous Gaelic exultation in uncouth rhymes that she strung together as easily as most old people of her kind can do such things in times of passion or trance. She must have lived like a vulture, for no share would she have in our pots, though sometimes she added a relish to them by fetching dainties from houses by the way, whose larders in our masculine ignorance we had overlooked.

" I would give thee the choicest of the world," she would say. " What is too good for my heroes, O heroes of the myrtle-badge ? "

" Sit down and pick," John Splendid bade her once, putting a roysterer's playful arm round her waist, and drawing her to the fire where a dinner stewed.

Up she threw her claws, and her teeth were at his neck with a weasel's instinct. But she drew back at a gleam of reason.

" Oh, darling, darling," she cried, patting him with her foul hands, " did I not fancy for the moment thou wert of the spoilers of my home and honour—thou, the fleet foot, the avenger, the gentleman with an account to pay —on thee this mother's blessing, for thee this widow's prayers ! "

M'Iver was more put about at her friendliness than at her ferocity, as he shook his plaiding to order and fell back from her worship.

" I've seldom seen a more wicked cat," said he ; " go home, grandam, and leave us to our business. If they find you in Lochaber they will gralloch you like a Yule hind."

She leered, witch-like, at him, clutched suddenly at his sword-hilt, and kissed it with a frenzy of words, then sped off, singing madly as she flew.

We left the Dark Dame on Levenside as we ferried over to Lochaber, and the last we saw of her, she stood knee-deep in the water, calling, calling, calling, through the grey dun morning, a curse on Clan Donald and a blessing on Argile.

His lordship sat at the helm of a barge, his face pallid and drawn with cold, and he sighed heavily as the bel-dame's cries came after us.

" There's little of God's grace in such an omen," said he, in English, looking at the dim figure on the shore, and addressing Gordon.

" It could happen nowhere else," said the cleric, " but in such a ferocious land. I confess it, my lord—I con-fess it with the bitter shame of surrender, that I behold generations of superstition and savagery still to beat down ere your people are so amenable to the Gospel as the folks of the Lowland shires. To them such a shriek-ing harridan would be an object of pity and stern measure ; they would call her mad as an etter-cap, and keep her in bounds : here she is made something of a prophetess——"

" How ? " asked Argile, shortly, and he was looking wistfully at the hills we were leaving—the hills that lay between him and his books.

" There's not a Highlander in your corps but has bowed his head to her blessing ; there's not one but looks upon her curse of the MacDonalds as so much of a gain in this enterprise."

"Oh," said his lordship, "you are a little extravagant. We have our foolish ways, Gordon, but we are not altogether heathen; and do you think that after all there might not be something in the portents of a witch like yon in her exaltation?"

"No more than's in the howling of the wind in the chimney," said Gordon, quickly.

"Perhaps not," said Argile, after a little, "perhaps not; but even the piping of the vent has something of prophecy in it, though the wind bloweth where it listeth. I have only a scholar's interest in these things, I give you my word, and——"

He laughed with a little restraint before he went on.

"Do you know, John," he called out to M'Iver—"do you know what our *cailleach* friend says of our jaunt? She put a head in at my tent last night, and 'Listen, MacCailein,' said she, 'and keep on high roads,' said she, 'and Inverlochy's a perilous place,' said she, 'and I'd be wae to see the heather above the gall.'"

John Splendid's back was to him as he sat at the prow of a boat coming close on our stern, but I saw the skin of his neck flame. He never turned: he made no answer for a moment, and when he spoke it was with a laughing allusion in English to the folly of portents.

This was so odd an attitude for a man usually superstitious to take up, that I engaged him on the point whenever we landed.

"You seem to have no great respect for the Dark Dame's wizardy," said I.

He took me aside from some of the clansmen who could overhear.

"Never let these lads think that you either lightly Dame Dubh or make overmuch of her talk about the heather and gall, for they prize her blessing, strangely enough, and they might lay too great stress on its failure. You catch me?"

I nodded to keep him going, and turned the thing over in my mind.

"What do you think of the prophecy yourself?" he asked; "is it not familiar?"

In a flash it came to my mind that I had half-hinted to him at what the Macaulay woman had said in the fold of Elrigmore.

"I think," said I, "the less the brooding on these things the better."

If we had our own misgivings about the end of this jaunt, our companions had none. They plunged with hearts almost jocular into the woods on Lochaber's edge, in a bright sunshine that glinted on the boss of the target and on the hilt of the knife or sword, and we came by the middle of the day to the plain on which lay the castle of Inverlochy—a staunch quadrangular edifice with round towers at the angles, and surrounded by a moat that smelled anything but freshly. And there we lay for a base, and thence we sent out round Keppoch and Locheil some dashing companies that carried on the work we began in Athole.

Auchinbreac's notion, for he was more than my lord the guide of this enterprise, was to rest a day or two in the castle and then follow on the heels of Montrose, who, going up Loch Ness-side, as we knew he was, would find himself checked in front by Seaforth, and so hemmed between two fires.

It was about three o'clock on Wednesday afternoon when Argile sent for M'Iver and myself to suggest a reconnoitring excursion up the Great Glen by the side of the lochs, to see how far the enemy might have reached before us.

"I'm sorry to lose your company, gentlemen," said he, "even for a day; but this is a delicate embassy, and I can fancy no one better able to carry it through successfully than the two gentlemen who have done more delicate and dangerous work in the ranks of the honourable Scots Brigade."

"I can say for myself," said John, "that there's not a man in Keppoch could guess my nativity or my politics if I had on another tartan than that of the Diarmaid."

"Ah! you have the tongue, no doubt of it," said Argile, smiling; "and if a change of colour would make your task less hazardous, why not effect it? I'm sure we could accommodate you with some neutral fabric for kilt and plaid."

"For the humour of the thing," said John, "I would like to try it; but I have no notion of getting hanged for a spy. James Grahame of Montrose has enough knowledge of the polite arts of war to know the difference between a spy in his camp in a false uniform and a scout taking all the risks of the road by wearing his own colours. In the one case he would hang us offhand, in the other there's a hair's-breadth of chance that he might keep us as hostages."

"But in any tartan, cousin, you're not going to let yourself be caught," said Argile. "We have too much need for you here. Indeed, if I thought you were not certain to get through all right, I would send cheaper men in your place."

John laughed.

"There's no more cure," said he, "for death in a common herd than for the same murrain in an ensign of foot."

"A scholar's sentiment!" cried Argile. "Are you taking to the philosophies?"

"It's the sentiment, or something like it, of your chaplain, Master Gordon," said John; "he reproved me with it on Dunchuach. But to do myself justice, I was never one who would run another into any danger I was unwilling to face myself."

The Marquis said no more, so we set about preparing for the journey.

"Well, Elrigmore, here we are running the loupegarthe with MacDonalds on the one side of us and Camerons on the other," said my comrade, as we set out at the mouth of the evening, after parting from a number of the clan who went up to the right at Spean to do some harrying in Glen Roy.

No gavilliger or provost-marshal ever gave a more hazardous gauntlet to run, thought I, and I said as much, but my musings brought only a good-humoured banter from my friend.

All night we walked on a deserted rocky roadway under

moon and star. By the side of Loch Lochy there was
not a light to be seen ; even the solitary dwellings we
crept bye in the early part of our journey were without
smoke at the chimney or glimmer at the chink. And on
that loch-side, towards the head of it, there were many
groups of mean little hovels, black with smoke and rain,
with ragged sloven thatch, the midden at the very door
and the cattle routing within, but no light, no sign of
human occupation.

It was the dawning of the day, a fine day as it proved
and propitious to its close, that we ventured to enter one
such hut or bothy at the foot of another loch that lay
before us. Auchinbreac's last order to us had been to
turn wherever we had indication of the enemy's whereabouts, and to turn in any case by morning. Before we
could go back, however, we must have some sleep and
food, so we went into this hut to rest us. It stood alone
in a hollow by a burn at the foot of a very high hill, and
was tenanted by a buxom, well-featured woman with a
herd of duddy children. There was no man about the
place ; we had the delicacy not to ask the reason, and she
had the caution not to offer any. As we rapped at her
door we put our arms well out of sight below our neutral
plaids, but I daresay our trade was plain enough to the
woman when she came out and gave us the Gael's welcome somewhat grudgingly, with an eye on our apparel
to look for the tartan.

" Housewife," said John M'Iver, blandly, " we're a bit
off our way here by no fault of our own, and we have
been on the hillside all night, and——"

" Come in," she said, shortly, still scrutinising us very
closely, till I felt myself flushing wildly. She gave us
the only two stools in her dwelling, and broke the peats
that smouldered on the middle of her floor. The chamber
—a mean and contracted interior—was lit mainly from
the door and the smoke-vent, that gave a narrow glimpse
of heaven through the black *cabar* and thatch. Round
about the woman gathered her children, clinging at her
gown, and their eyes stared large and round in the gloom
at the two of us who came so appallingly into their nest.

We sat for a little with our plaids about us, revelling in

the solace of the hearty fire that sent wafts of odorous reek round the dwelling; and to our dry rations the woman added whey, that we drank from birch cogies.

"I am sorry I have no milk just now," she said. "I had a cow till the day before yesterday; now she's a cow no more, but pith in Colkitto's heroes."

"They lifted her?" asked John.

"I would not say they lifted her," said the woman, readily, "for who would be more welcome to my all than the gentlemen of Keppoch and Seumais Grahame of Montrose?" And again she looked narrowly at our close-drawn plaids.

I stood up, pulled out my plaid-pin, and let the folds off my shoulder, and stood revealed to her in a Diarmaid tartan.

"You see we make no pretence at being other than what we are," I said, softly; "are we welcome to your whey and to your fire-end?"

She showed no sign of astonishment or alarm, and she answered with great deliberation, choosing her Gaelic, and uttering it with an air to impress us.

"I dare grudge no one at my door," said she, "the warmth of a peat and what refreshment my poor dwelling can give; but I've seen more welcome guests than the spoilers of Appin and Glencoe. I knew you for Campbells when you knocked."

"Well, mistress," said M'Iver, briskly, "you might know us for Campbells, and might think the worse of us for that same fact (which we cannot help), but it is to be hoped you will know us for gentlemen too. If you rue the letting of us in, we can just go out again. But we are weary and cold and sleepy, for we have been on foot since yesterday, and an hour among bracken or white hay would be welcome."

"And when you were sleeping," said the woman; "what if I went out and fetched in some men of a clan who would be glad to mar your slumber?"

John studied her face for a moment. It was a sonsy and simple face, and her eyes were not unkindly.

"Well," he said, "you might have some excuse for a deed so unhospitable, and a deed so different from the

spirit of the Highlands as I know them. Your clan would
be little the better for the deaths of two gentlemen whose
fighting has been in other lands than this, and a wife with
a child at her breast would miss me, and a girl with her
wedding-gown at the making would miss my friend here.
These are wild times, goodwife, wild and cruel times, and
a widow more or less is scarcely worth troubling over. I
think we'll just risk you calling in your men, for, God
knows, I'm wearied enough to sleep on the verge of the
Pit itself."

The woman manifestly surrendered her last scruple at
his deliverance. She prepared to lay out a rough bedding
of the bleached bog-grass our people gather in the dry
days of spring.

"You may rest you a while, then," said she. "I have
a husband with Keppoch, and he might be needing a bed
among strangers himself."

"We are much in your reverence, housewife," said
John, nudging me so that I felt ashamed of his double-
dealing. "That's a bonny bairn," he continued, lifting
one of the children in his arms; "the rogue has your
own good looks in every lineament."

"Aye, aye," said the woman, drily, spreading her
blankets; "I would need no sight of tartan to guess *your*
clan, master. Your flattery goes wrong this time, for by
ill-luck you have the only bairn that does not belong to
me of all the brood."

"Now that I look closer," he laughed, "I see a difference; but I'll take back no jot of my compliment to
yourself."

"I was caught yonder," said he to me a little later in a
whisper in English, as we lay down in our corner. "A
man of my ordinary acuteness should have seen that
the brat was the only unspoiled member of all the
flock."

We slept, it might be a couple of hours, and wakened
together at the sound of a man's voice speaking with the
woman outside the door. Up we sat, and John damned
the woman for her treachery.

"Wait a bit," I said. "I would charge her with no
treachery till I had good proofs for it. I'm mistaken if

your lie about your wife and weans has not left her a more honest spirit towards us."

The man outside was talking in a shrill, high voice, and the woman in a softer voice was making excuses for not asking him to go in. One of her little ones was ill of a fever, she said, and sleeping, and her house, too, was in confusion, and could she hand him out something to eat?

"A poor place Badenoch nowadays!" said the man, petulantly. "I've seen the day a bard would be free of the best and an honour to have by any one's fire. But out with the bannocks and I'll be going. I must be at Kilcumin with as much speed as my legs will lend me."

He got his bannocks and he went, and we lay back a while on our bedding, and pretended to have heard none of the incident. It was a pleasant feature of the good woman's character that she said never a word of her tactics in our interest.

"So you did not bring in your gentlemen?" said John, as we were preparing to go. "I was half afraid some one might find his way unbidden, and then it was all bye with two poor soldiers of fortune."

"John MacDonald the bard, John Lom, as we call him, went bye a while ago," she answered simply, "on his way to the clan at Kilcumin."

"I have never seen the bard yet that did not demand his bardic right to kail-pot and spoon at every passing door."

"This one was in a hurry," said the woman, reddening a little in confusion.

"Just so," said M'Iver, fumbling in his hand some coin he had taken from his sporran; "have you heard of the gold touch for fever? A child has been brought from the edge of the grave by the virtue of a dollar rubbed on its brow. I think I heard you say some neighbour's child was ill? I'm no physician, but if my coin could—what?"

The woman flushed deeper than ever, an angered pride this time in her heat.

"There's no child ill that I know of," said she; "if there was, we have gold of our own."

She bustled about the house and put past her blankets, and out with a spinning-wheel and into a whirr of it, with a hummed song of the country at her lips—all in a mild temper, or to keep her confusion from showing itself undignified.

"Come away," I said to my comrade in English; "you'll make her bitterly angry if you persist in your purpose."

He paid no heed to me, but addressed the woman again with a most ingenious story, apparently contrived, with his usual wit, as he went on with it.

"Your pardon, goodwife," said he, "but I see you are too sharp for my small deceit. I daresay I might have guessed there was no child ill; but for reasons of my own I'm anxious to leave a little money with you till I come back this road again. We trusted you with our lives for a couple of hours there, and surely, thinks I, we can trust you with a couple of yellow pieces."

The woman stopped her wheel and resumed her good-humour. "I thought," said she,—"I thought you meant payment for——"

"You're a bit hard on my manners, goodwife," said John. "Of course I have been a soldier, and might have done the trick of paying forage with a sergeant's bluntness, but I think I know a Gaelic woman's spirit better."

"But are you likely to be passing here again at any time?" cried the woman, doubt again darkening her face, and by this time she had the money in her hand. "I thought you were going back by the Glen?"

"That was our notion," said my comrade, marvellously ready, "but to tell the truth we are curious to see this Keppoch bard, whose songs we know very well in real Argile, and we take a bit of the road to Kilcumin after him."

The weakness of this tale was not apparent to the woman, who I daresay had no practice of such trickery as my friend was the master of, and she put the money carefully in a napkin and in a recess beneath one of the roof-joists. Our thanks she took carelessly, no doubt, because we were Campbells.

I was starting on the way to Inverlochy when M'Iver

protested we must certainly go a bit of the way to Kilcumin.

"I'm far from sure," said he, "that that very particular bit of MacDonald woman is quite confident of the truth of my story. At any rate, she's no woman if she's not turning it over in her mind by now, and she'll be out to look the road we take before very long or I'm mistaken."

We turned up the Kilcumin road, which soon led us out of sight of the hut, and, as my friend said, a glance behind us showed us the woman in our rear, looking after us.

"Well, there's no turning so long as she's there," said I. "I wish your generosity had shown itself in a manner more convenient for us. There's another example of the error of your polite and truthless tongue! When you knew the woman was not wanting the money, you should have put it in your sporran again, and——"

"Man, Elrigmore," he cried, "you have surely studied me poorly if you would think me the man to insult the woman—and show my own stupidity at the same time—by exposing my strategy when a bit fancy tale and a short daunder on a pleasant morning would save the feelings of both the lady and myself."

"You go through life on a zigzag," I protested, "aiming for some goal that another would cut straight across for, making deviations of an hour to save you a second's unpleasantness. I wish I could show you the diplomacy of straightforwardness: the honest word, though hard to say sometimes, is a man's duty as much as the honest deed of hand."

"Am I not as honest of my word as any in a matter of honour? I but gloze sometimes for the sake of the affection I have for all God's creatures."

I was losing patience of his attitude and speaking perhaps with bitterness, for here were his foolish ideas of punctilio bringing us a mile or two off our road and into a part of the country where we were more certain of being observed by enemies than in the way behind us.

"You jink from ambuscade to ambuscade of phrase like a fox," I cried.

"Call it like a good soldier, and I'll never quarrel with your compliment," he said, good-humouredly. "I had the second excuse for the woman in my mind before the first one missed fire."

"Worse and worse!"

"Not a bit of it: it is but applying a rule of fortification to a peaceful palaver. Have bastion and ravelin as sure as may be, but safer still the sally-port of retreat."

I stood on the road and looked at him, smiling very smug and self-complacent before me, and though I loved the man I felt bound to prick a hole in his conceit.

But at that moment a dead branch snapped in a little plantation that lay by the way, and we turned quickly to see come to us a tall lean man in MacDonald clothing.

CHAPTER XVIII.

BARD OF KEPPOCH.

HE was a lantern-jawed, sallow-faced, high-browed fellow in his prime, with the merest hint of a hirple or halt in his walk, very shabby in his dress, wearing no sporran, but with a dagger bobbing about at his groin. I have never seen a man with surprise more sharply stamped on his visage than was betrayed by this one when he got close upon us and found two of a clan so unlikely to have stray members out for a careless airing on a forenoon in Badenoch.

" You're taking your walk ? " he said, with a bantering tone, after a moment's pause.

" You couldn't have guessed better," said John. " We are taking all we're likely to get in so barren a country."

The stranger chuckled sourly as the three of us stood in a group surveying each other. " My name," said he, in his odd north Gaelic, and throwing out his narrow chest, " is John MacDonald. I'm Keppoch's bard, and I've no doubt you have heard many of my songs. I'm namely in the world for the best songs wit ever strung together. Are you for war ? I can stir you with a stave to set your sinews straining. Are you for the music of the wood ? The thrush itself would be jealous of my note. Are you for the ditty of the lover ? Here's the songster to break hearts. Since the start of time there have been 'prentices at my trade : I have challenged North and East, South and the isle-flecked sea, and they cry me back their master."

M'Iver put a toe on one of mine, and said he, " Amn't I the unlucky man, for I never heard of you ? "

"Tut, tut," cried the bard in a fret, "perhaps you think so much in Argile of your hedge-chanters that you give the lark of the air no ear."

"We have so many poets between Knapdale and Cruachan," said John, "that the business is fallen out of repute, and men brag when they can make an honest living at prose."

"Honest living," said the bard, "would be the last thing I would expect Clan Campbell to brag of."

He was still in an annoyance at the set-back to his vanity, shuffling his feet restlessly on the ground, and ill at ease about the mouth, that I've noticed is the first feature to show a wound to the conceit.

"Come, come," he went on, "will you dare tell me that the sheiling singers on Loch Finne-side have never heard my 'Harp of the Trees'? If there's a finer song of its kind in all Albainn I've yet to learn it."

"If I heard it," said John, "I've forgotten it."

"Name of God!" cried the bard in amaze, "you couldn't; it goes so "—and he hummed the tune that every one in Argile and the west had been singing some years before.

We pretended to listen with eagerness to recall a single strain of it, and affected to find no familiar note. He tried others of his budget—some rare and beautiful songs, I must frankly own : some we knew by fragments ; some we had sung in the wood of Creag Dubh—but to each and all John Splendid raised a vacant face and denied acquaintance.

"No doubt," said he, "they are esteemed in the glens of Keppoch, but Argile is fairly happy without them. Do you do anything else for a living but string rhymes ? "

The bard was in a sweat of vexation. "I've wandered far," said he, "and you beat all I met in a multitude of people. Do you think the stringing of rhymes so easy that a man should be digging and toiling in the field and the wood between his *duans* ? "

"I think," said Splendid (and it was the only time a note of earnestness was in his utterance)—"I think his songs would be all the better for some such manly inter-regnum. You sing of battles : have you felt the blood rush behind the eyes and the void of courageous alarm at the pit of the stomach? You hum of grief: have you known the horror of a desolate home? Love,—sir, you are young, young——"

"Thanks be with you," said the bard; "your last word gives me the clue to my answer to your first. I have neither fought nor sorrowed in the actual fact; but I have loved, not a maid (perhaps), nor in errant freaks of the mind, but a something unnameable and remote, with a bounteous overflowing of the spirit. And that way I learned the splendour of war as I sat by the fire; and the widows of my fancy wring my heart with a sorrow as deep as the ruined homes your clan have made in my country could confer."

I'm afraid I but half comprehended his meaning, but the rapture of his eye infected me like a glisk of the sun. He was a plain, gawky, nervous man, very freckled at the hands, and as poor a leg in the kilt as well could be. He was fronting us with the unspoken superiority of the fowl on its own midden, but he had a most heartsome and invigorating glow.

"John Lom, John Lom!" I cried, "I heard a soldier sing your songs in the ship Archangel of Leith that took us to Elsinore."

He turned with a grateful eye from M'Iver to me, and I felt that I had one friend now in Badenoch.

"Do you tell me?" he asked, a very child in his pleasure, that John Splendid told me after he had not the heart to mar. "Which one did they sing—'The Harp of the Trees' or 'Macrannul Og's Lament'? I am sure it would be the Lament: it is touched with the sorrow of the starless night on a rain-drummed, wailing sea. Or perhaps they knew—the gentle hearts—my 'Farewell to the Fisher.' I made it with yon tremor of joy, and it is telling of the far isles beyond Uist and Barra, and the Seven Hunters, and the white sands of Colomkill."

M'Iver sat down on the wayside and whittled a stick with a pretence at patience I knew he could scarcely feel, for we were fools to be dallying thus on the way in broad morning when we should be harking back to our friends as secretly as the fox.

" Were you on the ocean ? " he asked the bard, whose rapture was not abated.

" Never," said he, " but I know Linnhe and Loch Eil and the fringe of Morar."

" Mere dubs," said M'Iver, pleasantly—" mere dubs or ditches. Now I, Barbreck, have been upon the deeps, tossed for days at hazard without a headland to the view. I may have made verse on the experience,—I'll not say yea or nay to that,—but I never gave a lochan credit for washing the bulged sides of the world."

" You hadn't fancy for it, my good fellow," said the bard, angry again. " I forgot to say that I saw Loch Finne too, and the Galley of Lorn taking MacCailein off from his castle. I'm making a song on that now."

" Touched ! " thinks I, for it was a rapier-point at my comrade's very marrow. He reddened at once, pulled down his brows, and scanned the bard of Keppoch, who showed his knowledge of his advantage.

" If I were you," said John in a little, " I would not put the finish on that ditty till I learned the end of the transaction. Perhaps MacCailein (and God bless my chief !) is closer on Lochiel and Lochaber to-day than you give him credit for."

" Say nothing about that," said I warningly in English to my friend, never knowing (what I learned on a later occasion) that John Lom had the language as well as myself.

" When MacCailein comes here," said the bard, " he'll get a Badenoch welcome."

" And that is the thief's welcome, the shirt off his very back," cried M'Iver.

" Off his back very likely," said the bard ; " it's the back we see oftenest of the bonny gentleman."

M'Iver grew livid to the very lip, and sprang to his feet, clutching with great menace the black knife he had been whittling with. Not a bit abashed, the bard pulled out his dirk, and there was like to be a pretty to-do when I put between them.

The issue of the quarrel that thus I retarded was postponed altogether by a circumstance that changed the whole course of our adventure in this wild country,—severed us at a sharp wrench from the Campbell regiments, and gave us the chance—very unwelcome it was—of beholding the manner of war followed by Alasdair MacDonald's savage tribes. It happened in a flash, without warning. No blow had been struck by the two gentlemen at variance, when we were all three thrown to the ground, and the bound prisoners of a squad of Macgregors who had got out of the thicket and round us unobserved in the heat of the argument.

They treated us all alike—the bard as curt as the Campbells, in spite of his tartan,—and without exchanging any words with us marched us before them on a journey of several hours to Kilcumin.

Long or ever we reached Kilcumin we were manifestly in the neighbourhood of Montrose's force. His pickets held the road ; the hillsides moved with his scouts. On a plain called Leiter-nan-lub the battalion lay camped, a mere fragment of the force that brought ruin to Argile : Athol men under the Tutor of Struan, Stewarts of Appin, MacIans of Glencoe, a few of the more sedate men of Glengarry, Keppoch, and Maclean, as well as a handful of the Gregaraich who had captured us. It was the nightfall when we were turned into the presence of Sir Alasdair, who was sitting under a few ells of canvas playing cartes with some chieftains by the light of a fir-root fire.

" Whom have we here ? " said he, never stopping for more than a glimpse of us.

" Two Campbells and a man who says he's bard of Keppoch," he was told.

" A spy in an honest tartan, no doubt," said Sir Alasdair ; " but we'll put it to the test with Keppoch himself : tell him to come over and throw an eye on the fellow."

Keppoch was sent for, and came across from a fire at another part of the field, a hiccough at his throat and a blear look in his eye as one that has been overly brisk with the bottle, but still and on the gentleman and in a very good humour.

" Here's my bard sure enough ! " he cried. " John, John, what do you seek in Kilcumin, and in Campbell company too ? "

"The company is none of my seeking," said John Lom, very short and blunt. "And we're like to have a good deal more of the same clan's company than we want before long, for Argile and his clan to three times your number are at Inverlochy. I have tramped a weary day to tell you the tale, and I get but a spy's reception."

The tale went round the camp in the time a man would whistle an air. Up came Montrose on the instant, and he was the first to give us a civil look. But for him we had no doubt got a short quittance from MacColkitto, who was for the tow gravatte on the spot. Instead we were put on parole when his lordship learned we had been Cavaliers of fortune. The moon rose with every sign of storm, the mountains lay about white to their foundations, and ardent winds belched from the glens, but by mountain and glen MacDonald determined to get round on the flank of Argile.

CHAPTER XIX.

THE MIRACULOUS JOURNEY.

THE month of January, as our old Gaelic notion has it, borrows three days from July for a bribe of three young lambs. Those three days we call *Faoilteach*, and often they are very genial and cheerful days, with a sun that in warmth is a sample of the mellow season at hand. But this year, as my history has shown, we had no sign of a good *Faoilteach*, and on the morning of the last day of January, when Alasdair MacDonald's army set over the hills, it was wild, tempestuous weather. A wind rose in the dawning and increased in vehemence as the day aged, and with it came a storm of snow—the small bitter sifting snow that, encountered on the hill, stings like the ant and drifts in monstrous and impassable wreaths. Round about us yawned the glens, to me nameless, mysterious, choked to the throat with snow-mist that flapped and shook like grey rags. The fields were bleak and empty ; the few houses that lay in the melancholy plain were on no particularly friendly terms with this convocation of Ersemen and wild kerns : they shut their doors steadfastly on our doings, and gave us not even the compliment of looking on at our strange manœuvres. There was but one exception, in a staunch and massive dwelling,—a manifest baron keep or stout domicile of that nature, just on the border of the field in which the camp was pitched : it was apparently in the charge of two old spinster sisters whose men-folk were afield somewhere else, for they had shuttered the windows, barricaded the gates, and ever and anon would they show blanched faces as the tumult of our preparation disturbed them, and they came to the door and cunningly pulled it open a little and looked out on this warlike array. If a soldier made a step in their direction they fled inside with terror, and their cries rang in the interior.

Those two spinsters—very white, very thin clad for a morn so rigorous, and with a trepidation writ on every feature—were all that saw us off on our march to the south-east. They came out and stood hand in hand on the door-stoop, and I have little doubt the honest bodies thanked the God of Israel that the spoilers were departed furth their neighbourhood.

The country we now plunged into, as may be guessed, was a *terra incognita* to me. Beyond that it was Badenoch and an unhealthy clime for all that wear the Campbell tartan, I could guess no more. It was after these little wars were over I discovered the names of the localities—the glens, mounts, passes, streams, and drove-roads—over which we passed in a march that Gustavus never faced the like of.

With good judgment enough our captors put a small advance-guard ahead, a score of Airlie's troopers, swanky blaspheming persons, whose horses pranced very gaily up Glen Tarf, guided by John Lom. M'Iver and I walked together with the main body, quite free and unfettered, sometimes talking with affability to our captors. The Irish were in good humour; they cracked jokes with us in their peculiar Gaelic that at first is ill for a decent Gael of Albion to follow, if uttered rapidly, but soon becomes as familiar as the less foreign language of the Athole men, whose tongue we Argiles find some strange conceits in. If the Irish were affable, the men of our own side of the ocean were most singularly morose—small wonder, perhaps, for we have little reason to love each other. Sour dogs! they gloomed at us under their bonnets and swore in their beards. I have no doubt but for their gentry there had been dirks in us before we reached Corryarick.

It was with the repartee of the Irish and the scowls of the Gaels we went up the rough valley of the Tarf, where the wind moaned most drearily and drove the thin fine snow like a smoke of burning heather. But when we

M

got to the pass of Corryarick our trials began, and then such spirit did M'Iver put in the struggle with the task before us, such snatches of song, sharp saying and old story,—such comradary as it might be named,—that we were on good terms with all. For your man of family the Gael has ever some regard. M'Iver (not to speak of myself) was so manifestly the *duine-uasail* that the coarsest of the company fell into a polite tone, helped to their manners to some degree no doubt by the example of Montrose and Airlie, who at the earliest moments of our progress walked beside us and discoursed on letters and hunting, and soldiering in the foreign wars.

The pass of Corryarick met us with a girning face and white fangs. On Tarf-side there was a rough bridle-path that the wind swept the snow from, and our progress was fairly easy. Here the drifts lay waist high, the horses plunged to the belly-bands, the footmen pushed through in a sweat. It was like some Hyperborean hell, and we the doomed wretches sentenced to our eternity of toil. We had to climb up the shoulder of the hill, now among tremendous rocks, now through water unfrozen, now upon wind-swept ice, but the snow—the snow—the heartless snow was our constant companion. It stood in walls before, it lay in ramparts round us, it wearied the eye to a most numbing pain. Unlucky were they who wore trews, for the same clung damply to knee and haunch and froze, while the stinging sleet might flay the naked limb till the blood rose among the felt of the kilted, but the suppleness of the joints was unmarred.

It was long beyond noon when we reached the head of the pass, and saw before us the dip of the valley of the Spey. We were lost in a wilderness of mountain-peaks; the bens started about us on every hand like the horrors of a nightmare, every ben with its death-sheet, menacing us, poor insects, crawling in our pain across the landscape.

I thought we had earned a halt and a bite of meat by this forenoon of labour; and Montrose himself, who had walked the pass on foot like his fellows, seemed anxious to rest, but Sir Alasdair pushed us on like a fate relentless.

"On, on," he cried, waving his long arms to the prospect before; "here's but the start of our journey; far is

the way before ; strike fast, strike hot ! Would ye eat a
meal with appetite while the Diarmaids wait in the way ? ''

M'Iver, who was plodding beside MacDonald when he
said these words, gave a laugh. "Take your time, Sir
Sandy," said he ; "you'll need a bowl or two of brose ere
you come to grips with MacCailein."

"We'll never come to grips with MacCailein," said
MacDonald, taking the badinage in good part, "so long as
he has a back-gate to go out at or a barge to sail off in."

"I could correct you on that point in a little affair of
arms as between gentlemen—if the time and place were
more suitable," said M'Iver, warmly.

"Let your chief defend himself, friend," said Mac-
Donald. "Man, I'll wager we never see the colour of
his face when it comes to close quarters."

"I wouldn't wonder," I ventured. "He is in no great
trim for fighting, for his arm is——"

Sir Alasdair gave a gesture of contempt and cried,
"Faugh ! we've heard of the raxed arm : he took care
when he was making his tale that he never made it a
raxed leg."

Montrose edged up at this, with a red face and a somewhat annoyed expression. He put his gloved hand lightly
on MacDonald's shoulder and chided him for debate with
a prisoner of war.

"Let our friends be, Alasdair," he said, quietly. "They
are, in a way, our guests : they would perhaps be more
welcome if their tartan was a different hue, but in any
case we must not be insulting them. Doubtless they have
their own ideas of his lordship of Argile——"

"I never ask to serve a nobler or a more generous
chief," said M'Iver, firmly.

"I would expect no other sentiment from a gentleman
of Argile's clan. He has ever done honestly enough by
his own people. But have we not had enough of this ?
We are wasting our wind that should be more precious,
considering the toils before us."

We found the descent of Corryarick even more ill than
its climbing. The wind from the east had driven the
snow into the mouth of it like a wedge. The horses,
stepping ahead, more than once slipped into drifts that

rose to their necks. Then they became wild with terror, dashed with frantic hooves into deeper trouble, or ran back, quivering in every sinew and snorting with affright till the troopers behove to dismount and lead them. When we in the van reached the foot of the corrie we looked back on a spectacle that fills me with new wonder to this day when I think of it,—a stream of black specks in the distance dropping, as it were, down the sheer face of white ; nearer, the broken bands of different clansmen winding noiselessly and painfully among the drifts, their kilts pinned between their thighs, their plaids crossed on their chests—all their weapons a weariness to them.

In the afternoon the snow ceased to fall, but the dusk came on early notwithstanding, for the sky was blotted over with driving clouds.

At the head of Glen Roy the MacDonalds, who had lost their bauchles of brogues in the pass, started to a trot, and as the necessity was we had to take up the pace too. Long lank hounds, they took the road like deer, their limbs purple with the cold, their faces pinched to the aspect of the wolf, their targets and muskets clattering about them. " There are Campbells to slay, and suppers to eat," the Major-General had said. It would have given his most spiritless followers the pith to run till morning across a strand of rock and pebble. They knew no tiring, they seemingly felt no pain in their torn and bleeding feet, but put mile after mile below them.

But the Campbells were not in Glen Roy. They had been there and skirmished for a day among their old foes, and had gone back to Lochyside, little thinking the fires they left in the Cameron barns at morning would light the enemy on ere night. The roofs still smouldered, and a granary here and there on the sides of the valley sent up its flames,—at once a spur to the spirit of the MacDonalds and a light to their vengeance.

We halted for the night in Glen Spean, with Ben Chlinaig looming high to the south, and the river gulping in ice beside our camp. Around was plenty of wood : we built fires and ate as poor a meal as the Highlands ever granted in a bad year, though it was the first break in our fast for the day. Gentle and simple, all fared alike—a whang of barley bannock, a stirabout of oat-and-water, without salt, a quaich of spirits from some kegs the troopers carried, that ran done before the half of the corps had been served. Sentinels were posted, and we slept till the morning pipe with sweet weariness in our bones.

Our second day was a repetition of the first. We left without even a breakfast whenever the pipers set up the Cameron rant, " Sons of the dogs, O come and get flesh ! " The Campbells had spoiled the bridge with a charge of powder, so we had to ford the river among the ice-lumps, MacDonald showing the way with his kilt-tail about his waist. A hunter from a hamlet at the glen foot gladly left the smoking ruin of his home and guided us on a drove-road into the wilds of Lochaber, among mountains more stupendous than those we had left behind. These relentless peaks were clad with blinding snow. The same choking drifts that met us in Corryarick filled the passes between Stob Choire and Easan Mor and Stob Ban, that cherish the snow in their crannies in the depths of midsummer. Hunger was eating at our hearts when we got to Glen Nevis, but the glen was empty of people, and the second night fell ere we broke fast.

I have hungered many times on weary marches, but yon was the most cruel hunger of my life. And though the pain of the starving could be dulled a little by draughts of water from the wayside springs, what there was no remede for was the weakness that turned the flesh in every part of me to a nerveless pulp. I went down Nevis Glen a man in a delirium. My head swam with vapours, so that the hillside seemed to dance round and before me. If I had fallen in the snow I should assuredly have lain there and died, and the thought of how simple and sweet it would be to stretch out my heavy limbs and sleep the sleep for ever, more than once robbed me of my will. Some of the Stewarts and Camerons, late recruits to the army, and as yet not inured to its toils, fell on the wayside halfway down the glen. MacDonald was for leaving them —" We have no need for weaklings," he said, cruelly, fuming at the delay ; but their lairds gave him a sharp answer, and said they would bide bye them till they had recovered. Thus a third of our force fell behind us in the march, and I would have been behind too, but for M'Iver's encouragement. His songs were long done; his stories chilled on his lip. The hunger had him at the heart, but he had a lion's will and a lion's vigour.

"For the love of God!" he said to me, "do not let them think we are so much of the Covenanter that we cannot keep up! For a Scots Cavalier you are giving in over early."

"Campaigning with Mackay was never like this," I pleaded, wearily; "give me the open road and an enemy before me, and I would tramp gaily to the world's end. Here's but a choked ravine the very deer abhor in such weather, and before us but a battle we must not share in."

He said never a word for a few moments, but trudged on. My low-heeled shoon were less fitted for the excursion than his close-thonged brogues that clung to the feet like a dry glove, and I walked lamely. Ever and anon he would look askance at me, and I was annoyed that he should think me a poorer mountaineer than those unwearied knaves who hurried us. I must have shown my feeling in my face, for in a little he let-on to fall lame too, and made the most grievous complaint of ache and weariness. His pretence deceived me but for a little. He was only at his old quirk of keeping me in good repute with myself, but he played the part with skill, letting us both fall behind the general company a little, so that the MacDonalds might not witness the indignity of it.

Glen Nevis, as I saw it that night in the light of the moon, is what comes to me now in my dreams. I smell the odour of the sweat-drenched, uncleanly cleeding of those savage clans about us; I see the hills lift on either hand with splintered peaks that prick among the stars—gorge and ravine and the wide ascending passes filled ever with the sound of the river, and the coarse, narrow drove-road leads into despair. That night the moon rode at the full about a vacant sky. There was not even a vapour on the hills; the wind had failed in the afternoon.

At the foot of the hill Carn Dearg (or the Red Mount), that is one of three gallant mountains that keep company for Nevis Ben the biggest of all, the path we followed made a twist to the left into a gully from which a blast of the morning's wind had cleaned out the snow as by a giant's spade.

So much the worse for us, for now the path lay strewn with boulders that the dragoons took long to thread through, and the bare feet of the private soldiers bled redly anew. Some lean high fir-trees threw this part into a shadow, and so it happened that as I felt my way wearily on, I fell over a stone. The fall lost me the last of my senses : I but heard some of the Stewarts curse me for an encumbrance as they stumbled over me and passed on, heedless of my fate, and saw, as in a dwam, one of them who had abraded his knees by his stumble over my body, turn round with a drawn knife that glinted in a shred of moonlight.

I came to, with M'Iver bent over me, and none of our captors at hand.

" I had rather this than a thousand rix-dollars," said he, as I sat up and leaned on my arm.

" Have they left us ? " I asked, with no particular interest in the answer. It could work little difference whatever it might be. " I thought I saw one of them turn on me with a knife."

" You did," said M'Iver. " He broke his part of the parole, and is lying on the other side of you, I think with a hole in his breast. An ugly and a treacherous scamp ! It's lucky for us that Montrose or MacColkitto never saw the transaction between this clay and John M'Iver, or their clemency had hardly been so great. ' You can bide and see to your friend,' was James Grahame's last words, and that's the reason I'm here."

M'Iver lifted me to my feet, and we stood a little to think what we should do. My own mind had no idea save the one that we were bound to keep in touch with the company whose prisoners we were, but M'Iver hinted at an alternative scarce so honest—namely, a desertion and a detour to the left that would maybe lead us to the Campbell army before active hostilities began.

" You would surely not break parole ? " said I, surprised, for he was usually as honourable in such matters as any Highlander I ever met.

"Bah!" he cried, pretending contempt at hesitation, though I could perceive by his voice he was somewhat ashamed of the policy he proposed. "Who quitted the contract first? Was it not that Stewart gentleman on your other side who broke it in a most dastardly way by aiming at your life?"

"I'm thankful for the life you saved, John," said I, "little worth though it seems at this time, but Montrose is not to be held responsible for the sudden impulse of a private. We made our pact as between gentleman and gentleman—let us be going."

"Oh, very well!" said he, shortly. "Let us be going. After all, we are in a trap anyway we look at all; for half the Stewarts and Camerons are behind in the wood there, and our flank retreat among these hills might be a tempting of Providence. But are you thinking of this Athole corp and what his kin will be doing to his slayers?"

"I'll risk it," I said, shortly. "We may be out of their hands one way or other before they miss him."

On a sudden there rose away before us towards the mouth of the glen the sound of a bagpipe. It came on the tranquil air with no break in its uproar, and after a preparatory tuning it broke into an air called "Cogadh no Sith"—an ancient braggart pibroch made by one Macruimen of the Isle of Sky,—a tune that was commonly used by the Campbells as a night-retreat or tattoo.

My heart filled with the strain. It gave me not only the simple illusion that I saw again the regimentals of my native country—many a friend and comrade among them in the shelter of the Castle of Inverlochy—but it roused in me a spirit very antique, very religious and moving too, as the music of his own land must in every honest Gael.

"Cruachan for ever!" I said lightly to M'Iver, though my heart was full.

He was as much touched by that homely lilt as myself. "The old days, the old styles!" said he. "God! how that pibroch stings me to the core!" And as the tune came more clearly in the second part, or Crunluadh as we call it, and the player maybe came round a bend of the road, my comrade stopped in his pace and added with what in another I might have thought a sob—"I've trudged the world; I have learned many bravadoes, so that my heart never stirred much to the mere trick of an instrument but one, and the *piob mhor* conquers me. What is it, Colin, that's in us, rich and poor, yon rude cane-reeds speak so human and friendly to?"

"'Tis the Gaelic," I said, cheered myself by the air. "Never a roar of the drone or a sob of the chanter but's in the Gaelic tongue."

"Maybe," said he, "maybe: I've heard the scholars like yourself say the sheepskin and the drones were Roman—that or Spanish, it's all one to me. I heard them at Boitzenburg when we gave the butt of the gun to Tilly's *soldadoes*, they played us into Holstein, and when the ditch of Stralsund was choked with the tartan of Mackay, and our lads were falling like corn before the hook, a Reay piper stood valiantly in front and played a salute. Then and now it's the pipes, my darling!"

"I would as lief have them in a gayer strain. My fondest memories are of reels I've danced to their playing," I said, and by now we were walking down the glen.

"And of one reel you danced," said he, quizzingly, "not more than two months gone in a town that was called Inneraora?"

"Two months!" I cried,—"two months! I could have sworn offhand we have been wandering in Lorn and Badenoch for as many years!"

Such spirit did my native pipes, played by a clansman, put in me that my weariness much abated, and we made great progress down the glen, so that before the tune had ceased we were on the back of Montrose's men as they crept on quietly in the night.

The piper stopped suddenly enough when some shots rang out,—an exchange of compliments between our pickets ahead and some wandering scouts of Argile.

And yonder below us, Loch Linnhe and Locheil glanced in the moonlight, and the strong towers of Inverlochy sat like a scowl on the fringe of the wave!

CHAPTER XX.

INVERLOCHY.

WHEN we came up with the main body of MacDonald's army, the country, as I say, was shining in the light of the moon, with only a camp-fire down in the field beside the castle to show in all the white world a sign of human life. We had got the Campbells in the rear, but they never knew it. A few of their scouts came out across the fields and challenged our pickets ; there was an exchange of musketry, but, as we found again, we were thought to be some of the Lochaber hunters unworthy of serious engagement.

For the second time in so many days we tasted food, a handful of meal to the quaich of water—no more and no less ; and James Grahame, Marquis of Montrose, supped his brose like the rest of us, with the knife from his belt doing the office of a horn-spoon.

Some hours after us came up the Camerons, who had fallen behind, but fresher and more eager for fighting than our own company, for they had fallen on a herd of roe on the slope of Sgur an Iolair, and had supped savagely on the warm raw flesh.

" You might have brought us a gigot off your take," Sir Alasdair said to the leader of them, Dol Ruadh. He was a short-tempered man of no great manners, and he only grunted his response.

" They may well call you Camerons of the soft mouth," said Alasdair, angrily, " that would treat your comrades so."

" You left us to carry our own men," said the chief, shortly ; " we left you to find your own deer."

We were perhaps the only ones who slept at the mouth of Glen Nevis that woeful night, and we slept because, as my comrade said, "What cannot be mended may be well slept on ; it's an ease to the heart." And the counsel was so wise and our weariness so acute, that we lay on the bare ground till we were roused to the call of a trumpet.

It was St Bridget's Day, and Sunday morning. A myriad bens around gave mists, as smoke from a censer, to the day. The Athole pipers high-breastedly strutted with a vain port up and down their lines and played incessantly. Alasdair laid out the clans with amazing skill, as M'Iver and I were bound to confess to ourselves, —the horse (with Montrose himself on his charger) in the centre, the men of Clanranald, Keppoch, Locheil, Glengarry, and Maclean, and the Stewarts of Appin behind. MacDonald and O'Kyan led the Irish on the wings.

In the plain we could see Argile's forces in a somewhat similar order, with the tartan as it should be in the midst of the bataille and the Lowland levies on the flanks. Over the centre waved the black galley of Lorne on a gold standard.

I expressed some doubt about the steadfastness of the Lowlanders, and M'Iver was in sad agreement with me.

"I said it in Glenaora when we left," said he, "and I say it again. They would be fairly good stuff against foreign troops ; but they have no suspicion of the character of Gaelic war. I'm sore feared they'll prove a poor reed to lean on. Why, in heaven's name, does Mac-Cailein take the risk of a battle in such an awkward corner ? An old soldier like Auchinbreac should advise him to follow the Kilcumin road and join forces with Seaforth, who must be far down Glen Albyn by now."

As we were standing apart thus, up to us came Ian Lom, shaking the brogue-money he got from Grahame in his dirty loof. He was very bitter.

"I never earned an honester penny," he said, looking up almost insolently in our faces, so that it was a temptation to give him a clout on the cunning jowl.

"So Judas thought too, I daresay, when he fingered his filthy shekels," said I. "I thought no man from Keppoch would be skulking aside here when his pipers blew the onset."

"Och!" said M'Iver, "what need ye be talking? Bardery and bravery don't very often go together."

Ian Lom scowled blackly at the taunt, but was equal to answer it.

"If the need arise," said he, "you'll see whether the bard is brave or not. There are plenty to fight; there's but one to make the song of the fight, and that's John MacDonald, with your honours' leave."

We would, like enough, have been pestered with the scamp's presence and garrulity a good deal longer; but Montrose came up at that moment and took us aside with a friendly enough beckon of his head.

"Gentlemen," he said in English, "as cavaliers you can guess fairly well already the issue of what's to happen below there, and as Cavaliers who, clansmen or no clansmen of the Campbell chief, have done well for old Scotland's name abroad, I think you deserve a little more consideration at our hands at this juncture than common prisoners of war can lay claim to. If you care you can quit here as soon as the onset begins, abiding of course by your compact to use no arms against my friends. You have no objection?" he added, turning about on his horse and crying to Alasdair.

The Major-General came up and looked at us. "I suppose they may go," said he,—"though, to tell my mind on the matter, I could devise a simpler way of getting rid of them. We have other methods in Erin O, but as your lordship has taken the fancy, they may go, I daresay. Only they must not join their clan or take arms with them until this battle is over. They must be on the Loch Linnhe road before we call the onset."

Montrose flushed at the ill-breeding of his officer, and waved us away to the left on the road that led to Argile by Loch Linnhe-side, and took us clear of the coming encounter.

We were neither of us slow to take advantage of the opportunity, but set off at a sharp walk at the moment that O'Kyan on the right flank was slowly moving in the direction of Argile's line.

John broke his sharp walk so quickly into a canter that I wondered what he meant. I ran close at his heels, but I forbore to ask, and we had put a good lump of moorland between us and the MacDonalds before he explained.

"You perhaps wondered what my hurry was," he said, with the sweat standing in beads on his face, though the air was full of frost. "It wasn't for exercise, as you might guess at anyrate. The fact is, we were within five minutes of getting a wheen Stewart dirks in our doublets, and if there was no brulzie on foot we were even yet as good as lost on Brae Lochaber."

"How does that happen?" I asked. "They seemed to let us away generously enough and with no great ill-will."

"Just so! But when Montrose gave us the *congé*, I happened to turn an eye up Glen Nevis and I saw some tardy Stewarts (by their tartan) come running down the road. These were the lads Dol Ruadh left behind last night, and they could scarcely miss in daylight the corpse we left by the road, and their clansmen missed in the mirk. That was my notion at the first glance I got of them, and when we ran they ran too, and what do you make of that?"

"What we should make of it," I said in alarm, "is as good a pace into Lorn as we can: they may be on the heels of us now,"—for we were in a little dip of the ground from which the force we had just parted so gladly were not to be seen.

On that point M'Iver speedily assured me.

"No, no!" he said. "If Seumas Grahame himself were stretched out yonder instead of a Glenart cearnoch of no great importance to any one, Alasdair MacDonald would be scarcely zealous fool enough to spoil his battle order to prosecute a private feud. Look at that," he proceeded, turning round on a little knowe he ran lightly up on and I after him—"Look at that! the battle's begun."

We stood on that knowe of Brae Lochaber, and I saw from thence a spectacle whose like, by the grace of God, I have never seen before nor since in its agony for any eye that was friendly to Diarmaid Clan. I need not here set down the sorry end of that day at Inverlochy. It has been written many times, though I harbour no book on my shelves that tells the story. We saw MacDonald's charge; we saw the wings of Argile's army—the rotten Lowland levies—break off and skurry along the shore; we saw the lads of the Diarmaid tartan hewn down on the edge of the tide till its waves ran red; but we were as helpless as the rush that waved at our feet. Between us and our friends lay the enemy and our parole—I daresay our parole was forgotten in that terrible hour.

John M'Iver laid him down on the *tulaich* and clawed with his nails the stunted grass that in wind-blown patches came through the snow. None of my words made any difference on his anguish. I was piping to the surrender of sorrow, nigh mad myself.

The horses of Ogilvie—who himself fell in the brulzie —chased the Lowlanders along the side of Loch Linnhe, and so few of the flying had the tartan that we had no great interest in them, till we saw six men with their plaiding cast run unobserved up the plain, wade waist-deep through the Nevis, and come somewhat in our direction. We went down to join them, and ran hard and fast and came on them at a place called the Rhu at the water of Kiachnish.

CHAPTER XXI.

SEVEN BROKEN MEN.

AT last there was but one horseman in chase of the six men who were fleeing without a look behind them—a frenzied blackavised trooper on a short-legged garron he rode most clumsily, with arms that swung like wings from the shoulders, his boots keeping time to the canter with grotesque knockings against the gaunt and sweating flanks of his starven animal. He rode with a shout, and he rode with a fool's want of calculation, for he had left all support behind him and might readily enough have been cut off by any judicious enemy in the rear. Before we could hurry down to join the fugitives they observed for themselves that the pursuit had declined to this solitary person, so up they drew (all but one of them), with dirks or sgians out to give him his welcome. And yet the dragoon put no check on his horse. The beast, in a terror at the din of the battle, was indifferent to the rein of its master, whom it bore with thudding hooves to a front that must certainly have appalled him. He was a person of some pluck, or perhaps the drunkenness of terror lent him the illusion of valour; at least, when he found a bloody end inevitable he made the best of the occasion. Into the heaving sides of the brute he drove desperate spurs, anew he shouted a scurrilous name at Clan Campbell, then fired his pistol as he fell upon the enemy.

The *dag* failed of its purpose, but the breast of the horse struck an elderly man on the brow and threw him on his back, so that one of the hind-hooves of the animal crushed in his skull like a hazel-nut.

Who of that fierce company brought the trooper to his end we never knew, but when M'Iver and I got down to the level he was dead as knives could make him, and his horse, more mad than ever, was disappearing over a mossy moor with a sky-blue lochan in the midst of it.

Of the five Campbells three were gentlemen—Forbes the baron-bailie of Ardkinglas, Neil Campbell in Sonachan, Lochowside, and the third no other than Master Gordon the minister, who was the most woe-begone and crest-fallen of them all. The other two were small tacksmen from the neighbourhood of Inneraora—one Callum Mac-Iain vic Ruarie vic Allan (who had a little want, as we say of a character, or natural, and was ever moist with tears), and a Rob Campbell in Auchnatra, whose real name was Stewart, but who had been in some trouble at one time in a matter of a neighbour's sheep on the braes of Appin, had discreetly fled that country, and brought up a family under a borrowed name in a country that kept him in order.

We were, without doubt, in a most desperate extremity. If we had escaped the immediate peril of the pursuing troopers of MacDonald, we had a longer, wearier hazard before us. Any one who knows the countryside I am writing of, or takes a glance at my relative Neill Bane's diagram or map of the same, will see that we were now in the very heart of a territory hotching (as the rough phrase goes) with clans inimical to the house of Argile. Between us and the comparative safety of Bredalbane lay Stewarts, MacDonalds, Macgregors, and other families less known in history, who hated the name of MacCailein more than they feared the wrath of God. The sight of our tartan in any one of their glens would rouse hell in every heart about us.

Also our numbers and the vexed state of the times were against us. We could hardly pass for peaceable drovers at such a season of the year; we were going the wrong airt for another thing, and the fact that not we alone but many more of Argile's forces in retreat were fleeing home would be widely advertised around the valleys in a very few hours after the battle had been fought. For the news of war—good or ill—passes among the glens with a magic speed. It runs faster than the fiery cross itself—so fast and inexplicable on any natural law, that more than once I have been ready to believe it a witches' premonition more than a message carried on young men's feet.

"But all that," said Sonachan, a pawky, sturdy little gentleman with a round ruddy face and a great store of genealogy that he must be ever displaying—"But all that makes it more incumbent on us to hang together. It may easily be a week before we get into Glenurchy ; we must travel by night and hide by day, and besides the heartening influence of company there are sentinels to consider and the provision of our food."

Ardkinglas, on the other hand, was a fushionless, stupid kind of man : he was for an immediate dispersion of us all, holding that only in individuals or in pairs was it possible for us to penetrate in safety to real Argile.

"I'm altogether with Sonachan," said M'Iver, "and I could mention half a hundred soldierly reasons for the policy ; but it's enough for me that here are seven of us, no more and no less, and with seven there should be all the luck that's going."

He caught the minister's eyes on him at this, and met them with a look of annoyance.

"Oh yes, I know, Master Gordon, you gentlemen of the lawn bands have no friendliness to our old Highland notions. Seven or six, it's all the same to you, I suppose, except in a question of merks to the stipend."

"You're a clever man enough, M'Iver——"

"Barbreck," corrected my friend, punctiliously.

"Barbreck let it be then. But you are generally so sensitive to other folk's thoughts of you that your skin tingles to an insult no one dreamt of paying. I make no doubt a great many of your Gaelic beliefs are sheer paganism or Popery or relics of the same, but the charm of seven has a Scriptural warrant that as minister of the Gospel I have some respect for, even when twisted into a portent for a band of broken men in the extremity of danger."

We had to leave the dead body of our friend, killed by the horse, on the hillside. He was a Knapdale man, a poor creature, who was as well done, perhaps, with a world that had no great happiness left for him, for his home had been put to the torch and his wife outraged and murdered. At as much speed as we could command, we threaded to the south, not along the valleys but in the braes, suffering anew the rigour of the frost and the snow. By midday we reached the shore of Loch Leven, and it seemed as if now our flight was hopelessly barred, for the ferry that could be compelled to take the army of Mac-Cailein over the brackish water at Lettermore was scarce likely to undertake the conveying back of seven fugitives of the clan that had come so high-handedly through their neighbourhood four days ago. On this side there was not a boat in sight; indeed there was not a vestige on any side of human tenancy. Glencoe had taken with him every man who could carry a pike, not to our disadvantage perhaps, for it left the less danger of any strong attack.

On the side of the loch, when we emerged from the hills, there was a cluster of whin-bushes spread out upon a machar of land that in a less rigorous season of the year, by the feel of the shoe-sole, must be velvet-piled with salty grass. It lay in the clear, grey forenoon like a garden of fairydom to the view—the whin-bushes at a distant glance floating on billows of snow, touched at their lee by a cheering green, hung to the windward with the silver of the snow, and some of them even prinked off with the gold flower that gives rise to the proverb about kissing being out of fashion when the whin wants bloom. To come on this silent, peaceful, magic territory, fresh out of the turmoil of a battle, was to be in a region haunted, in the borderland of morning dreams, where care is a vague and far-off memory, and the elements study our desires. The lake spread out before us without a ripple, its selvedge at the shore repeating the picture on the brae. I looked on it with a mind peculiarly calm, rejoicing in its aspect. Oh, love and the coming years, thought I, let them be here or somewhere like it—not among the savage of the hills, fighting, plotting, contriving; not among snow-swept mounts and crying and wailing brooks, but by the sedate and tranquil sea in calm weather. As we walked, my friends with furtive looks to this side and yon, down to the shore, I kept my face to the hills of real Argile, and my heart was full of love. I got that glimpse that comes to most of us (had we the wit to comprehend it) of the future of my life. I beheld in a wave of the emotion the picture of my coming years, going down from day to day very unadventurous and calm, spent in some peaceful valley by a lake, sitting at no rich-laden board but at bien and happy viands with some neighbour heart. A little bird of hope fluted within me, so that I knew that if every clan in this countryside was arraigned against me, I had the breastplate of fate on my breast. " I shall not die in this unfriendly country," I promised myself. " There may be terror, and there may be gloom, but I shall watch my children's children play upon the braes of Shira Glen."

" You are very joco," said John to me as I broke into a little laugh of content with myself.

" It's the first time you ever charged me with jocosity, John," I said. " I'm just kind of happy thinking."

" Yon spectacle behind us is not humorous to my notion," said he, " whatever it may be to yours. And perhaps the laugh may be on the other side of your face before the night comes. We are here in a spider's web."

" I cry pardon for my lightness, John," I answered ; " I'll have time enough to sorrow over the clan of Argile. But if you had the Sight of your future, and it lay in other and happier scenes than these, would you not feel something of a gaiety ? "

He looked at me with an envy in every feature, from me to his companions, from them to the country round about us, and then to himself as to a stranger whose career was revealed in every rag of his clothing.

" So," said he ; " you are the lucky man to be of the breed of the elect of heaven, to get what you want for the mere desire of it, and perhaps without deserve. Here am I at my prime and over it, and no glisk of the future before me. I must be ever stumbling on, a carouser of life in a mirk and sodden lane."

" You cannot know my meaning," I cried.

" I know it fine," said he. " You get what you want

because you are the bairn of content. And I'm but the child of hurry (it's the true word), and I must be seeking and I must be trying to the bitter end."

He kicked, as he walked, at the knolls of snow in his way, and lashed at the bushes with a hazel wand he had lifted from a tree.

"Not all I want, perhaps," said I; "for do you know that fleeing thus from the disgrace of my countrymen, I could surrender every sorrow and every desire to one notion about—about—about——"

"A girl of the middle height," said he, "and her name is——"

"Do not give it an utterance," I cried. "I would be sorry to breathe her name in such a degradation. Degradation indeed, and yet if I had the certainty that I was a not altogether hopeless suitor yonder, I would feel a conqueror greater than Hector or Gilian-of-the-Axe."

"Ay, ay," said John. "I would not wonder. And I'll swear that a man of your fate may have her if he wants her. I'll give ye my notion of wooing; it's that with the woman free and the man with some style and boldness, he may have whoever he will."

"I would be sorry to think it," said I; "for that might apply to suitors at home in Inneraora as well as me."

M'Iver laughed at the sally, and "Well, well," said he, "we are not going to be debating the chance of love on Leven-side, with days and nights of slinking in the heather and the fern between us and our home."

Though this conversation of ours may seem singularly calm and out of all harmony with our circumstances, it is so only on paper, for in fact it took but a minute or two of our time as we walked down among those whins that inspired me with the peaceful premonition of the coming years. We were walking, the seven of us, not in a compact group, but scattered, and at the whins when we rested we sat in ones and twos behind the bushes, with eyes cast anxiously along the shore for sign of any craft that might take us over.

What might seem odd to any one who does not know the shrinking mood of men broken with a touch of disgrace in their breaking, was that for long we studiously said nothing of the horrors we had left behind us. Five men fleeing from a disastrous field and two new out of the clutches of a conquering foe, we were dumb or discoursed of affairs very far removed from the reflection that we were a clan at extremities.

But we could keep up this silence of shame no longer than our running: when we sat among the whins on Leven-side, and took a breath and scrutinised along the coast, for sign of food or ferry, we must be talking of what we had left behind.

Gordon told the story with a pained, constrained, and halting utterance: of the surprise of Auchinbreac when he heard the point of war from Nevis Glen, and could not believe that Montrose was so near at hand; of the wavering Lowland wings, the slaughter of the Campbell gentlemen.

"We were in a trap," said he, drawing with a stick on the smooth snow a diagram of the situation. "We were between brae and water. I am no man of war, and my heart swelled at the spectacle of the barons cut down like nettles. And by the most foolish of tactics, surely, a good many of our forces were on the other side of the loch."

"That was not Auchinbreac's doing, I'll warrant," said M'Iver; "he would never have counselled a division so fatal."

"Perhaps not," said the cleric, drily; "but what if a general has only a sort of savage army at his call? The gentry of your clan——"

"What about MacCailein?" I asked, wondering that there was no word of the chief.

"Go on with your story," said M'Iver, sharply, to the cleric.

"The gentry of your clan," said Gordon, paying no heed to my query, "were easy enough to guide; but yon undisciplined kerns from the hills had no more regard for martial law than for the holy commandments. God help them! They went their own gait, away from the main body, plundering and robbing."

"I would not just altogether call it plundering, nor yet robbing," said John, a show of annoyance on his face.

"And I don't think myself," said Sonachan, removing, as he spoke, from our side, and going to join the three others, who sat apart from us a few yards, "that it's a gentleman's way of speaking of the doings of other gentlemen of the same name and tartan as ourselves."

"Ay, ay," said the minister, looking from one to the other of us, his shaven jowl with lines of a most annoying pity on it—"Ay, ay," said he, "it would be pleasing you better, no doubt, to hint at no vice or folly in your army; that's the Highlands for you! I'm no Highlander, thank God, or at least with the savage long out of me; for I'm of an honest and orderly Lowland stock, and my trade's the Gospel and the truth, and the truth you'll get from Alexander Gordon, Master of the Arts, if you had your black joctilegs at his neck for it!"

He rose up, pursing his face, panting at the nostril, very crouse and defiant in every way.

"Oh, you may just sit you down," said M'Iver, sharply, to him. "You can surely give us truth without stamping it down our throats with your boots, that are not, I've noticed, of the smallest size."

"I know you, sir, from boot to bonnet," said Gordon.

"You're well off in your acquaintance," said M'Iver, jocularly. "I wish I kent so good a man."

"From boot to bonnet," said Gordon, in no whit abashed by the irony. "Man, do you know," he went on, "there's a time comes to me now when by the grace of God I can see to one's innermost as through a lozen. I shudder, sometimes, at the gift. For there's the fair face, and there's the smug and smiling lip, and there's the flattery at the tongue, and below that masked front is Beelzebub himself, meaning well sometimes— perhaps always — but by his fall a traitor first and last."

"God!" cried M'Iver, with a very ugly face, "that sounds awkwardly like a roundabout way of giving me a bad character."

"I said, sir," answered Gordon, "that poor Beelzebub does not sometimes ken his own trade. I have no doubt that in your heart you are touched to the finest by love of your fellows."

"And that's the truth—when they are not clerics," cried John.

"Touched to the finest, and set in a glow too, by a manly and unselfish act, and eager to go through this world on pleasant footings with yourself and all else."

"Come, come," I cried; "I know my friend well, Master Gordon. We are not all that we might be; but I'm grateful for the luck that brought me so good a friend as John M'Iver."

"I never cried down his credit," said the minister, simply.

"Your age gives you full liberty," said John. "I would never lift a hand."

"The lifting of your hand," said the cleric with a flashing eye, "is the last issue I would take thought of. I can hold my own. You are a fair and shining vessel (of a kind), but Beelzebub's at your heart. They tell me that people like you; this gentleman of Elrigmore claims you for his comrade. Well, well, so let it be! It but shows anew the charm of the glittering exterior: they like you for your weaknesses and not for your strength. Do you know anything of what they call duty?"

"I have starved to the bone in Laaland without complaint, stood six weeks on watch in Stralsund's Franken gate, eating my meals at my post, and John M'Iver never turned skirts on an enemy."

"Very good, sir, very good," said the minister; "but duty is most ill to do when it is to be done in love and not in hate."

"Damn all schooling!" cried John. "You're off in the depths of it again, and I cannot be after you. Duty is duty in love or hate, is it not?"

"It would take two or three sessions of St Andrews to show you that it makes a great differ whether it is done in love or hate. You do your duty by your enemy well enough, no doubt,—a barbarian of the blackest will do no less,—but it takes the better man to do his duty sternly by those he loves and by himself above all. Argile——"

"Yes," cried I, "what about Argile?"

The minister paid no heed to my question.

"Argile," said he, "has been far too long flattered by you and your like, M'Iver."

"Barbreck," put in my comrade.

"Barbreck be it then. A man in his position thus never learns the truth. He sees around him but plausible faces and the truth at a cowardly compromise. That's the sorrow of your Highlands; it will be the black curse of your chiefs in the day to come. As for me, I'm for duty first and last—even if it demands me to put a rope at my brother's neck or my hand in the fire."

"Maybe you are, maybe you are," said John, "and it's very fine of you; and I'm not denying but I can fancy some admirable quality in the character. But if I'm no great hand at the duty, I can swear to the love."

"It's a word I hate to hear men using," said I.

The minister relaxed to a smile at John's amiability, and John smiled on me.

"It's a woman's word, I daresay, Colin," said he; "but there's no man, I'll swear, turning it over more often in his mind than yourself."

"Where we lay, the Pap of Glencoe—Sgor-na-ciche, as they call it in the Gaelic—loomed across Loch Leven in wisps of wind-blown grey. Long-beaked birds came to the sand and piped a sharp and anxious note, or chattered like children. The sea-banks floated on the water, rising and dipping to every wave; it might well be a dream we were in on the borderland of sleep at morning.

"What about Argile?" I asked again.

The minister said never a word. John Splendid rose to his feet, shook the last of his annoyance from him, and cast an ardent glance to those remote hills of Lorn.

"God's grandeur!" said he, turning to the Gaelic it was proper to use but sparingly before a Saxon. "Behold the unfriendliness of those terrible mountains and ravines! I am Gaelic to the core, but give me in this mood of mine the flat south soil and the dip of the sky round a bannock of country. Oh, I wish I were where Aora runs! I wish I saw the highway of Loch Finne that leads down the slope of the sea where the towns pack close together and fires are warm!" He went on and sang a song of the low country, its multitude of cattle, its friendly hearths, its frequented walks of lovers in the dusk and in the spring.

Sonachan and Ardkinglas and the tacksmen came over to listen, and the man with the want began to weep with a child's surrender.

" And what about Argile ? " said I, when the humming ceased.

" You are very keen on that bit, lad," said the baron-bailie, smiling spitefully with thin hard lips that revealed his teeth gleaming white and square against the dusk of his face. " You are very keen on that bit ; you might be waiting for the rest of the minister's story."

" Oh," I said, " I did not think there was any more of the minister's tale to come. I crave his pardon."

" I think, too, I have not much more of a story to tell," said the minister, stiffly.

" And I think," said M'Iver, in a sudden hurry to be off, " that we might be moving from here. The head of the loch is the only way for us if we are to be off this unwholesome countryside by the mouth of the night."

It is likely we would have taken him at his word, and have risen and gone on his way to the east, where the narrowing of the loch showed that it was close on its conclusion ; but the Stewart took from his knapsack some viands that gave a frantic edge to our appetite and compelled us to stay and eat.

The day was drawing to its close, the sun, falling behind us, was pillowed on clouds of a rich crimson. For the first time, we noticed the signs of the relaxation of the austere season in the return of bird and beast to their familiar haunts. As the sun dipped the birds came out to the brae-side to catch his last ray, as they ever love to do. Whaups rose off the sand, and, following the gleam upon the braes, ascended from slope to slope, and the plover followed too, dipping his feet in the golden tide receding. On little fir-patches mounted numerous black-cock of sheeny feather, and the owls began to hoot in the wood beyond.

CHAPTER XXII.

DAME DUBH.

WE had eaten to the last crumb, and were ready to be going, when again I asked Gordon what had come over Argile.

"I'll tell you that," said he, bitterly; but as he began, some wildfowl rose in a startled flight to our right and whirred across the sky.

"There's some one coming," said M'Iver; "let us keep close together."

From where the wildfowl rose, the Dame Dubh, as we called the old woman of Carnus, came in our direction, half-running, half-walking through the snow. She spied us while she was yet a great way off, stopped a second as one struck with an arrow, then continued her progress more eagerly than ever, with high-piped cries and taunts at us.

"O cowards!" she cried; "do not face Argile, or the glens you belong to. Cowards, cowards, Lowland women, Glencoe's full of laughter at your disgrace!"

"Royal's my race, I'll not be laughed at!" cried Stewart.

"They cannot know of it already in Glencoe!" said M'Iver, appalled.

"Know it!" said the crone, drawing nearer and with still more frenzy; "Glencoe has songs on it already. The stench from Inverlochy's in the air; it's a mock in Benderloch and Ardgour, it's a nightmare in Glenurchy, and the women are keening on the slopes of Cladich. Cowards, cowards, little men, cowards! all the curses of Conan on you and the black rocks; die from home, and Hell itself reject you!"

We stood in front of her in a group, slack at the arms and shoulders, bent a little at the head, affronted for the first time with the full shame of our disaster. All my bright portents of the future seemed, as they flashed again before me, muddy in the hue, an unfaithful man's remembrance of his sins when they come before him at the bedside of his wife; the evasions of my friends revealed themselves what they were indeed, the shutting of the eyes against shame.

The woman's meaning Master Gordon could only guess at, and he faced her composedly.

"You are far off your road," he said to her mildly, but she paid him no heed.

"You have a bad tongue, mother," said M'Iver.

She turned and spat on his vest, and on him anew she poured her condemnation.

"*You*, indeed, the gentleman with an account to pay, the hero, the avenger! I wish my teeth had found your neck at the head of Aora Glen." She stood in the half-night, foaming over with hate and evil words, her taunts stinging like asps.

"Take off the tartan, ladies!" she screamed; "off with men's apparel and on with the short-gown."

Her cries rang so over the land that she was a danger bruiting our presence to the whole neighbourhood, and it was in a common panic we ran with one accord from her in the direction of the loch-head. The man with the want took up the rear, whimpering as he ran, feeling again, it might be, a child fleeing from maternal chastisement: the rest of us went silently, all but Stewart, who was a cocky little man with a large bonnet pulled down on the back of his head like a morion, to hide the absence of ears that had been cut off by the law for some of his Appin adventures. He was a person who never saw in most of a day's transactions aught but the humour of them, and as we ran from this shrieking beldame of Carnus, he was choking with laughter at the ploy.

"Royal's my race," said he at the first ease to our running—"Royal's my race, and I never thought to run twice in one day from an enemy. Stop your greeting, Callum, and not be vexing our friends the gentlemen."

"What a fury!" said Master Gordon. "And that's the lady of omens! What about her blessing now?"

"Ay, and what about her prophecies?" asked M'Iver, sharply. "She was not so far wrong, I'm thinking, about the risks of Inverlochy; the heather's above the gall indeed."

"But at any rate," said I, "MacCailein's head is not on a pike."

"You must be always on the old key," cried M'Iver, angrily. "Oh man, man, but you're sore in want of tact." His face was throbbing and hoved. "Here's half-a-dozen men," said he, "with plenty to occupy their wits with what's to be done and what's to happen them before they win home, and all your talk is on a most vexatious trifle. Have you found me, a cousin of the Marquis, anxious to query our friends here about the ins and outs of the engagement? It's enough for me that the heather's above the gall. I saw this dreary morning the sorrow of my life, and I'm in no hurry to add to it by the value of a single tear."

Sonachan was quite as bitter. "I don't think," said he, "that it matters very much to you, sir, what Argile may have done or may not have done; you should be glad of your luck (if luck it was and no design), that kept you clear of the trouble altogether." And again he plunged ahead of us with Ardkinglas, to avoid my retort to an impertinence that, coming from a younger man, would have more seriously angered me.

The minister by now had recovered his wind, and was in another of his sermon moods, with this ruffling at Mac-Cailein's name as his text.

"I think I can comprehend," said he, "all this unwillingness to talk about my lord of Argile's part in the disaster of to-day. No Gael though I am, I'm loath myself to talk about a bad black business, but that's because I love my master—for master he is in scholarship, in gifts, in every attribute and intention of the Christian soldier. It is for a different reason, I'm afraid, that our friend Barbreck shuffles."

"Barbreck never shuffles," said John, stiffly. "If he did in this matter, it would be for as true an affection for his chief as any lalland cleric ever felt for his patron."

"And yet, sir, you shuffle for another reason too. You do not want to give your ridiculous Highland pride the shock of hearing that your chief left in a galley before the battle he lost had well begun."

A curious cry came from M'Iver's lips. He lifted his

face, lined with sudden shadows, to the stars that now were lighting to the east, and I heard his teeth grind.

"So that's the bitter end of it!" said I to myself, stunned by this pitiful conclusion. My mind groped back on the events of the whole waeful winter. I saw Argile again at peace among his own people; I heard anew his clerkly but wavering sentiment on the trade of the sword; I sat by him in the mouth of Glen Noe, and the song and the guess went round the fire. But the picture that came to me first and stayed with me last was Argile standing in his chamber in the castle of Inneraora, the pallor of the study on his face, and his little Archie, with his gold hair and the night-gown, running out and clasping him about the knees.

We struggled through the night, weary men, hungry men. Loch Leven-head may be bonny by day, but at night it is far from friendly to the unaccustomed wanderer. Swampy meadows frozen to the hard bone, and uncountable burns, and weary ascents, and alarming dips, lie there at the foot of the great forest of Mamore. And to us, poor fugitives, even these were less cruel than the thickets at the very head where the river brawled into the loch with a sullen surrender of its mountain independence.

About seven or eight o'clock we got safely over a ford and into the hilly country that lies tumbled to the north of Glencoe. Before us lay the choice of two routes, either of them leading in the direction of Glenurchy, but both of them hemmed in by the most inevitable risks, especially as but one of all our party was familiar (and that one but middling well) with the countryside. "The choice of a cross-road at night in a foreign land is Tall John's pick of the farmer's daughters," as our homely proverb has it; you never know what you have till the morn's morning. And our picking was bad indeed, for instead of taking what we learned again was a drove-road through to Tynree, we stood more to the right and plunged into what after all turned out to be nothing better than a corrie among the hills. It brought us up a most steep hillside, and landed us two hours' walk later far too much in the heart and midst of Glencoe to be for our comfort. From the hillside we emerged upon, the valley lay revealed, a great hack among the mountains.

CHAPTER XXIII.

THE WIDOW OF GLENCOE.

OF the seven of us, Stewart was the only one with a notion of the lie of the country. He had bought cattle in the glen, and he had borrowed (as we may be putting it) in the same place, and a man with the gifts of observation and memory, who has had to guess his way at night among foreign clans and hills with a drove of unwilling and mourning cattle before him, has many a feature of the neighbourhood stamped upon his mind. Stewart's idea was that to-night we might cross Glencoe, dive into one of the passes that run between the mountains called the Big and Little Herdsman, or between the Little Herd and Ben Fhada, into the foot of the forest of Dalness, then by the corries through the Black Mount of Bredalbane to Glenurchy. Once on the Brig of Urchy, we were as safe, in a manner, as on the shores of Loch Finne. On Neill Bane's map this looks a very simple journey, that a vigorous mountaineer could accomplish without fatigue in a couple of days if he knew the drove-roads ; but it was a wicked season for such an enterprise, and if the Dame Dubh's tale was right (as well enough it might be, for the news of Argile's fall would be round the world in a rumour of wind), every clan among these valleys and hills would be on the hunting-road to cut down broken men seeking their way back to the country of MacCailein Mor. Above all was it a hard task for men who had been starving on a half-meal drammock for two or three days. I myself felt the hunger gnawing at my inside like a restless red-hot conscience. My muscles were like iron, and with a footman's feeding, I could have walked to Inneraora without more than two or three hours' sleep at a time; but my weakness for food was so great that the prospect before me was appalling.

It appalled, indeed, the whole of us. Fancy us on barren hills, unable to venture into the hamlets or townships where we had brought torch and pike a few days before; unable to borrow or to buy, hazarding no step of the foot without a look first to this side and then to yon, lest enemies should be up against us. Is it a wonder that very soon we had the slouch of the gangrel and the cunning aspect of the thief? But there's something in gentle blood that always come out on such an occasion. The baron-bailie and Neil Campbell, and even the minister, made no ado about their hunger, though they were suffering keenly from it; only the two tacksmen kept up a ceaseless grumbling.

M'Iver kept a hunter's ear and eye alert at every step of our progress. He had a hope that the white hares, whose footprints sometimes showed among the snow, might run, as I have seen them do at night, within reach of a cudgel; he kept a constant search for badger-hamlets, for he would have dug from his sleep that gluttonous fat-haunched rascal who gorges himself in his own yellow moon-time of harvest. But hare nor badger fell in our way.

The moon was up, but a veil of grey cloud overspread the heavens and a frosty haze obscured the country. A clear cold hint at an odour of spring was already in the air, perhaps the first rumour the bush gets that the sap must rise. Out of the haze now and then, as we descended to the valley, there would come the peculiar cry of the red-deer, or the flaff of a wing, or the bleat of a goat. It was maddening to be in the neighbourhood of the meal that roe, or bird, or goat would offer, and yet be unable to reach it.

Thus we were stumbling on, very weary, very hungry, the man with the want in a constant wail, and Sonachan lamenting for suppers he had been saucy over in days of rowth and plenty, when a light oozed out of the grey-dark ahead of us, in the last place in the world one would look for any such sign of humanity.

We stopped on the moment, and John Splendid went ahead to see what lay in the way. He was gone but a little when he came back with a hearty accent to tell us that luck for once was ours.

"There's a house yonder," said he, talking English for the benefit of the cleric ; "it has a roaring fire and every sign of comfort, and it's my belief there's no one at home within but a woman and a few bairns. The odd thing is that as I get a look of the woman between the door-post and the wall, she sits with her back to the cruisie-light, patching clothes and crooning away at a dirge that's broken by her tears. If it had been last week, and our little adventures in Glencoe had brought us so far up this side of the glen, I might have thought she had suffered something at our hands. But we were never near this tack-house before, so the housewife's sorrow, whatever it is, can scarcely be at our door. Anyway," he went on, "here are seven cold men, and weary men and hungry men too (and that's the worst of it), and I'm going to have supper and a seat, if it's the last in the world."

"I hope there's going to be no robbery about the affair," said the minister, in an apparent dread of rough theft and maybe worse.

M'Iver's voice had a sneer in every word of it when he answered in a very affected tongue of English he was used to assume when he wished to be at his best before a Saxon.

"Is it the logic of your school," he asked, "that what's the right conduct of war when we are in regiments is robbery when we are but seven broken men ? I'm trying to mind that you found fault with us for helping ourselves in this same Glencoe last week, and refused to eat Corry-oick's beef in Appin, and I cannot just recall the circumstance. Are we not, think ye, just as much at war with Glencoe now as then ? And have seven starving men not an even better right, before God, to forage for themselves than has an army ? "

"There's a difference," said the minister, stiffly. "We were then legitimate troops of war, fighting for the Solemn League and Covenant under a noble lord with Letters. It was the Almighty's cause, and——"

"Was it indeed?" said John Splendid. "And was Himself on the other side of Loch Leven when His tulzie was on?"

"Scoffer!" cried Gordon, and M'Iver said no more, but led us through the dark to the house whose light so cheerfully smiled before us.

The house, when we came to it, proved a trig little edifice of far greater comfort than most of the common houses of the Highlands—not a dry-stone bigging but a rubble tenement, very snugly thacked and windowed, and having a piece of kail-plot at its rear. It was perched well up on the brae, and its light at evening must have gleamed like a friendly star far up the glen, that needs every touch of brightness to mitigate its gloom. As we crept close up to it in the snow, we could hear the crooning John Splendid had told us of, a most doleful sound in a land of darkness and strangers.

"Give a rap, and when she answers the door we can tell our needs peaceably," said the minister.

"I'm not caring about rapping, and I'm not caring about entering at all now," said M'Iver, turning about with some uneasiness. "I wish we had fallen on a more cheery dwelling, even if it were to be coerced with club and pistol. A prickle's at my skin that tells me here is dool, and I can smell mort-cloth."

Sonachan gave a grunt, and thumped loudly on the fir boards. A silence that was like a swound fell on the instant, and the light within went out at a puff. For a moment it seemed as if our notion of occupancy and light and lament had been a delusion, for now the grave itself was no more desolate and still.

"I think we might be going," said I in a whisper, my heart thud-thudding at my vest, my mind sharing some of John Splendid's apprehension that we were intruders on some profound grief. And yet my hunger was a furious thing that belched red-hot at my stomach.

"Royal's my race!" said Stewart. "I'll be kept tirling at no door-pin in the Highlands,—let us drive in the bar."

"What does he say?" asked the cleric, and I gave him the English of it.

"You'll drive no doors in here," said he firmly to Stewart. "We can but give another knock and see what comes of it. Knock you, M'Iver."

"Barbreck."

"Barbreck be it then."

"I would sooner go to the glen foot, and risk all," said John.

Sonachan grunted again; out he drew his dirk, and he rapped with the hilt of it loud and long at the door. A crying of children rose within, and, behold, I was a child again! I was a child again in Shira Glen, alone in a little chamber with a window uncurtained and unshuttered, yawning red-mouthed to the outer night. My back was almost ever to the window, whose panes reflected a peat-fire and a face as long as a fiddle, and eyes that shone like coal; and though I looked little at the window yawning to the wood, I felt that it never wanted some curious spy outside, some one girning or smiling in at me and my book. I must look round, or I must put a hand on my shoulder to make sure no other hand was there,—then the Terror that drives the black blood from the heart through all the being, and a boy unbuckling his kilt with fevered fingers and leaping with frantic sobs to bed! One night when the black blood of the Terror still coursed through me, though I was dovering over to sleep, there came a knocking at the door, a knock commanding, a knock never explained. It brought me to my knees with a horror that almost choked me at the throat, a cold dew in the very palms of the hands. I dare not ask who rapped for fear I should have an answer that comes some day or other to every child of my race,—an answer no one told me of, an answer that then I guessed.

All this flashed through my mind when the children's crying rose in the dark interior—that cry of children old and young as they go through the mysteries of life and the alley-ways of death.

The woman soothed her children audibly, then called out, asking what we wanted.

"I'm a man from Appin," cried out Stewart with great promptness and cunning, "and I have a friend or two with me. I was looking for the house of Kilinchean, where a cousin of mine—a fine spinner and knitter, but thrawn in the temper—is married on the tenant, and we lost our way. We're cold and we're tired, and we're hungry, and——"

"Step in," said the woman, lifting back the door. "You are many miles from Kilinchean, and I know Appin Mary very well."

But three of us entered, Stewart, M'Iver, and myself, the others on a sudden inspiration preferring not to alarm the woman by betraying the number of us, and concealing themselves in the byre that leaned against the gable of the dwelling.

"God save all here!" said M'Iver as we stepped in, and the woman lit the cruisie by sticking its nose in the peat-embers. "I'm afraid we come on you at a bad time."

She turned with the cruisie in her hands and seemed to look over his head at vacancy, with large and melting eyes in a comely face.

"You come," said she, "like grief, just when we are not expecting it, and in the dead of night. But you are welcome at my door."

We sat down on stools at her invitation, bathed in the yellow light of cruisie and peat. The reek of the fire rose in a faint breath among the pot-chains, and lingered among the rafters, loath, as it were, to emerge in the cold night. In a cowering group beneath the blankets of a bed in a corner were four children, the bed-clothes hurriedly clutched up to their chins, their eyes staring out on the intruders. The woman put out some food before us, coarse enough in quality but plenty of it, and was searching in a press for platters when she turned to ask how many of us there were. We looked at each other a little ashamed, for it seemed as if she had guessed of our divided company and the four men in the byre. It is likely she would have been told the truth, but her next words set us on a different notion.

"You'll notice," said she, still lifting her eyes to a point over our heads, "that I have not my sight."

"God! that's a pity," said M'Iver in genuine distress, with just that accent of fondling in it that a Highlander in his own tongue can use like a salve for distress.

" I am not complaining of it," said the woman ; " there are worse hardships in this world."

" Mistress," said John, " there are. I think I would willingly have been bl—— dim in the sight this morning if it could have happened."

" Ay, ay ! " said the woman in a sad abstraction, standing with plates in her hand listening (I could swear) for a footstep that would never come again.

We sat and warmed ourselves and ate heartily, the heat of that homely dwelling—the first we had sat in for days —an indulgence so rare and precious that it seemed a thing we could never again tear ourselves away from to encounter the unkindness of those Lorn mounts anew. The children watched us with an alarm and curiosity no way abated, beholding in us perhaps (for one at least was at an age to discern the difference our tartan and general aspect presented from those of Glencoe) that we were strangers from a great distance, maybe enemies, at least with some rigour of warfare about our visage and attire. The mother, finding her way with the readiness of long familiarity about the house, got ease for her grief, whatever it was, in the duties thus suddenly thrust upon her ; she spoke but seldom, and she never asked—in that she was true Gael—any more particulars about ourselves than Stewart had volunteered. And when we had been served with our simple viands, she sat composedly before us with her hands in her lap, and her eyes turned on us with an appearance of sedate scrutiny no whit the less perplexing because we knew her orbs were but fair clean windowpanes shuttered and hasped within.

" You will excuse my dull welcome," she said, with a wan smile, speaking a very pleasant accent of North Country Gaelic, that turned upon the palate like a sweet. " A week or two ago you would have found a very cheerful house, not a widow's sorrow, and, if my eyes were useless, my man (*beannachd leis !*) had a lover's eyes, and these were the eyes for himself and me."

" Was he at Inverlochy ? " I asked softly ; " was he out with Montrose ? "

" He died a week come Thursday," said the woman. " They're telling me of wars—weary on them and God's pity on the widow women they make, and the mothers they must leave lonely—but such a thing is sorrow that the world, from France to the Isles, might be in flames and I would still be thinking on my man that's yonder in the cold clods of the yard. . . . Stretch your hands ; it's your welcome, gentlemen."

" I have one or two other friends out-bye there in the byre," put in Stewart, who found the vigilance of the youths in the bed gave no opportunity for smuggling provand to the others of our party.

The woman's face flamed up a little and took on the least of a look of alarm that Stewart—who was very cunning and quick in some matters—set about removing at once with some of those convenient lies that he seemed never out of the want of.

" Some of our lads," said he, with a duck of apology at M'Iver and myself for taking liberties with the reputation of our friends. " They're very well where they are among the bracken, if they had but the bite and sup, and if it's your will I could take them that."

" Could they not be coming in and sitting by the fire ? " asked the woman, set at rest by Stewart's story ; but he told her he would never think of filling her room with a rabble of plain men, and in a little he was taking out the viands for our friends in the byre.

The woman sat anew upon her stool and her hands on her lap, listening with a sense so long at double exercise that now she could not readily relax the strain on it. M'Iver was in a great fidget to be off. I could see it in every movement of him. He was a man who ever disliked to have his feelings vexed by contact with the everlasting sorrows of life, and this intercourse with new widowhood was sore against his mind. As for me, I took, in a way of speaking, the woman to my heart. She stood to me for all the griefs I had known in life, and was yet the representative, the figure of love—revealing an element of nature, a human passion so different from those tumults and hatreds we had been encountering. I had been thinking as I marched among the wilds of Lochaber and Badenoch that vengeance and victory and dominion by the strong hand were the main spurs to action, and now, on a sudden, I found that affection was stronger than them all.

" Are you keeping the place on ? " I asked the widow, " or do you go back to your folks, for I notice from your tongue that you are of the North ? "

" I'm of the Grants," she said ; " but my heart's in Glencoe, and I'll never leave it. I am not grieving at the future, I am but minding on the past, and I have my bairns. . . . More milk for the lads outside ; stretch your hands. . . . Oh yes, I have my bairns."

" Long may they prosper, mistress," said M'Iver, drumming with a horn spoon on his knee, and winking and smiling very friendly to the little fellows in a row in the bed, who, all but the oldest, thawed to this humour of the stranger. " It must be a task getting a throng like yon bedded at evening. Some day they'll be off your hand, and it'll be no more the lullaby of Crodh Chailein, but them driving at the beasts for themselves."

" Are you married ? " asked the woman.

" No," said John, with a low laugh, " not yet. I never had the fortune to fill the right woman's eye. I've waited at the ferry for some one who'll take a man over without the ferry fee, for I'm a poor gentleman though I'm of a good family, and had plenty, and the ones with the tocher won't have me, and the tocherless girls I dare not betray."

" You ken the old word," said the woman ; " the man who waits long at the ferry will get over some day."

Stewart put down a cogie and loosened a button of his vest, and with an air of great joviality, that was marred curiously by the odd look his absence of lugs conferred, he winked cunningly at us and slapped the woman in a rough friendship on the shoulder.

" Are you thinking yourself——" he began, and what he would finish with may be easily guessed. But M'Iver fixed him with an eye that pricked like a rapier.

" Sit ye down, Stewart," said he ; " your race is royal, as ye must be aye telling us, but there's surely many a droll bye-blow in the breed."

" Are you not all from Appin ? " asked the woman, with a new interest, taking a corner of M'Iver's plaiding in her hand and running a few checks through fine delicate fingers of a lady. Her face dyed crimson; she drew back her stool a little, and cried out—

"That's not off a Stewart web—it was never waulked in Appin. Whom have I here?"

John Splendid bent to her very kindly and laid a hand on hers.

"I'll tell you the God's truth, mother," said he; "we're broken men: we have one Stewart of a kind with us, but we belong to parts far off from here, and all we want is to get to them as speedily as may be. I'll put you in mind (but troth I'm sure it's not needed) of two obligations that lie on every Gaelic household. One of them is to give the shelter of the night and the supper of the night to the murderer himself, even if the corpse on the heather was your son; and the other is to ask no question off your guest till he has drunk the *deoch-an-doruis*."

"I'm grudging you nothing," said the woman; "but a blind widow is entitled to the truth and frankness."

M'Iver soothed her with great skill, and brought her back to her bairns.

"Ay," said he, "some day they'll be off your hands, and you the lady with sons and servants."

"Had you a wife and bairns of your own," said the woman, "you might learn some day that a parent's happiest time is when her children are young. They're all there, and they're all mine when they're under the blanket; but when they grow up and scatter, the nightfall never brings them all in, and one pair of blankets will not cover the cares of them. I do not know that," she went on, "from what I have seen in my own house; but my mother told me, and she had plenty of chance to learn the truth of it, with sons who died among strangers, and sons who bruised her by their lives more than they could by their deaths."

"You have some very ruddy and handsome boys there," said M'Iver. And aye he would be winking and smiling at the young rogues in the corner.

"I think they are," said the woman. "I never saw but the eldest, and he was then at the breast, the dear, his father's image."

"Then the father of him must have been a well-fared and pretty man," said John, very promptly, not a bit abashed by the homeliness of the youth, who was the plainest of the flock, with a freckled skin, a low hang-dog brow, and a nose like the point of a dirk.

"He was that," said the woman, fondly—"the finest man in the parish. He had a little lameness, but——"

"I have a bit of a halt myself," said M'Iver, with his usual folly; "and I'm sure I'm none the worse for it."

The oldest boy sat up in bed and gloomed at us very sullenly. He could scarcely be expected to understand the conceits of M'Iver's tale about his lameness, that any one with eyes could behold had no existence.

"But I never think of my man," the woman went on, "but as I saw him first before he met with his lameness. Eyes are a kind of doubtful blessing too in some ways. Mine have forgotten all the ugly things they knew, and in my recollection are but many bonny things : my man was always as young to me as when he came courting in a new blue bonnet and a short coat ; my children will be changing to every one but to me."

Stewart, with his own appetite satisfied, was acting lackey to the gentlemen in the byre—fetching out cogies of milk and whangs of bear-meal bannock, and the most crisp piquant white cheese ever I put tooth to. He was a man without a conscience, and so long as his own ends and the ends of his friends were served, he would never scruple to empty the woman's girnel or toom her last basin, and leave her no morsel of food or drink at the long-run. But M'Iver and I put an end to that, and so won, as we thought, to the confidence of the elder lad in the bed, who had glunched low-browed among his franker brethren.

We slept for some hours, the seven of us, among the bracken of the byre, wearied out and unable to go farther that night, even if the very dogs were at our heels. We slept sound, I'm sure, all but M'Iver, whom, waking twice in the chill of the night, I found sitting up and listening like any sentinel.

"What are you watching for there ? " I asked him on the second time.

"Nothing at all, Colin, nothing at all. I was aye a

poor sleeper at the best, and that snore of Rob Stewart is the very trump of the next world."

It was in the dawn again he confessed to his real apprehension,—only to my private ear, for he wished no more to alarm the others by day than to mar my courtship of slumber by night.

"The fact is," said he, "I'm not very sure about our young gentleman yonder in the bed. He's far too sharp in the eye and black in the temper, and too much of Clan Donallachd generally, to be trusted with the lives and liberties of seven gentlemen of a tartan he must know unfriendly to Glencoe. I wish I saw his legs that I might guess the length of him, or had had the wit to ask his mother his age, for either would be a clue to his chance of carrying the tale against us down the valley there. He seemed tremendous sharp and wicked lying yonder looking at us, and I was in a sweat all night for fear he would be out and tell on us. But so far he's under the same roof as ourselves."

Sonachan and the baron-bailie quarrelled away about some point of pedigree as they sat, a towsy, unkempt pair, in a dusty corner of the byre, with beards of a most scraggy nature grown upon their chins. Their uncouthness gave a scruple of foppishness to M'Iver, and sent him seeking a razor in the widow's house. He found the late husband's, and shaved himself trimly, while Stewart played lackey again to the rest of us, taking out a breakfast the housewife was in the humour to force on us. He had completed his scraping, and was cracking away very freely with the woman, who was baking some bannocks on the stone, with sleeves rolled up from arms that were rounded and white. They talked of the husband (the one topic of new widowhood), a man, it appeared, of a thousand parts, a favourite with all, and yet, as she said, "When it came to the black end they left me to dress him for the grave, and a stranger had to bury him."

M'Iver, looking fresh and spruce after his cleansing, though his eyes were small for want of sleep, aroused at once to an interest in the cause of this unneighbourliness.

The woman stopped her occupation with a sudden start and flared crimson.

"I thought you knew," said she, stammering, turning a

rolling-pin in her hand—" I thought you knew; and then how could you? . . . I maybe should have mentioned it, . . . but, . . . but could I turn you from my door in the night-time and hunger?"

M'Iver whistled softly to himself, and looked at me where I stood in the byre-door.

"Tuts," said he, at last turning with a smile to the woman, as if she could see him; "what does a bit difference with Lowland law make after all? I'll tell you this, mistress, between us,—I have a name myself for private foray, and it's perhaps not the first time I have earned the justification of the kind gallows of Crief by small diversions among cattle at night. It's the least deserving that get the tow gravatte."

(Oh you liar! I thought.)

The woman's face looked puzzled. She thought a little, and said, "I think you must be taking me up wrong; my man was never at the trade of reiving, and——"

"I would never hint that he was, goodwife," cried John, quickly, puzzled-looking himself. "I said I had a name for the thing; but they were no friends of mine who gave me the credit, and I never stole stot or quey in all my life."

(I have my doubts, thinks I.)

"My man died of the plague," said the woman, blurting out her news, as if eager to get over an awkward business.

I have never seen such a sudden change in a person's aspect as came over John Splendid in every feature. The vain trim man of a minute ago, stroking his chin and showing a white hand (for the entertainment of the woman he must always be forgetting was without her sight), balancing and posturing on well-curved legs, and jauntily pinning his plaid on his shoulder, in a flash lost backbone. He stepped a pace back, as if some one had struck him a blow, his jaw fell, and his face grew ashen. Then his eyes went darting about the chamber, and his nostrils sniffed as if disease was a presence to be seen and scented, a thing tangible in the air, maybe to be warded off by a sharp man's instruction in combat of arms.

"God of grace!" he cried, crossing himself most vigorously for a person of the Protestant religion, and muttering what I have no doubt was some charm of his native glen for the prevention of fevers. He shut his mouth thereafter very quickly on every phrase he uttered, breathing through his nose; at the same time he kept himself, in every part but the shoe-soles he tiptoed on, from touching anything. I could swear the open air of the most un-friendly glen in Christendom was a possession to be envious of for John M'Iver of Barbreck.

Stewart heard the woman's news that came to him as he was carrying in from the byre the vessels from which he had been serving his companions. He was in a stew more extraordinary than John Splendid; he blanched even to the scars of his half-head, as we say, spat vehe-mently out of his mouth a piece of bread he was chewing, turned round about in a flash, and into the byre past me as I stood (not altogether alarmed, but yet a little dis-turbed and uneasy) in the doorway. He emptied his clothing and knapsack of every scrap of food he had pur-loined, making a goodly heap upon the floor,—the very oaten flour he dusted off his finger-tips, with which he had handled cake that a little ago he was risking his soul's salvation to secure. And—except the minister—the other occupants of the byre were in an equal terror.

For in this matter of smittal plagues we Highlanders are the most arrant cowards. A man whose life we would save on the field, or the rock-face, or the sea, at the risk of our own lives or the more abominable peril of wound and agony, will die in a ditch of the Spotted Death or a fever before the most valiant of us would put out a hand to cover him again with his blanket. He will get no woman to sound his coronach, even if he were Lord of the Isles. I am not making defence or admitting blame, though I have walked in Hamburg when the pitch-barrels blazed in the street, fuming the putrid wind; but there is in the Gaelic character a dread of disfiguration more than of sudden and painful death. What we fear is the black mystery of such disorders: they come on cunning winds unheralded, in fair weather or bad, day or night, to the rich and to the poor, to the strong as to the weak. You may be robust to-day in a smiling country and to-morrow in a twist of agony, coal-black, writhing on the couch, every fine interest in life blotted out by a yellow film upon the eyes. A vital gash with a claymore confers a bloodier but a more comely and natural end. Thus the Gael

abhors the very roads that lead to a plague-struck dwelling.
If plagues do not kill, they will mar—yes, even against
the three charms of Island I, and that, too, makes heavier
their terror, for a man mutilated even by so little as the
loss of a hand is an object of pity to every hale member of
his clan. He may have won his infirmity in a noble hour,
but they will pity him, and pity to the proud is worse
than the glove in the face.

Instantly there was a great to-do in getting away from
this most unfortunate dwelling. The lads in the byre
shook tartan and out to the fresh air, and rejoiced in the
wind with deep-drawn gulping breaths, as if they might
wash the smallest dust of disease from their bodily systems.
So at last only M'Iver and I were left standing at the
door.

"Well," said John, with an effort, "we must be going.
I never thought it was so late. And we must be on the
other side of Dalness before very long. You have been
very good to us, and my name's John M'Iver of Barbreck
—a kind of a Campbell with a great respect for the Mac-
Donalds, of whom I kent a few perfect gentry in foreign
wars I have been at the fighting of. And—good day,
mistress, we must be going. My friends have the very
small manners surely, for they're off down the road.
We'll just let them go that way. What need ye expect
off small men and gillies?"

He signed to me with a shake of his sporran to show
it was empty, and, falling to his meaning, I took some
silver from my own purse and offered it to the glum-
faced lad in the blankets. Beetle-brow scowled, and
refused to put a hand out for it, so I left it on a table
without a clink to catch the woman's ear.

"Would you not have a *deoch-an-doruis?*" asked the
woman, making to a press and producing a bottle.

M'Iver started in a new alarm. "No, no. You're
very good," said he; "but I never take it myself in
the morning, and—good day, mistress—and my friend
Elrigmore, who's left with me here, is perhaps too free
with it sometimes; and indeed maybe I'm that way
myself too—it's a thing that grows on you. Good-bye,
mistress."

She put out her hand, facing us with uplifted eyes. I

felt a push at my shoulder, and the minister, who had left the four others down the brae, stepped softly into the room. M'Iver was in a high perplexity. He dare not shake the woman's hand, and still he dare not hurt her feelings. "My thong's loose," said he, stooping to fumble with a brogue that needed no such attention. He rose with the minister at his shoulder.

"And good day to you again, mistress," said M'Iver, turning about to go, without heeding the outstretched hand.

Master Gordon saw the whole play at a glance. He took the woman's hand in his without a word, wrung it with great warmth, and, seized as it seemed by a sudden whim, lifted the fingers to his lips, softly kissed them, and turned away.

"O," cried the woman, with tears welling to her poor eyes—"O Clan Campbell, I'll never call ye down! Ye may have the guile they claim for ye, but ye have the way with a widow's heart!"

I did it with some repugnance, let me own; but I, too, shook her hand, and followed the minister out at the door. M'Iver was hot with annoyance and shame, and ready to find fault with us for what we had done; but the cleric carded him like wool in his feelings.

"Oh, valour, valour!" he said in the midst of his sermon, "did I not say you knew your duty in hate better than in affection?"

John Splendid kept a dour-set jaw, said never a word, and the seven of us proceeded on our way.

It was well on in the morning, the land sounding with a new key of troubled and loosening waters. Mists clogged the mountain-tops, and Glencoe far off to its westward streamed with a dun vapour pricked with the tip of fir and ash. A moist feel was in the air; it relapsed anon to a smirr of rain.

"This is a shade better than clear airs and frost and level snow for quarries on a hunting," said I.

"I'm glad it suits you," said M'Iver. "I've seen the like before, and I'm not so sure about the advantage of it."

CHAPTER XXIV.

A NIGHT'S SHELTER.

THE rain that was a smirr or drizzle on the north side
of Glencoe grew to a steady shower in the valley itself,
and when we had traversed a bit in the airt of Tynree
it had become a pouring torrent—slanting in our faces
with the lash of whips, streaming from the hair and
crinkling the hands, and leaving the bonnet on the head
as heavy as any French soldier's salade. I am no great
unlover of a storm in the right circumstances. There is
a long strath between Nordlingen and Donauworth of
Bavaria, where once we amazed our foreign allies by
setting out, bare to the kilt and sark, in threshing hail,
running for miles in the pelt of it out of the sheer content of encounter—and perhaps a flagon or two of wine.
It was a bravado, perhaps, but a ploy to brace the spirit ;
we gathered from it some of the virtues of our simple but
ample elders, who were strong men when they lay asleep
with a cheek to the naked earth and held their faces
frankly up to sun or rain. But if we rejoiced in the
rains of Bavaria, there was no cause for glee in those
torrents of Glencoe, for they made our passage through
the country more difficult and more dangerous than it
was before. The snow on the ground was for hours a
slushy compost, that the foot slipped on at every step,
or that filled the brogue with a paste that nipped like
brine. And when the melting snow ran to lower levels,
the soil itself, relaxing the rigour of its frost, became as
soft as butter and as unstable to the foot. The burns
filled to the lip and brawled over, new waters sprung up
among the rocks and ran across our path, so that we were

for ever wading and slipping and splashing and stumbling on a route that seemed never to come to any end or betterment.

Seven more pitiful men never trod Highlands. The first smirr soaked our clothing; by the middle of the glen we were drenched to the hide, and the rain was flowing from the edges of our kilts in runnels. Thus heaven scourged us with waters till about the hour of noon, when she alternated water with wind and gales burst from the west, the profound gorges of Stob Dubh belching full to the throat with animus. There were fir-plantings by the way, whose branches twanged and boomed in those terrific blasts, that on the bare brae-side lifted up the snow with an invisible scoop and flung it in our faces.

Stewart and the man with the want led the way, the latter ever with his eyes red a-weeping, looking about him with starts and tremors, moaning lamentably at every wail of wind, but pausing, now and then, to gnaw a bone he had had enough of a thief's wit to pouch in the house of the blind widow. Stewart, a lean wiry man, covered the way with a shepherd's long stride—heel and toe and the last spring from the knee—most poverty-struck and mean in a kilt that flapped too low on his leg and was frayed to ribbons, a man with but one wish in the world, to save his own unworthy skin, even if every one else of our distressed corps found a sodden and abominable death in the swamps or rocks of that doleful valley. Then on the rear behind those commoners came the minister and John Splendid and myself, the minister with his breeks burst at the knees, his stockings caught up with a poor show of trimness by a braid of rushes, contrived by M'Iver, and his coat-skirts streaming behind him. You could not but respect the man's courage: many a soldier I've seen on the dour hard leagues of Germanie—good soldiers too, heart and body—collapse under hardships less severe. Gordon, with a drawn and curd-white face, and eyes burning like lamps, surrendered his body to his spirit, and it bore him as in a dream through wind and water, over moor and rock, and amid the woods that now and again we had to hide in.

That we had to hide so little was one of the miracles of our traverse. At any other time perhaps Glencoe and the regions round about it would be as well tenanted as any low-country strath, for it abounded on either hand with townships, with crofts that perched on brief plateaux, here and there with black bothy-houses such as are (they say) the common dwellings over all the Hebrid Isles. Yet, moving, not in the ultimate hollow of the valley, but in fighting fashion upon the upper levels, we were out of the way of molestation, and in any case it was a valley for the time deserted of men. Women we could see in plenty, drawing water or bearing peats in from the bogs behind their dwellings, or crossing from house to house or toun to toun, with plaids drawn tightly over their heads, their bodies bent to meet the blasts that made their clothing banner and full. Nor children either were there in that most barren country, or they kept within, sheltering the storms assailing, and the want of them (for I have ever loved the little ones) added twenty-fold to my abhorrence of the place.

We had to hide but rarely, I say : two or three times when down in the valley's depths there showed a small group of men who were going in the same direction as ourselves by the more natural route, at a quarter of a league's distance in advance of us. They were moving with more speed than we, and for a time we had the notion that they might be survivors, like ourselves, of Argile's clan. But at last this fancy was set at flight by the openness of their march, as well as by their stoppage at several houses by the way, from which they seemed to be joined by other men, who swelled their numbers so that after a time there would be over a score of them on the mission, whatever it might be. In that misty rain-swept day the eye could not carry far, and no doubt they were plainer to our view than we were to theirs among the drab vapours of the hillside. But once or twice we thought they perceived us, for they stopped and looked to the left and up the brae-face we were on, and then it was we had to seek the shelter of tree or bush. If they saw us, they seemed to suspect no evil, for they held on their way, still ahead of us, and making for Tynree. Whoever they were, they became at last so manifest a danger to our escape out of the head of the glen that we fell back anew on the first plan of going through the corries on the south side of the glen and piercing by them to Dalness. In the obscurity of a great shower that set up a screen between us and the company marching to Tynree, we darted down the brae, across the valley, and over to the passage they call the Lairig Eilde, that is on the west of the great Little Herd hill of Etive, and between it and Ben Fhada or the Long Mount, whose peaks you will find with snow in their gullies in the height of summer.

It was with almost a jocund heart I turned my back on Glencoe as we took a drove-path up from the river. But I glanced with a shiver down its terrible distance upon that nightmare of gulf and eminence, of gash, and peaks afloat upon swirling mists. It lay, a looming terror, forgotten of heaven and unfriendly to man (as one might readily imagine), haunted for ever with wailing airs and rumours, ghosts calling in the deeps of dusk and melancholy, legends of horror and remorse.

"Thank God," said I, as we gave the last look at it— "thank God I was not born and bred yonder. Those hills would crush my heart against my very ribs."

"It's good enough for the people who are in it," said John. "What are they but MacDonalds? 'Take and not give' is their motto. They can have Glencoe for me, with M'Millan's right to Knapdale,—as long as wave beats on rock."

Master Gordon, though we had spoken in the Gaelic, half guessed our meaning. "A black place and mournful," said he; "but there may be love there too and warm hearts, and soil where the truth might flourish as in the champaign over against Gilgal beside the plains of Moreh."

Now we were in a tract of country mournful beyond my poor description. I know corries in Argile that whisper silken to the winds with juicy grasses, corries where the deer love to prance deep in the cool dew, and the beasts of far-off woods come in bands at their seasons and together rejoice. I have seen the hunter in them and the shepherd too, coarse men in life and occupation, come sudden among the blowing rush and whispering reed, among the bog-flower and the cannoch, unheeding the moor-hen and the cailzie-cock rising, or the stag of ten at pause, while they stood, passionate adventurers in a rapture of the mind, held as it were by the spirit of such places as they lay in a sloeberry bloom of haze, the spirit of old good songs, the baffling surmise of the piper and the bard. To those corries of my native place will be coming in the yellow moon of brock and foumart—the beasts that dote on the autumn eves—the People of Quietness ; have I not seen their lanthorns and heard their laughter in the night ?—so that they must be blessed corries, so endowed since the days when the gods dwelt in them without tartan and spear in the years of the peace that had no beginning.

But the corries of Lorn ; black night on them, and the rain rot ! They were swamps of despair as we went struggling through them. The knife-keen rushes whipped us at the thigh, the waters bubbled in our shoes. Round us rose the hills grey and bald, sown with boulders and crowned with sour mists. Surely in them the sun never peeps even in the long days of summer : the star, I'll warrant, never rains on them his calm influence !

Dolour left us speechless as we trudged, even when for a time we were lost. We essayed in a silence at openings here and there, at hacks and water-currents, wandering off from each other, whistling and calling, peering from rock-brows or spying into wounds upon the hills, so that when we reached Dalness it was well on in the day. If in summer weather the night crawls slowly on the Highlands, the winter brings a fast black rider indeed. His hoofs were drumming on the hills when first we saw sight of Dalness ; he was over and beyond us when we reached the plain. The land of Lorn was black dark to the very roots of its trees, and the rivers and burns themselves got lost in the thick of it, and went through the night calling from hollow to hollow to hearten each other till the dawn.

Dalness lies in Glen Etive, at a gusset of hills on either side of which lie paths known to the drover and the adventurer. The house receded from the passes and lay back in a pleasance walled by whin or granite, having a wattled gate at the entrance. When we were descending the pass we could see a glare of light come from the place even though the mist shrouded, and by the time we got to the gate it was apparent that the house was lit in every chamber. The windows that pierced the tall gables threw beams of light into the darkness, and the open door poured out a yellow flood. At the time we came on it first we were unaware of our propinquity to it, and this mansion looming on us suddenly through the vapours seemed a cantrip of witchcraft, a dwelling's ghost, grey, eerie, full of frights, a phantom of the mind rather than a habitable home. We paused in a dumb astonishment to look at it lying there in the darkness, a thing so different from the barren hills and black bothies behind us.

We gathered in a cluster near the wattle gate, the minister perhaps the only man who had the wit to acknowledge the reality of the vision. His eyes fairly gloated on this evidence of civilised state, so much recalling the surroundings in which he was most at home. As by an instinct of decency, he drew up his slack hose and bound them anew with the rushen garters, and pulled his coat-lapels straight upon his chest, and set his dripping peruke upon his head with a touch of the dandy's air, all the time with his eyes on those gleaming windows, as if he feared to relinquish the spectacle a moment, lest it should fly like a dream.

We had thought first of pushing across the glen, over the river, through Corrie Ghuibhasan, and into the Black Mount ; but the journey in a night like what was now fallen was not to be attempted. On the hills beyond the river the dog-fox barked with constancy, his vixen screeching like a child—signs of storm that no one dare gainsay. So we determined to seek shelter and concealment somewhere in the policies of the house. But first of all we had to find what the occasion was of this brilliancy in Dalness, and if too many people for our safety were not in the neighbourhood. I was sent forward to spy the place, while my companions lay waiting below a cluster of alders.

I went into the grounds with my heart very high up on my bosom, not much put about at any human danger, let me add, for an encounter with an enemy of flesh and blood was a less fearsome prospect than the chance of an encounter with more invulnerable foes, who, my skin told me, haunted every heugh and howe of that still and sombre demesne of Dalness. But I set my teeth tight in my resolution, and with my dirk drawn in my hand— it was the only weapon left me—I crept over the grass from bush to bush and tree to tree as much out of the revelation of the window-lights as their numbers would let me.

There was not a sound in the place, and yet those lights might have betokened a great festivity, with pipe and harp going, and dancers' feet thudding on the floor.

At one of the gables there was a low window, and I made for it, thinking it a possible eye to a lobby or passage, and therefore not so hazardous to look in at. I crept up and viewed the interior.

My window, to my astonishment, looked in on no bare plain lobby, but on a spacious salmanger or hall, very rosy with sconce-light and wood-fire—a hall that extended the whole length of the house, with a bye-ordinar high ceil of black oak carved very handsomely. The walls at the far end were hung with tapestry very like MacCailein's rooms at home in Inneraora, and down the long sides, whose windows streamed the light upon the hall, great stag-heads glowered with unsleeping eyes, stags of numerous tines. The floor was strewn with the skins of the chase, and on the centre of it was a table laden with an un-touched meal, and bottles that winked back the flicker of the candle and the hearth.

The comfort of the place, by contrast with our situation, seemed, as I looked hungrily on it through the thick glass of the lozen, more great and tempting than anything ever I saw abroad in the domains of princes. Its air was charged with peace and order ; the little puffs and coils and wisps of silver-grey smoke, coming out of the fire-place into the room, took long to swoon into nothingness in that tranquil interior.

But the most wonderful thing of all was, that though the supper seemed ready waiting for a company, and could not have been long left, I waited five or ten minutes

with my face fast to the pane and no living footstep
entered the room. I watched the larger door near the
far-off end eagerly ; it lay ajar, smiling a welcome to the
parts of the house beyond, but no one came in.

" Surely they are throng in some other wing," I thought,
" and not so hungry as we, or their viands did not lie so
long untouched in that dainty room."

I went round the house at its rear, feeling my way slowly
among the bushes. I looked upon parlours and bed-
closets, kitchens and corridors ; they were lighted with
the extravagance of a marriage-night, and as tenantless
and silent as the cells of Kilchrist. The beds were straightened out, the hearths were swept, the floors were scrubbed,
on every hand was the evidence of recent business, but
the place was relinquished to the ghosts.

How it was I cannot say, but the mystery of the house
made me giddy at the head. Yet I was bound to push
my searching further, so round with a swithering heart
went Elrigmore to the very front door of the mansion of
Dalness—open, as I have said, with the light gushing
lemon-yellow on the lawn. I tapped softly, my heart this
time even higher than my bosom, with a foot back ready to
retreat if answer came. Then I rasped an alarm on the
side of the yett with a noise that rang fiercely through the
place and brought the sweat to my body, but there was
even then no answer.

So in I went, the soft soles of my brogues making no
sound on the boards, but leaving the impress of my footsteps in a damp blot.

Now, to me, brought up in a Highland farm-steading
(for the house of Elrigmore is without great spaciousness
or pretence), large and rambling castles and mansions
ever seem eerie. I must in them be thinking, like any
boy, of the whisperings of wraiths in their remote upper
rooms ; I feel strange airs come whipping up their long
or crooked lobbies at night ; the number of their doors
are, to my Highland instinct, so many unnecessary en-
trances for enemies and things mischancy.

But to wander over the house of Dalness, lit from tolbooth to garret with lowe—to see the fires, not green but
at their prime with high-banked peat that as yet had not

thrown an ash—to see so fine a supper waiting in a mansion utterly desolate and its doors open to the wilds, seemed a thing so magical that I felt like taking my feet from the place in a hurry of hurries and fleeing with my comrades from so unco a countryside. High and low I ranged in the interior. I had found a nut without a kernel, and at last I stood dumfoundered and afraid, struck solemn by the echo of my own hail as it rang unfamiliar through the interior.

I might have been there fifteen minutes or half an hour when M'Iver, impatient at my delay or fearing some injury to my person, came in and joined me. He too was struck with amazement at the desertion of the house. He measured the candles, he scrutinised the fires, he went round the building out and in and he could but conclude that we must be close upon the gate when the house was abandoned.

" But why abandon it ? " I asked.

" That's the Skyeman's puzzle ; it would take seven men and seven years to answer it," said he. " I can only say it's very good of them (if there's no ambuscade in it) to leave so fine an inn and so bonny a supper with a bush above the door and never a bar against entrance. We'll just take advantage of what fortune has sent us."

" The sooner the better," said I, standing up to a fire that delighted my body like a caress. " I have a trick of knowing when good fortune's a dream, and I'll be awake and find myself lying on hard heather before the bite's at my mouth."

M'Iver ran out and brought in our companions, none of them unwilling to put this strange free hostel to the test for its warmth and hospitality. We shut and barred the doors, and set ourselves down to such a cold collation as the most fortunate of us had not tasted since the little wars began. Between the savage and the gentleman is but a good night's lodging. Give the savage a peaceful hearth to sit by, a roof to his head, and a copious well-cooked supper, and his savagery will surrender itself to the sleek content of a Dutch merchantman. We sat at a table whose load would have rationed a company of twice our number, and I could see the hard look of hunting relax in the aspect of us all: the peering, restless, sunken eyes came out of their furrowed caverns, turned calm, full, and satisfied; the lines of the brow and mouth, the contour of the cheek, the carriage of the head, the disposition of the hands, altered and improved. An hour ago, when we were the sport of ferocious nature in the heart of a country infernal, no more than one of us would have swithered to strike a blow at a fellow-creature and to have robbed his corpse of what it might have of food and comfort. Now we gloated in the airs benign of Dalness house, very friendly to the world at large, the stuff that tranquil towns are made of. We had even the minister's blessing on our food, for Master Gordon accepted the miracle of the open door and the vacant dwelling with John Splendid's philosophy, assuring us that in doing so he did no more than he would willingly concede any harmless body of broken men such as we were, even his direst enemies, if extremity like ours brought them to his neighbourhood.

"I confess I am curious to know how the thing happened, but the hand of the Almighty's in it anyway," he said; and so saying he lay back in his chair with a sigh of satisfaction that lost nothing of its zest by the influence of the rain that blattered now in drumming violence on the window-panes.

John Splendid, at the table-end, laughed shortly between his sups at a flagon of wine.

"All the same," said he, "I would advise you to put some of the Almighty's provand in your pouch, for fear the grace that is ours now may be torn suddenly enough from us."

Sonachan pointed at Stewart, who had already filled every part of his garments with broken meat, and his wallet as well. "There's a cautious man," said he, "whatever your notion of sudden ceasing may be. He has been putting bite about in his wallet and his stomach since ever we sat down. Appin ways, no doubt."

"*Biadh an diugh, cogadh a maireach*—food to-day, war to-morrow," said the son of kings. "Royal's my race! A man should aye be laying in as he goes: if I had not had my wallet on Loch Leven-side, I ken some gentry who would have been as hungry as common herds, and with nothing to help it."

John Splendid laughed again. "Wise man, Rob!" said he; "you learnt the first principles of campaigning in Appin as nicely as ever I did in the wars of the Invincible Lion (as they called him) of the North. Our reverend comrade here, by the wisdom of his books, never questions, it seems, that we have a lease of Dalness house as long as we like to stay in it, its pendicles and pertinents, lofts, crofts, gardens, mills, multures, and sequels, as the lawyers say in their damned sheep-skins, that have been the curse of the Highlands even more than books have been. Now I've had an adventure like this before. Once in Regenwalde, between Danzig and Stettin, where we lay for two months, I spent a night with a company of Hepburn's blades in a castle abandoned by a cousin of the Duke of Pomerania. Roystering dogs! Stout hearts! Where are they now, those fine lads in corslet and morgensterne, who played havoc with the casks in the Regenwalde cellar? Some of them died of the pest in Schiefelbein, four of them fell under old Jock Hepburn at Frankfort, the lave went wandering about the world, kissing and drinking, no doubt, and lying and sorrowing and dying, and never again will we foregather in a vacant house in foreign parts! For that is the hardship of life, that it's ever a flux and change. We are here to-day and away to-morrow, and the bigger the company and the more high-hearted the merriment, the less likely is the experience to be repeated. I'm sitting here in a miraculous dwelling in the land of Lorn, and I have but to shut my eyes and round about me are cavaliers of fortune at the board. I give you the old word, Elrigmore: 'Claymore and the Gael'; for the rest—pardon me—you gentlemen are out of the ploy I shut my eyes and I see Fowlis and Farquhar, Mackenzie, Obisdell, Ross, the two *balbiren* and *stabknechten*, with their legs about the board; the wind's howling up from Stettin road; to-morrow we may be carrion in the ditch at Guben's Gate, or wounded to a death by slow degrees in night scaladoe. That was soldiering. You fought your equals with art and science; here's—— Well, well, God's grace for MacCailein Mor!"

" God's grace for us all ! " said the minister.

The man with the want fell fast asleep in his chair, with his limbs in gawky disposition. Stewart's bullet-head, with the line of the oval unbroken by ears, bobbed with affected eagerness to keep up with the fast English utterance and the foreign names of M'Iver, while all the time he was fingering some metal spoons and wondering if money was in them and if they could be safely got to Inneraora. Sonachan and the baron-bailie dipped their beaks in the jugs, and with lifted heads, as fowls slocken their thirst, they let the wine slip slowly down their throats, glucking in a gluttonous ecstasy.

" God's grace for us all ! " said the minister again, as in a benediction.

M'Iver pushed back his chair without rising, and threw a leg across its arm with a complacent look at the shapely round of the calf, that his hose still fitted with wonderful neatness considering the stress they must have had from wind and rain.

" We had grace indeed," said he, " in Pomerania. We came at night, just as now, upon this castle of its most noble and puissant lord. It was Palm Sunday, April the third, Old Style. I mind, because it was my birthday ; the country all about was bursting out in a most rare green ; the gardens and fields breathed sappy odours, and the birds were throng at the bigging of their homes in bush and eave ; the day sparkled, and river and cloud too, till the spirit in a person jigged as to a fiddle ; the nights allured to escapade."

" What was the girl's name ? " I asked M'Iver, leaning forward, finding his story in some degree had parallel with my own.

" Her name, Colin—I did not mention the girl, did I ? How did you guess there was a girl in it ? " said John, perplexed.

I flushed at my own transparency, and was glad to see that none but the minister (and M'Iver a little later) had observed the confession of my query. The others were too busy on carnal appetites to feel the touch of a sentiment wrung from me by a moment's illusion.

"It is only my joke," I stammered; "you have a reputation among the snoods."

M'Iver smiled on me very warm-heartedly, yet cunningly too.

"Colin, Colin," he cried. "Do I not know *you* from boot to bonnet? You think the spring seasons are never so fond and magic as when a man is courting a girl; you are minding of some spring day of your own and a night of twinkling stars. I'll not deny but there was a girl in my case in the parlour of Pomerania's cousin at Regenwalde; and I'll not deny that a recollection of her endows that season with something of its charm. We had ventured into this vacant house, as I have said: its larders were well plenished; its vaults were full of marshalled brigades of bottles and battaglia of casks. Thinking no danger, perhaps careless if there was, we sat late, feasted to the full, and drank deep in a house that like this was empty in every part. It was 1631—I'll leave you but that clue to my age at the time—and, well I was an even prettier lad than I am to-day. I see you smile, Master Gordon; but that's my bit joke. Still there's some relevance to my story in my looks too. Though I was but a sergeant of pikes (with sons of good families below me, as privates, mind you), I was very trim and particular about my apparel. I carried myself with a good chest, as we say,—my features and my leg speak for themselves. I had sung songs—trifles of my own, foolishly esteemed, I'm hearing, in many parts of Argile. I'll not deny but I like to think of that, and to fancy young folks humming my ditties by warm fires when I'm maybe in the cold with the divot at my mouth. And I had told a tale or two—a poor art enough, I'll allow, spoiled by bookcraft. It was a cheery company as you may guess, and at last I was at a display of our Highland dancing. I see dancing to-day in many places that is not the thing as I was taught it by the strongest dancer in all Albainn. The company sat facing me as I stepped it over a couple of sword-blades, and their backs were to the door. Mackenzie was humming a *port-a-bheul* with a North Country twang even in his nose, and I was at my last step when the door opened with no noise and a girl looked in, her eyes staring hard at me alone, and a finger on her lips for silence. A man of less discernment would have stopped his dance incontinent and betrayed the presence of the lady to the others, who never dreamt so interesting a sight was behind them. But I never let on. I even put an extra flourish on my conclusion, that came just as the girl backed out at the door beckoning me to follow her. Two minutes later, while my friends were bellowing a rough Gaelic chorus, I was out following my lady of silence up a little stair and into a room below the eaves. There she narrated to me the plot that we unhappy lads were to be the victims of. The house was a trap : it was to be surrounded at night, when we had eaten and drunken over-well, and the sword was our doom arranged for. The girl told me all this very quietly in the French she learned I was best master of next to my own Gaelic, and—what a mad thing's the blood in a youth—all the time I was indifferent to her alarum, and pondering upon her charms of lip and eye. She died a twelvemonth later in Glogoe of Silesia, and—— God give her peace ! "

" You may save your supplication," said Gordon ; " her portion's assigned, a thing fixed and unalterable, and your prayer is a Popish conceit."

" God give her peace ! I'll say it, Master Gordon, and I'll wish it in the face of every Covenanter ever droned a psalm ! She died in Silesia, not careless, I'm thinking, of the memory of one or two weeks we spent in Frankfort, whose outer lanes and faubourgs are in my recollection blossoming with the almond-flower and scented at eve."

He rose to his feet and paced the floor beside us, strong, but loosened a little at the tongue by the generous wine of Dalness ; his mien a blending of defiance against the cheatry of circumstance and a display of old ancient grief.

" Heart of the rose, *gramachree*, bird-song at the lip, star eye and wisdom, yet woman to the core ! I wish I were so young as then I was, and *ochanie*, what availed my teens, if the one woman that ever understood me were no more but a dust in Glogoe ! "

" Come, come, man," I cried ; " it's a world full of very choice women."

" Is it indeed ? " asked he, turning on me a pitiful eye ; " I'm wrong if you ever met but one that was quite so fine as you must have them—— Tuts, tuts, here I'm on the key of old man's history. I cheat myself at times of leisure into the notion that once I loved a foreign girl who died a spotless maiden. You'll notice, Master Gordon, I have something of the sentiment you Lowlanders make such show of, or I play-act the thing very well. Believe me, I'll hope to get a wife out of your parish some day yet ; but I warn you she must have a tocher in her stocking as well as on her father's hill."

The minister surveyed him through half-shut eyes, leaning back on the rungs of his chair. I think he saw the truth as clearly as I did myself, for he spoke with more than common softness when he answered.

" I like your tale," he said, " which had a different conclusion and a more noble one than what I looked for at the opening." Then he leaned out and put a hand on John Splendid's sleeve. " Human nature," said he, " is the most baffling of mysteries. I said I knew you from boot to bonnet, but there's a corner here I have still to learn the secret of."

" Well, well," cried M'Iver, lifting a glass confusedly, and seating himself again at the board, " here's a night-cap—MacCailein Mor and the Campbell cause ! "

" And a thought for the lady of Regenwalde," I whispered, pressing his foot with my toe beneath the table, and clinking my glass with his.

We drank, the two of us, in a silence, and threw the glasses on the hearth.

The windows, that now were shuttered, rattled to gowsty airs, and the rain drummed on. All about the house, with its numerous corners, turrets, gussets, and corbie-stepped gables, the fury of the world rose and wandered, the fury that never rests but is ever somewhere round the ancient universe, jibing night and morning at man's most valiant effort. It might spit and blow till our shell shook and creaked, and the staunch walls wept, and the garden footways ran with bubbling waters, but we were still to conquer. Our lanthorn gleamed defiance to that brag of night eternal, that pattern-piece of the last triumph of the oldest enemy of man—Blackness the Rider, who is older than the hoary star.

Fresh wood hissed on the fire, but the candles burned low in their sockets. Sonachan and the baron-bailie slept with their heads on the table, and the man with the want, still sodden at the eyes, turned his wet hose upon his feet with a madman's notion of comfort.

"I hope," said M'Iver, "there's no ambuscade here, as in the house of the cousin of his Grace of Pomerania. At least we can but bide on, whatever comes, and take the night's rest that offers, keeping a man-about watch against intrusion."

"There's a watch more pressing still," said Master Gordon, shaking the slumber off him and jogging the sleeping men upon the shoulders. "My soul watcheth for the Lord more than they that watch for the morning. We have been wet with the showers of the mountain, like Job, and embracing the rock for want of a shelter. We are lone-haunted men in a wild land encompassed by enemies; let us thank God for our safety thus far, and ask His continued shield upon our flight."

And in the silence of that great house, dripping and rocking in the tempest of the night, the minister poured out his heart in prayer. It had humility and courage too; it was imbued with a spirit strong and calm. For the first time my heart warmed to the man who in years after was my friend and mentor—Alexander Gordon, Master of the Arts, the man who wedded me and gave my children Christian baptism, and brought solace in the train of those little ones lost for a space to me among the grasses and flowers of Kilmalieu.

CHAPTER XXV.

THE ANGRY EAVESDROPPER.

It may seem, in my recounting of these cold wanderings, of days and nights with nothing but snow and rain, and always the hounds of fear on every hand, that I had forgotten to exercise my mind upon the blunder and the shame of Argile's defeat at Inverlochy. So far is this from the fact that M'Iver and I on many available occasions disputed—as old men at the trade of arms will do—the reasons of a reverse so much unexpected, so little to be condoned, considering the advantage we had in numbers compared with the fragments of clans Alasdair MacDonald brought down from the gorges of Lochaber to the waters of Loch Linnhe and Locheil. It was useless to bring either the baron-bailie or Sonachan into our deliberations ; neither of them had any idea of how the thing had happened, though they were very well informed indeed about certain trivial departures from strict forms of Highland procedure in the hurried marshalling of the troops.

" Cheap trash of pennyland men from Lochow-side were put on the right of gentlemen cadets of the castle and Loch Finne-side lairds," was the baron-bailie's bitter protestation.

Sonachan, who was naturally possessed of a warm side to the people, even common quality, of his own part of the country, would sniff at this with some scorn.

" Pennyland here, pennyland there, they were closer in blood on Black Duncan than any of your shore-side partans, who may be gentrice by sheepskin right but never by the glaive."

So the two would be off again into the tanglements of Highland pedigree.

The mind of the man with the want was, of course, a vacant tablet, washed clean of every recollection by the copious tears he had wept in his silliness since ever the shock of the battle came on him; Stewart was so much of an unscrupulous liar that no word of his could be trusted; and the minister alone could give us any idea of what had been the sentiment in the army when the men of Montrose (who were really the men of Sir Alasdair, his major-general) came on them. But, for reasons every true Gael need not even have a hint of, we were averse from querying this dour, sour, Lowland cleric on points affecting a Highland retreat.

So it was, I say, that the deliberations of M'Iver and myself were without any outside light in somewhat dark quarters: we had to guide us only yon momentary glimpse of the stricken field with its flying men, seen in a stupid blur of the senses,—as one lying by a dark hill tarn at night, waiting for mallard or teal, sees the birds wheeling above the water ere he has appreciated the whirr of their presence, lets bang his piece at the midst of them, and is in a dense stillness again before he comprehends that what he has waited for in the cold night has happened.

"The plan of old Gustavus did it, I'll wager my share of the silver-mine," would John insist; "and who in heaven's name would think Alasdair *mosach* knew the trick of it? I saw his horseman fire one pistol-shot and fall on at full speed. That's old Gustavus for you, isn't it? And yet," he would continue, reflecting, "Auchinbreac knew the Swedish tactics too. He had his musketeers and pikemen separate, as the later laws demand; he had even a hint from myself of the due proportion of two pikes to three muskets."

"But never a platoon fired a volley," I recalled. "It was steel and targe from the onset." And then I would add, "What's to be said for MacCailein?"

On this John Splendid would ruffle up wrothily with blame for my harping on that incident, as if it were a crime to hint at any weakness in his chief.

" You are very much afraid of a waff of wind blowing on your cousin's name," I would cry.

" My chief, Elrigmore, my chief. I make no claim to consideration for a cousin, but I'll stand up for Argile's name so long as the gyrony of eight and the galley for Lorn are in his coat of arms."

Inverlochy, Inverlochy, Inverlochy—the black name of it rang in my head like a tolling bell as I sought to doze for a little in Dalness house. The whole events of the scandalous week piled up on me : I no sooner wandered one thought away in the mists of the nether mind than a new one, definite and harassing, grew in its place, so that I was turning from side to side in a torture-rack of reflection when I should be lost in the slumber my travel and weariness so well had earned me. Something of an eeriness at our position in that genteel but lonely house lay heavy on me too : it had no memories of friendship in any room for me ; it was haunted, if haunted at all, with the ghosts of people whose names we only breathed with bitterness in the shire of Argile. And constantly the wind would be howling in it, piping dismally in the vent of the room the minister and I were in together ; constant the rain would be hissing on the embers of the fire ; at a long distance off a waterfall, in veering gusts of greater vehemence, crashed among its rocks and thundered in its linn.

M'Iver, who was the first to take watch for the night, paced back and forth along the lobbies or stood to warm himself at the fire he fed at intervals with peat or pineroot. Though he had a soldier's reverence for the slumbers of his comrades, and made the least of noises as he moved around in his deer-skins, the slightest movement so advertised his zeal, and so clearly recalled the precariousness of our position, that I could not sleep. In an hour or more after I lay down M'Iver alarmed the advanceguard of my coming sleep by his unconscious whistle of a pibroch, and I sat up to find that the cleric was sharing my waukrife rest. He had cast his peruke. In the light of a cruisie that hung at the mantel-breas he was a comical-looking fellow with a high bald head, and his eyes, that were very dark and profound, surrounded by the red rings of weariness, all the redder for the pallor of his face. He stretched his legs and rubbed his knees slowly, and smiled on me a little mournfully.

"I'm a poor campaigner," said he; "I ought to be making the best of the chance we have; but instead I must be thinking of my master and patron, and about my flock in Inneraora town."

I seized the opportunity as a gled would jump at a dove.

"You're no worse than myself," I said, rising to poke up the fire; "I'm thinking of Argile too, and I wish I could get his defalcation—if that it may be called—out of my mind. Was it a—was it—what you might call a desertion without dignity, or a step with half an excuse in policy? I know MacCailein had an injured arm."

Gordon rose and joined me at the fireside. He seemed in a swither as to whether I was a fit confidant or not in such a matter, but at last would appear to decide in my favour.

"You have heard me speak well of Argile," he said, quietly. "I never said a word in his praise that was not deserved; indeed I have been limited in my valuation of his virtues and ornaments, lest they should think it the paid chaplain who spoke and not the honest acquaintance. I know pious men, Highland and Lowland, but my lord of Argile has more than any of them the qualities of perfection. At home yonder, he rises every morning at five and is in private till eight. He prays in his household night and morning, and never went abroad, though but for one night, but he took his write-book, standish, and English New Bible, and Newman's Concordance with him. Last summer, playing one day with the bullats with some gentlemen, one of them, when the Marquis stopped to lift his bullat, fell pale, and said to them about him, ' Bless me, it is that I see my lord with his head off and all his shoulder full of blood.' A wicked man would have counted that the most gloomy portent and a fit occasion for dread, for the person who spoke was the Laird of Drimmindorren's seventh son, with a reputation for the second sight. But Argile laughed at the thing, no way alarmed, and then with a grave demeanour he said, said he, ' The wine's in your head, sir; and even if it was an omen, what then? The axe in troublous times is no disgrace, and a chief of Clan Diarmaid would be a poor chief indeed if he failed to surrender his head with some show of dignity.' "

"But to leave his people twice in one war with no apparent valid excuse must look odd to his unfriends," I said, and I toasted my hose at the fire.

"I wish I could make up my mind whether an excuse is valid or not," said the cleric; "and I'm willing to find more excuses for MacCailein than I'll warrant he can find for himself this morning, wherever he may happen to be. It is the humour of God Almighty sometimes to put two men in the one skin. So far as I may humbly judge, Argile is the poor victim of such an economy. You have seen the sort of man I mean: to-day generous to his last plack, to-morrow the widow's oppressor; Sunday a soul humble at the throne of grace, and writhing with remorse for some child's sin, Monday riding vaingloriously in the glaur on the road to hell, bragging of filthy amours, and inwardly gloating upon a crime anticipated. Oh, but were the human soul made on less devious plan, how my trade of Gospel messenger were easy! And valour, too, is it not in most men a fever of the moment; at another hour the call for courage might find them quailing and flying like the coney of the rocks."

"Then Argile, you think, was on those occasions the sport of his weaker self?" I pushed. I found so many obstacles in the way of satisfaction to my natural curiosity that I counted no persistence too rude now.

"He was the result of his history," said the minister, quickly, his face flushing with a sudden inspiration. "From the start of time those black moments for the first Marquis of Argile have been preparing. I can speak myself of his more recent environment. He has about him ever flatterers of the type of our friend the sentinel out there, well-meaning but a woeful influence, keeping from him every rumour that might vex his ear, colouring every event in such a manner as will please him. They kept the man so long in a delusion that fate itself was under his heel, that when the stress of things came——"

"Not another word!" cried M'Iver from the doorway.

We turned round and found him standing there wrapped up in his plaid, his bonnet over a frowning brow, menace in his eye.

"Not another word, if it must be in that key. Has Archibald Marquis of Argile and Lord of Lochow no friends in this convocation? I would have thought his own paid curate and a neighbour so close as Elrigmore would never waste the hours due to sleep upon treason to the man who deserved better of them."

"You should have eavesdropped earlier and you would have learned that there was no treason in the matter. I'm as leal friend to my lord of Argile as you or any of your clan. What do I care for your bubbly-jock Highland vanity?" said Gordon.

"We were saying nothing of MacCailein that we would not say to you," I explained to M'Iver, annoyed in some degree by his interference.

"Ay, ay," said he, with a pitying shrug of the shoulder, and throwing off his last objection to my curiosity; "you're on the old point again. Man, but you're ill to satisfy! And yet we must have the story sooner or later, I suppose. I would rather have it anywhere than in this wauf and empty foreign domicile, that is a melancholy in itself enough for any man. But since the minister's in a key for history let him on."

"I'm in no key for history at all," said Master Gordon, very shortly. "If you would have the truth, I'm searching my wits for some accounting for the conduct of a nobleman I love more than a brother."

"And that's no great credit to you: have you ever known his equal?" cried M'Iver, always in the mood for bickering with this Lowland scholar—the only person, or almost the only person, I found him unwilling to pick and choose words for.

"You're speaking there as a kinsman and clansman," said Master Gordon; "I'm speaking as man of man. I like this one for his struggle, sometimes successful, sometimes not all that way, to keep a manly and religious front before those contending passions within him. He is a remnant of the old world of Highland sturt and strife, and still to a degree in the midst of it, and at the same time a man endowed by heaven with a genius of peace and intellect. Fighting with a horde of savages against reivers no more dishonest than his own clans, is it a wonder that sometimes MacCailein's spirit, the spirit of the thinker and the scholar, should sink at the horror of his position? For all that, he has a courageous front nine times out of ten, and it would have been a miracle itself if he had not taken to the galley at Inverlochy yesterday morning."

"Yesterday morning!" I cried. "Good God! I thought it was years ago, or something in a dream."

"And it was just yesterday morning," spoke on the cleric, "and to-day there's a marquis on his way south somewhere thinking of yesterday (I make no doubt) even on, with every recollection of his life lost for a space below that salt sea of remorse. And so simple the thing too, like every pregnant moment of life. We lay on the flat land yonder as you left us on your reconnoitre, changed shots on the Saturday night with wandering malcontents as we thought them, and found Montrose on the braes above us as the dawn broke. We had but a shot or two apiece to the musket, they tell me. Dunbarton's drums rolled, the pipes clamoured, the camp rose from its sleep in a confusion, and a white moon was fainting behind us. Argile, who had slept in a galley all night, came ashore in a wherry with his left arm in a sling. His face was like the clay, but he had a firm lip, and he was buckling a hauberk with a steady hand as the men fell under arms. Left alone then, I have a belief that he would have come through the affair gallantly; but the Highland double-dealings were too much for him. He turned to Auchinbreac and said 'Shall I take the command, or——?' leaving an alternative for his relative to guess at. Auchinbreac, a stout soldier but a vicious, snapped him very short. 'Leave it to me, leave it to me,' he answered, and busied himself again in disposing his troops, upon whom I was well aware he had no great reliance. Then Sir James Rollock-Niddry and a few others pushed the Marquis to take his place in his galley again, but would he? Not till Auchinbreac came up a second time, and seeing the contention of his mind, took your Highland way of flattering a chief, and made a poltroon act appear one of judgment and necessity. ' As a man and soldier only, you might be better here at the onset,' said Auchinbreac, who had a wily old tongue ; ' but you are disabled against using sword or pistol ; you are the mainstay of a great national movement, depending for its success on your life, freedom, and continued exertion.' Argile took to the galley again, and Auchinbreac looked after him with a shamed and dubious eye. Well, well, Sir Duncan has paid for his temporising ; he's in his place appointed. I passed the knowe where he lay writhing to a terrible end, with a pike at his vitals, and he was moaning for the chief he had helped to a shabby flight."

" A shabby flight ! " said M'Iver, with a voice that was new to me, so harsh was it and so high-set.

" You can pick the word for yourself," said the minister ; " if by heaven's grace I was out of this, in Inneraora I should have my own way of putting it to Argile, whom I love and blame."

" Oh you Lowland dog ! " cried John Splendid, more high-keyed than ever, "*you* to blame Argile ! " And he stepped up to the cleric, who was standing by the chimney-jambs, glowered hellishly in his face, then with a fury caught his throat in his fingers, and pinned him up against the wall.

CHAPTER XXVI.

TRAPPED.

I CAUGHT M'Iver by the coat-lapels, and took him off the gasping cleric.

"Oh man!" I cried, "is this the Highland brigadier to be throttling an old soldier of Christ?"

"Let me get at him and I'll set him in the way of putting the last truth of his trade to its only test," said he, still with a face corp-white, tugging at my hold and eyeing Master Gordon with a very uplifted and ferocious demeanour.

I suppose he must, in the midst of his fury, have got just a glisk of the true thing before him—not a worthy and fair opponent for a man of his own years, but an old wearied man of peace, with a flabby neck, and his countenance blotched, and his wig ajee upon his head so that it showed the bald pate below, for he came to himself as it were with a start. Then he was ashamed most bitterly. He hung his head and scraped with an unconscious foot upon the floor. The minister recovered his wind, looked with contempt in every line at the man who had abused him, and sat down without a word before the fire.

"I'm sorry about this," said M'Iver, fumbling about his waist-belt with nervous fingers; "I'm sorry about this, Master Gordon. A Highlander cannot be aye keeping God's gift of a temper in leash, and yet it's my disgrace to have laid a hand on a gentleman of your age and calling, even for the name of my chief. Will you credit me when I say I was blind to my own act? Something in me rose uncontrollable, and had you been Hector in armour, or my grandfather from the grave, I was at your neck."

"Say no more about it," answered Gordon. "I have seen the wolf so often at the Highlander's heart that I need not be wondering to find him snarling and clawing now. And still—from a gentleman—and a person of travel——"

"Say away, sir," said M'Iver, bitterly; "you have the whole plea with you this time, and I'm a rogue of the blackest. I can say no more than I'm sorry for a most dirty action."

Gordon looked at him, and seemed convinced that here was a genuine remorse; at least his mien softened and he said quietly, "You'll hear no more of it from me."

We were standing, M'Iver and I, in front of the hearth, warming to the peat glow, and the cleric sat in an oak arm-chair. Out in the vacant night the rain still pattered and the gale cried. And all at once, above the sound of wind and water, there came a wild rapping at the main door of the house, the alarum of a very crouse and angry traveller finding a hostel barred against him at unseasonable hours. A whole childhood of fairy tale rose to my mind in a second; but the plain truth followed with more conviction, that likely here was no witch, warlock, nor fairy, but some one with a better right to the tenancy of Dalness than seven broken men with nor let nor tack. We were speedily together, the seven of us, and gathered in the hall, and listening with mouths open and hearts dunting, to the rapping that had no sign of ceasing.

"I'll have a vizzy from an upper window of who this may be," said John, sticking a piece of pine in the fire till it flared at the end, and hurrying with it thus lighted up the stair. I followed at his heels, while the rest remained below ready to give whatever reception was most desirable to the disturbers of our night's repose. The window we went to looked out on the most utter blackness, a blackness that seemed to stream in at the window as we swung it softly back on its hinge. M'Iver put out his head and his torch, giving a warder's keek at the door below where the knocking continued. He drew in his head quickly and looked at me with astonishment.

"It's a woman," said he. "I never saw a campaign where so many petticoats of one kind or another were going. Who, in God's name, can this one be, and what's her errand to Dalness at this hour? One of its regular occupants would scarcely make such to-do about her summons."

"The quickest answer could be got by asking her," I said.

"And about a feint?" he said, musing. "Well, we can but test it."

We went down and reported to our companions, and Gordon was for opening the door on the moment. "A wanderer like ourselves," said he, "perhaps a widow of our own making from Glencoe. In any case a woman, and out in the storm."

We stood round the doors while M'Iver put back the bars and opened as much as would give entry to one person at a time. There was a loud cry, and in came the Dark Dame, a very spectacle of sorrow! Her torn garments clung sodden to her skin, her hair hung stringy at her neck, the elements had chilled and drowned the frenzied gleaming of her eyes. And there she stood in the doorway among us, poor woman, poor wretch, with a frame shaking to her tearless sobs!

"You have no time to lose," she said to our query, "a score of Glencoe men are at my back. They fancy they'll have you here in the trap this house's owner left you. Are you not the fools to be advantaging yourselves of comforts you might be sure no fairy left for Campbells in Dalness? You may have done poorly at Inverlochy —though I hear the Lowlanders and not you were the poltroons—but blood is thicker than water, and have we not the same hills beside our doors at home, and I have run many miles to warn you that MacDonald is on his way." She told her story with sense and straightness, her frenzy subdued by the day's rigour. Our flight from her cries, she said, had left her a feeling of lonely helplessness; she found, as she sped, her heart truer to the tartan of her name than her anger had let her fancy, and so she followed us round Loch Leven-head, and over the hills to Glencoe. At the blind woman's house in the morning, where she passed readily enough for a natural, she learned that the eldest son in the bed had set about word of our presence before we were long out of his mother's door. The men we had seen going down in the airt of Tynree were the lad's gathering, and they would have lost us but for the beetle-browed rogue, who, guessing our route through the hills to Dalness, had run before them, and, unhampered by arms or years, had reached the house of Dalness a little before we came out of our journey in swamp and corry. A sharp blade, certes! he had seen that unless something brought us to pause a while at Dalness we would be out of the reach of his friends before they had gained large enough numbers and made up on him. So he had planned with the few folk in the house to leave it temptingly open in our way, with the shrewd guess that starved and wearied men would be found sleeping beside the fire when the MacDonalds came round the gusset. All this the Dame Dubh heard and realised even in her half frenzy as she spent some time in the company of the marching MacDonalds, who never dreamt that her madness and her denunciations of Clan Diarmaid were mixed in some degree with a natural interest in the welfare of every member of that clan.

M'Iver scrutinised the woman sharply, to assure himself there was no cunning effort of a mad woman to pay off the score her evil tongue of the day before revealed she had been reckoning; but he saw only here dementia gone to a great degree, a friend anxious for our welfare —so anxious, indeed, that the food Master Gordon was pressing upon her made no appeal to her famishing body.

"You come wonderfully close on my Frankfort story," said M'Iver, whimsically. "I only hope we may win out of Dalness as snugly as we won out of the castle of the cousin of Pomerania."

For a minute or two we debated on our tactics. We had no muskets, though swords were rife enough in Dalness, so a stand and a defence by weapons was out of the question. M'Iver struck on a more pleasing and cleanly plan. It was to give the MacDonalds tit for tat, and decoy them into the house as their friends had decoyed us into it, and leave them there in durance while we went on our own ways.

We jammed down the iron pins of the shutters in the

salmanger, so that any exit or entrance by this way was made a task of the greatest difficulty; then we lit the upper flats, to give the notion that we were lying there. M'Iver took his place behind a door that led from the hall to other parts of the house, and was indeed the only way there, while the rest of us went out into the night and concealed ourselves in the dark angle made by a turret and gable—a place where we could see, without being seen, any person seeking entry to the house.

All the paths about the mansion were strewn with rough sand or gravel from the river, and the rain, in slanting spears, played hiss upon them with a sound I never hear to-day but my mind's again in old Dalness. And in the dark, vague with rain and mist, the upper windows shone blear and ghostly, dull vapours from a swamp, corp-candles on the sea, more than the eyes of a habitable dwelling warm and lit within. We stood, the seven of us, against the gable (for the woman joined us and munched a dry crust between the chittering of her teeth), waiting the coming of the MacDonalds.

I got to my musing again, puzzled in this cold adventure, upon the mystery of life. I thought it must be a dream such as a man has lying in strange beds, for my spirit floated and cried upon that black and ugly air, lost and seeking as the soul of a man struggling under sleep. I had been there before, I felt, in just such piteous case among friends in the gable of a dwelling, yet all alone, waiting for visitors I had no welcome for. And then again (I would think), is not all life a dream, the sun and night of it, the seasons, the faces of friends, the flicker of fires and the nip of wine; and am not I now stark awake for the first time, the creature of God, alone in His world before the dusk has been divided from the day and bird and beast have been let loose to wander about a new universe? Or again (I would think), am I not dead and done with? Surely I fell in some battle away in Low Germanie, or later in the sack of Inneraora town, that was a town long, long ago, before the wave threshed in upon Dunchuach?

The man with the want, as usual, was at his tears, whispering to himself reproach and memory and omens of fear, but he was alert enough to be the first to observe the approach of our enemy. Ten minutes at least before they appeared on the sward, lit by the lights of the upper windows, he lifted a hand, cocked an ear, and told us he heard their footsteps.

There were about a score and a half of the MacDonalds altogether, of various ages, some of them old gutchers that had been better advised to be at home snug by the fire in such a night or saying their prayers in preparation for the looming grave, some of them young and strapping, all well enough armed with everything but musketry, and guided to the house by the blind woman's son and a gentleman in a laced coat, whom we took to be the owner of Dalness because two men of the bearing and style of servants were in his train and very pretentious about his safety in the course of a debate that took place a few yards from us as to whether they should demand our surrender or attack and cut us down without quarter.

The gentleman sent his two lackeys round the house, and they came back reporting (what we had been very careful of) that every door was barred.

"Then," said the gentleman, "we'll try a bland knock, and if need be, force the main door."

He was standing now in a half dusk, clear of the light of the windows, with a foot on the step of the door; behind him gathered the MacDonalds with their weapons ready, and I dare say, could we have seen it, with no very pretty look on their faces. As he spoke, he put his hand on the hasp, and, to his surprise, the heavy door was open. We had taken good care of that too.

The band gathered themselves together and dived into the place, and the plaiding of the last of them had scarcely got inside the door than Stewart ran up with the key and turned the lock, with a low whistle for the guidance of M'Iver at the inner door. In a minute or less, John was round in our midst again with his share of the contract done, and our rats were squealing in their trap.

For a little there was nothing but crying and cursing, wild beating against the door, vain attack on the windows, a fury so futile that it was sweet to us outsiders, and we forgot the storm and the hardship.

At last M'Iver rapped on the door and demanded attention.

"Is there any one there with the English?" he asked.

The gentleman of Dalness answered that he could speak English with the best cateran ever came out of MacCailein Mor's country, and he called for instant release, with a menace added that Hell itself could not excel the punishment for us if they were kept much longer under lock and bar. "We are but an advanced guard," said he, with a happy thought at lying, "and our friends will be at your back before long."

M'Iver laughed pawkily.

"Come, come, Dalness," said he, "do you take us for girls? You have every man left in Glencoe at your back there; you're as much ours as if you were in the tolbooth of Inneraora O; and I would just be mentioning that if I were in your place I would be speaking very soft and soothing."

"I'll argue the thing fairly with you if you let us out," said Dalness, stifling his anger behind the door, but still with the full force of it apparent in the stress of his accent.

M'Iver laughed again.

"You have a far better chance where you are," said he. "You are very snug and warm there; the keg of brandy's on the left-hand side of the fire, though I'm afraid there's not very much left of it now that my friend of Achnatra here has had his will of it. Tell those gentry with you that we intend to make ourselves cosy in other parts of the house till the morn's morning, and that if they attempt to force a way out by door or window before we let them, we'll have sentinels to blow out the little brains they have. I'm putting it to you in the English, Dalness—and I cry pardon for making my first gossip with a Highland gentleman in such a tongue—but I want you to put my message in as plausible a way as suits you best to the lads and *bodachs* with you."

The man drew away from the neighbourhood of the door; there was a long silence, and we concluded they were holding parley of war as to what was next to be done. Meantime we made preparations to be moving from a place that was neither safe nor homely. We took food from the pantries, scourged Stewart from a press he was prying in with clawing fingers and bulging pockets, and had just got together again at the rear of the house when a cry at the front told us that our enemies, in some way we never learned the manner of, had got the better of our bolted doors and shutters.

Perhaps a chance of planning our next step would have been in our favour; perhaps on the other hand it would have been the worse for us, because in human folly we might have determined on staying to face the odds against us, but there was no time for balancing the chances; whatever was to be done was to be done quickly.

"Royal's my race!" cried Stewart, dropping a pillow-slip full of goods he carried with him—"Royal's my race—and here's one with great respect for keeping up the name of it." And he leaped to a thicket on his left. The man with the want ran weeping up to the Dark Dame and clung to her torn gown, a very child in the stupor of his grief and fear. The baron-bailie and Sonachan and the minister stood spellbound, and I cursed our folly at the weakness of our trap. Only M'Iver kept his wits about him.

"Scatter," said he in English—"scatter without adieux, and all to the fore by morning search back to the Brig of Urchy, comrades there till the middle of the day, then the devil take the hindmost."

More than a dozen MacDonalds came running round the gable end, lit by the upper windows, and we dispersed like chaff to the wind before M'Iver's speech concluded, He and I ran for a time together, among the bushes of the garden, through the curly kail, under low young firs that clutched at the clothing. Behind us the night rang with pursuing cries, with challenge and call, a stupid clamour that gave a clue to the track we could follow with greatest safety. M'Iver seemingly stopped to listen, or made up his mind to deviate to the side after a little; for I soon found myself running alone, and two or three men—to judge by their cries—keeping as close on me as they could by the sound of my plunging among twig and bracken. At last, by striking to an angle down a field that suddenly rolled down beside me, I found soft carpeting for my feet, and put an increasing distance between us. With no relaxation to my step, however, I kept running till I seemed a good way clear of Dalness policies, and on a bridle-path that led up the glen—the very road, as I learned later, that our enemy had taken on their way from Tynree. I kept on it for a little as well as I could, but the night was so dark (and still the rain was pouring though the wind had lowered) that by-and-by I lost the path, and landed upon rough water-broken rocky land, bare of tree or bush. The tumult behind me was long since stilled in distance, the storm itself had abated, and I had traversed for less than an hour when the rain ceased. But still the night was solemn black, though my eyes by usage had grown apt and accustomed to separate the dense black of the boulder from the drab air around it. The country is one threaded on every hand by *eas* and brook that drop down the mountain-sides at almost every yard of the way. Nothing was to hear but the sound of running and falling waters, every brook with its own note, a tinkle of gold on a marble stair as I came to it, declining to a murmur of sweethearts in a bower as I put its banks behind me after wading or leaping ; or a song sung in a clear spring morning by a girl among heather hills, muffling behind me to the blackguard discourse of banditty waiting with poignards out upon a lonely highway.

I was lost somewhere north of Glen Etive ; near me I knew must be Tynree, for I had been walking for two hours and yet I dare not venture back on the straight route to to-morrow's rendezvous till something of daylight gave me guidance. At last I concluded that the way through the Black Mount country to Bredalbane must be so close at hand it would be stupidity of the densest to go back by Dalness. There was so much level land round me that I felt sure I must be rounding the Bredalbane hills, and I chanced a plunge to the left. I had not taken twenty steps when I ran up against the dry-stone dyke that bordered the Inns of Tynree.

CHAPTER XXVII.

A TAVERN IN THE WILDS.

TYNREE is the Gaelic of a name that in the English is King's House. What humour gave so gaudy a title to so humble a place I have been always beat to know. For if the poorest of the chiefs of the poor isles had his choice of the gallows at once or Tynree for a long habitation, I'm thinking he would cry, " Out with your rope." Standing all its lee lone on the edge of the wildest moor of all the Scottish kingdom, blustered on by the winds of Glencoe and Glen Etive, the house, far apart from any other (even a hunter's bothy among the corries), must be eerie, empty of all but its owner at most seasons of the year. He will have nothing about him but the flying plover that is so heart-breaking in its piping at the grey of morn, for him must the night be a dreariness no rowth of cruisie or candle may mitigate. I can fancy him looking out day after day upon plains of snow and cruel summits, blanching and snarling under sodden skies, and him wishing that God so good was less careless, and had given him a home and trade back among the cosy little glens, if not in the romping towns. But they tell me—people who rove and have tried Tynree in all weathers—that often it is cheerful with song and story ; and there is a tale that once upon a time a little king, out adventuring in the kingly ways of winter stories, found this tavern in the wilds so warm, so hospitable, so resounding with the songs of good fellows, that he bided as a guest for a week of the winter weather.

When I came on Tynree, it was sounding with music, just, it might be, as in the day of the king in the story.

Three of the morning, yet the hostel sent out a most hearty reek and firelight, the odours of stewing meats and of strong waters, and the sound of piping and trumping and laughing.

I stood back a piece from the house and debated with myself whether or not it was one where the tartan of Diarmaid would be sure of a welcome even if his sporran jingled with gold to the very jaws. All I wanted was shelter till the day broke and—this may seem odd to any one who has not known the utter wearisomeness of being a hunted man jinking in the dark among woods and alleys —the easy conversation of some human beings with no thought bothering them but what would be for the next meal, or the price of cattle at a town tryst. And song and trump—come, I'll tell the God's own truth upon that! They called me Sobersides in those days: M'Iver gave me the name and kept it on me till the very last, and yet sobriety of spirit (in one way) was the last quality in those old days of no grace to find in my nature. I liked to sit in taverns, drinking not deeply, but enough to keep the mood from flagging, with people of the young heart, people fond of each other, adrift from all commercial cunning, singing old staves and letting their fancy go free to a tune twanged on a Jew's-trump or squeezed upon a bagpipe or zigged upon a fiddle. So the merriment of Tynree held me like a charm, and a mad whim at last seized me, and in I went, confident that my instinct of comradery would not deceive me, and that at least I had the boon-companion's chance.

The company never even stopped their clamour to look at me; the landlord put a jug at my elbow, and a whang of bread and cheese, and I was joining with an affected gusto in a chorus less than ten minutes after I had been a hunted man on the edge of Moor Rannoch, ready to toss up a bawbee to learn whither my road should be.

It was an orra and remarkable gathering, convened surely by the trickery of a fantastic and vagabond providence,—" not a great many, but well picked," as Macgregor the Mottled said of his band of thieves. There were men and women to the number of a score, two or three travelling merchants (as they called themselves, but I think in my mind they were the kind of merchants who bargain with the dead corp on the abandoned battle-field, or follow expeditions of war to glean the spoil from burning homesteads) ; there were several gangrels, an Irishman with a silver eye, a strolling piper with poor skill of his noble instrument, the fiddler who was a drunken native of the place, a gipsy and his wife and some randy women who had dropped out of the march of Montrose's troops. Over this notable congregation presided the man of the house—none of your fat and genial-looking gentlemen, but a long lean personage with a lack-lustre eye. You would swear he would dampen the joy of a penny wedding, and yet (such a deceit is the countenance) he was a person of the finest wit and humour, otherwise I daresay Tynree had no such wonderful party in it that night.

I sat by the fire-end and quaffed my ale, no one saying more to me for a little than " There you are ! " Well enough they knew my side in the issue—my tartan would tell them that—but wandering bodies have no politics beyond the conviction that the world owes them as easy a living as they can cheat it out of, and they never mentioned war. The landlord's dram was on, and 'twas it I had shared in, and when it was over I pulled out a crown and bought the heartiest goodwill of a score of rogues with some flagons of ale.

A beetle-browed chamber, long, narrow, stifling with the heat of a great fire, its flagged floor at intervals would slap with bare or bauchled feet dancing to a short reel. First one gangrel would sing a verse or two of a Lowland ballant, not very much put out in its sentiment by the presence of the random ladies ; then another would pluck a tune upon the Jew's-trump, a chorus would rise like a sudden gust of wind, a jig would shake upon the fiddle. I never saw a more happy crew, nor yet one that—judging from the doctrine that thrift and sobriety have their just reward—deserved it less. I thought of poor Master Gordon somewhere dead or alive in or about Dalness, a very pupil of Christ, and yet with a share of His sorrows, with nowhere to lay his head, but it did not bitter me to my company.

By-and-by the landlord came cannily up to me and whispered in my ear a sort of apology for the rabble of his house.

"You ken, sir," said he in very good English—"you ken yourself what the country's like just now, given over to unending brawl, and I am glad to see good-humoured people about me, even if they are penniless gangrels."

"My own business is war," I acknowledged; "I'll be frank enough to tell you I'm just now making my way to Inneraora as well as the weather and the MacDonalds will let me."

He was pleased at my candour, I could see; confidence is a quality that rarely fails of its purpose. He pushed the bottle towards me with the friendliest of gestures, and took the line of the fellow-conspirator.

"Keep your thumb on that," said he; "I'm not supposed to precognosce every lodger in Tynree upon his politics. I'm off Clan Chattan myself, and not very keen on this quarrel—that's to say, I'll take no side in it, for my trade is feeding folk and not fighting them. Might I be asking if you were of the band of Campbells a corps of MacDonalds were chasing down the way last night?"

I admitted I was.

"I have nothing to do with it," said he; "and I'll do a landlord's duty by any clan coming my way. As for my guests here, they're so pleased to see good order broken in the land and hamlets half-harried that they'll favour any man whose trade is the sword, especially if he's a gentleman," he added. "I'm one myself, though I keep a sort of poor hostel here. I'm a young son."

We were joined by the gipsy, a bold tall man with very black and lambent eyes, hiccoughing with drink but not by any means drunken, who took out a wallet and insisted on my joining now in his drink. I dare not refuse the courtesy.

"Would you like your fortune spaed, sir?" asked my black friend, twitching his thumb in the direction of his wife, who was leering on me with a friendliness begot of the bottle. The place was full of deafening noises and peat-smoke. Fiddle jigged and pipes snored in the deep notes of debauchery, and the little Jew's-trump twanged between the teeth of a dirty-faced man in a saffron shirt and hodden breeks, wanting jacket and hose—a wizen little old man, going around the world living like a poet in realms whereto trump and tipple could readily bring him.

"Spae my fortune!" said I, laughing; "such swatches of the same as I had in the past were of no nature to make me eager to see what was to follow."

"Still and on," said he, "who knows but you may find a wife and a good fortune in a little lurk of the thumb? Jean! Jean! woman," he cried across the chamber to his callet, and over she came to a very indifferent and dubious client.

I had got my hand read a score of times ere this (for I am of a nature curious and prying), and each time the reading was different, but it did not altogether shake my faith in wise women; so, half for the fun of it, I put some silver pieces in the loof of my hand and held it before the woman, the transaction unnoticed by the company. She gave the common harangue to start with. At last, "There's a girl with a child," said she.

"Faith, and she never went to the well with the dish-clout then," said the black man, using a well-known Gaelic proverb, meaning a compliment in his dirty assumption.

"She's in a place of many houses now," went on the woman, busy upon the lines of my hand, "and her mind is taken up with a man in the ranks of Argile."

"That's not reading the hand at all, goodwife," said I; "those small facts of life are never written in a line across the loof."

"Jean is no apprentice at the trade," said her man across her shoulder. "She can find a life's history in the space of a hair."

"The man found the woman and the child under a root of fir," said the woman, "and if the man is not very quick to follow her, he may find kinship's courting get the better of a far-off lover's fancy."

"*Dhè!*" said I; "you have your story most pat. And what now, would you say, would be the end of it all —coming to the real business of the palmist, which, I take it, is not to give past history but to forecast fate?"

I'll not deny but I was startled by the woman's tale,

for here was Betty and here was MacLachlan put before me as plainly as they were in my own mind day and night since we left Inneraora.

The woman more closely scrutinised my hand, paused a while, and seemed surprised herself at its story.

"After all," said she, "the woman is not going to marry the man she loves."

I plucked my hand away with a "Pshaw! what does it matter? If I doubled your fee you would give me the very best fortune in your wit to devise."

The Irishman with the silver eye here jostled a merchantman, who drew his gully-knife, so that soon there was a fierce quarrel that it took all the landlord's threats and vigour of arm to put an end to. By this time I was becoming tired of my company; now that the spae-wife had planted the seed of distress in my mind, those people were tawdry, unclean, wretched. They were all in rags, foul and smelling; their music was but noise demented. I wondered at myself there in so vicious a company. And Betty—home—love—peace—how all the tribe of them suddenly took up every corner of my mind. Oh! fool, fool, I called myself, to be thinking your half-hearted wooing of the woman had left any fondness behind it. From the beginning you were second in the field, and off the field now—a soldier of a disgraced army, has the cousin not all the chances in the world? He'll be the true friend in trouble, he'll console her loneliness in a sacked burgh town; a woman's affection is so often her reward for simple kindness that he has got her long ago at no greater cost than keeping her company in her lonely hours. And you are but the dreamer, standing off trembling and flushing like a boy when you should be boldly on her cheek, because you dare not think yourself her equal. The father's was the true word: "There's one thing a woman will not abide, that her lover should think lightly either of himself or her."

All that black stream of sorry thought went rushing through me as I sat with an empty jug in my hand in a room that was sounding like a market-place. With a start I wakened up to find the landlord making a buffoon's attempt at a dance in the middle of the floor to the tune of the Jew's-trump, a transparent trick to restore the good-humour of his roysterers, and the black man who had fetched the spae-wife was standing at my side surveying me closely out of the corners of his eyes. I stood to my feet and ganted with great deliberation to pretend I had been half-sleeping. He yawned too, but with such obvious pretence that I could not but laugh at him, and he smiled knowingly back.

"Well," said he in English, "you'll allow it's a fair imitation, for I never heard that a put-on gant was smittal. I see that you are put about at my wife's fortune : she's a miracle at the business, as I said ; she has some secrets of fate I would rather with her than me. But I would swear a man may sometime get the better even of fate if he has a warning of its approach."

"I can scarcely see that by the logic of Porphyrius or Peter Hispanus with the categories, two scholars I studied at Glascow. But you are surely a queer man to be a vagabond at the petticoat-tails of a spae-wife," said I.

"I've had my chance of common life, city and town, and the company of ladies with broidery and camisole and washen faces," he answered with no hesitation, "and give me the highroad and freedom and the very brute of simplicity. I'm not of these parts. I'm not of the Highlands at all, as you may guess, though I've been in them and through them for many a day. I see you're still vexed about my woman's reading of your palm. It seems to have fitted in with some of your experience."

I confessed her knowledge of my private affairs surprised me, and his black eyes twinkled with humour.

"I'll explain the puzzle for just as much money as you gave her," said he, "and leave you more satisfied at the end than she did. And there's no black art at the bottom of my skill either."

"Very well," said I ; "here's your drink-money ; now tell me the trick of it, for trick I suppose it is."

He pocketed the money after a vagabond's spit on the coin for luck, and in twenty words exposed his by-love's device. They had just come from Inneraora two or three days before, and the tale of the Provost's daughter in Strongara had been the talk of the town.

" But how did your wife guess the interest of the lady in a man of Argile's army ? " I asked.

" Because she spaed the lady's fortune too," he answered, " and she had to find out in the neighbourhood what it was like to be before she did so ; you know that is half the art of the thing."

" Yet your woman's guess that I was the man—that's beyond me ! "

" I was struck myself when she out with that," he confessed. " Oh, she's a deep one, Jean ! But your manner and tongue betrayed the returned soldier of fortune ; of such officers in the ranks of Argile there are not so many that it was risking too much to believe all of them knew the story of the Provost's daughter, and your conduct, once she got that length, did the rest."

" And about kinship's courting ? " I asked, amazed at the simplicity of the thing.

The man dashed his fee on the board and ordered more liquor.

" Drink up," said he, " and drown care if you're the man my goodwife thought you, for faith there's a little fellow from over the loch making himself very snug in the lady's company in your absence."

There was no more drinking for me ; the fumes of this wretched company stank in my nostril, and I must be off to be alone with melancholy. Up I got and walked to the door with not fair-good-e'en nor fair-good-day, and I walked through the beginnings of a drab disheartening dawn in the direction that I guessed would lead me soonest to Bredalbane. I walked with a mind painfully downcast, and it was not till I reached a little hillock a good distance from the Inns at Tynree, a hillock clothed with saugh saplings and conspicuously high over the flat countryside, that I looked about me to see where I was.

CHAPTER XXVIII.

LOST ON THE MOOR OF RANNOCH.

I stood on the hillock clothed with its stunted saugh-trees and waited for the day that was mustering somewhere to the east, far by the frozen sea of moss and heather tuft. A sea more lonely than any ocean the most wide and distant, where no ship heaves, and no isle lifts beckoning trees above the level of the waves; a sea soundless, with no life below its lamentable surface, no little fish or proud leviathan plunging and romping and flashing from the silver roof of fretted wave dishevelled to the deep profound. The moorfowl does not cry there, the coney has no habitation. It rolled, that sea so sour, so curdled, from my feet away to mounts I knew by day stupendous and not so far, but now in the dark so hid that they were but troubled clouds upon the distant marge. There was a day surely when, lashing up on those hills around, were waters blue and stinging, and some plague-breath blew on them and they shivered and dried and cracked into this parched semblance of what they were in the old days when the galleys sailed over. No galleys now. No white birds calling eagerly in the storm. No silver bead of spray. Only in its season the cannoch tuft, and that itself but sparsely; the very bluebell shuns a track so desolate, the sturdy gall itself finds no nourishment here.

The grey day crept above the land; I watched it from my hillock, and I shrunk in my clothing that seemed so poor a shielding in a land so chill. A cold clammy dawn, that never cleared even as it aged, but held a hint of mist to come that should have warned me of the danger I faced in venturing on the untravelled surface of the moor, even upon its safer verge. But it seemed so simple a thing to keep low to the left and down on Glenurchy that I thought little of the risk, if I reflected upon it at all.

Some of the stupidity of my venturing out on the surface of Rannoch that day must have been due to my bodily state. I was not all there, as the saying goes. I was suffering mind and body from the strain of my adventures, and most of all from the stormy thrashings of the few days before—the long journey, the want of reasonable sleep and food. There had come over all my spirit a kind of dwam, so that at times my head seemed as if it were stuffed with wool; what mattered was of no account, even if it were a tinker's death in the sheuch. No words will describe the feeling except to such as themselves have known it; it is the condition of the man dead with care and weariness so far as the body is concerned, and his spirit, sorry to part company, goes lugging his flesh about the highways.

I was well out on Rannoch before the day was full awake on the country, walking at great trouble upon the coarse barren soil, among rotten bog-grass, lichened stones, and fir-roots that thrust from the black peatlike skeletons of antiquity. And then I came on a cluster of lochs—grey, cold, vagrant lochs—still to some degree in the thrall of frost. Here's one who has ever a fancy for such lochans, that are lost and sobbing, sobbing, even-on among the hills, where the reeds and the rushes hiss in the wind, and the fowls with sheeny feather make night and day cheery with their call. But not those lochs of Rannoch, those black basins crumbling at the edge of a rotten soil. I skirted them as far off as I could, as though they were the lochans of a nightmare that drag the traveller to their kelpie tenants' arms. There were no birds among those rushes; I think the very deer that roamed in the streets of Inneraora in the November's blast would have run far clear of so stricken a territory. It must be horrible in snow, it must be lamentable in the hottest days of summer, when the sun rides over the land, for what does the most kindly season bring to this forsaken place except a scorching for the fugitive wild-flower, if such there be?

These were not my thoughts as I walked on my way; they are what lie in my mind of the feelings the Moor of Rannoch will rouse in every stranger. What was in my mind most when I was not altogether in the swound of wearied flesh was the spae-wife's story of the girl in Inneraora, and a jealousy so strong that I wondered where, in all my exhausted frame, the passion for it came from. I forgot my friends left in Dalness, I forgot that my compact and prudence itself called for my hurrying the quickest way I could to the Brig of Urchy; I walked in an indifference until I saw a wan haze spread fast over the country in the direction of the lower hills that edged the desert. I looked with a careless eye on it at first, not reflecting what it might mean or how much it might lead to. It spread with exceeding quickness, a grey silver smoke rolling out on every hand, as if puffed continually from some glen in the hills. I looked behind me, and saw that the same was happening all around. Unless I made speed out of this sorrowful place I was caught in the mist. Then I came to the full understanding that trouble was to face. I tightened the thongs of my shoes, pinched up a hole in my waist-belt, scrugged my bonnet, and set out at a deer-stalker's run across the moor. I splashed in hags and stumbled among roots; I made wild leaps across poisonous-looking holes stewing to the brim with coloured water; I made long detours to find the most fordable part of a stream that twisted back and forth, a very devil's cantrip, upon my way. Then a smirr of rain came at my back and chilled me to the marrow, though the sweat of travail a moment before had been on every part of me, and even dripping in beads from my chin. At length I lifted my eyes from the ground that I had to scan most carefully in my running, and behold! I was swathed in a dense mist that cut off every view of the world within ten yards of where I stood. This cruel experience dashed me more than any other misadventure in all my wanderings, for it cut me off, without any hope of speedy betterment, from the others of our broken band. They might be all at Urchy Bridge by now, on the very selvedge of freedom, but I was couped by the heels more disastrously than ever. Down I sat on a tuft of moss, and I felt cast upon the dust by a most cruel providence.

How long I sat there I cannot tell; it may have been a full hour or more, it may have been but a pause of some minutes, for I was in a stupor of bitter disappointment. And when I rose again I was the sport of chance, for whether my way lay before me or lay behind me, or to left or right, was altogether beyond my decision. It was well on in the day: high above this stagnant plain among tall bens there must be shining a friendly and constant sun; but Elrigmore, gentleman and sometime cavalier of Mackay's Scots, was in the very gullet of night for all he could see around him. It was folly, I knew; but on somewhere I must be going, so I took to where my nose led, picking my way with new caution among the bogs and boulders. The neighbourhood of the lochs was a sort of guidance in some degree, for their immediate presence gave to a nostril sharpened by life in the wild a moist and peaty odour fresh from the corroding banks. I sought them and I found them, and finding them I found a danger even greater than my loss in that desolate plain. For in the grey smoke of mist those treacherous pools crept noiselessly to my feet, and once I had almost walked blindly into an ice-clear turgid little lake. My foot sank in the mire of it almost up to the knees ere I jumped to the nature of my neighbourhood, and with an effort little short of miraculous in the state of my body, threw myself back on the safe bank, clear of the death-trap. And again I sat on a hillock and surrendered to the most doleful meditations. Noon came and went, the rain passed and came again, and passed once more, and still I was guessing my way about the lochs, making no head-way from their neighbourhood, and, to tell the truth, a little glad of the same, for they were all I knew of the landscape in Moor Rannoch, and something of friendship was in their treacherous presence, and to know they were still beside me, though it said little for my progress to Glenurchy, was an assurance that I was not making my position worse by going in the wrong airt.

All about me, when the rain was gone for the last time,

there was a cry of waters, the voices of the burns running into the lochans, tinkling, tinkling, tinkling merrily, and all out of key with a poor wretch in draggled tartans, fleeing he knew not whither, but going about in shortened circles like a hedgehog in the sea.

The mist made no sign of lifting all this time, but shrouded the country as if it were come to stay for ever, and I was doomed to remain till the end, guessing my way to death in a silver-grey reek. I strained my ears, and far off to the right I heard the sound of cattle bellowing, the snorting low of a stirk upon the hillside when he wonders at the lost pastures of his calfhood in the merry summer before. So out I set in that direction, and more bellowing arose, and by-and-by, out of the mist but still far off, came a long low wail that baffled me. It was like no sound nature ever conferred on the Highlands, to my mind, unless the rare call of the Benderloch wolf in rigorous weather. I stopped and listened, with my inner head cracking to the strain, and as I was thus standing in wonder, a great form leaped out at me from the mist, and almost ran over me ere it lessened to the semblance of a man, and I had John M'Iver of Barbreck, a heated and hurried gentleman of arms, in my presence.

He drew up with a shock, put his hand to his vest, and I could see him cross himself under the jacket.

"Not a bit of it," I cried; "no wraith nor warlock this time, friend, but flesh and blood. Yet I'm bound to say I have never been nearer ghostdom than now; a day of this moor would mean death to me."

He shook me hurriedly and warmly by the hand, and stared in my face, and stammered, and put an arm about my waist as if I were a girl, and turned me about and led me to a little tree that lifted its barren branches above the moor. He was in such a confusion and hurry that I knew something troubled him, so I left him to choose his own time for explanation. When we got to the tree, he showed me his black knife—a very long and deadly weapon—laid along his wrist, and "Out dirk," said he; "there's a dog or two of Italy on my track here." His mind, by the stress of his words, was like a hurricane.

Now I knew something of the Black Dogs of Italy, as

they were called, the abominable hounds that were kept
by the Camerons and others mainly for the hunting down
of the Gregarich.

"Were they close on you?" I asked, as we prepared
to meet them.

"Do you not hear them bay?" said he. "There were
three on my track: I struck one through the throat with
my knife and ran, for two Italian hounds to one knife is
a poor bargain. Between us we should get rid of them
before the owners they lag for come up on their tails."

"You should thank God who got you out of a trouble
so deep," I said, astounded at the miracle of his escape
so far.

"Oh ay," said he; "and indeed I was pretty clever
myself, or it was all bye with me when one of the black
fellows set his fangs in my hose. Here are his partners;
short work with it, on the neck or low at the belly with
an up cut, and ward your throat."

The two dogs ran with ferocious growls at us as we
stood by the little tree, their faces gaping and their
quarters streaked with foam. Strong cruel brutes, they
did not swither a moment, but both leaped at M'Iver's
throat. With one swift slash of the knife, my companion
almost cut the head off the body of the first, and I reckoned
with the second. They rolled at our feet, and a silence
fell on the country. Up M'Iver put his shoulders, dighted
his blade on a tuft of bog-grass, and whistled a stave
of the tune they call "The Desperate Battle."

"If I had not my lucky penny with me I would wonder
at this meeting," said he at last, eyeing me with a look
of real content that he should so soon have fallen into my
company at a time when a meeting was so unlikely.
"It has failed me once or twice on occasions far less
important; but that was perhaps because of my own
fumbling, and I forgive it all because it brought two brave
lads together like barks of one port on the ocean. 'Up
or down?' I tossed when it came to putting fast heels
below me, and 'up' won it, and here's the one man in
all broad Albainn I would be seeking for, drops out of
the mist at the very feet of me. Oh, I'm the most wonderful fellow ever stepped heather, and I could be making a

song on myself there and then if occasion allowed. Some people have genius, and that, I'm telling you, is well enough so far as it goes; but I have luck too, and I'm not so sure but luck is a hantle sight better than genius. I'm guessing you have lost your way in the mist now?"

He looked quizzingly at me, and I was almost ashamed to admit that I had been in a maze for the greater part of the morning.

"And no skill for getting out of it?" he asked.

"No more than you had in getting into it," I confessed.

"My good scholar," said he, "I could walk you out into a drove-road in the time you would be picking the bog from your feet. I'm not making any brag of an art that's so common among old hunters as the snaring of conies; but give me a bush or a tree here and there in a flat land like this, and an herb here and there at my feet, and while winds from the north blow snell, I'll pick my way by them. It's my notion that they learn one many things at colleges that are no great value in the real trials of life. You, I make no doubt, would be kenning the name of an herb in the Latin, and I have but the Gaelic for it, and that's good enough for me; but I ken the use of it as a traveller's friend whenever rains are smirring and mists are blowing."

"I daresay there's much in what you state," I confessed, honestly enough; "I wish I could change some of my schooling for the art of winning off Moor Rannoch."

He changed his humour in a flash. "Man," said he, "I'm maybe giving myself overmuch credit at the craft; it's so seldom I put it to the trial that if we get clear of the Moor before night it'll be as much to your credit as to mine."

As it happened, his vanity about his gift got but a brief gratification, for he had not led me by his signs more than a mile on the way to the south when we came again to a cluster of lochans, and among them a large fellow called Loch Ba, where the mist was lifting quickly. Through the cleared air we travelled at a good speed, off the Moor, among Bredalbane braes, and fast though we went it was a weary march, but at last we reached Loch

Tulla, and from there to the Bridge of Urchy was no more than a meridian daunder.

The very air seemed to change to a kinder feeling in this, the frontier of the home-land. A scent of wet birk was in the wind. The river, hurrying through grassy levels, glucked and clattered and plopped most gaily, and bubble chased bubble as if all were in a haste to reach Lochow of the bosky isles and holy. Oh! but it was heartsome, and as we rested ourselves a little on the banks we were full of content to know we were now in a friendly country, and it was a fair pleasure to think that the dead leaves and broken branches we threw in the stream would be dancing in all likelihood round the isle of Innishael by nightfall.

We ate our chack with exceeding content, and waited for a time on the chance that some of our severed company from Dalness would appear, though M'Iver's instruction as to the rendezvous had been given on the prospect that they would reach the Brig earlier in the day. But after an hour or two of waiting there was no sign of them, and there was nothing for us but to assume that they had reached the Brig by noon as agreed on and passed on their way down the glen. A signal held together by two stones on the glen-side of the Brig indeed confirmed this notion almost as soon as we formed it, and we were annoyed that we had not observed it sooner. Three sprigs of gall, a leaf of ivy from the bridge arch where it grew in dark green sprays of glossy sheen, and a bare twig of oak standing up at a slant, were held down on the parapet by a peeled willow withy, one end of which pointed in the direction of the glen.

It was M'Iver who came on the symbols first, and "We're a day behind the fair," said he. "Our friends are all safe and on their way before us; look at that."

I confessed I was no hand at puzzles.

"Man," he said, "there's a whole history in it! Three sprigs of gall mean three Campbells, do they not? and that's the baron-bailie and Sonachan, and this one with the leaves off the half-side is the fellow with the want. And oak is Stewart—a very cunning clan to be fighting or foraying or travelling with, for this signal is Stewart's work

or I'm a fool : the others had not the gumption for it.
And what's the ivy but Clan Gordon, and the peeled
withy but hurry, and—surely that will be doing for the
reading of a very simple tale. Let us be taking our ways.
I have a great admiration for Stewart that he managed
to do so well with this thing, but I could have bettered
that sign, if it were mine, by a chapter or two more."

"It contains a wonderful deal of matter for the look
of it," I confessed.

"And yet," said he, "it leaves out two points I consider of the greatest importance. Where's the Dark
Dame, and when did our friends pass this way ? A
few chucky-stones would have left the hour plain to our
view, and there's no word of the old lady."

I thought for a second, then, "I can read a bit further
myself," said I ; "for there's no hint here of the Dark
Dame because she was not here. They left the *suaicheantas*
just of as many as escaped from——"

"And so they did ! Where are my wits to miss a tale
so plain ? " said he. "She'll be in Dalness yet, perhaps
better off than scouring the wilds, for after all even the
MacDonalds are human, and a half-wit widow woman
would be sure of their clemency. It was very clever
of you to think of that now."

I looked again at the oak-stem, still sticking up at the
slant. "It might as well have lain flat under the peeled
wand like the others," I thought, and then the reason for
its position flashed on me. It was with just a touch of
vanity I said to my friend, "A little colleging may be of
some use at woodcraft too, if it sharpens Elrigmore's wits
enough to read the signs that Barbreck's eagle eye can
find nothing in. I could tell the very hour our friends
left here."

"Not on their own marks," he replied sharply, casting
his eyes very quickly again on twig and leaf.

"On nothing else," said I.

He looked again, flushed with vexation, and cried himself beat to make more of it than he had done.

"What's the oak branch put so for, with its point to
the sky if—— ? "

"I have you now ! " he cried ; "it's to show the situation of the sun when they left the rendezvous. Three o'clock, and no mist with them; good lad, good lad! Well, we must be going. And now that we're on the safe side of Argile there's only one thing vexing me, that we might have been here and all together half a day ago if yon whelp of a whey-faced MacDonald in the bed had been less of the fox."

"Indeed and he might have been," said I, as we pursued our way. "A common feeling of gratitude for the silver——"

"Gratitude!" cried John, "say no more; you have fathomed the cause of his bitterness at the first trial. If I had been a boy in a bed myself, and some reckless soldiery of a foreign clan, out of a Sassenach notion of decency, insulted my mother and my home with a covert gift of coin to pay for a night's lodging, I would throw it in their faces and follow it up with stones."

Refreshed by our rest and heartened by our meal, we took to the drove-road almost with lightness, and walked through the evening till the moon, the same that gleamed on Loch Linnhe and Lochiel, and lighted Argile to the doom of his reputation for the time being, swept a path of gold upon Lochow, still hampered with broken ice. The air was still, there was no snow, and at Corryghoil, the first house of any dignity we came to, we went up and stayed with the tenant till the morning. And there we learned that the minister and the three Campbells and Stewart, the last with a bullet in his shoulder, had passed through early in the afternoon on their way to Cladich.

CHAPTER XXIX.

THE RETURN.

WE got a cold welcome from the women of our own clan and country. They had been very warm and flattering as we passed north—the best they had was not good enough for us; now they eyed us askance as we went among them in the morning. Glenurchy at its foot was wailing with one loud unceasing coronach made up of many lamentations, for no poor croft, no keep, no steading in all the countryside almost, but had lost its man at Inverlochy. It was terrible to hear those sounds and see those sights of frantic women setting every thought of life aside to give themselves wholly to their epitaphs for the men who would come no more.

For ordinary our women keen but when they are up in years and without the flowers of the cheek that the salt tear renders ugly; women who have had good practice with grief, who are so far off from the fore-world of childhood where heaven is about the dubs of the door that they find something of a dismal pleasure in making wails for a penny or two or a cogie of soldier's brose. They would as soon be weeping as singing; have you not seen them hurrying to the hut to coronach upon a corpse, with the eager step of girls going to the last dance of the harvest? Beldames, witches, I hate your dirges, that are but an old custom of lamentation! But Glenurchy and Lochow to-day depended for their sorrow upon no hired mourners, upon no aged play-actors at the passion of grief; cherry-cheeked maidens wept as copiously as their grand-dames, and so this universal coronach that rose

267   S

and fell on the wind round by Stronmealchan and Inishtrynich, and even out upon the little isles that snuggle in the shadow of Cruachan Ben, had many an unaccustomed note; many a cry of anguish from the deepest well of sorrow came to the ear. To walk by a lake and hear grief's chant upon neighbouring isles is the chief of the Hundred Dolours. Of itself it was enough to make us melancholy and bitter, but it was worse to see in the faces of old women and men who passed us surly on the road, the grudge that we had been spared, we gentlemen in the relics of fine garments, while their own lads had been taken. It was half envy that we, and not their own, still lived, and half anger that we had been useless in preventing the slaughter of their kinsmen. As we walked in their averted or surly looks, we had no heart to resent them, for was it not human nature? Even when a very old crooked man with a beard like the foam of the linn, and eyes worn deep in their black sockets by constant staring upon care, and through the black mystery of life, stood at his door among his wailing daughters, and added to his rhyming a scurrilous verse whereof we were the subjects, we did no more than hurry our pace.

By the irony of nature it was a day bright and sunny; the *londubh* parted his beak of gold and warbled flutey from the grove, indifferent to all this sorrow of the human world. Only in far-up gashes of the hills was there any remnant of the snow we had seen cover the country like a cloak but a few days before. The crows moved briskly about in the trees of Cladich, and in roupy voices said it might be February of the full dykes but surely winter was over and gone. Lucky birds! they were sure enough of their meals among the soft soil that now followed the frost in the fields and gardens; but the cotters, when their new grief was weary, would find it hard to secure a dinner in all the country once so well provided with herds and hunters, now reft of both.

I was sick of this most doleful expedition; M'Iver was no less, but he mingled his pity for the wretches about us with a shrewd care for the first chance of helping some of them. It came to him unexpectedly in a dark corner of the way through Cladich wood, where a yeld hind lay with a broken leg at the foot of a creag or rock upon which it must have stumbled. Up he hurried, and despatched and gralloched it with his *sgian dubh* in a twinkling, and then he ran back to a cot where women and children half craved us as we passed, and took some of them up to this lucky find and divided the spoil. It was a thin beast, a prey no doubt to the inclement weather, with ivy and acorn, its last meal, still in its paunch.

It was not, however, till we had got down Glenaora as far as Carnus that we found either kindness or conversation. In that pleasant huddle of small cothouses, the Macarthurs, aye a dour and buoyant race, were making up their homes again as fast as they could, inspired by the old philosophy that if an inscrutable God should level a poor man's dwelling with the dust of the valley, he should even take the stroke with calmness and start to the building again. So the Macarthurs, some of them back from their flight before Antrim and Athole, were throng bearing stone from the river and turf from the brae, and setting up those homes of the poor, that have this advantage over the homes of the wealthy, that they are so easily replaced. In this same Carnus, in later years, I have made a meal that showed curiously the resource of its people. Hunting one day, I went to a little cothouse there and asked for something to eat. A field of unreaped barley stood ripe and dry before the door. Out the housewife went and cut some straws of it, while her daughter shook cream in a bottle, chanting a churn-charm the while. The straw was burned to dry the grain, the breeze win'd it, the quern ground it, the fire cooked the bannocks of it. Then a cow was milked, a couple of eggs were found in the loft, and I sat down in a marvellously short space of time to bread and butter, milk, eggs, and a little drop of spirits that was the only ready-made provand in the house. And though now they were divided between the making of coronachs and the building of their homes, they had still the art to pick a dinner, as it were, off the lichened stone.

There was one they called Niall Mor a Chamais (Big Neil of Kames), who in his day won the applause of

courts by slaying the Italian bully who bragged Scotland
for power of thew, and I liked Niall Mor's word to us
as we proceeded on our way to Inneraora.

"Don't think," said he, "that MacCailein's beat yet,
or that the boar's tusks are reaped from his jaw. I am
of an older clan than Campbell, and closer on Diarmaid
than Argile himself; but we are all under the one banner
now, and I'll tell you two gentlemen something. They
may tear Castle Inneraora out at the roots, stable their
horses in the yard of Kilmalieu, and tread real Argile in
the clay, but we'll be even with them yet. I have an
arm here " (and he held up a bloody-looking limb, hashed
at Inverlochy) ; " I'll build my home when this is mended,
and I'll challenge MacDonald till my mouth is gagged with
the clod."

"And they tell me your son is dead yonder," I said,
pitying the old man who had now no wife nor child.

"So they tell me," said he ; "that's the will of God,
and better a fast death on the field than a decline on the
feather-bed. I'll be weeping for my boy when I have
bigged my house again and paid a call to some of his
enemies."

Niall Mor's philosophy was very much that of all
the people of the glen, such of them as were left. They
busily built their homes and pondered, as they wrought,
on the score to pay.

"That's just like me," M'Iver would say after speeches
like that of Niall Mor. He was ever one who found of a
sudden all another person's traits in his own bosom when
their existence was first manifested to him. "That's just
like me myself ; we are a beaten clan (in a fashion), but
we have our chief and many a thousand swords to the fore
yet. I declare to you I am quite cheery thinking we will
be coming back again to those glens and mounts we have
found so cruel because of our loneliness, and giving the
MacDonalds and the rest of the duddy crew the sword in
a double dose."

"Ay, John," said I, "it's easy for you to be light-
hearted in the matter. You may readily build your
bachelor's house at Barbreck, and I may set up again the
barn at Elrigmore ; but where husband or son is gone it's

a different story. For love is a passion stronger than hate. Are you not wondering that those good folk on either hand of us should not be so stricken that they would be sitting in ashes, weeping like Rachel ? "

" We are a different stuff from the lady you mention," he said ; " I am aye thinking the Almighty put us into this land of rocks and holds, and scalloped coast, cold, hunger, and the chase, just to keep ourselves warm by quarrelling with each other. If we had not the recreation now and then of a bit splore with the sword, we should be lazily rotting to decay. The world's well divided after all, and the happiness as well as the dule of it. It is because I have never had the pleasure of wife nor child I am a little better off to-day than the weeping folks about me, and they manage to make up their share of content with reflections upon the sweetness of revenge. There was never a man so poor and miserable in this world yet but he had his share of it, even if he had to seek it in the bottle. Amn't I rather clever to think of it now ? Have you heard of the idea in your classes ? "

" It is a notion very antique," I confessed, to his annoyance ; " but it is always to your credit to have thought it out for yourself. It is a notion discredited here and there by people of judgment, but a very comfortable delusion (if it is one) for such as are well off, and would salve their consciences against the miseries of the poor and distressed. And perhaps, after all, you and the wise man of old are right ; the lowest state—even the swineherd's—may have as many compensations as that of his master the Earl. It is only sin, as my father would say, that keeps the soul in a welter——"

" Does it indeed ? " said John, lightly ; " the merriest men ever I met were rogues. I've had some vices myself in foreign countries, though I aye had the grace never to mention them, and I ken I ought to be stewing with remorse for them, but am I ? "

" Are you ? " I asked.

" If you put it so straight, I'll say No—save at my best, and my best is my rarest. But come, come, we are not going into Inneraora on a debate-parade ; let us change the subject. Do you know I'm like a boy with a sweet-cake in this entrance to our native place. I would like not to gulp down the experience all at once like a glutton, but to nibble round the edges of it. We'll take the highway by the shoulder of Creag Dubh, and let the loch slip into our view."

I readily enough fell in with a plan that took us a bit off our way, for I was in a glow of eagerness and apprehension. My passion to come home was as great as on the night I rode up from Skipness after my seven years of war, even greater perhaps, for I was returning to a home now full of more problems than then. The restitution of my father's house was to be set about, six months of hard stint were perhaps to be faced by my people, and, above all, I had to find out how it stood between a certain lady and me.

Coming this way from Lochow, the traveller will get his first sight of the waters of Loch Finne by standing on a stone that lies upon a little knowe above his lordship's stables. It is a spot, they say, Argile himself had a keen relish for, and after a day of chasing the deer among the hills and woods, sometimes would he come and stand there and look with satisfaction on his country. For he could see the fat, rich fields of his policies there, and the tumultuous sea that swarms with fish, and to his left he could witness Glenaora and all the piled-up numerous mountains that are full of story if not of crop. To this little knowe M'Iver and I made our way. I would have rushed on it with a boy's impetuousness, but he stopped me with a hand on the sleeve.

"Canny, canny," said he, "let us get the very best of it. There's a cloud on the sun that'll make Finne as cold, flat, and dead as lead; wait till it passes."

We waited but a second or two, and then the sun shot out above us, and we stepped on the hillock and we looked, with our bonnets in our hands.

Loch Finne stretched out before us, a spread of twinkling silver waves that searched into the curves of a myriad bays; it was dotted with skiffs. And the yellow light of the early year gilded the remotest hills of Ardno and Ben Ime, and the Old Man Mountain lifted his ancient rimy chin, still merrily defiant, to the sky. The parks had a greener hue than any we had seen to the north ; the town revealed but its higher chimneys and the gable of the kirk, still its smoke told of occupation ; the castle frowned as of old, and over all rose Dunchuach.

" O Dunchuach ! Dunchuach ! " cried M'Iver, in an ecstasy, spreading out his arms, and I thought of the old war-worn Greeks who came with weary marches to their native seas.

" Dunchuach ! Dunchuach ! " he said ; " far have I wandered, and many a town I've seen, and many a prospect that was fine, and I have made songs to maids and mountains, and foreign castles too, but never a verse to Dunchuach. I do not know the words, but at my heart is lilting the very tune, and the spirit of it is here at my breast."

Then the apple rose in his throat, and he turned him round about that I might not guess the tear was at his eye.

" Tuts," said I, broken, " 'tis at my own ; I feel like a girl."

" Just a tickling at the pap o' the hass," he said in English ; and then we both laughed.

It was the afternoon when we got into the town. The street was in the great confusion of a fair-day, crowded with burgesses and landward tenants, men and women from all parts of the countryside still on their way back from flight, or gathered for news of Inverlochy from the survivors, of whom we were the last to arrive. Tradesmen from the Lowlands were busy fitting shops and houses with doors and windows, or filling up the gaps made by fire in the long lands, for MacCailein's first thought on his return from Edinburgh had been the comfort of the common people. Seamen clamoured at the quay, loud-spoken mariners from the ports of Clyde and Leven and their busses tugged at anchor in the upper bay or sat shoulder to shoulder in a friendly congregation under the breast-wall, laden to the beams with merchandise and provender for this hungry country. If Inneraora had been keening for the lost of Inverlochy, it had got over it ; at least we found no public lamentation such as made our traverse on Lochow-side so dreary.

Rather was there something eager and rapt about the comportment of the people. They talked little of what was over and bye with, except to curse our Lowland troops, whose unacquaintance with native war had lost us Inverlochy. The women went about their business, red-eyed, wan, silent, for the most part ; the men mortgaged the future, and drowned care in debauchery in the alehouses. A town all out of its ordinary, tapsilteerie. Walking in it, I was beat to imagine clearly what it had been like in its placid day of peace. I could never think of it as ever again to be free from this most tawdry aspect of war, a community in good order, with the day moving from dawn to dusk with douce steps, and no sharp agony at the public breast.

But we had no excuse for lingering long over our entrance upon its blue flagstone pavements ; our first duty was to report ourselves in person to our commander, whose return to Inneraora Castle we had been apprised of at Cladich.

CHAPTER XXX.

ARGILE'S BEDROOM.

THIS need for waiting upon his lordship so soon after the great reverse was a sour bite to swallow, for M'Iver as well as myself. M'Iver, had he his own way of it, would have met his chief and cousin alone; and he gave a hint delicately of that kind, affecting to be interested only in sparing me the trouble and helping me home to Elrigmore, where my father and his men had returned three days before. But I knew an officer's duty too well for that, and insisted on accompanying him, certain (with some mischievous humour in spoiling his fair speeches) that he dared scarcely be so fair-faced and flattering to MacCailein before me as he would be alone with him.

The castle had the stillness of the grave. Every guest had fled as quickly as he could from this retreat of a naked and ashamed soul. Where pipers played as a custom, and laughter rang, there was the melancholy hush of a monastery. The servants went about a-tiptoe, speaking in whispers lest their master should be irritated in his fever; the very banner on the tower hung limp about its pole, hiding the black galley of its blazon, now a lymphad of disgrace. As we went over the bridge a little dog, his lordship's favourite, lying at the door, weary, no doubt, of sullen looks and silence, came leaping and barking about us at John's cheery invitation, in a joy, as it would appear, to meet any one with a spark of life and friendliness.

Argile was in his bed-chamber and between blankets, in the hands of his physician, who had been bleeding him. He had a minister for mind and body, for Gordon was with him too, and stayed with him during our visit, though the chirurgeon left the room with a word of caution to his patient not to excite himself.

"Wise advice, is it not, gentlemen ? " said the Marquis. "As if one stirred up his own passions like a dame waiting on a drunken husband. I am glad to see you back, more especially as Master Gordon was just telling me of the surprise at Dalness, and the chance that you had been cut down there by the MacDonalds, who, luckily for him and Sonachan and the others, all followed you in your flight, and gave them a chance of an easy escape."

He shook hands with us warmly enough, with fingers moist and nervous. A raised look was in his visage, his hair hung upon a brow of exceeding pallor. I realised at a half-glance the commotion that was within.

" A drop of wine ? "

"Thank you," said I, "but I'm after a glass in the town." I was yet to learn sorrow for this unhappy nobleman whose conduct had bittered me all the way from Lorn.

MacCailein scrutinised me sharply, and opened his lips as it were to say something, but changed his mind, and made a gesture towards the bottle, which John Splendid speedily availed himself of with a "Here's one who has no swither about it. Lord knows I have had few enough of life's comforts this past week ! "

Gordon sat with a Bible in his hand, abstracted, his eyes staring on a window that looked on the branches of the highest tree about the castle. He had been reading or praying with his master before the physician had come in ; he had been doing his duty (I could swear by his stern jaw), and making MacCailein Mor writhe to the flame of a conscience revived. There was a constraint on the company for some minutes, on no one more than Argile, who sat propped up on his bolsters, and, fiddling with long thin fingers with the fringes of his coverlet, looked every way but in the eyes of M'Iver or myself. I can swear John was glad enough to escape their glance. He was as little at ease as his master, made all the fuss he could with his bottle, and drank his wine with far too great a deliberation for a person generally pretty brisk with the beaker.

"It's a fine day," said he at last, breaking the silence. "The back of the winter's broken fairly." Then he started and looked at me, conscious that I might have some contempt for so frail an opening.

"Did you come here to speak about the weather?" asked MacCailein, with a sour wearied smile.

"No," said M'Iver, ruffling up at once; "I came to ask when you are going to take us back the road we came?"

"To—to—overbye?" asked MacCailein, baulking at the name.

"Just so; to Inverlochy," answered M'Iver. "I suppose we are to give them a call when we can muster enough men?"

"Hadn't we better consider where we are first?" said MacCailein. Then he put his fair hand through his ruddy locks and sighed. "Have you nothing to say (and be done with it) about my—my—my part in the affair? His reverence here has had his will of me on that score."

M'Iver darted a look of annoyance at the minister, who seemed to pay no heed, but still to have his thoughts far off.

"I have really nothing to say, your lordship, except that I'm glad to see you spared to us here instead of being left a corpse with our honest old kinsman Auchinbreac (*beannachd leas!*) and more gentry of your clan and house than the Blue Quarry will make tombs for in Kilmalieu. If the minister has been preaching. it's his trade; it's what you pay him for. I'm no homilist, thank God, and no man's conscience."

"No, no; God knows you are not," said Argile, in a tone of pity and vexation. "I think I said before that you were the poorest of consciences to a man in a hesitancy between duty and inclination. . . . And all my guests have left me, John; I'm a lonely man in my castle of Inneraora this day, except for the prayers of a wife— God bless and keep her!—who knows and comprehends my spirit. And I have one more friend here in this room——"

"You can count on John M'Iver to the yetts of Hell," said my friend, "and I am the proud man that you should think it."

"I am obliged to you for that, kinsman," said his lordship in Gaelic, with a by-your-leave to the cleric. "But do not give your witless vanity a foolish airing before my chaplain." Then he added in the English, "When the fairy was at my cradle-side and gave my mother choice of my gifts, I wish she had chosen rowth of real friends. I could be doing with more about me of the quality I mention; better than horse and foot would they be, more trusty than the claymores of my clan. It might be the slogan 'Cruachan' whenever it wist, and Archibald of Argile would be more puissant than he of Homer's story. People have envied me when they have heard me called the King of the Highlands—fools that did not know I was the poorest, weakest man of his time, surrounded by flatterers instead of friends. Gordon, Gordon, I am the victim of the Highland liar, that smooth-tongued——"

"Call it the Campbell liar," I cried bitterly, thinking of my father. "Your clan has not the reputation of guile for nothing, and if you refused straightforward honest outside counsel sometimes, it was not for the want of its offering."

"I cry your pardon," said MacCailein, meekly; "I should have learned to discriminate by now. Blood's thicker than water, they say, but it's not so pure and transparent; I have found my blood drumly enough."

"And ready enough to run freely for you," said M'Iver, but half comprehending this perplexed mind. "Your lordship should be the last to echo any sentiment directed against the name and fame of Clan Campbell."

"Indeed they gave me their blood freely enough—a thousand of them lying yonder in the north—I wish they had been so lavish, those closest about me, with truth and honour. For that I must depend on an honest servant of the Lord Jesus Christ, the one man in my pay with the courage to confront me with no cloaked speech, but his naked thought, though it should lash me like whips. Oh, many a time my wife, who is none of our race, warned me against the softening influence, the blight and rot of this eternal air of flattery that's round about Castle Inneraora like a swamp vapour. She's in Stirling to-day—I ken it in my heart that to-night she'll weep upon her pillow because she'll know fate has found the weak joint in her goodman's armour again."

John Splendid's brow came down upon a most perplexed face; this seemed all beyond him, but he knew his master was somehow blaming the world at large for his own error.

"Come now, John," said his lordship, turning and leaning on his arm and looking curiously at his kinsman. "Come now, what do you think of me here without a wound but at the heart, with Auchinbreac and all my gallant fellows yonder?"

"Auchinbreac was a soldier by trade and a good one too," answered M'Iver, at his usual trick of prevarication.

"And a flatterer like yourself, you mean," said his lordship. "He and you learned the lesson in the same school, I'm thinking. And as ill-luck had it, his ill counsel found me on the swither, as yours did when Colkitto came down the glens there to rape and burn. That's the Devil for you; he's aye planning to have the minute and the man together. Come, sir, come, sir, what do you think, what do you think?"

He rose as he spoke and put his knees below him, and leaned across the bed with hands upon the blankets, staring his kinsman in the face as if he would pluck the truth from him out at the very eyes. His voice rose to an animal cry with an agony in it; the sinister look that did him such injustice breathed across his visage. His knuckle and collar-bones shone blae through the tight skin.

"What do I think?" echoed M'Iver. "Well, now——"

"On your honour now," cried Argile, clutching him by the shoulder.

At that M'Iver's countenance changed: he threw off his soft complacence, and cruelty and temper stiffened his jaw.

"I'll soon give you that, my Lord of Argile," said he. "I can lie like a Dutch major for convenience sake, but put me on honour and you'll get the truth if it cost me my life. Purgatory's your portion, Argile, for a Sunday's work that makes our name a mock to-day across the envious world. Take to your books and your preachers, sir—you're for the cloister and not for the field ; and if I live a hundred years, I'll deny I went with you to Inverlochy. I left my sword in Badenoch, but here's my dagger" (and he threw it with a clatter on the floor) ; "it's the last tool I'll handle in the service of a scholar. To-morrow the old big wars for me ; Hebron's troopers will welcome an umquhile comrade, and I'll find no swithering captains among the cavaliers in France."

Back sat my lord in bed, and laughed with a surrender shrill and distraught, until Master Gordon and I calmed him, and there was his cousin still before him in a passion, standing in the middle of the floor.

"Stop, stop, John," he cried ; "now that for once I've got the truth from you, let us be better friends than ever before."

"Never the same again," said M'Iver, firmly, "never the same again, for you ken my estimate of you now ; and what avails my courtesy ? "

"Your flatteries, you mean," said Argile, good-natured. "And, besides, you speak only of my two blunders ; you know my other parts,—you know that by nature I am no poltroon."

"That's no credit to you, sir—it's the strong blood of Diarmaid ; there was no poltroon in the race but what came in on the wrong side of the blanket. I've said it first, and I'll say it to the last, your spirit is smoored among the books. Paper and ink will be the Gael's undoing ; my mother taught me, and my mother knew. So long as we lived by our hands we were the world's invincibles. Rome met us and Rome tried us, and her corps might come in winter torrents, but they never tore us from our hills and keeps. What Rome may never do, that may paper and sheepskin ; you, yourself, MacCailein, have the name of plying pen and ink very well to your own purpose in the fingers of old lairds who have small skill of that contrivance."

He would have passed on in this outrageous strain without remission, had not Gordon checked him with a determined and unabashed voice. He told him to sit down in silence or leave the room, and asked him to look upon his master and see if that high fever was a condition to inflame in a fit of temper. John Splendid cooled a little, and went to the window, looking down with eyes of far surmise upon the pleasance and the town below, chewing his temper between his teeth.

"You see, Elrigmore, what a happy King of the Highlands I am," said the Marquis, despondently. "Fortunate Auchinbreac, to be all bye with it after a moment's agony!"

"He died like a good soldier, sir," I said; "he was by all accounts a man of some vices, but he wiped them out in his own blood."

"Are you sure of that? Is it not the old folly of the code of honour, the mad exaltation of mere valour in arms, that makes you think so? What if he was spilling his drops on the wrong side? He was against his king at least, and—oh, my wits, my wits, what am I saying? . . . I saw you did not drink my wine, Elrigmore; am I so low as that?"

"There is no man so low, my lord," said I, "but he may be yet exalted. We are, the best of us, the instruments of a whimsical providence" ("What a rank doctrine," muttered the minister), "and Cæsar himself was sometimes craven before his portents. You, my lord, have the one consolation left, that all's not bye yet with the cause you champion, and you may yet lead it to the highest victory."

Argile took a grateful glance at me. "You know what I am," he said, "not a man of the happy, single mood like our friend Barbreck here, but tossed between philosophies. I am paying bitterly for my pliability, for who so much the sport of life as the man who knows right well the gait he should gang, and prays fervently to be permitted to follow it, but sometimes stumbles in the ditch? Monday, oh Monday; I must be at Edinburgh and face them all! 'Tis that dauntons me." His eyes seemed to swim in blood, as he looked at me, or through me, aghast at the horror of his situation, and sweat stood in blobs upon his brow. "That," he went on, "weighs me down like lead. Here about me my people know me, and may palliate the mistake of a day by the recollection of a lifetime's honour. I blame Auchinbreac; I blame the chieftains,—they said I must take to the galley; I blame——"

"Blame no one, Argile," said Master Gordon, standing up before him, not a second too soon, for his lordship had his hand on the dirk M'Iver had thrown down. Then he turned to us with ejecting arms. "Out you go," he cried sternly, "out you go; what delight have you in seeing a nobleman on the rack?"

As the door closed behind us we could hear Argile sob.

Seventeen years later, if I may quit the thread of my history and take in a piece that more properly belongs to the later adventures of John Splendid, I saw my lord die by the maiden. Being then in his tail, I dined with him and his friends the day before he died, and he spoke with exceeding cheerfulness of that hour M'Iver and I found him in bed in Inneraora. "You saw me at my worst," said he, "on two occasions; bide till to-morrow and you'll see me at my best. I never unmasked to mortal man till that day Gordon put you out of my room." I stayed and saw him die; I saw his head up and his chin in the air as behoved his quality, that day he went through that noisy, crowded, causied Edinburgh—Edinburgh of the doleful memories, Edinburgh whose ports I never enter till this day but I feel a tickling at the nape of my neck, as where a wooden collar should lie before the shear fall.

"A cool enough reception this," said M'Iver, as we left the gate. "It was different last year, when we went up together on your return from Low Germanie. Then MacCailein was in the need of soldiers, now he's in the need of priests, who gloze over his weakness with their prayers."

"You are hardly fair either to the one or the other," I said. "Argile, whom I went in to meet to-day with a poor regard for him, turns out a better man than I gave him credit for being; he has at least the grace to grieve about a great error of judgment, or weakness of the spirit, whichever it may be. And as for Master Gordon, I'll take off my hat to him. Yon's no type of the sour, dour, anti-prelatics; he comes closer on the perfect man and soldier than any man I ever met."

M'Iver looked at me with a sign of injured vanity.

"You're not very fastidious in your choice of comparisons," said he. "As for myself, I cannot see much more in Gordon than what he is paid for—a habit of even temper, more truthfulness than I have myself, and that's a dubious virtue, for see the impoliteness that's always in its train! Add to that a lack of any clannish regard for MacCailein Mor, whom he treats just like a common merchant, and that's all. Just a plain, stout, fozy, sappy burrow-man, keeping a gospel shop, with scarcely so much of a man's parts as will let him fend a blow in the face. I could march four miles for his one, and learn him the A B *ab* of every manly art."

"I like you fine, man," I cried; "I would sooner go tramping the glens with you any day than Master Gordon; but that's a weakness of the imperfect and carnal man, that cares not to have a conscience at his coat-tail every hour of the day: you have your own parts and he his, and his parts are those that are not very common on our side of the country—more's the pity."

M'Iver was too busy for a time upon the sudden rupture with Argile to pay very much heed to my defence of Master Gordon. The quarrel—to call that a quarrel in which one man had all the bad temper and the other nothing but self-reproach—had soured him of a sudden as thunder turns the morning's cream to curd before noon. And his whole demeanour revealed a totally new man. In his ordinary John was very pernicketty about his clothing, always with the most shining of buckles and buttons, always trim in plaiding, snod and spruce about his hair and his hosen, a real dandy who never overdid the part, but just contrived to be pleasant to the eye of women, who, in my observation, have, the most sensible of them, as great a contempt for the mere fop as they have for the sloven. It took, indeed, trimness of apparel to make up for the plainness of his face. Not that he was ugly or harsh-favoured,—he was too genial for either; he was simply well-favoured enough to pass in a fair, as the saying goes, which is a midway between Apollo and plain Donald. But what with a jacket and vest all creased for the most apparent reasons, a plaid frayed to ribbons in dashing through the wood of Dalness, brogues burst at the toes, and a bonnet soaked all out of semblance to itself by rains, he appeared more common. The black temper of him transformed his face too : it lost the geniality that was its main charm, and out of his eyes flamed a most wicked, cunning, cruel fellow.

He went down the way from the castle brig to the arches cursing with great eloquence. A soldier picks up many tricks of blasphemy in a career about the world with foreign legions, and John had the reddings of three or four languages at his command, so that he had no need to repeat himself much in his choice of terms about his chief. To do him justice he had plenty of condemnation for himself too.

" Well," said I, " you were inclined to be calm enough with MacCailein when first we entered his room. I suppose all this uproar is over his charge of flattery, not against yourself alone but against all the people about."

" That's just the thing," he cried, turning round and throwing his arms furiously about. " Could he not have charged the clan generally, and let who would put the cap on ? If yon's the policy of Courts, heaven help princes ! "

" And yet you were very humble when you entered," I protested.

" Was I that ? " he retorted. " That's easy to account for. Did you ever feel like arguing with a gentleman when you had on your second-best clothes and no ruffle ? The man was in his bed, and his position as he cocked up there on his knees was not the most dignified I have seen ; but even then he had the best of it, for I felt like a beggar before him in my shabby duds. Oh, he had the best of us all there ! You saw Gordon had the sense to put on a new surtout and clean linen and a freshly dressed peruke before he saw him ; I think he would scarcely have been so bold before Argile if he had his breek-bands a finger-length below his belt, and his wig on the nape of his neck as we saw him in Glencoe."

"Anyhow," said I, "you have severed from his lordship; are you really going abroad?"

He paused a second in thought, smiled a little, and then laughed as if he had seen something humorous.

"Man," said he, "didn't I do the dirk trick with a fine touch of nobility? Maybe you thought it was done on the impulse and without any calculation. The truth was, I played the whole thing over in my mind while he was in the preliminaries of his discourse. I saw he was working up to an attack, and I knew I could surprise him. But I must confess I said more than I intended. When I spoke of the big wars and Hebron's troopers—well, Argile's a very nice shire to be living in."

"What, was it all play-acting then?"

He looked at me and shrugged his shoulders.

"You must be a singularly simple man, Elrigmore," he said, "to ask that of any one. Are we not play-acting half our lives once we get a little beyond the stage of the ploughman and the herd? Half our tears and half our laughter and the great bulk of our virtues are like your way of cocking your bonnet over your right ear; it does not come by nature, and it is done to pleasure the world in general. Play-acting! I'll tell you this, Colin, I could scarcely say myself when a passion of mine is real or fancied now. But I can tell you this too; if I began in play to revile the Marquis, I ended in earnest. I'm afraid it's all bye with me yonder. No more mine-managing for me; I struck too close on the marrow for him to forget it."

"He has forgotten and forgiven it already," I cried. "At least, let us hope he has not forgotten it (for you said no more than was perhaps deserved), but at least it's forgiven. If you said to-morrow that you were sorry for your temper——"

"Said ten thousand fiends in Hell!" cried M'Iver. "I may be vexed I angered the man; but I'll never let him know it by my words, if he cannot make it out from my acts."

CHAPTER XXXI.

MISTRESS BETTY.

I DRESSED myself up in the morning with scrupulous care,
put my hair in a queue, shaved cheek and chin, and put
at my shoulder the old heirloom brooch of the house,
which, with some other property, the invaders had not
found below the *bruach* where we had hid it on the day
we had left Elrigmore to their mercy. I was all in a
tremor of expectation, hot and cold by turns in hope and
apprehension, but always with a singular uplifting at the
heart, because for good or ill I was sure to meet in the
next hour or two the one person whose presence in
Inneraora made it the finest town in the world. Some
men tell me they have felt the experience more than
once; light o' loves they, errant gallants, I'll swear (my
dear) the tingle of it came to me but at the thought
of meeting one woman. Had she been absent from
Inneraora that morning I would have avoided it like a
leper-house because of its gloomy memorials; but the
very reek of its repairing tenements as I saw them from
the upper windows of my home floating in a haze against
the blue over the shoulder of Dun Torvil seemed to call
me on. I went about the empty chambers carolling like
the bird. Aumrie and clothes-press were burst and
vacant, the rooms in all details were bereft and cheerless
because of the plenishing stolen, and my father sat among
his losses and mourned, but I made light of our spoiling.

As if to heighten the rapture of my mood, the day was
full of sunshine, and though the woods crowding the
upper glen were leafless and slumbering, they were touched

to something like autumn's gold. Some people love the country but in the time of leafage; I find it laden with delights in every season of the year, and the end of winter as cheery a period as any, for I know that the buds are pressing at the bark, and that the boughs in rumours of wind stretch out like the arms of the sleeper who will soon be full awake.

Down I went stepping to a merry lilt, banishing every fear from my thoughts, and the first call I made was on the Provost. He was over in Askaig's with his wife and family pending the repair of his own house, and Askaig was off to his estate. Master Brown sat on the balusters of the outer stair, dangling his squat legs and studying through horn specs the tale of thig and theft which the town officer had made up a report on. As I put my foot on the bottom step he looked up, and his welcome was most friendly.

"Colin! Colin!" he cried, hastening down to shake me by the hand, "come your ways in. I heard you got home yesterday, and I was sure you would give us a call in the by-going to-day. And you're little the waur of your jaunt—hale and hearty. We ken all about your prisoning; M'Iver was in last night and kept the crack going till morning—a most humorous devil."

He pinched rappee as he spoke, in rapid doses from a snuff-box, and spread the brown powder in extravagant carelessness over his vest. He might affect what light-heartedness he could; I saw that the past fortnight had made a difference for the worse on him. The pouches below the eyes had got heavier and darker, the lines had deepened on his brow, the ruddy polish had gone off his cheek, and it was dull and spotted; by ten o'clock at night—when he used to be very jovial over a glass—I could tell he would be haggard and yawning. At his years men begin to age in a few hours; a sudden wrench to the affections, or shock to a long-disciplined order of things in their lives, will send them staggering down off the braehead whereon they have been perched with a good balance so long that they themselves have forgot the natural course of human man is to be progressing some-where.

" Ah, lad, lad ! haven't we the times ? " he said, as he led me within to the parlour. " Inneraora in the stour in her reputation as well as in her tenements. I wish the one could be amended as readily as the other ; but we mustn't be saying a word against princes, ye ken," he went on in the discreet whisper of the conspirator. " You were up and saw him last night, I'm hearing. To-day they tell me he's himself again, and coming down to a session meeting at noon. I must put myself in his way to say a friendly word or two. Ah ! you're laughing at us. I understand, man, I understand. You travellers need not practise the art of civility ; but we're too close on the castle here to be out of favour with MacCailein Mor. Draw in your chair, and—Mary, Mary, goodwife ! bring in the bottle with you and see young Elrigmore."

In came the goodwife with even greater signs of trouble than her husband, but all in a flurry of good-humoured welcome. They sat, the pair of them, before me in a little room poorly lit by a narrow window but half-glazed, because a lower portion of it had been destroyed in the occupation of the Irish, and had to be timbered up to keep the wind outside. A douce pathetic pair ; I let my thoughts stray a little even from their daughter as I looked on them, and pondered on the tragedy of age that is almost as cruel as war, but for the love that set Provost Brown with his chair haffit close against his wife's, so that less noticeably he might take her hand in his below the table and renew the glow that first they learned, no doubt, when lad and lass awandering in summer days, oh long ago, in Eas-a-chosain glen.

They plied me with a hundred questions, of my adventures, and of my father, and of affairs up in Shira Glen. I sat answering very often at hazard, with my mind fixed on the one question I had to ask, which was a simple one as to the whereabouts and condition of their daughter. But I leave to any lad of a shrinking and sensitive nature if this was not a task of exceeding difficulty. For you must remember that here were two very sharp-eyed parents, one of them with a gift of irony discomposing to a lover, and the other or both perhaps, with no reason, so far as I knew, to think I had any special feeling for the girl. But I knew as well as if I had gone over the thing a score of times before, how my manner of putting that simple question would reveal me at a flash to the irony of the father and the wonder of the mother. And in any case they gave me not the smallest chance of putting it. As they plied me with affairs a thousand miles beyond the limits of my immediate interest, and I answered them with a brevity almost discourteous, I was practising two or three phrases in my mind.

"And how is your daughter, sir?" might seem simple enough, but it would be too cold for an inquirer to whom hitherto she had always been Betty; while to ask for Betty outright would—a startling new spring of delicacy in my nature told me—be to use a friendly warmth only the most cordial relations with the girl would warrant. No matter how I mooted the lady, I knew something in my voice and the very flush in my face would reveal my secret. My position grew more pitiful every moment, for to the charge of cowardice I levelled first at myself for my backwardness, there was the charge of discourtesy. What could they think of my breeding that I had not mentioned their daughter? What could I think from their silence regarding her but that they were vexed at my indifference to her, and with the usual Highland pride were determined not even to mention her name till she was asked for. Upon my word, I was in a trouble more distressing than when I sat in the mist in the Moor of Rannoch and confessed myself lost! I thought for a little, in a momentary wave of courage, of leading the conversation in her direction by harking back to the day when the town was abandoned, and she took flight with the child into the woods. Still the Provost, now doing all the talking, while his wife knit hose, would ever turn a hundred by-ways from the main road I sought to lead him on.

By-and-by, when the crack had drifted hopelessly away from all connection with Mistress Betty, there was a woman's step on the stair. My face became as hot as fire at the sound, and I leaned eagerly forward in my chair before I thought of the transparency of the movement.

The Provost's eyes closed to little slits in his face; the corner of his mouth curled in amusement.

" Here's Peggy back from Bailie Campbell's," he said to his wife, and I was convinced he did so to let me know the new-comer, who was now moving about in the kitchen across the lobby, was not the one I had expected. My disappointment must have shown in my face ; I felt I was wasting moments the most precious, though it was something to be under the same roof as my lady's relatives, under the same roof as she had slept below last night, and to see some of her actual self almost, in the smiles and eyes and turns of the voice of her mother. I stood up to go, slyly casting an eye about the chamber for the poor comfort of seeing so little as a ribbon or a shoe that was hers, but even that was denied me. The Provost, who, I'll swear now, knew my trouble from the outset, though his wife was blind to it, felt at last constrained to relieve it.

" And you must be going," he said ; " I wish you could have waited to see Betty, who's on a visit to Carlunnan and should be home by now."

As he said it, he was tapping his snuff-mull and looking at me pawkily out of the corners of his eyes, that hovered between me and his wife, who stood with the wool in her hand, beaming mildly up in my face. I half turned on my heel and set a restless gaze on the corner of the room. For many considerations were in his simple words. That he should say them at all relieved the tension of my wonder ; that he should say them in the way he did, was, in a manner, a manifestation that he guessed the real state of my feelings to the lady whose very name I had not dared to mention to him, and that he was ready to favour any suit I pressed. I was even inclined to push my reading of his remark further, and say to myself that if he had not known the lady herself favoured me, he would never have fanned my hope by even so little as an indifferent sentence.

" And how is she—how is Betty ? " I asked, lamely.

He laughed with a pleasing slyness, and gave me a dunt with his elbow on the side, a bit of the faun, a bit of the father, a bit of my father's friend.

" You're too blate, Colin," he said, and then he put his arm through his wife's and gave her a squeeze to take her into his joke. I would have laughed at the humour of it but for the surprise in the good woman's face. It fair startled me, and yet it was no more than the look of a woman who learns that her man and she have been close company with a secret for months, and she had never made its acquaintance. There was perhaps a little more, a hesitancy in the utterance, a flush, a tone that seemed to show the subject was one to be passed bye as fast as possible.

She smiled feebly a little, picked up a row of dropped stitches, and " Oh, Betty," said she, " Betty—is—is— she'll be back in a little. Will you not wait ? "

" No, I must be going," I said ; " I may have the happiness of meeting her before I go up the glen in the afternoon."

They pressed me both to stay, but I seemed, in my mind, to have a new demand upon me for an immediate and private meeting with the girl ; she must be seen alone, and not in presence of the old couple, who would give my natural shyness in her company far more gawki- ness than it might have if I met her alone.

I went out and went down the stair, and along the front of the land, my being in a tumult, yet with my observation keen to everything, no matter how trivial, that happened around me. The sea-gulls, that make the town the playground of their stormy holidays, swept and curved among the pigeons in the gutter and quarrelled over the spoils ; tossed in the air wind-blown, then dropped with feet outstretched upon the black joists and window- sills. Fowls of the midden, new brought from other parts to make up the place of those that had gone to the kail- pots of Antrim and Athole, stalked about with heads high, foreign to this causied and gravelled country, clucking eagerly for meat. I made my way amid the bird of the sea and the bird of the wood and common bird of the yard with a divided mind, seeing them with the eye for future recollection, but seeing them not. Peats were at every close-mouth, at every door almost that was half- habitable, and fuel cut from the wood, and all about the thoroughfare was embarrassed.

I had a different decision at every step, now to seek

the girl, now to go home, now finding the most heartening hints in the agitation of the parents, anon troubled exceedingly with the reflection that there was something of an unfavourable nature in the demeanour of her mother, however much the father's badinage might soothe my vanity.

I had made up my mind for the twentieth time to go the length of Carlunnan and face her plump and plain, when behold she came suddenly round the corner at the Maltland where the surviving Lowland troops were gathered! M'Iver was with her, and my resolution shrivelled and shook within me like an old nut kernel. I would have turned but for the stupidity and ill-breeding such a movement would evidence, yet as I held on my way at a slower pace and the pair approached, I felt every limb an encumbrance, I felt the country lout throbbing in every vein.

Betty almost ran to meet me as we came closer together, with an agreeableness that might have pleased me more had I not the certainty that she would have been as warm to either of the two men who had rescued her from her hiding in the wood of Strongara, and had just come back from her country's battles with however small credit to themselves in the result. She was in a very happy mood, for, like all women, she could readily forget the large and general vexation of a reverse to her people in war if the immediate prospect was not unpleasant and things around were showing improvement. Her eyes shone and sparkled, the ordinary sedate flow of her words was varied by little outbursts of gaiety. She had been visiting the child at Carlunnan, where it had been adopted by her kinswoman, who made a better guardian than its grandmother, who died on her way to Dunbarton.

"What sets you on this road?" she asked blandly.

"Oh, you have often seen me on this road before," I said, boldly and with meaning. Ere I went wandering we had heard the rivers sing many a time, and sat upon its banks and little thought life and time were passing as quickly as the leaf or bubble on the surface. She flushed ever so little at the remembrance, and threw a stray curl back from her temples with an impatient toss of her fingers.

" And so much of the dandy too ! " put in M'Iver, himself perjink enough about his apparel. " I'll wager there's a girl in the business." He laughed low, looked from one to the other of us, yet his meaning escaped, or seemed to escape, the lady.

" Elrigmore is none of the kind," she said, as if to protect a child. " He has too many serious affairs of life in hand to be in the humour for gallivanting."

This extraordinary reading of my character by the one woman who ought to have known it better, if only by an instinct, threw me into a blend of confusion and chagrin. I had no answer for her. I regretted now that my evil star had sent me up Glenaora, or that having met her with M'Iver, whose presence increased my diffidence, I had not pretended some errand or business up among the farm-lands in the Salachry hills, where distant relatives of our house were often found. But now I was on one side of the lady and M'Iver on the other, on our way towards the burgh, and the convoy must be concluded, even if I were dumb all the way. Dumb, indeed, I was inclined to be. M'Iver laughed uproariously at madame's notion that I was too seriously engaged with life for the recreation of love-making ; it was bound to please him, coming, as it did, so close on his own estimate of me as the Sobersides he christened me at almost our first acquaintance. But he had a generous enough notion to give me the chance of being alone with the girl he knew very well my feelings for.

" I've been up just now at the camp," he said, " anent the purchase of a troop-horse, and I had not concluded my bargain when Mistress Brown passed. I'm your true cavalier in one respect, that I must be offering every handsome passenger an escort ; but this time it's an office for Elrigmore, who can undertake your company down the way bravely enough, I'll swear, for all his blateness."

Betty halted, as did the other two of us, and bantered my comrade.

" I ask your pardon a thousand times, Barbreck," she

said ; " I thought you were hurrying on your way down behind me, and came upon me before you saw who I was."

" That was the story," said he, coolly ; " I'm too old a hand at the business to be set back on the road I came by a lady who has no relish for my company."

" I would not take you away from your marketing for the world," she proceeded. " Perhaps Elrigmore may be inclined to go up to the camp too ; he may help you to the pick of your horse—and we'll believe you the soldier of fortune again when we see you one."

She, at least, had no belief that the mine-manager was to be a mercenary again. She tapped with a tiny toe on the pebbles, affecting a choler the twinkle in her eyes did not homologate. It was enough for M'Iver, who gave a " Pshaw," and concluded he might as well, as he said, " be in good company so long as he had the chance," and down the way again we went. Somehow the check had put him on his mettle. He seemed to lose at once all regard for my interests in this. I became, in truth, more frequently than was palatable, the butt of his little pleasantries ; my mysterious saunter up that glen, my sobriety of demeanour, my now silence—all those things, whose meaning he knew very well, were made the text for his amusement for the lady. As for me, I took it all weakly, striving to meet his wit with careless smiles.

For the first time, I was seized with a jealousy of him. Here was I, your arrant rustic ; he was as composed as could be, overflowing with happy thoughts, laughable incident, and ever ready with the compliment or the retort women love to hear from a smart fellow of even indifferent character. He had the policy to conceal the vanity that was for ordinary his most transparent feature, and his trick was to admire the valour and the humour of others. Our wanderings in Lorn and Lochaber, our adventures with the MacDonalds, all the story of the expedition, he danced through, as it were, on the tiptoe of light phrase, as if it had been a strong man's scheme of recreation, scarcely once appealing to me. With a flushed cheek and parted lips the lady hung upon his words, arched her dark eyebrows in fear, or bubbled into the merriest laughter as the occasion demanded. Worst of all, she seemed to share his amusement at my silence, and then I could have wished rather than a bag of gold I had the Mull witch's invisible coat, or that the earth would swallow me up. The very country people passing on the way were art and part in the conspiracy of circumstances to make me unhappy. Their salutes were rarely for Elrigmore, but for the lady and John Splendid, whose bold quarrel with MacCailein Mor was now the rumour of two parishes, and gave him a wide name for unflinching bravery of a kind he had been generally acknowledged as sadly wanting in before. And Mistress Betty could not but see that high or low, I was second to this fellow going off—or at least with the rumour of it—to Hebron's cavaliers in France before the week-end.

M'Iver was just, perhaps, carrying his humour at my cost a little too far for my temper, which was never readily stirred, but flamed fast enough when set properly alowe, and Betty—here too your true woman wit—saw it sooner than he did himself, quick enough in the uptake though he was. He had returned again to his banter about the supposititious girl I was trysted with up the glen, and my face showed my annoyance.

" You think all men like yourself," said the girl to him, " and all women the same—like the common soldier you are."

" I think them all darlings," he confessed, laughing ; " God bless them, kind and foolish——"

" As you've known them oftenest," she supplied, coldly.

" Or sedate and sensible," he went on. " None of them but found John M'Iver of Barbreck their very true cavalier."

" Indeed," said Mistress Betty, colder than ever, some new thought working within her, judging from the tone. " And yet you leave to-morrow, and have never been to Carlunnan." She said the last words with a hesitancy, blushing most warmly. To me they were a dark mystery, unless I was to assume, what I did wildly for a moment, only to relinquish the notion immediately, that she had been in the humour to go visiting her friends with him. M'Iver's face showed some curious emotion that it baffled

me to read, and all that was plain to me was that here
were two people with a very strong thought of a distressing
kind between them.

" It would be idle for me," he said in a little, " to deny
that I know what you mean. But do you not believe you
might be doing me poor justice in your suspicions ? "

" It is a topic I cannot come closer upon," she answered ;
" I am a woman. That forbids me and that same compels
me. If nature does not demand your attendance up
there, then you are a man wronged by rumour or a man
dead to every sense of the human spirit. I have listened
to your humour and laughed at your banter, for you have
an art to make people forget ; but all the way I have been
finding my lightness broken in on by the feeble cry of a
child without a mother—it seems, too, without a father."

" If that is the trouble," he said, turning away with a
smile he did not succeed in concealing either from the
lady or me, " you may set your mind at rest. The child
you mention has, from this day, what we may be calling a
godfather."

" Then the tale's true ? " she said, stopping on the
road, turning and gazing with neither mirth nor warmth
in her countenance.

M'Iver hesitated, and looked upon the woman to me
as if I could help him in the difficulty ; but I must have
seemed a clown in the very abjection of my ignorance of
what all this mystery was about. He searched my face
and I searched my memory, and then I recollected that
he had told me before of Mistress Brown's suspicions of
the paternity of the child.

" I could well wish your answer came more readily,"
said she again, somewhat bitterly, " for then I know it
would be denial."

" And perhaps untruth, too," said John, oddly. " This
time it's a question of honour, a far more complicated
turn of circumstances than you can fancy, and my answer
takes time."

" Guilty ! " she cried, " and you go like this. You
know what the story is, and your whole conduct in
front of my charges shows you take the very lightest view
of the whole horrible crime."

"Say away, madame," said M'Iver, assuming an indifference his every feature gave the lie to. "I'm no better nor no worse than the rest of the world. That's all I'll say."

"You have said enough for me, then," said the girl. "I think, Elrigmore, if you please, I'll not trouble you and your friend to come farther with me now. I am obliged for your society so far."

She was gone before either of us could answer, leaving us like a pair of culprits standing in the middle of the road. A little breeze fanned her clothing, and they shook behind her as to be free from some contamination. She had overtaken and joined a woman in front of her before I had recovered from my astonishment. M'Iver turned from surveying her departure with lowered eyebrows, and gave me a look with half-a-dozen contending thoughts in it.

"That's the end of it," said he, as much to himself as for my ear, "and the odd thing of it again is that she never seemed so precious fine a woman as when it was ' a' bye wi' auld days and you,' as the Scots song says."

"It beats me to fathom," I confessed. "Do I understand that you admitted to the lady that you were the father of the child ? "

"I admitted nothing," he said, cunningly, "if you'll take the trouble to think again. I but let the lady have her own way, which most of her sex generally manage from me in the long-run."

"But, man ! you could leave her only one impression, that you are as black as she thinks you, and am I not sure you fall far short of that ? "

"Thank you," he said ; "it is good of you to say it. I am for off whenever my affairs here are settled, and when I'm the breadth of seas afar from Inneraora, you'll think as well as you can of John M'Iver, who'll maybe not grudge having lost the lady's affection if he kept his friend's and comrade's heart."

He was vastly moved as he spoke. He took my hand and wrung it fiercely ; he turned without another word, good or ill, and strode back on his way to the camp, leaving me to seek my way to the town alone.

CHAPTER XXXII.

A SCANDAL AND A QUARREL.

FOR some days I kept to Glen Shira as the tod keeps to the cairn when heather burns, afraid almost to let even my thoughts wander there lest they should fly back distressed, to say the hope I cherished was in vain. I worked in the wood among the pines that now make rooftrees for my home, and at nights I went on *ceilidh* among some of the poorer houses of the Glen, and found a drug for a mind uneasy in the tales our peasants told around the fire. A drug, and yet a drug sometimes with the very disease in itself I sought for it to kill. For the love of a man for a maid is the one story of all lands, of all ages, trick it as we may, and my good people, telling their old ancient histories round the fire, found, although they never knew it, a young man's quivering heart a score of times a night.

Still at times, by day and night—ay! in the very midmost watches of the stars—I walked, in my musing, as I thought, upon the causeyed street, where perhaps I had been sooner in the actual fact if M'Iver's departure had not been delayed. He was swaggering, they told me, about the town in his old regimentals, every pomp of the foreign soldier assumed again as if they had never been relaxed in all those years of peace and commerce. He drank stoutly in the taverns, and 'twas constantly, "Landlady, I'm the lawing," for the fishermen, that they might love him. A tale went round, too, that one morning he went to a burial in Kilmalieu, and Argile was there seeing the last of an old retainer to his long home, and old Macnachtan came riding down past corpse and mourner with his only reverence a finger to his cap. "Come down off your horse when death or Argile goes bye," cried M'Iver, hauling the laird off his saddle. But between Argile and him were no transactions; the pride of both would not allow it, though it was well known that their affections were stronger than ever they had been before, and that Gordon made more than one attempt at a plan to bring them together.

It is likely, too, I had been down—leaving M'Iver out of consideration altogether—had there not been the tales about MacLachlan, tales that came to my ears in the most miraculous way, with no ill intention on the part of the gossips—about his constant haunting of Inneraora and the company of his cousin. He had been seen there with her on the road to Carlunnan. That venue of all others! God! did the river sing for him too among its reeds and shallows; did the sun tip Dunchuach like a thimble and the wild beast dally on the way? That was the greatest blow of all! It left plain (I thought in my foolishness) the lady's coolness when last I met her; for me henceforth (so said bitterness) the serious affairs of life, that in her notion set me more than courtship. I grew solemn, so gloomy in spirit that even my father observed the ceasing of my whistle and song, and the less readiness of my smile. And he, poor man, thought it the melancholy of Inverlochy and the influence of this ruined countryside.

When I went down to the town again the very house-fronts seemed inhospitable, so that I must pass the time upon the quay. There are days at that season when Loch Finne, so calm, so crystal, so duplicate of the sky, seems like water sunk and lost for ever to wind and wave, when the sea-birds doze upon its kindly bosom like bees upon the flower, and a silence hangs that only breaks in distant innuendo of the rivers or the low of cattle on the Cowal shore. The great bays lapse into hills that float upon a purple haze, forest nor lea has any sign of spring's extravagance or the flame of the autumn that fires Dunchuach till it blazes like a torch. All is in the light sleep of the year's morning, and what, I have thought, if God in His pious whim should never awake it any more?

It was such a day when I went up and down the rough cobble of the quay, and to behold men working there at their noisy and secular occupations seemed, at first, a Sabbath desecration. But even they seemed affected by this marvellous peace of sea and sky, as they lifted from the net or rested on the tackle to look across greasy gunnels with some vague unquiet of the spirit at the marvellous restfulness of the world. Their very voices learned a softer note from that lulled hour of the enchanted season, and the faint blue smoke of their den fires rose and mingled in the clustered masts or nestled wooing in the drying sails. Then a man in drink came roaring down the quay, an outrage on the scene, and the magic of the day was gone ! The boats bobbed and nudged each other or strained at the twanging cord as seamen and fishers spanged from deck to deck ; rose cries in loud and south-ward Gaelic or the lowlands of Air. The world was no longer dreaming but stark awake, all but the sea and the lapsing bays and the brown floating hills. Town Inner-aora bustled to its marge. Here was merchandise, here the pack and the bale ; snuffy men in perukes, knee-breeched and portly, came and piped in high English, managing the transport of their munitions ashore.

I was standing in the midst of the throng of the quay-head, with my troubled mind finding ease in the industry and interest of those people without loves or jealousies, and only their poor merchandise to exercise them, when I started at the sound of a foot coming up the stone slip from the water-edge. I turned, and who was there but MacLachlan ? He was all alone but for a haunch-man, a gillie-wet-foot as we call him, and he had been set on the slip by a wherry that had approached from Cowal side unnoticed by me as I stood in meditation. As he came up the sloping way, picking his footsteps upon the slimy stones, he gave no heed to the identity of the person before him ; and with my mood in no way favourable to polite discourse with the fellow, I gave a pace or two round the elbow of the quay, letting him pass on his way up among the clanking rings and chains of the moored gaberts, the bales of the luggers, and the brawny and crying mariners. He was not a favourite among the quay-folk, this pompous little gentleman, with his nose in the air and his clothing so very gaudy. The Lowlands men might salute his gentility if they cared ; no residenters of the place did so, but turned their shoulders on him and were very busy with their affairs as he passed. He went bye with a waff of wind in his plaiding, and his haunch-man as he passed at a discreet distance got the double share of jibe and glunch from the mariners.

At first I thought of going home ; a dread came on me that if I waited longer in the town I might come upon this intruder and his cousin, when it would sore discomfort me to do so. Thus I went slowly up the quay, and what I heard in the bye-going put a new thought in my head.

Two or three seamen were talking together as I passed, with nudges and winks and sly laughs, not natives of the place but from farther up the loch, yet old frequenters with every chance to know the full ins and outs of what they discoursed upon. I heard but three sentences as I passed ; they revealed that MacLachlan at Kilmichael market had once bragged of an amour in Inneraora. That was all ! But it was enough to set every drop of blood in my body boiling. I had given the dog credit for a decent affection, and here he was narrating a filthy and impossible story. Liar ! liar ! liar ! At first the word rose to my mouth, and I had to choke it at my teeth for fear it should reveal my passion to the people as I passed through among them with a face inflamed ; then doubt arose, a contention of recollections, numb fears— but the girl's eyes triumphed : I swore to myself she at least should never know the villainy of this vulgar and lying rumour set about the country by a rogue.

Now all fear of facing the street deserted me. I felt a man upright, imbued with a strong sense of justice ; I felt I must seek out John Splendid and get his mind, of all others, upon a villainy he could teach me to avenge. I found him at Askaig's corner, a flushed man with perhaps (as I thought at first) too much spirits in him to be the most sensible of advisers in a matter of such delicacy.

" Elrigmore ! " he cried ; " sir, I give you welcome to

Inneraora! You will not know the place, it has grown so much since you last visited its humble street."

"I'm glad to see you now, John," I said, hurriedly. "I would sooner see you than any other living person here."

He held up a finger and eyed me pawkily. "Come, man, come!" he said, laughing. "On your oath now, is there not a lady? And that minds me; you have no more knowledge of the creatures, no more pluck in their presence, than a child. Heavens, what a soldier of fortune is this! Seven years among the army; town to town, camp to camp, here to-day and away to-morrow, with a soldier's pass to love upon your back and haunch, and yet you have not learned to lift the sneck of a door, but must be tap-tapping with your finger-nails."

"I do not know what you mean," said I.

"Lord! Lord!" he cried, pretending amazement, "and here's schooling! Just think it over for yourself. You are not an ill-looking fellow (though I think I swing a kilt better myself), you are the proper age (though it's wonderful what a youngish-looking man of not much over forty may do), you have a name for sobriety, and Elrigmore carries a good many head of cattle and commands a hundred swords—would a girl with any wisdom and no other sweetheart in her mind turn her back on such a list of virtues and graces? If I had your reputation and your estate, I could have the pick of the finest women in Argile—ay, and far beyond it."

"Never mind about that just now," I demanded, gripping my preacher by the hand and forcing him with me out of the way of the passers-by, whose glance upon us would have seemed an indelicacy when we were discussing so precious a thing as my lady's honour.

"But I shall mind it," insisted M'Iver, pursing his lips as much to check a hiccough as to express his determination. "It seems I am the only man dare take the liberty. Fie on ye! man, fie! you have not once gone to see the Provost or his daughter since I saw you last. I dare not go myself for the sake of a very stupid blunder; but I met the old man coming up the way an hour ago, and he was asking what ailed you at them. Will I tell you something, Colin? The Provost's a gleg man, but he's not so gleg as his wife. The dame for me! say I, in every household, if it's her daughter's love-affairs she's to keep an eye on."

"You know so much of the lady and her people," said I, almost losing patience, "that it's a wonder you never sought her for yourself."

He laughed. "Do you think so?" he said. "I have no doubt of the result; at least I would have had no doubt of it a week or two ago, if I had taken advantage of my chances." Then he laughed anew. "I said the goodwife was gleg; I'm just as gleg myself."

This tipsy nonsense began to annoy me; but it was useless to try to check it, for every sentence uttered seemed a spark to his vanity.

"It's about Betty I want to speak," I said.

"And it's very likely too; I would not need to be very gleg to see that. She does not want to speak to me, however, or of me, as you'll find out when once you see her. I am in her black books sure enough, for I saw her turn on the street not an hour ago to avoid me."

"She'll not do that to MacLachlan," I put in, glad of the opening, "unless she hears—and God forbid it—that the scamp lightlies her name at common fairs."

M'Iver drew himself up, stopped, and seemed to sober. "What's this you're telling me?" he asked, and I went over the incident on the quay. It was enough. It left him as hot as myself. He fingered at his coat-buttons and his cuffs, fastening and unfastening them; he played nervously with the hilt of his dirk; up would go his brows and down again like a bird upon his prey; his lips would tighten on his teeth, and all the time he was muttering in his pick of languages sentiments natural to the occasion. Gaelic is the poorest of tongues to swear in: it has only a hash of borrowed terms from Lowland Scots; but my cavalier was well able to make up the deficiency.

"Quite so; very true and very comforting," I said at last; "but what's to be done?"

"What's to be done?" said he, with a start. "Surely to God there's no doubt about that!"

"No, sir; I hope you know me better. But how's it

to be done? I thought of going up in front of the whole quay and making him chew his lie at the point of my dagger. Then I thought more formality was needed—a friend or two, a select venue, and careful leisure time for so important a meeting."

"But what's the issue upon which the rencontre shall take place?" asked M'Iver, it seemed to me with ridiculous scrupulosity.

"Why need you ask?" said I. "You do not expect me to invite him to repeat the insult or exaggerate the same."

M'Iver turned on me almost roughly and shook me by the shoulder. "Man!" said he, "wake up, and do not let your wits hide in the heels of your boots. Are you clown enough to think of sending a lady's name around the country tacked on to a sculduddry tale like this? You must make the issue somewhat more politic than that."

"I agree with you," I confessed; "it was stupid of me not to think of it, but what can I do? I have no other quarrel with the man."

"Make one, then," said M'Iver. "I cannot comprehend where you learned your trade as cavalier, or what sort of company you kept in Mackay's, if you did not pick up and practise the art of forcing a quarrel with a man on any issue you cared to choose. In ten minutes I could make this young fellow put down his gage in a dispute about the lacing of boots."

"But in that way at least I'm the poorest of soldiers; I never picked a quarrel, and yet here's one that sets my gorge to my palate, but cannot be fought on."

"Tuts, tuts! man," he cried, "it seems that, after all, you must leave the opening of this little play to John M'Iver. Come with me a bit yont the Cross here and take a lesson."

He led me up the wide pend close and round the back of old Stonefield's dwelling, and into a corner of a lane that gave upon the fields, yet at the same time kept a plain view of the door of Askaig's house, where we guessed MacLachlan was now on his visit to the Provost's family.

"Let us stand here," said he, "and I'll swear I'm not

very well acquainted with our friend's habits if he's not passing this way to Carlunnan sometime in the next ten minutes, for I saw Mistress Betty going up there, as I said, not so very long ago."

This hint at MacLachlan's persistency exasperated me the more. I felt that to have him by the throat would be a joy second only to one other in the world.

M'Iver saw my passion—it was ill to miss seeing it— and seemed struck for the first time by the import of what we were engaged upon.

"We were not given to consider the end of a duello from the opening when abroad," he said ; " but that was because we were abroad, and had no remonstrance and reminder in the face of familiar fields and houses and trees, and the passing footsteps of our own people. Here, however, the end's to be considered from the beginning— have you weighed the risks in your mind ? "

" I've weighed nothing," said I, shortly, " except that I feel in me here I shall have his blood before nightfall."

" He's a fairly good hand with his weapon, they tell me."

" If he was a wizard, with the sword of Great Donald, I would touch him to the vitals. Have I not learned a little, if you'll give me the credit, from Alasdair Mor ? "

" I forgot that," said M'Iver ; " you'll come through it all right. And here's our man coming up the lane. No anger now ; nothing to be said on your side till I give you a sign, and then I can leave the rest to your wisdom."

MacLachlan came staving up the cobbles in a great hurry, flailing the air, as he went, with a short rattan, for he affected some of the foppish customs the old officers brought back from the Continent. He was for passing us with no more than a jerk of the head, but M'Iver and I between us took up the mouth of the lane, and as John seemed to smile on him like one with gossip to exchange, he was bound to stop.

" Always on the going foot, MacLachlan," said John, airily. " I never see a young gentleman of your age and mettle but I wish he could see the wisdom of putting both to the best purpose on the field."

" With your cursed foreigners, I suppose you mean,"

said the young fellow. " I could scarcely go as a private pikeman like yourself."

" I daresay not, I daresay not," answered M'Iver, pricked at his heart (I could tell by his eye) by this reflection upon his humble office, but keeping a marvellously cool front to his cockerel. " And now when I think of it, I am afraid you have neither the height nor width for even so ornamental a post as an ensign's."

MacLachlan restrained himself too, unwilling, no doubt, as I thought, to postpone his chase of the lady by so much time as a wrangle with John M'Iver would take up. He affected to laugh at Splendid's rejoinder, turned the conversation upon the disjasket condition of the town and edged round to get as polite a passage as possible between us, without betraying any haste to sever himself from our company. But both John Splendid and I had our knees pretty close together, and the very topic he started seemed to be the short cut to the quarrel we sought.

" A poor town indeed," admitted M'Iver, readily, " but it might be worse. It can be built anew. There's nothing in nature, from a pigsty to a name for valour and honour, that a wise man may not patch up somehow."

MacLachlan's retort to this opening was on the tip of his tongue ; but his haste made him surrender a taunt as likely to cause trouble. " You're very much in the proverb way to-day," was all he said. " I'm sure I wish I saw Inneraora as hale and complete as ever it was : it never had a more honest friend than myself."

" That one has missed," thought I, standing by in a silent part of this three-cornered convention. M'Iver smiled mildly, half, I should think, at the manner in which his thrust had been foiled, half to keep MacLachlan still with us. His next attack was more adroit though roundabout, and it effected its purpose.

" I see you are on your way up to the camp," said he, with an appearance of indifference. " We were just thinking of a daunder there ourselves."

" No," said MacLachlan, shortly ; " I'm for farther up the Glen."

" Then at least we'll have your company part of the

way," said John, and the three of us walked slowly off, the young gentleman with no great warmth at the idea, which was likely to spoil his excursion to some degree. M'Iver took the place between us, and in the rear, twenty paces, came the *gille cas-fleuch*.

" I have been bargaining for a horse up here," said John in a while, " and I'm anxious that Elrigmore should see it. You'll have heard I'm off again on the old road."

" There's a rumour of it," said MacLachlan, cogitating on his own affairs, or perhaps wondering what our new interest in his company was due to.

" Ah ! it's in my blood," said John, " in my blood and bones ! Argile was a fairly good master—so to call him —but—well, you understand yourself : a man of my kind at a time like this feels more comfortable anywhere else than in the neighbourhood of his chief."

" I daresay," replied MacLachlan, refusing the hook, and yet with a sneer in his accent.

" Have you heard that his lordship and I are at variance since our return from the North ? "

" Oh ! there's plenty of gossip in the town," said Mac-Lachlan. " It's common talk that you threw your dagger in his face. My father, who's a small chief enough so far as wealth of men and acres goes, would have used the weapon to let out the hot blood of his insulter there and then."

" I daresay," said M'Iver. " You're a hot - headed clan. And MacCailein has his own ways."

" He's welcome to keep them too," answered the young fellow, his sneer in no ways abated. I became afraid that his carefully curbed tongue would not give us our opening before we parted, and was inclined to force his hand ; but M'Iver came in quickly and more astutely.

" How ? " said he ; " what's your meaning ? Are you in the notions that he has anything to learn of courtesy and gallantry on the other side of the loch at Strath-lachlan ? "

MacLachlan's eyes faltered a little under his pent brows. Perhaps he had a suspicion of the slightest that he was being goaded on for some purpose, but if he had, his temper was too raw to let him qualify his retort with calmness.

"Do you know, Barbreck," said he, "I would not care to say much about what your nobleman has to learn or unlearn? As for the gallantry—good Lord, now!—did you ever hear of one of my house leaving his men to shift for themselves when blows were going?"

M'Iver with an utterance the least thought choked by an anger due to the insult he had wrought for, shrugged his shoulders, and at the same time gave me his elbow in the side for his sign.

"I'm sorry to hear you say that about Gillesbeg Grua-mach," said he. "Some days ago, half as much from you would have called for my correction; but I'm out of his lordship's service, as the rumour rightly goes, and seeing the manner of my leaving it was as it was, I have no right to be his advocate now."

"But I have!" said I, hotly, stopping and facing Mac-Lachlan, with my excuse for the quarrel now ready. "Do you dare come here and call down the credit of MacCailein Mor?" I demanded in the English, with an idea of putting him at once in a fury at having to reply in a language he spoke but indifferently.

His face blanched; he knew I was doubling my insult for him. The skin of his jaw twitched and his nostrils expanded; a hand went to his dirk hilt on the moment.

"And is it that you are the advocate?" he cried to me in a laughable kind of Scots. I was bitter enough to mock his words and accent with the airs of one who has travelled far and knows other languages than his own.

"Keep to your Gaelic," he cried in that language; "the other may be good enough to be insolent in; let us have our own courtesies."

"Any language," said I, "is good enough to throw the lie in your face when you call MacCailein a coward."

"Grace of God!" said he; "I called him nothing of the kind; but it's what he is all the same."

Up came his valet and stood at his arm, his blade out, and his whole body ready to spring at a signal from his master.

I kept my anger out of my head, and sunk to the pit

of my stomach while I spoke to him. "You have said too much about Archibald, Marquis of Argile," I said. "A week or two ago, the quarrel was more properly M'Iver's; now that he's severed by his own act from the clan, I'm ready to take his place and chastise you for your insolence. Are you willing, John?" I asked, turning to my friend.

"If I cannot draw a sword for my cousin I can at least second his defender," he answered quickly.

MacLachlan's colour came back; he looked from one to the other of us, and made an effort to laugh with cunning.

"There's more here than I can fathom, gentlemen," said he. "I'll swear this is a forced quarrel; but in any case I fear none of you. Alasdair," he said, turning to his man, who it seemed was his *dalta* or foster-brother, "we'll accommodate those two friends of ours when and where they like."

"Master," cried the gillie, "I would like well to have this on my own hands," and he looked at me with great venom as he spoke.

MacLachlan laughed. "They may do their dangerous work by proxy in this part of the shire," said he; "but I think our own Cowal ways are better; every man his own quarrel."

"And now is the time to settle it," said I; "the very place for our purpose is less than a twenty minutes' walk off."

Not a word more was said; the four of us stepped out again.

CHAPTER XXXIII.

THE BROKEN SWORD.

WE went along the road two and two, M'Iver keeping company behind with the valet, who would have stabbed me in the back in all likelihood ere we had made half our journey, had there been no such caution. We walked at a good pace, and fast as we walked it was not fast enough for my eagerness, so that my long steps set the shorter ones of MacLachlan pattering beside me in a most humorous way that annoyed him much, to judge from the efforts he made to keep time and preserve his dignity. Not a word, good or bad, was exchanged between us ; he left the guidance to me, and followed without a pause when, over the tip of the brae at Tarra Dubh, I turned sharply to the left and plunged into the wood.

In this part of the wood there is a *larach* or site of an ancient church. No stone stands there to-day, no one lives who has known another who has heard another say he has seen a single stone of this umquhile house of God ; but the sward lies flat and square as in a garden, levelled, and in summer fringed with clusters of the nettle that grows over the ruins of man with a haste that seems to mock the brevity of his interests, and the husbandman and the forester for generations have put no spade to its soil. A *cill* or cell we call it in the language ; and the saying goes among the people of the neighbourhood that on the eve of Saint Patrick bells ring in this glade in the forest, sweet, soft, dreamy bells, muffled in a mist of years —bells whose sounds have come, as one might fancy, at their stated interval, after pealing in a wave about God's universe from star to star, back to the place of their first chiming. Ah! the monk is no longer there to hear them, only the mavis calls and the bee in its period hums where matins rose. A queer thought this, a thought out of all keeping with my bloody mission in the wood, which was to punish this healthy youth beside me ; yet to-day, looking back on the occasion, I do not wonder that, going a-murdering, my mind in that glade should soften by some magic of its atmosphere. For, ever was I a dreamer, as this my portion of history may long since have disclosed. Ever must I be fronting the great dumb sorrow of the universe, thinking of loves undone, of the weakness of man, poor man, a stumbler under the stars, the sickening lapse of time, the vast and awesome voids left by people dead, laughter quelled, eyes shut for evermore, and scenes evanished. And it was ever at the crisis of things my mind took on this mood of thought and pity.

It was not of my own case I reflected there, but of the great swooning silences that might be tenanted ere the sun dropped behind the firs by the ghost of him I walked with. Not of my own father, but of an even older man in a strath beyond the water hearing a rap at his chamber door to-night and a voice of horror tell him he had no more a son. A fool, a braggart, a liar the less, but still he must leave a vacancy at the hearth ! My glance could not keep off the shoulder of him as he walked cockily beside me, a healthy brown upon his neck, and I shivered to think of this hour as the end of him, and of his clay in a little stretched upon the grass that grew where psalm had chanted and the feet of holy men had passed. Kill him ! The one thrust of fence I dare not neglect was as sure as the arrow of fate ; I knew myself in my innermost his executioner.

It was a day, I have said, of exceeding calm, with no trace left almost of the winter gone, and the afternoon came on with a crimson upon the west, and numerous birds in flying companies settled upon the bushes. The firs gave a perfume from their tassels and plumes, and a little burn among the bushes gurgled so softly, so like a sound of liquor in a goblet, that it mustered the memories of good companionship. No more my mind was on the knave and liar, but on the numerous kindnesses of man.

We stepped in upon the bare *larach* with the very breath checked upon our lips. The trees stood round it and back, knowing it sanctuary; tall trees, red, and rough at the hide, cracked and splintered in roaring storms; savage trees, coarse and vehement, but respecting that patch of blessed memory vacant quite but of ourselves and a little bird who turned his crimson breast upon us for a moment then vanished with a thrill of song. Crimson sky, crimson-vested bird, the colour of that essence I must be releasing with the push of a weapon at that youth beside me!

John Splendid was the first to break upon the silence.

"I was never so much struck with the Sunday feeling of a place," he said; "I daresay we could find a less melancholy spot for our meeting if we searched for it, but the day goes, and I must not be putting off an interesting event both of you, I'm sure, are eager to begin."

"Indeed we might have got a more suitable place in many ways," I confessed, my hands behind me, with every scrap of passion gone from my heart.

MacLachlan showed no such dubiety. "What ails you at the place?" he asked, throwing his plaid to his servant, and running his jacket off its wooden buttons at one tug. "It seems to me a most particularly fine place for our business. But of course," he added with a sneer, "I have not the experience of two soldiers by trade, who are so keen to force the combat."

He threw off his belt, released the sword from its scabbard—a clumsy weapon of its kind, abrupt, heavy, and ill-balanced, I could tell by its slow response to his wrist as he made a pass or two in the air to get the feel of it. He was in a cold bravado, the lad, with his spirit up, and utterly reckless of aught that might happen him, now saying a jocular word to his man, and now gartering his hose a little more tightly.

I let myself be made ready by John Splendid without so much as putting a hand to a buckle, for I was sick sorry that we had set out upon this adventure. Shall any one say fear? It was as far from fear as it was from merriment. I have known fear in my time—the fear of the night, of tumultuous sea, of shot-ploughed space to be traversed inactively and slowly, so my assurance is no braggadocio, but the simple truth. The very sword itself, when I had it in my hand, felt like something alive and vengeful.

Quick as we were in preparing, the sun was quicker in descending, and as we faced each other, without any of the parades of foreign fence, the sky hung like a bloody curtain between the trees behind MacLachlan.

M'Iver and the servant now stood aside and the play began. MacLachlan engaged with the left foot forward, the trick of a man who is used to the targaid, and I saw my poor fool's doom in the antiquity of his first guard. In two minutes I had his whole budget of the art laid bare to me ; he had but four parries—quarte and tierce for the high lines, with septime and second for the low ones—and had never seen a counter-parry or lunge in the whole course of his misspent life.

" Little hero ! " thought I, " thou art a spitted cockerel already, and yet hope, the blind, the ignorant, has no suspicion of it ! "

A faint chill breeze rose and sighed among the wood, breathed from the west that faced me, a breeze bearing the odour of the tree more strong than before, and of corrupt leafage in the heughs. Our weapons tinkled and rasped, the true-points hissed and the pommels rang, and into the midst of this song of murderous game there trespassed the innocent love-lilt of a bird. I risked him the flash of an eye as he stood, a becking black body on a bough, his yellow beak shaking out a flutey note of passionate serenade. Thus the irony of nature ; no heed for us, the head and crown of things created : the bird would build its home and hatch its young upon the sapling whose roots were soaked by young MacLachlan's blood.

His blood ! That was now the last thing I desired. He fought with suppleness and strength, if not with art ; he fought, too, with venom in his strokes, his hair tossed high upon his temples, his eyes the whitest of his person, as he stood, to his own advantage, that I never grudged him, with his back against the sunset. I contented with defence till he cursed with a baffled accent. His man called piteously and eagerly; but M'Iver checked him, and the fight went on. Not the lunge, at least, I determined, though the punishment of a trivial wound was scarce commensurate with his sin. So I let him slash and sweat till I wearied of the game, caught his weapon in the curved guard of my hilt, and broke it in two.

He dropped the fragment in his hand with a cry of mingled anger and despair, snatched a knife from his stocking, and rushed on me to stab. Even then I had him at my mercy. As he inclosed, I made a complete volte with the left foot, passed back my right in rear of his, changed my sword into my left hand, holding it by the middle of the blade and presenting the point at his throat, while my right hand, across his body, seized his wrist.

For a moment I felt the anger at his treachery almost overmaster me. He thought himself gone. He let his head fall helplessly on my breast, and stood still as one waiting the stroke, with his eyes, as M'Iver told me again, closed and his mouth parted. But a spasm of disgust at the uncleanness of the task to be done made me retch and pause.

"Home, dog!" I gasped, and I threw him from me sprawling on the sod. He fell, in his weariness, in an awkward and helpless mass; the knife, still in his hand, pierced him on the shoulder, and thus the injury I could not give him by my will was given him by Providence. Over on his back he turned with a plash of blood oozing at his shirt, and he grasped with clawing fingers to stanch it, yet never relinquishing his look of bitter anger at me. With cries, with tears, with names of affection, the gillie ran to his master, who I saw was not very seriously injured.

M'Iver helped me on with my coat.

"You're far too soft, man!" he said. "You would have let him go scathless, and even now he has less than his deserts. You have a pretty style of fence, do you know, and I should like to see it paraded against a man more your equal."

"You'll never see it paraded by me," I answered, sorrowfully. "Here's my last duello, if I live a thousand years." And I went up and looked at my fallen adversary. He was shivering with cold, though the sweat hung upon the young down of his white cheeks, for the night air was more bitter every passing moment. The sun was all down behind the hills, the valley was going to rest, the wood was already in obscurity. If our butcher-work had seemed horrible in that sanctuary in the open light of day, now in the eve it seemed more than before a crime against Heaven. The lad weltering, with no word or moan from his lips; the servant stanching his wound, shaken the while by brotherly tears; M'Iver, the old man-at-arms, indifferent, practised to such sights, and with the heart no longer moved by man-inflicted injury; and over all a brooding silence; over all that place, consecrated once to God and prayer by men of peace, but now degraded to a den of beasts—over it shone of a sudden the new wan crescent moon! I turned me round, I turned and fell to weeping in my hands!

This abject surrender of mine patently more astounded the company than had the accident to MacLachlan. M'Iver stood dumfoundered, to behold a cavalier of fortune's tears, and MacLachlan's face, for all his pain, gave up its hate and anger for surprise, as he looked at me over the shoulder of his kneeling clansman plying rude leech-craft on his wound.

"Are you vexed?" said he, with short breaths.

"And that bitterly!" I answered.

"Oh, there is nothing to grieve on," said he, mistaking me most lamentably. "I'll give you your chance again. I owe you no less; but my knife, if you'll believe me, sprang out of itself, and I struck at you in a ruddy mist of the senses."

"I seek no other chance," I said; "our feuds are over: you were egged on by a subterfuge, deceit has met deceit, and the balance is equal."

His mood softened, and we helped him to his feet, M'Iver a silent man because he failed to comprehend this turn of affairs. We took him to a cothouse down at the foot of the wood, where he lay while a boy was sent for a skilly woman.

In life, as often as in the stories of man's invention, it is the one wanted who comes when the occasion needs, for God so arranges, and if it may seem odd that the skilly woman the messenger brought back with him for the dressing of MacLachlan's wound was no other than our Dark Dame of Lorn, the dubiety must be at the Almighty's capacity, and not at my chronicle of the circumstance. As it happened, she had come back from Dalness some days later than ourselves, none the worse for her experience among the folks of that unchristian neighbourhood, who had failed to comprehend that the crazy tumult of her mind might, like the sea, have calm in its depths, and that she was more than by accident the one who had alarmed us of their approach. She had come back with her frenzy reduced, and was now with a sister at Balantyre the Lower, whose fields slope on Aora's finest bend.

For skill she had a name in three parishes; she had charms sure and certain for fevers and hoasts; the lives of children were in her hands while yet their mothers bore them; she knew manifold brews, decoctions, and clysters; at morning on the saints' days she would be in the woods, or among the rocks by the rising of the sun, gathering mosses and herbs and roots that contain the very juices of health and the secret of age. I little thought that day when we waited for her, and my enemy lay bleeding on the fern, that she would bring me the cure for a sore heart, the worst of all diseases.

While M'Iver and I and the gillie waited the woman's coming, MacLachlan tossed in a fever, his mind absent and his tongue running on without stoppage, upon affairs of a hundred different hues, but all leading sooner or later to some babble about a child. It was ever " the dear child," the " m'eudail gheal," " the white treasure," " the orphan "; it was always an accent of the most fond and lingering character. I paid no great heed to this constant wail; but M'Iver pondered and studied, repeating at last the words to himself as MacLachlan uttered them.

" If that's not the young one in Carlunnan he harps on," he concluded at last, " I'm mistaken. He seems even

more wrapt in the child than does the one we know who
mothers it now, and you'll notice, by the way, he has
nothing to say of her."

"Neither he has," I confessed, well enough pleased
with a fact he had no need to call my attention to.

"Do you know, I'm on the verge of a most particular
deep secret?" said John, leaving me to guess what he
was at, but I paid no heed to him.

The skilly dame came in with her clouts and washes.
She dressed the lad's wound and drugged him to a more
cooling slumber, and he was to be left in bed till the next
day.

"What's all his cry about the child?" asked M'Iver,
indifferently, as we stood at the door before leaving. "Is
it only a fancy on his brain, or do you know the one he
speaks of?"

She put on a little air of vanity, the vanity of a woman
who knows a secret the rest of the world, and man particularly, is itching to hear. "Oh, I daresay he has some
one in his mind," she admitted; "and I daresay I know
who it might be too, for I was the first to sweel the baby
and the last to dress its mother—blessing with her!"

M'Iver turned round and looked her, with cunning
humour, in the face. "I might well guess that," he
said; "you have the best name in the countryside for
these offices, that many a fumbling dame botches. I
suppose," he added, when the pleasure in her face
showed his words had found her vanity—"I suppose
you mean the bairn up in Carlunnan?"

"That's the very one," she said with a start; "but
who told you?"

"Tuts!" said he, slyly, "the thing's well enough
known about the Castle, and MacLachlan himself never
denied he was the father. Do you think a secret like that
could be kept in a clattering parish like Inneraora?"

"You're the first I ever heard get to the marrow of
it," confessed the Dame Dubh. "MacLachlan himself
never thought I was in the woman's confidence, and I've
seen him in Carlunnan there since I came home, pretending more than a cousin's regard for the Provost's daughter
so that he might share in the bairn's fondling. He did it

so well, too, that the lady herself would talk of its father-less state with tears in her eyes."

I stood by, stunned at the revelation that brought joy from the very last quarter where I would have sought it. But I must not let my rapture at the idea of MacLachlan's being no suitor of the girl go too far till I confirmed this new intelligence.

"Perhaps," I said in a little to the woman, "the two of them fondling the bairn were chief enough, though they did not share the secret of its fatherhood."

"Chief!" she cried; "the girl has no more notion of MacLachlan than I have, if an old woman's eyes that once were clear enough for such things still show me any-thing. I would have been the first to tell her how things stood if I had seen it otherwise. No, no; Mistress Brown has an eye in other quarters. What do you say to that, Barbreck?" she added, laughing slyly to my friend.

A great ease came upon my mind; it was lightened of a load that had lain on it since ever my Tynree spaewife found, or pretended to find, in my silvered loof such an unhappy portent of my future. And then this rapture was followed by a gladness no less profound that Mac-Lachlan, bad as he had been, was not the villain quite I had fancied: if he had bragged of conquests, it had been with truth though not with decency.

Inneraora, as we returned to it that night, was a town enchanted; again its lights shone warm and happily. I lingered late in its street, white in the light of the stars, and looked upon the nine windows of Askaig's house. There was no light in all the place; the lower windows of the tenement were shuttered, and slumber was within. It gave me an agreeable exercise to guess which of the unshuttered nine would let in the first of the morning light on a pillow with dark hair tossed upon it and a rounded cheek upon a hand like milk.

CHAPTER XXXIV.

LOVE IN THE WOODS.

YOUNG LACHIE did not bide long on our side of the water: a day or two and he was away back to his people, but not before he and I, in a way, patched up once more a friendship that had never been otherwise than distant, and was destined so to remain till the end, when he married my aunt, Nannie Ruadh of the Boshang Gate, whose money we had been led to look for as a help to our fallen fortunes. She might, for age, have been his mother, and she was more than a mother to the child he brought to her from Carlunnan without so much as by your leave, the day after they took up house together. "That's my son," said he, " young Lachie." She looked at the sturdy little fellow beating with a knife upon the bark of an ashen sapling he was fashioning into a whistle, and there was no denying the resemblance. The accident was common enough in those days. "Who is the mother?" was all she said, with her plump hand on the little fellow's head. " She was So-and-so," answered her husband, looking into the fire ; " we were very young, and I've paid the penalty by my rueing it ever since."

Nannie Ruadh took the child to her heart that never knew the glamour of her own, and he grew up, as I could tell in a more interesting tale than this, to be a great and good soldier, who won battles for his country. So it will be seen that the Dame Dubh's story to us in the cot by Aora had not travelled very far when it had not in six years reached the good woman of Boshang Gate, who knew everybody's affairs between the two stones of the parish. M'Iver and I shared the secret with MacLachlan and the nurse of his dead lover; it went no farther, and it was all the more wonderful that John should keep his thumb on it, considering its relevancy to a blunder that made him seem a scoundrel in the eyes of Mistress Betty. Once I proposed to him that through her father she might have the true state of affairs revealed to her.

"Let her be," he answered, "let her be. She'll learn the truth some day, no doubt." And then, as by a second thought, "The farther off the better, perhaps," a saying full of mystery.

The Dark Dame, as I say, gave me the cure for a sore heart. Her news, so cunningly squeezed from her by John Splendid, relieved me at once of the dread that MacLachlan, by his opportunities of wooing, had made himself secure in her affections, and that those rambles by the river to Carlunnan had been by the tryst of lovers. A wholesome new confidence came to my aid when the Provost, aging and declining day by day to the last stroke that came so soon after, hinted once that he knew no one he would sooner leave the fortunes of his daughter with than with myself. I mooted the subject to his wife too, in one wild valour of a sudden meeting, and even she, once so shy of the topic, seemed to look upon my suit with favour.

"I could not have a goodson more worthy than yourself," she was kind enough to say. "Once I thought Betty's favour was elsewhere, in an airt that scarcely pleased me, and——"

"But that's all over," I said, warmly, sure she thought of MacLachlan.

"I hope it is; I think it is," she said. "Once I had sharp eyes on my daughter, and her heart's inmost throb was plain to me, for you see, Colin, I have been young myself, long since, and I remember. A brave heart will win the brawest girl, and you have every wish of mine for your good fortune."

Then I played every art of the lover, emboldened the more since I knew she had no tie of engagement. Remembering her father's words in the harvest-field of Elrigmore, I wooed her, not in humility, but in the confidence that, in other quarters, ere she ever came on the scene, had given me liberty on the lips of any girl I met in a lane without more than a laughing protest. Love, as I learned now, was not an outcome of the reason but will's mastership. Day by day I contrived to see my lady. I was cautious to be neither too hot nor too cold, and never but at my best in appearance and in conversation. All my shyness I thrust under my feet: there is one way to a woman's affections, and that is frankness to the uttermost. I thought no longer, ere I spoke, if this sentiment should make me ridiculous, or that sentiment too readily display my fondness, but spoke out as one in a mere gallantry.

At first she was half alarmed at the new mood I was in, shrinking from this, my open revelation, and yet, I could see, not unpleased altogether that she should be the cause of a change so much to my advantage. I began to find a welcome in her smile and voice when I called on the household of an afternoon or evening, on one pretext or another, myself ashamed sometimes at the very flimsiness of them. She would be knitting by the fire perhaps, and it pleased me greatly by some design of my conversation to make her turn at once her face from the flames whose rosiness concealed her flushing, and reveal her confusion to the yellow candle-light. Oh! happy days. Oh! times so gracious, the spirit and the joy they held are sometimes with me still. We revived, I think, the glow of that meeting on the stair when I came home from Germanie, and the hours passed in swallow flights as we talked of summer days gone bye.

At last we had even got the length of walking together in an afternoon or evening in the wood behind the town that has been the haunt in courting days of generations of our young people: except for a little melancholy in my lady, these were perhaps life's happiest periods. The wind might be sounding and the old leaves flying in the wood, the air might chill and nip, but there was no bitterness for us in the season's chiding. To-day, an old man, with the follies of youth made plain and contemptible, I cannot but think those eves in the forest had something precious and magic for memory. There is no sorrow in them but that they are no more, and that the world to come may have no repetition. How the trees, the tall companions, communed together in their heights among the stars! how the burns tinkled in the grasses and the howlets mourned! And we, together, walked sedate and slowly in those evening alleys, surrounded by the scents the dews bring forth, shone upon by silver moon and stars.

To-day, in my eld, it amuses me still that for long I never kissed her. I had been too slow of making a trial, to venture it now without some effort of spirit; and time after time I had started on our stately round of the hunting-road with a resolution wrought up all the way from my looking-glass at Elrigmore, that this should be the night, if any, when I should take the liberty that surely our rambles, though actual word of love had not been spoken, gave me a title to. A title! I had kissed many a bigger girl before in a caprice at a hedge-gate. But this little one, so demurely walking by my side, with never so much as an arm on mine, her pale face like marble in the moonlight, her eyes, when turned on mine, like dancing points of fire—Oh! the task defied me! The task I say—it was a duty, I'll swear now, in the experience of later years.

I kissed her first on the night before M'Iver set out on his travels anew, no more in the camp of Argile his severed chief, but as a Cavalier of the purchased sword.

It was a night of exceeding calm, with the moon, that I had seen as a corn-hook over my warfare with Mac-Lachlan in Tarra-dubh, swollen to the full and gleaming upon the country till it shone as in the dawn of day. We walked back and forth on the hunting-road, for long in a silence broken by few words. My mind was in a storm. I felt that I was losing my friend, and that, by itself, was trouble; but I felt, likewise, a shame that the passion of love at my bosom robbed the deprivation of much of its sorrow.

"I shall kiss her to-night if she spurns me for ever," I said to myself over and over again, and anon I would marvel at my own daring; but the act was still to do. It was more than to do—it was to be led up to, and yet my lady kept every entrance to the project barred, with a cunning that yet astounds me.

We had talked of many things in our evening rambles in that wood, but never of M'Iver, whose name the girl shunned mention of for a cause I knew but could never set her right on. This night, his last in our midst, I ventured on his name. She said nothing for a little, and for a moment I thought, " Here's a dour, little, unforgiving heart ! " Then, softly, said she, " I wish him well and a safe return from his travelling. I wish him better than his deserts. That he goes at all surprises me. I thought it but John Splendid's promise—to be acted on or not as the mood happened."

" Yes," I said ; " he goes without a doubt. I saw him to-day kiss his farewells with half-a-dozen girls on the road between the Maltland and the town."

" I daresay," she answered ; " he never lacked boldness."

My chance had come.

" No, indeed, he did not," said I ; " and I wish I had some of it myself."

" What ! for so common a display of it ? " she asked, rallying, yet with some sobriety in her tone.

" Not a bit," I answered ; " that—that—that I might act the part of a lover with some credit to myself, and kiss the one girl I know in that capacity."

" Would she let you ? " she asked, removing herself by a finger-length from my side, yet not apparently enough to show she thought herself the one in question.

" That, madame, is what troubles me," I confessed in anguish, for her words had burst the bubble of my courage.

" Of course you cannot tell till you try," she said, demurely, looking straight before her, no smile on the corners of her lips, that somehow maddened by their look of pliancy.

" You know whom I mean," I said, pursuing my plea, whose rustic simplicity let no man mock at, remembering the gawky errors of his own experience.

" There's Bell, the minister's niece, and there's Kilblaan's daughter, and——"

"Oh, my dear! my dear!" I cried, stopping and putting my hand daringly on her shoulder. "You know it is not any of these; you must know I mean yourself. Here am I, a man travelled, no longer a youth, though still with the flush of it, no longer with a humility to let me doubt myself worthy of your best thoughts; I have let slip a score of chances on this same path, and even now I cannot muster up the spirit to brave your possible anger."

She laughed a very pleasant soothing laugh and released her shoulder. "At least you give me plenty of warning," she said.

"I am going to kiss you now," I said, with great firmness.

She walked a little faster, panting as I could hear, and I blamed myself that I had alarmed her.

"At least," I added, "I'll do it when we get to Bealloch-an-uarain well."

She hummed a snatch of Gaelic song we have upon that notable well, a song that is all an invitation to drink the waters while you are young and drink you may, and I suddenly ventured to embrace her with an arm. She drew up with stern lips and back from my embrace, and Elrigmore was again in torment.

"You are to blame yourself," I said, huskily; "you let me think I might. And now I see you are angry."

"Am I?" she said, smiling again. "I think you said the well, did you not?"

"And may I?" eagerly I asked, devouring her with my eyes.

"You may—at the well," she answered, and then she laughed softly.

Again my spirits bounded.

"But I was not thinking of going there to-night," she added, and the howlet in the bush beside me hooted at my ignominy.

I walked in a perspiration of vexation and alarm. It was plain that here was no desire for my caress, that the girl was but probing the depth of my presumption, and I gave up all thought of pushing my intention to perform-ance. Our conversation turned to more common chan-nels, and I had hoped my companion had lost the crude impression of my wooing as we passed the path that led from the hunting-road to the Bealloch-an-uarain.

" Oh ! " she cried here, " I wished for some ivy ; I thought to pluck it farther back, and your nonsense made me quite forget."

" Cannot we return for it ? " I said, well enough pleased at the chance of prolonging our walk.

" No ; it is too late," she answered abruptly. " Is there nowhere else here where we could get it ? "

" I do not think so," I said, stupidly. Then I remembered that it grew in the richest profusion on the face of the grotto we call Bealloch-an-uarain. " Except at the well," I added.

" Of course it is so ; now I remember," said she ; " there is plenty of it there. Let us haste and get it." And she led the way up the path, I following with a heart that surged and beat.

When our countryside is changed, when the forest of Creag Dubh, where roam the deer, is levelled with the turf, and the foot of the passenger wears round the castle of Argile, I hope, I pray, that grotto on the brae will still lift up its face among the fern and ivy. Nowadays when the mood comes on me, and I must be the old man chafing against the decay of youth's spirit, and the recollection overpowers of other times and other faces than those so kent and tolerant about me, I put my plaid on my shoulders and walk to Bealloch-an-uarain well. My children's children must be with me elsewhere on my saunters ; here I must walk alone. I am young again when looking on that magic fountain, still the same as when its murmur sounded in my lover's ears. Here are yet the stalwart trees, the tall companions, that nodded on our shy confessions ; the ivy hangs in sheeny spray upon the wall. Time, that ranges, has here no freedom, but stands, shackled by links of love and memory to the rocks we sat on. I sit now there and muse, and beside me is a shadow that never ages, with a pale face averted, looking through leafless boughs at the glimpse of star and moon. I see the bosom heave ; I see the eyes flash full, then soften half-shut on some inward vision. For I am never there at Bealloch-an-uarain, summer or spring, but the season, in my thought, is that of my wife's first kiss, and it is always a pleasant evening and the birds are calling in the dusk.

I plucked my lady's ivy with a cruel wrench, as one would pluck a sweet delusion from his heart, and her fingers were so warm and soft as I gave her the leaves! Then I turned to go.

"It is time we were home," I said, anxious now to be alone with my vexation.

"In a moment," she said, plucking more ivy for herself; and then she said, "Let us sit a little; I am wearied."

My courage came anew. "Fool!" I called myself. "You may never have the chance again." I sat down by her side, and talked no love but told a story.

It is a story we have in the sheilings among the hills, the tale of "The Sea Fairy of French Foreland"; but I changed it as I went on, and made the lover a soldier. I made him wander, and wandering think of home and a girl beside the sea. I made him confront wild enemies and battle with storms, I set him tossing upon oceans and standing in the streets of leaguered towns, or at grey heartless mornings upon lonely plains with solitude around, and yet, in all, his heart was with the girl beside the sea.

She listened and flushed. My hero's dangers lit her eyes like lanthorns, my passions seemed to find an echo in her sighs.

Then I pitied my hero, the wandering soldier, so much alone, so eager, and unforgetting, till I felt the tears in my eyes as I imaged his hopeless longing.

She checked her sighs, she said my name in the softest whisper, laid her head upon my shoulder and wept. And then at last I met her quivering lips.

CHAPTER XXXV.

FAREWELL.

On the morrow, John Splendid came riding up the street on his way to the foreign wars. He had attired himself most sprucely; he rode a good horse, and he gave it every chance to show its quality. Old women cried to him from their windows and close-mouths. " Oh! *laochain*," they said, " yours be the luck of the seventh son! " He answered gaily, with the harmless flatteries that came so readily to his lips always, they seemed the very bosom's revelation. " Oh! women! " said he, " I'll be thinking of your handsome sons, and the happy days we spent together, and wishing myself soberly home with them when I am far away."

But not the old women alone waited on his going ; shy girls courtesied or applauded at the corners. For them his horse caracoled on Stonefield's causeway, his shoulders straightened, and his bonnet rose. " There you are ! " said he, " still the temptation and the despair of a decent bachelor's life. I'll marry every one of you that has not a man when I come home."

" And when may that be ? " cried a little, bold, fair one, with a laughing look at him from under the blowing locks that escaped the snood on her hair.

" When may it be ? " he repeated. " Say ' Come home, Barbreck,' in every one of your evening prayers, and heaven, for the sake of so sweet a face, may send me home the sooner with my fortune."

Master Gordon, passing, heard the speech. " Do your own praying, Barbreck——"

" John," said my hero. " John, this time, to you."

" John be it," said the cleric, smiling warmly. " I like you, truly, and I wish you well."

M'Iver stooped and took the proffered hand. " Master Gordon," he said, " I would sooner be liked and loved than only admired ; that's, perhaps, the secret of my life."

It was not the fishing season, but the street thronged with fishers from Kenmore and Cairndhu and Kilcatrine and the bays of lower Cowal. Their tall figures jostled in the causeway, their white teeth gleamed in their friendliness, and they met this companion of numerous days and nights, this gentleman of good-humour and even temper, with cries as in a schoolboy's playground. They clustered round the horse and seized upon the trappings. Then John Splendid's play-acting came to its conclusion, as it was ever bound to do when his innermost man was touched. He forgot the carriage of his shoulders ; indifferent to the disposition of his reins, he reached and wrung a hundred hands, crying back memory for memory, jest for jest, and always the hope for future meetings.

" O scamps ! scamps ! " said he, " fishing the silly prey of ditches when you might be with me upon the ocean and capturing the towns. I'll never drink a glass of Rhenish, but I'll mind of you and sorrow for your sour ales and bitter *aqua !* "

" Will it be long ? " said they—true Gaels, ever anxious to know the lease of pleasure or of grief.

" Long or short," said he, with absent hands in his horse's mane, " will lie with Fate, and she, my lads, is a dour jade with a secret. It'll be long if ye mind of me, and unco short if ye forget me till I return."

I went up and said farewell. I but shook his hand, and my words were few and simple. That took him, for he was always quick to sound the depth of silent feeling.

" *Mo thruadh ! mo thruadh !* Colin," said he. " My grief ! my grief ! here are two brothers closer than by kin, and they have reached a gusset of life, and there must be separation. I have had many a jolt from my fairy relatives, but they have never been more wicked than now. I wish you were with me, and yet, ah! yet——. Would her ladyship, think ye, forget for a minute, and shake an old friend's hand, and say good-bye ? "

I turned to Betty, who stood a little back with her father, and conveyed his wish. She came forward, dyed crimson to the neck, and stood by his horse's side. He slid off the saddle and shook her hand.

" It is very good of you," said he. " You have my heart's good wishes to the innermost chamber."

Then he turned to me, and while the fishermen stood back, he said, " I envied you twice, Colin—once when you had the foresight of your fortune on the side of Loch Leven, and now that it seems begun."

He took the saddle, waved his bonnet in farewell to all the company, then rode quickly up the street and round the castle walls.

It was a day for the open road, and, as we say, for putting the seven glens and the seven bens and the seven mountain moors below a young man's feet,—a day with invitation in the air and the promise of gifts around. The mallards at morning had quacked in the Dhuloch pools, the otter scoured the burn of Maam, the air-goat bleated as he flew among the reeds, and the stag paused above his shed antlers on Torvil-side to hide them in the dead bracken.

M'Iver rode beside flowering saugh and alder tree through those old arches, now no more, those arches that were the outermost posterns where good-luck allowed farewells. He dare not once look round, and his closest friends dare not follow him, as he rode alone on the old road so many of our people have gone to their country's wars or to sporran battles.

A silence fell upon the community, and in upon it broke from the river-side the wail of a bagpipe played by the piper of Argile. It played a tune familiar in those parts upon occasions of parting and encouragement, a tune they call " Come back to the Glen."

> Come back to the glen, to the glen, to the glen,
> And there shall the welcome be waiting for you.
> The deer and the heath-cock, the curd from the pen,
> The blaeberry fresh from the dew !

We saw the piper strut upon the gravelled walk beside the bridgegate, we saw Argile himself come out to meet the traveller.

"MacCailein! MacCailein! Ah the dear heart!" cried all our people, touched by this rare and genteel courtesy.

The Marquis and his clansman touched hands, lingered together a little, and the rider passed on his way with the piper's invitation the last sound in his ears. He rode past Kilmalieu of the tombs, with his bonnet off for all the dead that are so numerous there, so patient, waiting for the final trump. He rode past Boshang Gate, portal to my native glen of chanting birds and melodious waters and merry people. He rode past Gearron hamlet, where the folk waved farewells; then over the river before him was the bend that is ever the beginning of home-sickness for all that go abroad for fortune.

I turned to the girl beside me, and "Sweetheart," said I softly, "there's an elder brother lost. It is man's greed, I know; but rich though I am in this new heart of yours, I must be grudging the comrade gone."

"Gone!" said she, with scarcely a glance after the departing figure. "Better gone than here a perpetual sinner, deaf to the cry of justice and of nature."

"Good God!" I cried, "are you still in that delusion?" and I hinted at the truth.

She saw the story at a flash; she paled to the very lips, and turned and strained her vision after that figure slowly passing round the woody point; she relinquished no moment of her gaze till the path bent and hid John Splendid from her eager view.

THE END.

Printed in Great Britain by
WILLIAM BLACKWOOD & SONS LTD.